BETWEEN

THE

HELPLESS

&

THE

DARKNESS

BETWEEN

THE

HELPLESS

THE
DARKNESS

BRENT OLSON

© 2021 Brent Olson

Brent Olson
34596 690th Ave
Ortonville, MN 56278
www.independentlyspeaking.com

ISBN: 978-1-952976-18-6

LCCN: Pending

Cover and interior designed by Jonathan Sainsbury.

Typeset in Livory. Designed by Hannes von Döhren and Livius Dietzel.

Published by Kirk House Publihsers
1250 E 115th Street
Burnsville, MN 55337
612-781-2815
kirkhousepublishers.com

"A King is for fame, not longevity"

—Heimskringla,
The Saga of the Kings of Norway

PRELUDE

"TO ME, RANKS ON ME!" The king's voice soared above the tumult. "Strykar, now, bring them up now!" A foe moved to block his path and the Hardrada's sword licked out with an evil hiss. A fountain of blood erupted and he trod upon the fallen enemy, the man forgotten before he was dead. The iron center of his shield smashed another man to the ground. Amidst the bloody field he now occupied a small island of space, no one quite daring to challenge his reach or his fury. Towering above friend and foe alik,e he swept his black and bloody sword above his head. "To me, king's men to me!" Behind him the flag bearer waved LandWaster, the black raven on a field of red, stark against the afternoon sky.

Strykar cut his way through the throng, a bloody smile on his face. "My lord," he shouted, pointing, "the English archers have arrived."

The Hardrada whirled, saw the ranks of longbows and heard the first volley of arrows. All around him he heard the dull thuds of arrows entering unarmored flesh. He spared a moment to glance behind him, hoping to see the rest of his army coming up the road, armored and intact, but saw only an empty path winding into the hills. That was a fool's dream. . .the message would have only just reached them and it took time to bring up an army, even one as used to sudden surprises as his Vikings.

"No," he growled, "not now, not now, not today." He watched the English king on his horse, pointing with his sword, putting his troops in order. The Hardrada took a step, another, and as the killing rage overcame him, dropped his shield, took his sword in both hands, and plunged into the enemy lines. They melted before him, fearing the blue fury in his eyes nearly as much as the bloody swath of his sword.

"To the king!" Strykar bellowed, and widened the wedge with his axe. The panting, bloodied Norse followed, all order lost in their attempt to keep up with the Hardrada's mad dash for final victory, their eyes fixed on the bloody raven following in his wake.

The Hardrada surged ahead, clearing the ranks. Only the English king's personal bodyguard in his way. His pulse pounded in his head, his rasping breath filled his helmet and he saw the victory that could be his. Then, a flicker in the air, a shock to his neck and the feathered end of an English arrow like a shadow below his chin. His strength left him, he sank to his knees, and tumbled onto his side, his sword below him. The last thing he heard was Strykar's voice, shaking with emotion, shouting, "To the king. A shieldwall for the king." Above it all was the sound of volley after volley of arrows.

Then there was nothing.

Between The Helpless and The Darkness

ONE

Arnora shook her father.

"Wake up!" she shouted. "A message from the king! It was a trap; the English army ambushed him. The whole army is to come, with armor and bows, or all is lost. Father, GET UP!"

He snorted and rolled on his back but did not wake. All around her the camp boiled with activity, with men rushing down the long road as quickly as they could arm themselves. Horses reared and kicked as swearing men leaped on their backs and swatted them with the flat of their naked swords. Dust and wood smoke clouded the air and through it all her father sprawled across his sleeping robes. He had drunk so much the night before, laughing with his friends as they drunkenly speculated on the amount of treasure the king would extort from the English and how they would all be made wealthy. Somewhere in the night his mood had soured and now Arnora's body ached from the beating he'd given her shortly before he passed out. She shook him again and then sagged in frustration. Her red hair fell in tangles on her shoulders and she gathered her torn and stained dress around her sturdy body, a chill running through her despite the warmth of the air. The Norwegian king had earned his title, "The Hard Ruler" and he would not look with favor at one of his men at arms who missed battle because of a night-time encounter with a cask of English ale. Arnora had no idea what the reckoning would be, but it would be ferocious, particularly if the battle went bad.

But it must already be going badly. Arnora was very young, but she'd seen the face of the messenger, and felt the urgency of the men now vanished down the road. What if she succeeded in waking her father and he stumbled drunkenly into a battle only to be killed, and what if she let him slumber and the king came back to camp, bloodied and furious and found him lying there? She could see only two courses for her and both held the seeds of disaster.

She ran her fingers through her hair and sagged back against a tree, staring at her father and hearing nothing but his snores and groans. She hated this strange land he'd brought her to. She'd grown up high above Storfjord, on a small farm clinging to the edge of the mountain. A glacier fed waterfall of crystal-clear water had been a few feet from her house and she loathed the placid brown water of the streams around her. She and her mother had lived in a small tidy home, with goats to milk and fields to tend. For most of her life their neighbors had been women, children and old men. All those of fighting age had joined the king who led unending battles against those who would challenge his rule. Her father was an infrequent visitor, bringing trinkets from strange lands, a smell of unwashed man, and a tyrant's rule. She couldn't believe her mother hadn't even argued the last time he'd come home, saying that the king was no longer raiding but traveling to conquer, and there were riches and lands to be won in England. She'd packed up their small possessions and made their way down the steep, winding path to the fjord. Even though they started their trip on salt water it was two full days of travel before they reached the open ocean. Anora had never been more than a day's walk from home and had never seen more than fifty people in one place. Their farm had been on the far reaches of Tafjorden and the whole slow trip to the sea they'd been joined by more ships and men, the king's demands for soldiers reaching every remote farm and village. Anora had been in the belly of the stinking ship with livestock and she'd been sick the entire voyage. After their landing there was only a makeshift camp in the midst of a plundered land. Their food was badly cooked meat and stolen oats and Arnora spent most of her time trying to be invisible, surrounded by thousands of men whose eyes she could feel on her wherever she walked. Her mother became ill and, in less than a week had died, as quietly as she'd lived. And now here she sat, her mother dead less than a month. She had no other family and the man who was supposed to take care of her required more care than an infant and appreciated it less. She stood up and looked down at him and in a sudden spasm of anger kicked him in the side. He grunted and opened his eyes, but they were blurred and after a moment he settled back into his drunken stupor. Arnora looked around, anxious that one of the other camp women or boat guards had seen her action but for the moment she was quite alone.

Just so very alone.

STAMFORD BRIDGE, SEPTEMBER 1066
THE NEXT DAY

It was the worst thing he'd ever seen. A boy growing up in 11th century Norway, a time when every man had his pride, a sword, and little else, was no stranger to blood, but this was something new. Bodies were everywhere. Orm stood at the back of the small group of men and craned his neck to see. He was tall for his age, a slender youth with oversized hands and feet poking out of homespun linen. He gulped, sickened at what he was seeing. He'd seen dead men before, but this was the first battleground he'd ever been on; it stunned his senses. Before him, the River Derwent wound gently through the valley. The dead were scattered on both sides of the bridge, with an actual *pile* of corpses on the bridge itself. At a distance they looked peaceful, but the carnage close up belied that impression. Limbs, pools of blood, and scattered ropes of intestines littered the ground, and the dead faces he could see were frozen in their final shouts of rage and pain.

"Here comes the English king," a man said.

King Harold was not a big man and when he swung down from his horse he seemed even smaller. His armor was covered with dents and blood and he looked weary.

"What do we have here?" he asked.

A boy stepped forward from the small crowd. "I am Olaf Haraldsson, son of the Hardrada. I come to ask your mercy for his men." Orm was surprised that Prince Olaf appeared no older than his own thirteen years. He seemed much too young to be negotiating with the king who'd killed his father.

"Most of his men require mercy not from me, but from God. As for the rest, why should I grant that?" King Harold asked. "Your father did great harm this day. Have you viewed the field?"

"My Lord, I have. There have been enough widows made this day. What purpose will be served by making more?" The new made king stood very tall, his gaze direct. "We are under your hand, but even a dying dog will bite. Your mercy costs you nothing. Your revenge might cost more than you can afford." King Harold's bodyguard stirred. They greatly out-numbered the small group of Vikings, but that might mean little if swords were drawn. "If your wrath requires blood, take mine and let these others depart." Olaf knelt before the English king and bent his head. Orm stared at his pale neck, gleaming in the morning sun. It looked very vulnerable.

King Harold gazed at the sight. "Are you certain you are the Hardrada's son? If his knee would have so easily bent, much grief would have been avoided."

Without raising his head, Olaf replied, "I am his son, but I am not he. I've often heard I am but one-tenth the man he is. It is perhaps fit that I return to Norway with the tenth part of his army. What are your wishes, King Harold?"

"Rise, bury your dead, and depart. Trouble these shores no more. The world has changed and there is no room in it for men like your father. He should have remained king of Norway and not stretched his hand to grasp more than he could command."

"I go now to find my father. If you are correct, perhaps it is best he is dead."

"Do not seek his banner. LandWaster has flown over enough fields. I had it burned."

Olaf's shoulders stiffened. "Tell me, did you find it easy to burn?"

King Harold laughed, "Perhaps you are your father's son." He rose to leave. "No, it did not burn easily. It was soaked with the blood of Norway's finest. But it did burn."

"Your pardon, King Harold, but did you see how my father died?"

The king laughed again, "Did I see? Yes, boy, I did. Closer than I wanted. When he saw us bringing up the archers he turned berserker. He dropped his shield and charged my banner, swinging his sword with both hands and cutting a swath through my finest men like a farmer cutting hay. An arrow to the throat is what killed him, and a lucky thing for us, because I know of no man in my army who could have faced him and lived. Your father did many evil things in his life, and I confess to no sorrow at his death, but you need not be ashamed of him, boy. They will write songs about him."

An aide held his horse's reins for him; he mounted and rode away.

Olaf turned his gaze back to the battlefield. Now with

the sun fully up, some organized effort was in progress. Working parties from both armies were separating the piles of dead, removing their valuables, and carrying the bodies to common graves. He turned to Haakon. "This is work I do not know. Can anything be done to remove the stench of death or is this ground laid waste forever?"

Haakon looked around with a practiced eye. "My young Lord, this is a small thing. I was with your father in Constantinople when he commanded the Varangian Guard. The summer we harried Sicily there were a dozen battles worse than this one, whole populations put to the sword, cities burned simply to remove the smell of the dead. At least here armed men sought each other out. I have seen much worse: bodies of children trampled under cavalry, screaming slaves in flames, men cooked in their armor by boiling oil. This. . . this is a small thing. The grass will grow greener where blood soaked the ground; the cows will give more milk, and in a few years all that happened here will be forgotten." His gaze was bleak as he surveyed the field. "Perhaps not all will be forgotten. Perhaps the English king is right. Our day may be over. If so, it is best your father died. He will have songs written about him, and he would not have liked a world where he was not king." He clapped a massive hand on Olaf's back. "Give this no more thought. These men are dead. They died in service to their king, who was chosen by God. No sin rests with them, and even now they stand at the gates of Heaven."

Orm gathered his nerve and spoke. "Sirs," he said, "I'm here to look for my father."

They turned. "What's your name, boy?" Haakon asked.

"Orm Gudmundson. My father was in the king's guard." Haakon pointed into the valley. "Down there," he said, "I can give you no more guidance. If he lived until the king died, the guard made a shield wall around his body. The last of them fell there from English arrows."

Orm nodded and walked down the long hill into the

valley. He examined every corpse, hoping and dreading the time when he'd find a familiar face. Some of the wounded had survived the long night in the open. He touched these more carefully, but didn't stop to help. It was midmorning before he made his way to the pile of bodies that marked the last stand. Here there were fewer wounded. Most of the men had been struck by multiple arrows and lay in rows. The tattered remnants of the Hardrada's army had converged on the site of the last stand. Orm inspected body after body, becoming numb to the sight of ghastly wounds and agonized death.

He straightened up from the body of a man his father's age. "Take that gold, boy," another searcher advised, nodding toward a coil of metal on the upper arm of the corpse. "No sense leaving it for the English." Orm shuddered and moved away.

"Orm?" a faint voice said, "Boy, is that you?"

Orm turned and saw his father, pinned to the ground with arrows through both legs.

"Father," Orm said, "you live?"

"For now, boy. Get me out of here." Orm hurried to him and then stopped, unsure what to do next.

"Break the arrows, Orm, then get someone to carry me aboard ship. I admit, I tire of this place." His father chuckled, "I needed a bigger shield. When the arrow storm hit I could protect my head or my legs, not both. I confess, in the night there were several times when I felt I had chosen poorly."

A knot of the other searchers scattered like ants. One hurried over to Orm.

"Does this one live? I'll help you get him to the ships. We need to leave, now."

"Why hurry?" Gudmond asked, "Yesterday was when we needed urgency."

"Gudmond, is that you? I thought you were long dead." The man ripped Gudmond's pants open to expose the bloody and bruised wounds. He addressed the startled young man next to him. "My name is Dorrud, boy, and your father is a lucky man. Neither arrow is in the bone. This should be simple. Turn him on his side, sit on his feet."

Dorrud gripped each arrow in turn, breaking off the wooden shanks. He handed one of the feathered shafts to Gudmond and looked at him closely. "You know what I must do?"

Gudmond nodded and placed one of the arrows in his mouth. He bit down, hard. Dorrud wrapped a bit of cloth around his hand then slammed the heel against first one, then the other, of the arrows. Gudmond bucked and nearly threw Orm off. The bloody barbed heads came out the back of his legs and Dorrud pulled them completely out and cast them onto the grass. "Let the wounds bleed to clear the poison, then bind them tightly. I'll send someone to help you carry him to the ship."

Gudmond's face was pale and shiny with sweat. He spit out the broken arrow shaft and asked again, "Why do you hurry so?"

Dorrud looked around and leaned close.

"We have found the king."

He stepped closer. "The king still breathes."

CHAPTER TWO

HARALD THE HARDRADA woke to a world of pain.

He lay still, eyes closed, while he gathered his senses. Stillness was wise, for he had no idea if he was among friend or foe.

His armor was gone, and he lay on a pallet of some kind. He was aboard a ship and from the creak of the rigging and the feel of the swells knew the ship was on the open sea. He could hear activity around him and he tried to remember what had gone before.

The invasion had gone well; the Norse had captured York with only one pitched battle. He had left the city unburned, on the condition that noble hostages would surrender to him. They had promised to meet him at Stamford Bridge and he had marched half his army to the meeting place. Instead of hostages, the entire English army had surprised him. The bitter fight against the odds was a blur, except for the memory of when the killing rage had finally overwhelmed him. Because of the summer-like heat, most of his men were without their armor and when he'd seen the English archers coming he'd known the battle was lost. He'd dropped his shield as a pointless encumbrance and rushed the English, hoping to find and slay their king. They had melted before his rage, limbs and heads severed by his every swing. There had been a rush of fierce exultation when he saw the king's bodyguard fall back from him. Then, there had been a shock, and he'd seen the shadow of an arrow protruding from below his chin.

After that, all was blank.

Why was he not dead? His wound should have killed him.

"Lord Olaf, I think the king awakens." The voice close by his shoulder surprised him and he opened his eyes. As his vision swam into focus he saw his son, a somber look on his face, kneeling over him.

"Where are we?" Harald tried to say, but no words passed his tortured throat. The pain made him start and he reached a hand up, only to feel a mass of bandages.

"Father, do not try to speak. Your wound came close to ending your life. The arrow has been removed. If wound fever does not take you, you will live. I do not know if you will speak again. We are at sea, headed for the Orkneys with what remains of your army."

Harald raised an eyebrow. *What remains of my army?*

Olaf smiled, a particularly mirthless smile. "I'm afraid you have done ill, my lord. Of the men who followed your banner, one in ten return. The rest of us live due only to the mercy of the English king. Rest now, and make your peace with God. I fear you have much to answer for."

King Harald the Hardrada of Norway closed his eyes. *One in ten.* He did have much to answer for. Now that he was fully awake he could feel all the hurts his body had suffered. He was nearly fifty, and the battering he had taken while fighting at the forefront of his men had cost him dearly. He gritted his teeth against the pain. It felt like they were running with the wind, but even so it would be several days before they reached the Orkneys. He would have time to heal, time to think. *I have much to answer for, indeed.* The deck shifted beneath him and he fell back into a world of evil dreams and worse memories.

CHAPTER THREE

AT DAWN THE NEXT DAY Harald struggled to his feet. Except for the man at the helm, the boat was sleeping. He made his way to the side of the ship and relieved himself. Straightening up he surveyed the ocean. It was a fine fresh morning and when the ship was at the top of a swell he could see ships in every direction.

But, not enough of them.

Clutching the gunwale for support, he counted. Every fiber of his body ached and in his neck was a much sharper pain, but his eyes were as good as ever. Searching to the horizon in every direction he could count only twenty-four.

Olaf came up behind him. Harald turned a questioning eye to him.

Olaf caught his meaning immediately. "Yes, twenty-four is all. Twenty-four out of three hundred." He, too, looked out over the ocean. "I know the number of ships. I cannot count how many widows will sleep in empty beds or how many orphans will die from hunger." He turned to look at his father and saw the expression on his face. Despite his torment, he laughed. "Are you thinking that a week ago I would not have dared speak thus to you? You are right. A week ago, I was a child. Now. . .now I feel like the oldest man in the world. Shall I thank you for my maturity?" He handed his father a jug of water. Leaning over the railing he spit into the sea. "Queen Ellisif waits for us at the Brough of Birsay. If you cannot speak, you cannot rule. Then it will fall to the Queen to decide what to make of this. I do not care, one way or the other. I have now seen the works of a king and I want no part of them." He spit again and left for the stern of the ship.

Harald watched as Olaf relieved the helmsman, taking hold of the steering oar and leaning against the roll of the sea. Harald tipped the jug back and let the tiniest trickle of water run down his throat. His thirst required it, but still, the liquid burned all the way down to his stomach. As he turned, his knees weakened and he barely made it back to his pallet before darkness overcame him.

His sleep was troubled.

* * *

Orm leaned wearily against the side of the round-bellied freighter and watched the king's longship slicing through the morning sea a stone's throw away. A towering figure was at the rail drinking from a jug. As the ships passed the figure turned unsteadily and sank out of sight.

So, Orm thought, *the king does live. My father thought he was dying defending a corpse and he was wrong on both counts.*

He looked at the deck where his father lay. Blood stained bandages covered both legs and he tossed slightly in what seemed to be a combination sleep and fever dream. All Orm's life his father had been a figure of respect and power and to see him brought so low set his whole world askew. It had been a very long night, with Gudmond fading in and out, sometimes dozing and sometimes waking with a scream as the ship rolled and disturbed the tortured flesh of his legs. Orm had spent the night bracing his lanky body against the freighter's deck, trying to hold his father still. His shoulders and legs ached with the strain and now he wanted nothing more than for his father to lie quiet until they made landfall and he could put his charge in someone else's care. Orm watched as the king's longship became just a sail on the horizon. Traveling twice as fast as the lumbering freighter, its crew would be at their ease long before Orm and his father would struggle into port. Orm spared one last glance, spit into the sea, and knelt beside his father.

* * *

Arnora didn't see the king's ship pass. She lay pressed against the side of a ship, wrapped in a filthy cloak and trying with all her might to be invisible. Her father was keeping a low profile as well. By the time he'd come to his senses the battle was over and the sun was setting. In the smoky confusion of the night he'd been able to avoid anyone who might ask where he'd been during the day. He'd sworn Arnora to silence and when the English king allowed them to depart they'd climbed aboard a ship full of strangers. As the small contingent of ships sailed down the River Ouse they were haunted by the stench of hundreds of burning ships, the smoke turning the sun red and angry. It took until dark to reach The Humber and when the ships were safely in the in the estuary they anchored for the night. There was little rest for anyone, between tending wounds and keeping watch in case of treachery by the English. Morning had brought a fresh breeze and a clean morning sky. The battered flotilla made for the open sea and Arnora looked for a cranny in the ship where she could both get some sleep and avoid her father's ill-tempered attempts to punish her for his shortcomings. She pressed her face against the hull and if she wept, no one could see.

* * *

When Harald woke again it was to the creaks and squeals of the sail being lowered. The afternoon sun was in his face and the calls of seagulls came from overhead.

This time he kept his eyes closed.

He had no need of eyes to know what was going on. A lifetime of riding the waves told him all he needed to know. They were in sheltered waters, had lost the wind, and needed oars to maneuver. This meant they were among the Orkneys. Soon the world would require his presence again. For now, it could wait. He drifted off again.

Sometime later, a hand shook him awake.

Olaf said, "My lord, if you have the will to walk, now would be the time. We have landed at Brough of Birsay and all your people await you at cliff's edge."

Do I have the will? Harald asked himself. It was not a question he'd ever needed to ask before, not once in his life. He struggled to his feet, shrugging off his son's helping hand.

He looked around through squinted eyes. Thorfinn had built his stronghold on a tiny island, completely encircled by sheer cliffs and with no access except one small stairway leading from the narrow beach. It was usually a remote and desolate spot, but today it hummed with activity. The tiny beach was crowded with longships and the edge of the cliff was lined with hundreds of faces peering down. Harald walked down the gangplank to the sand below. The walk up the steep stairway was a torment. Anxious voices called down from above, asking for names of those who were lost. Occasionally there would be a shout of recognition or a scream of joy, but only occasionally.

Harald walked slowly, his will and his strength ebbing the closer he came to the top.

Ellisif waited for him at the cliff's edge. Her face was shadowed and she seemed to struggle for words.

"My lord," she said, "Maria is dead. Our daughter is dead."

Only a croak passed Harald's lips. He touched his throat and raised questioning hands.

"She died a week ago. A sudden fit, her face turned purple, and she died."

A week ago, Harald thought, *she died as we fought the English.*

Ellisif looked down at the scattering of ships. "It would appear all your luck has deserted you." With that she crumpled against his chest, sobs wracking her body. Harald held her up. Even her slight weight was more than he could hold. He turned. Olaf was behind him and at Olaf's shoulder was the giant Haakon. He was tall enough that his eyes were nearly level with Harald's own. Harald guided Ellisif into Haakon's arms. She started to sag to the ground. Haakon put one arm around her shoulders and scooped her up. Harald walked slowly towards Thorfinn's Hall. The crowd grew silent and parted before him. Behind him trailed Haakon and Olaf. The crowd turned their attention back to the cliff's edge as the weary remnant of Harald's army straggled to the top.

CHAPTER FOUR

HARALD RECLINED ON A seat of furs. Every now and then he sipped from a mug of water laced with honey.

He looked up as a figure came through the door.

"My lord," Strykar said, "I come to beg your forgiveness. I thought you were dead. I would never have left the field had I known you were yet alive."

Harald raised a dismissive hand, then lifted his eyebrow. He was becoming better at communication without words.

"How did I live, when so many others did not? When you went berserk I followed your wake." Strykar's voice was awestruck. "Truly, my lord, the English king owes much to the archer who struck you down. None would stand against you and for a moment I thought their whole army would drop their weapons and flee like a herd of cattle." Strykar paused for a moment, then shook off a sudden chill and went on. "I was struck in the head. When I regained my senses the thick of the battle had moved on. I fought until pure darkness then I sought my way back to the ships when it was impossible to tell friend from foe. I was weak from the cold. I thought how odd it would be to survive a battle and die of chills. Luckily, I met an English peasant who had a coat. He would not sell it to me. In fact, he said if he'd a weapon he would kill me." Strykar shrugged. "It seemed a foolish thing to say to a man with an axe.

"I struck off his head, took his coat, and departed. I returned to the ships as your son and Haakon were preparing for the English army. There was little for me to do except wait to be killed by the English, so I went to sleep. The next morning the English king gave quarter and we put out to sea." Strykar laughed. "My lord, when I saw you come down the gangplank of the ship, I thought I was seeing a ghost and wondered how I'd so ill-served you that you would come to haunt me."

Harald smiled. Truly, it was funny. Strykar Knattarson had been his marshal for years and never once ill-served him. A living sword and a trusted comrade, he was the only one of Harald's inner circle to survive the battle. In many ways he was a Viking of the Old North. Even though Strykar crossed himself at meals, Harald was confident that he had a Hammer of Thor hung around his neck as a good luck charm.

"By your leave, my lord," Strykar continued, "I will send ships to the Shetlands and to Norway, so our people know you yet live. We cannot stay here long. Winter approaches and we have several thousand people to feed. This place cannot hold us. What are your wishes, my lord? We could winter in either the Shetlands or in Scotland, but I see little point in it. We should return to Norway to gather our strength for the next campaign. No one will trouble your throne; you have placed the crown too firmly on your head. Yet, Svein of Denmark still lives and I see no reason to tempt him, or the northern earls. We can levy more troops come summer, after the crops are planted and the memory of this year's blood dims. It was simply ill-luck that cost us the victory.

The English came upon us unawares, in numbers, as well as heavily armed and armored. We had but half our army and most of them unarmored."

Harald stared at the man. Strykar was sounding like a fool. It was well he could not talk. None of what had happened had been ill luck. Could they not see that? All that had happened rested on his shoulders. He had been caught, like a child. Ten years as master of the Varangian Guard, twenty years as king of Norway, thirty-five years of warfare in all, and he had been out-thought and out-fought by an Englishman who had held his throne for a total of nine months. He took another sip of water and leaned back wearily.

Strykar looked at him with a searching gaze, then without a word rose from his bench and left the room.

Olaf was sitting outside the hall, his legs stretched out before him, head thrown back, enjoying the sun. The distant rumble of the surf was balanced by the shrill shrieks of seabirds.

Strykar squatted before him. "How old are you now, boy?"

"Fifteen," Olaf said, then chuckled dryly, "although in truth, I feel much older these past days."

Strykar laughed out loud. "Lad, if war aged a man, I would be a thousand."

Olaf looked at him warily. He had always been intimidated by the grizzled old warrior. Strykar had been at his father's side since the king was fourteen. In fact, he'd been the one to carry him off his first battlefield. His face was lined by the suns of a dozen lands and his blue eyes peered through a mass of wrinkles inflicted by countless hours squinting at a bright sun over blue water. His full beard was gray and a long scar puckered his forehead. He sat on his haunches, gently rolling the handle of his ever-present axe on the top of his thighs. Olaf noticed without surprise that he'd lost all of one finger and part of the next in the battle. The stumps were bound tightly with white cloth that was now stained red and yellow.

He continued, "I was just thinking of your father. The first time I saw him he was your age. He wanted to fight by his brother's side, but his brother told him his hands were too small to hold the sword tightly. With strips of leather he lashed the sword to his hand and said, 'See, now the sword will stay with me as long as I live.' When I carried him off the field the sword was still tied to his hand, and it was covered in blood that was not his own. He was but a boy, and I a warrior ten years his senior, but that was the day I decided that, should he live, here was a man I could follow."

Olaf looked out to sea. "I am not my father. I have done nothing except kneel before an English king."

"True, but think on this. That is something your father could not have done, but because you did there are a thousand wives who are not widows this day. To kill a man is an easy thing; I've done it a hundred times. I think you performed the harder task."

He went on, "You are a man today and I'll leave you with a man's thoughts. It is thus: I looked in your father's eyes just now, and he is no longer the Hardrada."

"What?"

"Oh, lad, don't tell me you haven't noticed. This has broken him. He still breathes, but he is a dead man. From now on Norway is in the hands of you and your brother." Strykar stood and looked down at the boy. "Not many men hold a kingdom at your age. Perhaps you have your father's luck... or the luck he used to have." He clapped Olaf on the shoulder and walked away.

CHAPTER FIVE

"So," Harald rasped, "I am not a mute."

His voice was hoarse and grating. Every word that passed his lips felt as if hot needles formed it. Still, a man in pain was a man alive.

"My lord," Olaf said, "what are your wishes?"

"What are yours?"

"We must leave this place."

"How many of our people are here?"

"Not many, here, but between here and the Shetlands there are over five thousand who came with us, a thousand fighting men. We have plenty of ships, but we lack hands to pull an oar."

"Women can row. Let us depart. We will form up again in the Shetlands."

"And your Queen?"

"Put her in a ship. Carry her if need be. Our child and my army have both been in their graves a week. I grow weary of this place and the Queen cannot live on a grave."

"Very well."

CHAPTER SIX

SEABIRDS SWARMED OVERHEAD. Harald leaned against the rail as the ship easily rode the waves. Overhead the stays hummed from the pressure of the sail and under his hands he could feel a slight trembling. He balanced against the rolling with unconscious competence as all around him strained the sails of the other ships in his fleet. Strykar stood at his elbow.

"My lord, what are your wishes?"

Harald shrugged, "Olaf can handle this. We need to land, pick up our people, reprovision, and depart. A day or two here should suffice." The pain had left his throat, although his voice was still a dark rasp.

"My lord, your people do need to hear from you. Many have lost their men, and many of the men have lost heart. You are still their king."

Harald turned and looked him in the eye. The implied rebuke in his voice was unfamiliar. Strykar looked at him, a slight smile on his face.

"A month ago," Harald rasped, "I would have killed you, for the tone in your voice alone."

Strykar shrugged, "A month ago, I wouldn't have needed to speak thus. I serve you, my lord, in every way, just as I have for over thirty years. If you wish to kill me, do so. Every man dies. Would I have ridden the roads we have ridden, if I feared death?"

Harald smiled, "You have always been a fool, Strykar. Yet always, my friend." He swallowed, a twinge in his throat, "So, as my friend, before you choose to follow me down another road, know this." He nodded down at the passing water. "It takes all my will to stop myself from jumping over the rail. How say you, old friend? Shall we leap into the sea and see which one of us can dive deepest before we try to breathe?"

Strykar looked at him. "I think not. You choose a road that would anger both Jesus and Thor."

The two men were silent. Below them, the sea washed by.

Finally, Strykar said, "I have another idea." A pause, then the crooked smile returned, "Instead, we will get drunk."

Harald's tired face smiled, "Very well, old friend. Let us drink."

Strykar looked into his eyes a moment longer, then leaped onto the rail and balanced there, knees flexing against the roll of the sea, one easy hand on the shrouds, "Strike the sail, you bastards, and break out the oars. The king wishes to get drunk and so do I!"

Tingwell Loch opened up before them.

CHAPTER SEVEN

THE FIRE HAD DIED down to embers.

Harald sat in the high seat. The air was thick with smoke and through the haze he could see the crowd had thinned. The sleeping benches were crowded, and the people who remained had begun to mute their voices. Strykar was at his usual post to the left and in front of Harald. His war axe was unsheathed and he casually leaned on the handle as his watchful eyes surveyed the hall. Each person in this hall had lost a comrade or a brother on the field of Stamford Bridge; it might require only a little alcohol to release their vengeance. Harald was not usually a man who needed protection, but at this moment Strykar was convinced he would but watch with mild curiosity if a sword came for his head.

Harald's throat burned from all the beer he'd drunk. He leaned against the backrest, lost in thought. *Am I still a man?* The question would have been unthinkable a few days ago. He had always dated the onset of his manhood from the first man he'd killed. He'd been fourteen, and in the years since he had killed more men than he could count. If skill at death were truly a test of manhood, he had enough and to spare. *I told Strykar I wished for death. I am not even sure that is true. I think, perhaps, what I wish for is nothing. An eternity of nothing. No dead men, no widows looking at me, no country to rule. No . . . anything. Does God grant such a wish?*

He was disturbed from his reverie by a loud argument in front of him. An aging man, unknown to him, was standing on trembling legs, stating his case with drunken ferocity.

"You people know nothing! All this," he waved an all-inclusive hand, "is shit! Iceland, Greenland, Scotland, even Norway, is nothing. I've been there, I've seen it!"

"Seen what?" Harald's voice was quiet, but the deadly undertones were evident.

The drunk wheeled around, suddenly, frighteningly, obviously aware that he had just told the Ruler of the North that all his possessions were shit.

"Your pardon, my lord." He tried to stand erect, but staggered. "I was just telling your men that they should not long for lands in England when much better land is there for the taking."

"Of what land do you speak?"

"Vinland, my lord."

Harald felt a slight spark of curiosity. It was the first emotion of any kind to stir him since he felt the arrow strike. "Do you mean the land Bjarni Herjolfsson said he found? That was before I was born. He was a liar, was he not, and a coward besides?"

"I do not know what other tales he might have, but his land exists. I was there. I was a small boy when my parents traveled with Thorfinn Karlsefni." He spoke slowly, trying not to slur his words. "We spent three years wintering in the huts built by Leif the Lucky. My lord, it is a wonderful land! Thick timber, fields of wild wheat, grape vines everywhere. We hardly needed to cut hay for the winter, for there was little snow."

"Why did you leave this paradise?"

"Skraelings, my lord," the man spat, "worthless, pagan wretches. Short, ugly, dirty, barbarians."

Despite himself, Harald was amused. "If these pagan wretches were so worthless, how did they drive you away?"

"They did not, at first. In the beginning they traded with us. Furs, mainly. But it was not long and they turned against us."

"For no reason?" Strykar asked. He had been drinking more than anyone else, but his voice remained steady.

The man shrugged. "I don't know. Some hard men were there with us, and they had little sympathy for pagan savages. There were killings, perhaps some goods taken without pay. Nothing of any consequence. Still, it was not long and we could not stir outside our stockade for fear of arrows from the forest. As I said, we stayed for three years, then loaded up what we could and returned to Iceland. That was fifty years ago, but I can still remember the sweet grape juice, the tall trees, and the lush meadows."

"I would hear more of this," Harold said in his harsh rasp. "Come closer. Strykar, quiet these drunken fools."

Harald never left the high seat all night. Strykar slept, like a dog, at the foot of his master's chair. He woke many times in the night, and each time he looked up he could see the gleam of Harald's gray eyes in his shadowed face as he listened to the murmurings of the drunken stranger.

Morning came. The quiet hall awoke. Cooks stirred the fire and added wood. A woman swung a massive kettle over the fire and began to cook porridge. Strykar rose and stretched, the bones in his back cracking loudly. With a grunt he bent over and picked up his axe from the floor.

"Strykar," Harold said.

"Yes, my lord?"

"After they break fast, I would speak with Olaf and Ellisif."

"Very well, my lord."

* * *

"Orm, wake up."

Orm struggled awake, his eyes sandy and his mouth foul. His mother knelt next to him. "Come, son," she said, "if you wish to see your father again." He lurched to his feet, his mind racing. Days at a sea followed by days helping his mother tend his father as he slipped deeper and deeper into a fever dream, his leg wounds swelling and stinking. He hadn't spoken for two days now, his body a shrunken and twitching imitation of the man who'd left for the invasion of England. Orm sank to his knees next to the pallet where his father lay. The smell from his wounds filled the shabby hut. His eyes were sunk deeply in their sockets and his skin was stretched tightly over the bones of his face. His mouth hung open and the sagging flesh made him look toothless. Orm hadn't grown accustomed to his father's drastic change and could barely keep from fleeing the room. Instead he stretched a faltering hand and touched his father's shoulder. Orm's mother knelt on the other side of the bed and gently wiped the sweat from her husband's brow. Orm sensed others behind him, comrades from the king's guard. The other wounded had died or begun their recovery. Orm's father alone had made his journey long and painful. Orm sat without moving. The only sounds were the crackle of the fire, his mother's quiet prayers and his father's tortured breathing, long, rattling, gasps. It wasn't long before one of the sounds ceased, dwindling away to nothing. Orm's eyes flickered back and forth, looking for life and movement and seeing none. A moment's relief was followed by shame at that relief that colored his cheeks. A hard hand on his shoulder and a voice said, "Move aside, son. We have work to do here." Orm slid backwards to the wall of the hut and watched as men surrounded his father's body. Moving gear and bandages out of the way, one of the men picked up Gudmond's sword. Sparing Orm a glance he handed it to him. "Here boy, this is yours."

Orm clutched the sword. Truthfully, it was not a very good sword but it had been his father's prized possession, because not every man owned a sword. And now it was his. He watched as his mother left the hut, followed by the men carrying her husband's body.

* * *

Ellisif was pale, but composed. She and Harald had not spoken since their first meeting in the Orkneys. She stood erect in front of the high seat. Olaf stood a step behind and to the side.

Harald looked at them both, his own face expressionless. "Olaf," he said, with no preamble, "you shall return to Norway and tell your brother he is now king. He is the elder, and I think better suited to the throne. It is my wish that you not contest his rule."

Olaf said, "Yes, my lord." His face was as expressionless as his father's.

Harald's lips bent in a slight smile. "Is that all you have to say? 'Yes, my lord.' Do you not dispute my wishes?"

"Do you wish me to?" Olaf asked. "I will not. I have no quarrel with your decision. I told you before, I have seen the works of kings and I take no pleasure in them."

Harald finally moved. He rose and came down from the high seat. He stood in front of his son and gazed at him. Olaf was not small, but his father towered above him.

"My son," Harald said, "I have spent much time in thought these past days. It may be that the man who wants least to be king will be the best king. I have striven my whole life to rule wherever I stand and it has brought me nothing except nightmares." Olaf was transfixed by his father's bleak whisper. "A few years before you were born I put my knee on an emperor's chest and gouged his eyes out. I did it for no better reason than to gain favor with the next emperor."

"I could not do that," Olaf said.

"I know," Harald said, "and that may make you a better man than I."

He turned his gaze to his queen. "Ellisif, I do not return to Norway. What are your wishes?"

Ellisif cocked her head to one side. "Where are you going, my lord?"

"Iceland, Greenland, and beyond. This land has no need of me and I weary of blood guilt." He leaned close to her ear. "This I tell you, and you alone. When I sleep, I see our daughter. I fear her death was God's punishment on me for reaching too far. For that, I beg your forgiveness." He knelt in front of her and bowed his head.

The entire hall was deathly still, held by the vision of Harald the Hardrada on bent knee.

Ellisif looked down at the scarred and weary body. Even kneeling he was not much shorter than she. Putting a soft hand on his shoulder, she leaned forward to whisper in his ear, "I will not forgive. I will, *never*, forgive."

There was the slightest tremor in Harald's shoulders, but when he regained his feet his face was again a mask. "I go to my grave with many stains on my soul."

Ellisif shrugged. "The stains on your soul have never been my concern. You made that clear years ago."

Strykar shifted uneasily. As the king's marshal, he knew far more than he wished about the state of his marriage, but even so this public. . .whipping was unseemly.

Ellisif continued, "I will not follow your road, my lord. I have obeyed your whims for twenty years, but now I long for home. By your leave, I will return to Kiev." She spoke with the slightest bit of an edge in her voice. "Truthfully, my lord, there is nothing to hold me here." A touch of irony entered her voice. "Perhaps, if that knee had bent years ago, I may have chosen otherwise. Tell me, was it so difficult?"

Harald met her eyes. "Easier than you can imagine." His bleak eyes turned to Strykar. "Tell our people. Let each one decide. Olaf returns to Norway. I go on to Iceland. We will winter there and when spring comes I will go on to find this Vinland. Make sure that all who travel with me understand, there will be no return."

Strykar spoke up. "My lord, what about the families of the slain? There are many of them with us, and truthfully, they may have nothing to return to in Norway, yet I cannot see how they will fit on this venture of yours. The risks are too great. The mutterings of a drunken stranger are no way to plan a campaign."

"Anyone who wishes can travel with us. This is not a campaign. We do not travel to conquer a kingdom, but to plow fields. Women and children will be no hindrance. Furthermore, the entire royal treasury is here. Ellisif and Olaf will return to Norway poor. We will use the money to provide for those who have losses and to supply our expedition."

Ellisif took a step closer, "My lord, this is most unlike you. Always, since I have known you, you have gathered up greater and greater treasures. And now you leave your sons with no inheritance, me with nothing at all, and give everything away to peasants?"

"I have given my sons all that I have—of value. Gold makes a heavy weight upon the shoulders of young men. They will make their way as best they can and become the better for it. As for you, the whole North knows that my hand is held over you in protection. That alone is enough to get you safely back to Kiev, and once among your family you have no need of my money. The treasure must go where it is needed." Harald smiled, but it was not a good smile to see. "No need for a long face. Think of the honor. How often are you invited to join in a king's penance?"

"Is that what this is? Penance?"

"Perhaps. Or perhaps my ears have grown tender in my old age. I find it difficult to sleep through the howling of hungry children."

Strykar cleared his throat. "One more thing before I leave," he said. "This is a small thing, but an answer would be a favor to me. Late in the night we were talking, of the things drunken men talk of, and a dispute arose and ended with a bet. Imagine a man, thinking of suicide. What would be the greater sin? To end his life in solitude or to end it just as surely by leading a hopeless mass to a certain death? We all know that suicide is a mortal sin, but what if in the search for an honest death, innocents also die? Both are surely sins, but which is the greater?" Strykar went on, no quaver in his voice though he knew he held his life in the balance. "It seemed like the sort of question a king could answer. What is your judgment?"

Harald looked at him. The two men faced each other. The hall was still. The moment stretched on, and then Harald spoke. "I am no longer a king. It does little good to ask such questions of me. It was a foolish wager and to debate it wastes our time. I want a ship to leave today to warn Iceland of our coming. Buy as many provisions and tools as these people can spare. We have little time to waste. Winter approaches and we need time to prepare."

Harald rose and walked toward the door. It opened before he reached it and a figure entered.

"My lord," the man said. "I am Orm Gudmondsson. My father sailed with you to England."

"I know him," Harald said, "He is my companion of old. He has sailed with me many times." With a closer look, Harald could see that Orm was not a man but a boy, man tall, but barely beginning to get any width to his shoulders. His feet were bare and his clothes patched.

"He will never sail again. An hour ago, he died, a straw death, as the wound fever took his leg and his life."

"I'm sorry, lad," Harald looked at the young man. "Your father was a good man. He will be mourned."

Orm met his eyes and said, "Not he alone," and brought the sword at his side around in a two- handed arc, hissing toward Harald's wounded neck.

Harald dropped straight down and his left leg swept out, scything the legs from underneath Orm. The sword clipped a few strands of his hair in passing. Orm's legs went up and the first thing that hit the ground was the back of his head. He lay sprawled on his back, the sword fallen from his loosened grip.

By instinct alone Harald was back on his feet before the shock of the sudden movement awakened the pain in his joints. Strykar was by his side, axe at the ready.

"My pardon, my lord," he said. "I did not see that coming."

"Small matter," Harald said. "He is very young." He gave Strykar a sideways glance. "Still, it is an answer of sorts to your question. A man who longs for death may be kept alive, simply by habit and impulse. God must laugh." He bent and grabbed Orm by the front of his woolen tunic and lifted him to his feet. When the young man tried to stand, he swayed and his knees buckled. Harald held him easily until Orm's eyes came into focus.

"Lad," Harald said, "I did not make light of your father's death. He was a good man and wound fever is an ugly way to die. Still, you must understand—I have seen more men die than you have seen live." He leaned closer to whisper. "I have killed more men with my own hand than live in your village." He pulled back away so he could look the boy in the eye. "With enough practice, death becomes an easy companion. Yet, he was your father and I am responsible for his death. Your desire for revenge is well placed. But you are not yet man enough to kill me. Be patient. Someday, you will be." A sudden mad impulse seized him, "Orm, why don't you join our venture to the West? I will not return, so it will be your only chance to pursue your vengeance. Think on it today; if you choose to accompany us you will have a place on my ship. A boy who would kill a king to avenge his father must have many other good qualities." Harald set the boy down, turned his back, walked out the door.

Strykar bent down and picked up Orm's sword. He held it out to the shaken boy.

Orm took the sword, "At what do you look?" he asked, humiliated and confused.

"I'm marking you, so that I never play a game of dice with you. Truly, you have the most extraordinary luck." Strykar patted the boy on the shoulder and followed Harald.

There was much to do.

CHAPTER EIGHT

HAROLD AND STRYKAR WALKED among the camp. It was near sunset. A few small fires flickered as the host settled down for the evening.

"We need to leave this place quickly," Harald said, "or it will go hard with them this winter."

"You are still their king. It is their duty to provide for you and yours."

"Duty is a bitter food for a child to eat in winter. We will leave some silver so they can bring supplies from the mainland."

"As you wish, my lord."

"Very good," Harald said. "How go the other preparations?"

"Olaf and Ellisif will also leave tomorrow. Many people go with them, and most of the wounded."

Haakon Snorrisson approached them.

"My lord," he said and fell into step.

Harald nodded at him, "Walk with us, Haakon."

They wound their way through the camp.

"My lord," Haakon asked, "what are your wishes? Your son sails in the morning and I would accompany him, if it suits you."

The three men came to the edge of the island. Below them small waves softly whispered against the rocky beach.

Harald looked at the evening sky and felt the breeze against his cheek. "The weather looks good for sailing tomorrow. Haakon, do you realize that Strykar and you are the last of those who first traveled to Byzantium with me? The others are dead or scattered."

"I know that, my lord. More than that, I feel it, in my bones. I have no great wish to go a'viking again. Your son is a good boy, and my counsel may be of some small use to him. But if you wish me at your side in this strange land, I will not tell you no."

Harald shook his head slowly. "Haakon, I may be done commanding people to bend to my will, and I want no one on this journey who does not wish to be. You will give good counsel to both my sons, and I will rest easier knowing you are at their sides, just as you spent so many years at mine. Go with my blessing, and remember us at your prayers." They perched comfortably on the rocks, looking out onto the quieting sea. Harald said, "We need to leave this place for our own sake. The season grows late for travel to Iceland."

Haakon said, "How many travel with you?"

"About fifty ships—perhaps a thousand people," Strykar said. "Of those, there are only about a hundred men who can still lift a sword. The rest are women, children, and cripples. Truly, this will be a strange expedition."

Harald said, "Remember, this is not a war on which we embark. I do not think we can take this land by force. We will have enough warriors for protection, but we will need to rely on negotiations and treaties if we are to make this new land a home. Now is when all those years in Byzantine should be rewarded. If we can live through Empress Zoe, we should be able to deal with a few naked Skraelings."

Strykar glanced sideways, "I remember how you dealt with Empress Zoe. You're not as young and pretty now—perhaps the same tactics won't work."

Haakon laughed out loud. "Yes, my lord, and I seem to remember when she lost patience with you there was an escape from prison, a night flight with a hostage, and a hard row back to Kiev. You truly are a master of diplomacy."

Harald chuckled, "With luck, the Skraelings are governed by men. I've always done much better with men than women." He flipped a small rock out into the water. "Take care of my sons, Haakon. The northern earls are angry, but perhaps their anger will die with me. Fare you well."

"You also, my lord," Haakon said.

Harald abruptly rose and stalked off into the darkness away from camp.

The two men watched him leave then Haakon said, "So Strykar, what is this you do? Are you accompanying your lord into the afterlife, like in the old times?"

"Perhaps," Strykar said, "or perhaps we do go to found a new country. Eric the Red did so, and Harald is a far greater man than he."

"Still," Haakon said, "he is very strange now. I welcome the chance to leave his company. I don't know his thoughts at all."

Strykar shrugged, "He thinks much of his daughter. He sleeps little and when he does his sleep is troubled. You are not wrong to leave. He lives in a different world than ever before. I have no idea where his whim will lead us, and neither does he. Glory, death or disgrace."

"Does he care?" Haakon asked.

"No," Strykar said, "no, I do not believe he cares at all."

The two men sat for a long time, talking of small things and listening to the night sounds of the camp and the sea.

CHAPTER NINE

THE NEXT MORNING DAWNED clear and bright.

The camp came alive long before light and the ships bound for Norway, with a great clatter of oars, departed as soon as the harbor markers could be seen.

Strykar stood beside Harald, watching as the ships cleared the safety of the bay. Without looking at him he said, "So, my lord, you have divested yourself of your wife, your sons, your kingdom, and your dreams, all in one day. What next?"

"Feel free to join them," Harald said. His eyes too, were locked on the departing vessels as they caught the breeze and deployed their sails. A figure that may or may not have been Olaf waved an arm in farewell.

"You miss my point," Strykar looked at his king, "When first we met, you had less than you have today. I look forward to seeing what you do now."

"Enough," Harald said. "Are we ready to depart?"

"Yes, my lord. There is seed grain loaded in each ship.

Every boat carries farming tools. I've purchased some cattle—we can certainly get sheep and horses in Iceland. Also, the smith known as Knut died last night. He had no sons so I purchased his tools from his widow."

"Ploughshares and looms?"

"Yes, my lord. One of each in every cargo ship."

"Very well. I want a minimum of two weeks food and water on board. We will plan to top off our water in the Faeroes, but we will not count on that. I want to sail with a heavy load. We need to support our people through the winter in Iceland, and we cannot count on a crop the first year in this new land."

"Already done."

A woman approached them. "Good day, Lord Harald." She was plainly dressed; the brooches that held her dress unadorned. Most of her hair was concealed under a woolen scarf, but Harald could see it was generously flecked with gray.

Harald nodded, then merely looked at her, waiting. "I am Vigdis Sigursdottor. Orm Gumnundsson is my son."

"Do you wish to kill me, too?" Harald asked.

"Why, yes, my lord," Vigdis said, surprised. "I would be a poor wife if I did not. Still," she continued, "Gumnund followed you with glee for many years. I cannot hold you responsible for his death. My son is a different matter. Should he decide to voyage with you, do I need fear a king's vengeance?"

"It is up to him. I have no taste for his blood, but I cannot promise that in the future he might hurry me enough to force me to hurt him. You have my word I bear him no ill will."

Vigdis looked at him carefully, judging his sincerity. "Very well. He has gathered his things and waits by your ship. I will go and say my farewells."

Harald cocked his head, "Your son goes without you? There is room enough for you and yours, as well."

She shrugged, "All that I own and all my responsibilities lie in Norway. There is nothing in Norway for Orm except the chance to die in a king's army. There are no kings in Iceland and Greenland. He is thirteen, old enough to leave and find a place to make his own."

Without another word she turned and walked back down the beach, past the long row of ships.

Strykar looked at Harald. "A woman of few words," he said.

"I'm glad she doesn't travel with us," Harald said. "She would succeed where her son and the entire English army failed."

The beach was busy, with people loading last-minute bundles. Some of the ships had been turned sideways to shore, so shaggy cattle could be urged up gangplanks. As the weight of the animals hit the ramp, the ships tipped over to leave only a slight incline for the cattle to climb. Once loaded they were rocked back upright and pushed off the beach. Soon the harbor was full of ships heading out to sea.

Strykar stopped by his ship, "We will meet you in Torshavn?"

"Yes," Harald said. "I will wait until all the ships clear the harbor. I will be the sheep dog and you the shepherd."

"Very well, my lord." The two men shook hands. Strykar swung aboard his ship for his own final preparations.

Harald continued down the beach alone. He saw a slender figure standing alone at the prow of his ship. It was Orm Gumnundsson, waiting to embark. When he came abreast of the lad he paused and looked at him in silence. The boy met his eyes defiantly. The bundle of his possessions was pitifully small. The cloak over his shoulders was thin and plain, without a single gold thread along the edge. The only spot of color was a flash of gold from the hilt of his father's sword that hung down his back.

"We need to talk," Harald said. "On the trip to Iceland, these people need me. Do I have your promise not to kill me aboard ship? I ask, not for myself, but for those who are in my charge."

Orm looked at him, sensitive to any hint of mockery, but heard none.

"I can wait," he said.

"Better gear than good sense, a traveler cannot carry," Harald quoted, then, putting a hand on the gunwale, swung aboard his ship. Orm followed more slowly, climbing up the anchor rope and swinging over the side. Once aboard, he looked around. He had traveled many times on coastal trading ships or broad beamed freighters, but this was the first time he'd been aboard a fighting longship. The bow towered over his head. He laid a hand on the intricate carving of the top strake that lead to the dragon's head on the bow. So perfectly balanced, it almost seemed like it was a living thing. The sides of the ship glowed with gilt; the stern was carved into a dragon's tail. The deck was crowded, with seamen's chests by every oarhole. Overhead, the mast, yard, and sail were unstepped and resting on their supports. Orm counted 25 oars on each side, with room on the chests for two men to sit side by side. Gaily-painted shields hung by ropes over the side, interlocked so as to keep spray out of the ship while under sail.

He turned to Harald, "Why is yours the last ship to leave?"

"This is a longship, Orm, not a fat-bellied freighter," Harald explained, "This is the warship of the king of Norway. Under sail it is the fastest ship in the world. This fact I know, for I've traveled most of the world and there are none her equal. We could leave tomorrow and still reach Iceland before any of the freighters.

"Lend a hand, lad," Harald said, nodding towards the gangplank at the center of the ship. A row of men passed water skins and tubs of dried fish and grain aboard ship. A portion of the deck planking was removed and Orm scurried aft to help stow gear below decks. He knew nothing of longships, but he did know how to work.

Shortly, the supplies were aboard and the crew found their places. Orm counted fewer than thirty men. It did not seem to be enough, but soon a trail of women and children tripled the size of the crew.

Harald caught the puzzled look in the boy's eyes. "This is a warship, made to carry nothing but warriors and weapons. We need to crowd more people on this ship to make room for supplies and livestock on the others. Do not worry; the ship is made for a crew this size. Although," he added, "it may get a little crowded at night. Now, get to an oar."

CHAPTER TEN

ARNORA FELT LIKE SHE WAS in a bad dream that would not go away. Once again, she was crouched by her father trying to rouse him from a drunken slumber. She shook him and shouted, "Father!" as loudly as she could. She was rewarded by a dark glower and a hard shove that toppled her sideways. All around her was an empty camp. Preparations had continued through the night and most of the people had left before daylight. With the coming of the dawn everyone else had streamed down to the harbor with all their possessions. There was nothing left within eyesight except a smattering of belongings not worth the bother of packing. She looked wearily at her father. Asbrand's friends, those that still lived, had fallen from him after the word of how he missed the Battle of Stamford Bridge came out. Although most of the king's sworn men had perished in the fighting and no one else cared sufficiently to punish him for his drunkenness, the episode had gained him no favor with those around him. He'd retreated further into strong drink and Arnora was the only person who seemed to care.

She left her father's side and went around their camp, gathering up belongings. There weren't many—she only had one dress, her father's sleep sack, and a smattering of arms and armor. She looked at the pitiful bundle of belongings and sagged with sadness. Their rapid flight from England had resulted in her having nothing at all of her mothers to remember her by except a green wool cloak which had served as her very best Sunday wear. It lay on the ground now and after a sideways glance at her father Arnora picked it up and put it on. It settled comfortably on her shoulders and she picked up the slightest hint of her mother's scent. It warmed her soul and brought tears to her eyes. She stood up straight and squared her shoulders. Feeling the cloak like a hug from her lost mother gave her the courage to walk back to her father and nudge him with her foot.

"Father," she said, as clearly and distinctly as she could, "you need to rise. We are all alone here and most of the ships have left the harbor. If you don't get up, we will die here, for we are in a land where we have no friends and winter is coming."

He rolled over on his back and his eyes slowly came into focus. He slowly turned his head from right to left, taking in his surroundings.

"Fool of a girl," he said, his voice rusty with sleep, "what have you done to us? Why did you let me sleep so long?"

He staggered to his feet, walked a little way away, turned his back and relieved himself against a tree. He lurched sideways as he turned back to Arnora and said, "Pick up your trash and hurry. We need to get on a ship." He bent over and grabbed his sword and a rusty mailshirt, leaving the rest for her to carry. Arnora saw only his back as he hurried down the trail towards the harbor. She gathered up what was left and followed him as quickly as she could.

She almost ran into him as she rounded a corner. He was standing stock still, staring at a harbor empty only but for one ship, the largest she'd ever seen.

"Only the king's ship is left," he said, "Lord Harald bears a grudge against me, through no fault of my own. Come along—we have no other choice. If I were alone, I could make my way easily—everyone has need of a good man. With you dragging me down my life is much harder."

Arnora felt tears start again.

Asbrand looked sideways at her and said, "Oh girl, it's not so bad. It's not entirely your fault. I should have left you and your mother in Norway and traveled light and alone. If it were your mother's fate to die, you could have been back in the mountains with a house and your goats, instead of hanging about my neck like a millstone. Come, now, we need to get onto that ship."

They hurried down the slope to the rocky beach. Men were splashing in the surf, pushing the huge ship out to sea. Asbrand threw his gear over the side and pushed Arnora after it.

"Find an oar," he said and turned to lend a hand. Arnora stood helplessly amidst the clutter and confusion. The ship grated and groaned its way off the beach and the oars bit deeply into the foaming surf. Men poured over the side of the ship, seawater dripping off them and running into the bilge. Asbrand grabbed Arnora by the arm and shoved her toward the stern. He nodded towards a slender, hooded figure sitting alone. "Help her," he said. "Hurry. The king won't throw us over the side once we are at sea, but if we are still close to shore and it pleases him, we'll go into the water. We have no friends in this land so if we're *lucky* we will die on that beach."

Arnora stumbled the length of the ship, avoiding piles of gear and dodging oars. When she reached the lonely figure struggling with a huge oar she realized it wasn't a woman, but a boy about her own age—tall, but still beardless. His face was streaming sweat and his teeth were clenched as he tried to keep up. He was the only person on the ship who looked as miserable as she felt and despite her shyness it was relatively easy for her to sit next to him and wrap her hands around the oar.

CHAPTER ELEVEN

HARALD JUMPED UP ON the top strake and bellowed, "We depart! Shields in, oars out, push off."

A dozen men leaped over the side of the ship as the shields were unhooked and brought aboard. This exposed the oarlocks, and soon all the oars were in the water. Orm caught the sharp edge of a seaman's tongue when he grabbed an oar at random and shoved it through the oarlock.

"Fool boy," he shouted, "open your eyes! That's a midships oar, not stern." Orm felt himself reddening. Taking a closer look, he saw that the oars were all different sizes. *Of course,* he realized, *the oars all strike the water in the same place, but the ship widens and narrows.* He corrected the mistake and then hurried back to his place in the stern. He felt the ship move beneath him as the men in the water heaved. Then, suddenly, it was free, skimming backward away from shore. Orm was speechless. The first rush of the boat as she came fully afloat was the finest feeling he'd ever experienced. Even adrift in the sheltered harbor he could feel the life and the spring in her. He'd spent much of his life aboard ships, but this was a greyhound compared to a village mutt.

She floated in the quiet harbor as the sailors clambered aboard and sorted themselves according to the oars. There weren't enough men for each oar. Harald gave no orders, simply stared silently until women and children filled in each blank spot. Orm picked out an oar by the stern and sat in the middle of the chest. *I nearly killed a king*, he said to himself, *I should be man enough to pull an oar alone.* He discovered his mistake with the first stroke. The oar was fully three times his height and not much over an arm's length was inside the hull. He strained to pull it and then strained to lift it for another stroke. On the third stroke he was slow and his oar collided with another. The "clunk" earned him a rap on the head from the sailor behind him. Other collisions followed and muffled oaths from the sailors.

Harald began to slowly tap a small drum. The rhythm resonated down the ship and soon the oars were moving to its beat. Orm planted his feet and heaved on the oar. After five minutes he felt blisters starting to form. Lost in misery, puffing from exertion, he didn't see the girl next to him until she sat on the sea chest and put her hands on the oar.

Startled, he looked up. "I don't need help," he said. "I can do it myself."

She merely smiled and leaned into the oar. "My name is Arnora. My father told me to make myself useful, and all the other places are full. Please, can I help you, so his anger doesn't grow?"

Orm shifted sideways so their bodies weren't touching. "Of course."

"Come about," Harald's hoarse voice somehow carried the length of the ship. The ship slowly came around, and then headed away from shore toward the open sea. From his seat on the sea chest Orm could watch Harald at the rudder. It was still pivoted up and out of the water, but as he watched, Harald let it down, pivoting on the rudder boss.

He secured it with a wide leather strap attached to the top strake. The tiller was shaped into a dragon head and it easily fit Harald's hand as he leaned back against the stern of the ship.

Even with the mismatched crew the ship was soon skimming across the water, faster than a man could walk.

Arnora and Orm didn't speak again, saving their breaths for the oar. When they cleared the harbor, another complication presented itself. The waves were not high, but high enough that the two inexperienced crew members had to be careful not to pull their oar through air rather than water.

Harald called out, "Step the mast," and ten men pulled their oars in. They grabbed the mast from its resting place. Four of them started walking it up while another four pulled on ropes attached to its top. Two men guided the base of the mast into a hole in the keelson. When the mast was fully erect, the slot in the mast partner was filled by the mast lock. The men swarmed to attach and tighten the shrouds and lines. Finally, the sail was raised. As it caught the wind, Harald yelled, "Oars in!"

Orm and Arnora pulled the oar in. It was longer than the ship was wide. Arnora stood up and guided it over the head of the oarsman on the other side of the ship while Orm twisted it so the blade came through the slot in the oarlock. Between the two of them they soon had the oar in and stored. Spray was coming over the side, and taking their cue from the others, Orm and Arnora hung shields back over the side, effectively raising the freeboard of the ship another two feet. When this was done, they sat back down on the sea chest. Orm was amazed as the ship gathered herself and picked up speed. Once they reached the open sea, he could feel every wave as the ship reacted like a living thing to the winds and water. He put a hand on the gunwale and felt it twist and buck under his hand as the ship pierced the waves.

Now that they were under way, the pace on board slowed. People moved leisurely about the deck, stowing gear and restoring order. Orm had his first good look at Arnora She was as tall as he, and heavier, with wide shoulders and hips. She had a full head of red hair and direct blue eyes. Orm looked down and away from those eyes and saw her hands were blistered and bleeding.

"You're hurt."

She looked down at her hands and blushed. "I'm afraid I haven't done much rowing before. They will heal. My father says I need to toughen up for this trip. He says a woman's hands are of no use."

Orm reflexively clenched his own hands, so she wouldn't see his blisters.

"I think, that hands can be useful even without calluses." He paused, trying to say the right thing. "There are different tasks for different hands, but work is work. My mother says no work is noble, but all work is honorable."

"Your mother is right," Harald's raspy voice joined the conversation, "Orm, who is your companion here?" Harald had relinquished the tiller to another sailor and was making his way to the bow, giving directions for the proper stowage of gear on the way.

"Her name is Arnora, I know nothing else. She just sat by me to help pull the oar."

Harald held out his hand. "Greetings, Arnora-without-a-father. I am Harald Sigurdsson."

Awestruck at being in the presence of the Hardrada, Arnora stammered, "Lord, I. . .I do have a father. I am Arnora Asbranddottor." She tentatively reached out her small hand where it was engulfed in Harald's massive one.

"Asbrand is aboard my ship?" Harald questioned. "I did not know he had a daughter."

"Yes, my lord. He is my father, but I have seen little of him in my life. His work kept him away from us."

More than work kept him away, Harald thought, *and no great loss for you.*

"What brings you to join him on this voyage?" he asked.

Arnora looked down. "My mother died of the camp fever. There was no one who would take me in and no dowry for a husband."

Of course not, any treasure for a dowry was long ago spent on whores and wine.

"He hopes to find a place for me in Iceland," Arnora continued. "Yours was the only ship on the beach, and we were the last ones aboard."

"Well, fare you well, Arnora Asbrandsdottor. You and Orm might have much to talk about. His father has also recently died." He nodded and his hand dropped briefly to Arnora's shoulder as he left.

"How do you know King Harald?" Arnora asked in a shocked whisper. She had been watching him covertly as she rowed. She had seen him often, but always from a distance. Up close he filled the eye in every way possible. Taller than any person she'd ever seen, his rasping voice and gleaming eyes dominated everything within view. The vicious scar from the arrow that should ended his life left a harsh red line across his throat and his shoulders seemed to sag as if a heavy weight pressed down on him.

"I, ahh, I tried to kill him yesterday."

"What!"

"My father was one of his liegemen. He was wounded fighting for the king's standard at Stamford Bridge. He fought on because he thought the king was already dead and honor required that he join him. The wound sickened. They cut off his leg to stop the rot, but he died anyway. I sought to. . ." Orm paused, struggling for the right words. "I don't know what I sought to do. I knew my father was dead and someone pressed his sword into my hands. The next thing I knew I was in the king's hall and my sword sought his neck."

"How do you still live?"

Orm shrugged. "A king's mercy. Perhaps just a king's whim."

"Do you still wish to kill him?"

"I do not know," Orm said honestly. "Truly, I do not. He is not who I thought he was. My whole life, he's been the king. Harald the Hardrada, the Ruthless, the Hard Ruler. All my life I have heard stories of how he brings fire and blood to any who oppose him, stories of his greed and treachery. He's a king many people would be glad to see gone. I know this, and I know his ambition killed my father and many others, but I've seen nothing of this in the time I've been around him. I suppose," He concluded, "when I know who he is, I will know if he should die or not."

Orm had been thinking out loud, trying to sort out his conflicting feelings, almost forgetting the girl next to him. He looked up and saw the look of horror on her face.

She struggled to find something to say.

"Perhaps, you should watch King Harald a long time before you make your decision. It would be a pity to make a mistake."

Despite his misery, Orm smiled. "Perhaps, you are right."

Asbrand was seated at an oar amidships. Harald paused by him.

"My lord," Asbrand said.

"I met your daughter, she seems a likely lass. She rowed hard enough to bloody her hands."

Asbrand said, "She could not stay in the Shetlands. I will leave her in Iceland. Surely there is a man there who needs a young wife, even one without a dowry."

Harald looked at him, "Are you sure this voyage is for you? Remember, 'Who travels widely needs his wits about him; the stupid should stay at home.'" Harald waited patiently to see if the man would take offense.

Asbrand said nothing, merely looked at Harald with a blank expression.

Harald leaned closer, looming over the other man, "Asbrand, my daughter just died. This would not be a good voyage to make light of a child's value."

"Yes, my lord."

Harald continued to the bow of the ship.

"Eric," he said to the sailor standing with his hand on the forestem, "how goes the voyage so far?"

Eric turned, "Fine, my lord. Even the merchantmen are making good time. Two days and we reach Torshavn."

Harald joined him. As far as they could see the sea around them was flecked with the sails of ships. Harald leaned over the side to spit into the curl of white water at the bow.

"So, Eric, how did you find our departure today?"

"Oh, my lord," Eric spat in disgust, "I didn't know whether to kill them all, or just myself. To kill them would have been more justice, but I thought if I jumped overboard there would be less disarray for you to clean up."

Harald laughed, "Truly, you are considerate, Eric. It would not have been a good omen if my kendtmann had started the voyage by killing all the new crewmen."

"Still, my lord," Eric asked, "do you remember how we left Oslo for England?"

Harald did remember. The ship had bristled with men and arms, their armor gleaming in the morning sun. The surface of the fjord had been as still as glass and the fifty oars had struck the water as one. Two strong men per oar and the ship had flown across the water.

Harald's banner had fluttered stiffly in the wind that day. The black raven on the field of red looked bright and new. Ellisif had repaired it over the winter.

A task for a queen.

With her own hands she had sewn the rips and washed out men's blood. Once, Harald had seen her silently weeping as she repeatedly rinsed the cloth in clean water. The water was changed many times until no tinge of pink remained.

As though he could read Harald's mind, Eric said, "It feels passing strange, my lord, not to be sailing under LandWaster."

Harald agree, "That was a good day, Eric. But all those strong men who beat the sea with their oars so we flew across the water, they are all dead. And they died under LandWaster. I think I am not sorry for its absence."

Orm and Arnora had followed Harald toward the prow of the ship, pausing under the great sail to stare at the assortment of weapons and other gear. Harald saw them and motioned them to him.

"Eric, here are two old veterans you can speak with. Eric is our kendtmann, the navigator, on this trip. Eric, show them a little of what you know, so if your despair over our new oarsmen overcomes you, there will be trained replacements."

Orm and Arnora stared at the navigator. He was tall and lean. Not so tall as Harald, but no one was. He wore a plain woolen shirt and trousers, but the cape that hung from his wide shoulders was a deep rich blue woven through with gold threads. His long nose angled down sharply over his full beard and mustache. His eyes were blue and they gazed with little joy at the boy and girl.

"This is Orm Gumnundsson and Arnora Asbrandsdottir. Instruct them a little; a longship and an open ocean voyage are new to them. A favor to them is a favor to me."

Harald left again on his rounds, not needing a hand to balance against the rolling of the ship.

"You have a powerful sponsor," Eric said, "and I know your fathers. What would you like to learn?"

"How do you know where you are going?" Arnora asked. "There is nothing but water, and it is all the same."

Orm tried to look uninterested, but in truth he was relieved he hadn't needed to expose his own ignorance of the sea.

"Girl, you are wrong," Eric explained. "The sea tells us much. The color shows us how far we are from land. Look at the bow wave; it tells us how fast we are traveling. See how the swells strike us? You can use that to set a steady course. That, and the wind. A warm, wet wind is usually from the southwest, a cold, wet wind comes out of the northeast."

"What of the stars?" Orm asked, "Can you not tell your course from them?"

"Yes, the stars are the best, when you can see them. If there are clouds or fog they are of no use, and if you are sailing in the north in the summer, the stars can seldom be seen so the sun is more useful. Wait till noon and then measure its height above the sea. With experience, that will tell you how far north you are. The Shetlands are about as far north as Bergen and the Faeroes are about the same as Trondheim. Iceland is even further north."

"It all sounds impossible," Arnora said.

"Like anything else." Eric said, "Very hard in the beginning, but if you work hard and pay attention you learn more and more. Orm, run to the stern. When this piece of wood passes by you, wave."

Orm scurried off, dodging people and barrels.

Eric took Arnora's finger and placed it on his wrist. "Now, can you feel my pulse?" Arnora's eyes lost their focus. She moved her finger around, and then nodded.

"Very well then, start counting the beats." He threw a small piece of wood in the water, even with the bow.

Eric watched intently. At the moment Orm waved, he pulled Arnora's fingers off his wrist.

"How many?"

"Twenty-seven."

Eric's mouth moved in silent arithmetic. Orm rejoined them, puffing slightly.

"What does that tell you?" Orm asked.

"It tells me that if this wind holds, we will sight the Faeroes shortly before dark tomorrow. I know how far away the Faeroes are, I know how long the boat is, I know how long it took to pass the wood, and I know how long a day is. And together, they tell me how long the voyage will be. See, none of it is magic. You can tell how far you are from land by seeing which seabirds fly with you. Some live always on the water, but many return to land every night. You need to stay aware of everything. All changes are important. Why, if the wind is right, you'll be able to smell the sheep on the Faeroes before you ever see the land."

"And knowing this, you can go wherever you want," Orm said.

"No, lad, sometimes the sea takes you where it wants. The winds and currents are sometimes too powerful to fight, but with luck you can always find your way back. I have sailed to Iceland in as little as a week and once it took me a month. And that time, half the ships in the fleet never got there at all. You cannot defeat the sea, but with courage you can win your way through in the end. Remember, children, courage is all. King Harald says it best. 'Courage is half of success.'"

Eric tapped Orm's chest. "Use this to stay the course and this," tapping Arnora's head, "to find your answers." Abruptly, he wearied of talking to children and stood and stretched, his eye on the horizon and his back to the rest of the ship. "Now go. Come back when you have learned a little and we'll talk again. But not today."

CHAPTER TEN

DIAMONDS SPARKLED IN THE drops of water reflecting the morning sun. The swell was about a man's length in height. Harald leaned comfortably against the stern, one hand on the tiller. As he steered, his fingers roamed gently over the smooth wood, cherishing the feel. Other than his clothes, it was the last thing in the world made for him alone. The dragon's neck was thick, fitting his huge hands, and the carved head swelled even larger.

They had begun to catch up and pass some of the slower merchantmen and Harald took a slight pleasure in weaving in and out amongst them. As long as the wind held and they were under sail, he had enough experienced sailors on board to play this game. Should the wind drop, however, out would come the oars and then Harald would want as much sea room and as few witnesses as possible.

With the exception of Eric at the bow and the men at the shrouds in case the sail needed to be trimmed, everyone else was settling down, finding what comfort they could on the crowded deck. Never before had he sailed with so many young ones on board. So far, all was well. After all, even though children, they were children of the North. In a country where most roads were saltwater, everyone learned to be comfortable on board ship. It was just that it was not the sort of a ship they were used to. The lines of a longship were constructed around speed and battle, not comfort. Even so, they could adapt. If not for the rolling and pitching, the dimensions of the deck weren't markedly different than many of the houses these people had come from. Built long and narrow, if the ship had a roof over it and a fire in the middle instead of a mast, it would have been just like home. Now, as the sun began to set, people relaxed against the hull, sat on sea chests, gazing idly at the sea. Even though it was only midafternoon a few dozed in their sleeping skins. Many of the women, unused to even a moment's idleness, were busy with needle and thread. They had no cooking to do. Harald had deemed the waves stiff enough that he wanted no fire aboard ship. Instead, people eased their hunger on dried fish and drank water or beer from the big barrels that had been rolled on board.

This was the longest voyage on the open sea many of them had ever taken. No one seemed seasick. A few small children toddled about, watched carefully by any adult within reach. Harald wasn't concerned about them falling overboard. With the shields in place the sides of the ship were higher than a small child's head.

Orm and Arnora were seated side by side on a seaman's chest a few feet away from Harald. They had done nothing but sit and talk since their navigation lesson. He watched them idly, not even aware of what he was doing.

Eric picked his way through the throng of legs and made his way to Harald.

"My lord, what are your wishes? We are traveling under a winter sky now; it will be dark in a short time. We have open sea, but I fear a collision in the dark."

Harald nodded, "I know. We will reef the sail so as not to outstrip the merchantmen, but we will continue to sail. I, too, fear a collision, but I fear October seas more. It is best we finish our journey."

Eric nodded and turned to Orm. "Boy, grab that rope."

Orm grabbed the one indicated. It was tied through a hole in the gunwale and went up to the middle of the sail. There it split into a noose and went through two holes, an arm's length apart.

"We need to slow our speed, so we want the wind to catch less of the sail. Pull that rope tighter; it gathers the cloth."

Orm pulled, but could feel the sail fighting him, like a fish on the end of a line. Arnora helped him pull and soon a portion of the sail was bunched in a small fold around the noose. Eric nodded approval and Orm tied the rope off again.

"Now, do the same on the other side." Orm and Arnora scurried over to the other gunwale, eager to prove their worth. Eric turned his back on them and questioned, "Torches? In the bow?"

"No, not yet, stand ready. If the need arises we can light one quickly. Choose good men for the watch tonight, then get some sleep. I will take the first watch and you the second." Orm and Arnora had the other reef rope tightened and tied off. Harald felt the ship settle under him, slowing perceptibly in her rush through the water.

Eric nodded and moved forward, stopping here and there to speak to some of the men scattered hither and yon. On the way, he unobtrusively checked Orm's knots. He reached the bow, nibbled a bit of fish, took a small drink of water, and slid into his sleeping sack. With the ease of long practice, he turned on his side, pillowed his head on his arm and was asleep.

As the sun dropped lower in the skies, the day quickly chilled. Orm was soon cold. His thin cloak was not enough protection from the damp sea breeze. Arnora was slightly better off. Her mother's cloak was thick, and she was warmed by more than just the wool.

"Open the chest, boy." Harald nodded toward their seat. Orm gave Harald a doubtful look.

"Go ahead, I know the owner well, and he would not mind."

Orm fumbled with the latches and opened the seaman's chest. It was full to the top. Orm looked up again and Harald shook his head. "Go ahead, boy. Find something to wear. The chattering of your teeth will keep the whole crew awake."

Orm gingerly pawed through the gear. The chest contained well-worn leather breeches, bits and pieces of armor and plunder, knives, and near the bottom, a heavy wool clock. Orm pulled it out of the chest and flung it over his shoulders. It hung loosely on him and a full arm's length dragged on the deck.

Harald laughed out loud, his wounded voice a harsh affront. "When you fill that cloak, you will be a man indeed."

"Whose. . . .?" Orm questioned.

"My liegeman, Gunnar Halsson. At Stamford Bridge, he held the entire English army on the opposite side while we formed our ranks. In the end, his chain mail was in tatters and he was fighting with an axe in either hand. An Englishman crawled beneath the bridge and stabbed at him through a crack in the timbers. The English had to push their pile of dead to one side before they could cross over his body. He was a good man. Many is the time he sat on that chest and sang to us while we rowed. He left no son, Orm. I give his goods to you. There should be a sleeping sack in there. They are big enough for two, and his will be big enough for four of you."

Orm was pushing the chest back in place when he noticed the huge bow strapped to the side. He reached out for it.

"No, boy." Harald's voice had an edge. "That is not for you. Not yet. When you are as tall as the bow, then you can lay your hand on it. If you are interested, we will find a bow your size when we get to Iceland."

They were interrupted by a bellow from amidships.

"Arnora, come to me now," Asbrand said, "It grows cold and your duty is to warm my feet."

Arnora started unhappily.

"Go on, girl. He is your father," Harald said, "while he lives."

She nodded and started to leave.

"Tomorrow, you and Orm should learn the rudder." Harald said. The cloud left Arnora's face and she hurried off.

"Arnora," Harald's voice stopped her, "tell your father what I said. All of it."

CHAPTER ELEVEN

"It's time," the sailor said, waking Eric. He rolled over on his back and checked the stars.

"You could have woken me sooner, it is past time." He slid out of his sleeping sack, rolled it up, and put it back in his sea chest.

The sailor shrugged. "We passed Strykar's ship a while ago and he and Lord Harald had a conversation, but I don't know what they said. It feels like we have altered course a bit towards the north. Other than that, nothing."

Eric stretched, rolled his shoulders, and began slowly picking his way in the darkness back to the stern. The ship was taking the swells a little more directly and the stars showed that it was the ship that had changed, not the waves.

In the darkness Eric couldn't see the sail, but a touch on the shroud lines gave him an indication of how it was set and the creak of the mast confirmed it. At midship, two other sailors were on watch, leaning against the mast and peering out into the night while they kept up a desultory conversation.

"What news?" Eric asked.

"We came within hailing distance of Strykar's ship not long ago. He and Lord Harald talked about not landing in the Faeroes, but continuing on to Iceland. Shortly after that we changed course, more to the north. Other than that, nothing."

Eric nodded. "Very well, wake your replacements and get some sleep."

On his way to the stern Eric checked the reef lines that Orm had tied off and retied one of them.

Harald's huge form loomed in front of him.

"I'm here to relieve you," Eric said.

"Good, I grow weary of this. How does the sea feel to you?"

Eric said, "The same, my lord. We're headed north, though, perhaps too far north to hit the Faeroes."

"I am not planning to make port at the Faeroes. If we arrive there in the late afternoon today, we run the risk of some of the ships seeking harbor in the dark. If the other crews are like ours, that is a real danger. Plus, we will lose the best part of a day filling water barrels and setting back out to sea. We will strike far enough north so as to not be worried about shoals, then head straight west for Iceland. We gain nearly an entire day, and catch a better wind."

"Is this wise, my lord?"

Harald snorted, "Is this wise? Is any part of this venture wise? The season grows very late, and we have used only a day's worth of water. I think the greater risk is to linger on the voyage and risk a fall storm." Eric's eyes were now fully adjusted to the darkness and he could see Harald's frosty breath in the night air. "These are not warriors who sail with us. Hard, cold weather will kill some of them. The wind is working for us now, and I think we should take advantage of any luck that comes our way."

"Very well. Any orders?"

"At first light, take the reefs out of the sail and we get all these people to Iceland as fast as possible. Use your judgment."

Eric took the tiller and settled his cloak around his body. Harald unwrapped his own sleeping skin and then settled on the deck next to the sleeping Orm. He lay a while, stars dancing against the inside of his closed eyes, as he tried to relax his body from the tension of night sailing in a fleet of ships. Nothing had happened, but the long hours of tension-filled darkness had left him as exhausted as if he'd been fighting a storm. At one point he thought he'd heard a far-off "crunch." He had listened carefully but heard no shouts of dismay nor saw any torches lit to search for survivors. With all the ships moving in the same direction at approximately the same speed, collisions weren't necessarily fatal but even that thought was not a comfort.

Harald pulled the hood of his cloak up, shadowing his face and drifted off to sleep, the rolling of the longship the closest thing to a cradle he'd ever known.

He awoke when Eric changed course.

His cloak was wet from the night air. He pushed his hood back and slid to a sitting position against the side of the ship. Eric still stood at the rudder, one casual hand controlling it.

"How went the night, Eric?" The sun was just coming over the horizon. The shadow of the mast neatly hit the dragon's head on the bow. "Are we far enough north to be traveling west again?"

"Yes, my lord," Eric said, "I waited until I saw the sun to make sure, but we will clear the Faeroes with ease, if that is still your wish."

Harald stood, the sleep skin puddling at his feet. He looked around at the sea and sky and breathed deeply through his nose. "I think so. This wind feels like it will hold. A long run before the wind and then a long winter's rest while we listen to the storms outside the door." After he stretched hugely he turned to the side of the ship to relieve himself over the edge.

"How many of our fleet are still in sight?" he asked, gazing off into the distance.

"Most of them; I am not sure if all are there. Now that they can see your change of course, they should close up. I think we should leave the reefs in the sail until they all pass us."

"Very well, I'll relieve you after I get something to eat." Harald walked toward the mast, stepping carefully to avoid the sleeping crew. Positioned nearly under the mast, he saw Arnora and her father sharing a sleeping sack. Asbrand was on his back, snoring, and Arnora was huddled as far away from him as she could get. She lay on her side with the hood of her cloak pulled tightly around her face. Harald could see only the tip of her nose and a wisp of red hair. He removed the lid from a water barrel and used the dipper inside to get a drink. As he drank he stared thoughtfully at the sleeping child and her father's slack face. The dipper was still nearly full and with what he recognized was a supreme act of will, he gently put it back inside the barrel and replaced the lid. He would need to keep his distance from Asbrand if the man were to survive the rest of the trip.

Three of the deck planks had been removed and two slaves were busy bailing out the bilge. They had evidently been at it for a while, because one of them was standing on a rib of the ship while the other crouched down next to the keel, scooping water with a wooden bucket. He could only manage to get the bucket half full, then he would hand it up to his partner who would dump it over the side. Harald watched them for a moment, but could see no flaw in their efforts.

He turned away and wrapped an arm around the mast. He leaned his face into the wood, taking strength from it. The stiff breeze was billowing the sail and the mast felt alive, a soundless humming. He could feel the tension in the wood from the force of the sail.

He had selected the tree for the mast himself. On a morning's ride he'd found a tall oak tree, in the midst of a forest of other, lesser trees. Few large oaks remained in Norway. Most of them had already been taken for ships. He didn't know how this one had avoided that fate for so long. He'd been standing on the ground inspecting it when he heard shouting. A moment later a would-be assassin's arrow had zipped past his head and sunk deeply into the tree. Harald ducked around the trunk and by the time he had his sword out his bodyguard had taken the man's head. The next day he had ordered the tree cut and made into a mast for his new warship.

Harald felt the mast with sensitive fingers and nodded approvingly to himself. The arrow head was still there, sunk deep into the wood, where he'd ordered it left. It seemed a good luck token to him, although others had thought him mad.

He lifted the lid of another barrel, peered within and began picking through the dried fish inside, looking for something even vaguely appetizing. He finally gave up and grabbed a piece at random.

As he turned away from the barrel, he gently tapped Arnora with the side of his boot.

She opened misty eyes. "Wake up child. You have much to do today. I will need your and Orm's assistance. Get something to eat and prepare for the day, then come to the stern."

Arnora nodded and quickly slid out of the sleeping sack. She looked around the sleeping boat. Only a few people were up and stirring about. She made a helpless face and asked, "How do I. . . .?"

Harald nodded, "Over the side. Wake one of the older women; you can guard each other's privacy. Try not to fall overboard."

Harald headed back to the stern. He handed half his fish to Eric and he accepted it without joy.

Harald laughed, "Ship food, Eric. Have you forgotten what an open sea voyage is?"

"That is why I wanted to land in the Faeroes. At least there we could have cooked some porridge and perhaps sent boys for birds. I know what a week on the open sea is," Eric said, "it's dried fish and stale water. It's wet clothes and bad sleep."

"Ah, you do remember, why are you a kendtmann? Anyone who likes good food and drink as much as you should have stayed a farmer."

Eric stretched, and relinquished his post at the rudder. "Did you ever see the farm where I grew up? Hard against the side of a mountain, only a small patch of land between rock and fjord, hungry all winter and tired all summer. When my father told me that as the youngest son there was no inheritance for me except his axe and a chance to go a'viking, I was the happiest man alive." Eric shook his head. "I should not have complained about the dried fish and wet clothes. Truly, this has been a good life. If the sea takes me tomorrow I would have no regret."

"Is that why you came on this voyage? Because there is nothing for you in Norway?"

"Is that not why we all came? The sea road doesn't call to the idle and well-to-do. It calls to those who have nothing to lose. Besides," he added, "I know where I came from, a poor farm in a poor land. Look at me now—I am the kendemann of the finest ship in the world."

"With the worst crew," Harald said.

Eric looked at him and started to laugh. Harald joined him and soon all the sleepers were jolted from their slumber by their mirth.

CHAPTER TWELVE

"No, no, boy," Harald snapped, "you're losing the wind."

Orm gulped and jerked the tiller. The great ship lurched into and shuddered through a wave. The sail lost its tension and flapped idly against the mast. The ship wallowed from side to side. Harald saw it coming and rode the roll, but other people were caught unaware and angry shouts filled the air. Orm almost lost his grasp on the tiller but Arnora braced him with her shoulder and he regained his grip.

"The other way," Harald said, his voice quiet but insistent, "turn the tiller the other way."

"Sorry," Orm swung the tiller hard the other direction. Two more rolls, the mast dipping dangerously towards the sea, and then the ship answered its rudder, a wave threw the stern to the side and the sail caught the wind again. Once again, the ship was a thing alive.

Eric stormed the length of the ship, dodging spilled gear and startled people. "What game do you play here!?"

"Orm now knows how close to the wind he can sail

with this ship," Harald replied. "A valuable lesson, and one he learned in but a few moments."

"Had the waves been any higher, he would be learning how long he could cling to the hull of a capsized longship! When you teach him that lesson, be sure to let me know, because it's one I already know and do not wish to learn again!"

Harald said nothing. Looking down at Eric from his great height, he waited patiently for whatever the next words would be. They locked eyes for a moment, and then Eric turned and stormed his way back to the bow.

"Orm," Harald said, "you now know what the rudder feels like when you've lost the wind in a heavy sea. It would be best if you never again know that feeling. Now, Arnora, you take the tiller."

"My lord," Arnora said, startled, "I cannot."

"Child, there is no 'cannot' in this world. There is 'I don't wish to,' and there is 'I am too scared to try,' but you are far too young to start dealing in 'cannot'. Now, take the tiller."

Arnora tentatively grabbed the tiller. Orm moved out of her way, but stayed close. Her small hands would not fit around the dragon's head.

Harald watched her closely, and when he saw her eyes widen as the ship answered to her touch, he laughed out loud.

She grabbed the tiller firmly.

"Lean back," Harald instructed, "Let your feet on the floor and your back against the stern tell you what you need to know. Where is the wind? And at what angle are we taking the waves? Turn a little to windward; that is the right course."

"Why did the breeze change direction when we lost the wind?" Arnora asked.

Harald looked at her with respect. "Very good, child, I'm surprised you noticed that amongst all the excitement. The wind blows, but we make our own as we sail against it.

When we slowed, the wind didn't change; we just stopped making our own so it felt different."

Arnora nodded, somewhat distantly. She stood erect, her face into the breeze. Her cheeks were flushed and red curls spilled over the top of her cloak. Her body swayed gracefully as the ship rode the waves. Her small hands on the tiller moved it gently in response to the sea. Harald noted with surprise that she was holding the ship on a perfect heading.

"Arnora!" came a bellow from midship, "Come now and tend to my gear!"

Arnora jumped, her hands twitching on the tiller, and then moved to obey.

"Stay," Harald commanded, "You have the helm. At this moment, you control the lives of everyone on this ship. You cannot jump to anyone's whim."

"But, my father calls," Arnora said, her voice trailing off.

"Were the Pope himself beckoning you, I would not care. Once your hand is on the tiller you keep it there until someone relieves you. Now, your lesson is not over so keep your place."

Arnora nodded, misery on her face. Her misery deepened as she saw Asbrand coming toward her. His face was pink with fury and when he reached her he grabbed her hair and pulled her head back.

"Girl," he snarled, his face close to hers, "did you not hear me summon you? Stop this playing and tend to my needs."

"Asbrand," Harald queried, "do you value that hand?"

"What?"

Harald's voice was quiet, but carried with utter clarity. The stern of the ship became the center of attention for everyone near.

"This is my daughter, Lord Harald."

"That is true, but she is not a dog. Furthermore, she is at the helm of my ship. So," he continued, "the question still stands. If you wish to keep that hand, remove it from my helmsman." Orm felt the hair stand up on the back of his neck. Harald's voice was still quiet, with the ever-present rasp harshening it slightly, but even so, it had become implacably dangerous.

"You are no longer the king, Lord Harald," Asbrand said, "Who are you to steal my daughter from her duties?"

Harald tipped his head slightly to one side, a look of vague interest on his face. "You are correct; I am no longer the king. Who I am is the man who is going to kill you if you do not release that child."

"You have no right!"

"Perhaps," Harald said, "and you have no more time."

With an oath, Asbrand gave Arnora's hair a final jerk, then released her and started back toward his nest.

Harald's big hand snaked out and grabbed him. Pulling him around, Harald clamped both hands on the front of his shirt and lifted him off the ground. The great muscles in his back knotted as he held the man at eye level. Asbrand's feet dangled a hand's width off the deck.

"Know this," Harald whispered, his hot breath filling Asbrand's nostrils. "Your daughter is under my hand. Any harm to her is an affront to me.

"No," he continued, "let there be no misunderstanding. Any harm to her means your death, as quickly as I get within a sword's length of you." He released his grip and Asbrand fell to the deck, staggering. Harald turned his back on him and faced Arnora.

"You have fallen off the wind," he said. "Pay attention to the course."

"Yes, my lord." Arnora faced into the wind, her hands firm on the tiller, her eyes bright and her shoulders square. She did not look towards her father as he regained his feet and walked slowly back to his berth. Perhaps she did not even see him go.

CHAPTER THIRTEEN

ARNORA WAS AT THE HELM when Eric first spotted the jagged hills of Iceland coming over the horizon. At his cry, Harald made his way to the bow through the crowd of wet, tired people. They were at the end of their second week at sea and even though the winds had been favorable and the weather moderate, everyone was tired of the crowded conditions. They still had plenty of salt fish, but the drinking water in the barrels was becoming brackish and foul.

Eric was standing at the bow, an easy hand holding onto the dragon's neck. Harald joined him.

"Where are we?" he asked.

Eric pointed. "Right where we should be, my lord. The gleam on the horizon is Vatnajokull, the glacier on the eastern edge of the island. The fleet takes its bearings from it and will split up to find winter quarters. Are your wishes still to go to Holar?"

Harald nodded. "Yes, we have enough silver on board to buy a roof for the winter, even if there should be no real hospitality waiting for us. Set our course for Skagafjord and if the good Christians at Holar do not welcome us, we will find shelter in one of the fishing villages."

Eric said, "So, a few days and then with luck our feet are under a table for the winter." He glanced back to the stern. "Does that child have the helm?"

Harald's laugh filled the air. "It drives you mad, doesn't it? That child does have the helm, and she was born to it. After two weeks she reads the wind better than anyone on this boat except you and me."

"Being the third best helmsman among *this* crew is no great compliment, my lord. Truthfully, it matters not to me, but I wonder if you have thought this through. We leave this ship soon and then the girl returns to being servant to a worthless father. Do you favor her by showing her a world that will never be hers?"

"Do not speak so quickly, Eric. Worlds change and if a hand is made to hold a tiller, do I not do God's will by giving it the opportunity?"

"You mock God. This is a lowborn child, a girl, and heir to nothing but bad debts and a dull sword. This . . .. whim of yours will cause talk and gives you good will with no one."

"I seek no one's good will, Eric. I leave my kingdom-making dreams behind. My desires do not extend beyond a warm bed for the winter and fair seas in the spring." Harald gazed serenely towards the distant hills, his voice gentle, his manner untroubled. "As for my whim, I am who I am. Stay with me or leave my employment, but do not seek to bend me to your will."

Eric turned away and headed for midships. After two steps he turned and looked back.

"I hope you know what you are doing. We journey to Iceland, a country of laws and one with no patience for kings, but much respect for power. There are many people betting their lives on your prowess. I hope you do not cause trouble and lead us all into outlawry simply because of a quirk made serious by the memory of a dead child. Children do die, Lord Harald. Everyone's children die. You cannot dwell on the lost one; it will drive you mad. The death of your daughter does not mean God is punishing you. It is just the way of the world." Harald's gaze was blank and without expression and he turned away to gaze over the bow. Eric finished his speech to his broad back.

"In one thing I know you are mistaken. You say you have left your dreams of a kingdom behind. If you truly believe that, you are lying to yourself. You are a king, wherever you stand, and that will not change as long as you draw breath."

Harald gave no indication that he had heard. He stayed in the bow, arm wrapped around the dragon's neck, as the snows and rock of Iceland slowly approached.

CHAPTER FOURTEEN

"When will we arrive?" Orm asked.

"Patience, boy," Eric said. "We will be there when we are there. This is no time for haste. Landsmen fear the deep blue, but a true sailor knows that most of the danger is close to shore. A properly made and manned boat can live through any storm, but the rocks and shoals in shallow water can gut her in a moment."

The ship rocked gently, beating upwind and across the mild waves.

"Still," Orm said, "We have been within sight of Iceland for almost as long as it took to sail here from Scotland! I tire of this."

"As do we all. But, at least now there is land near so you're sleeping on shore and eating hot food almost every day. Shall we hurry? Perhaps you would enjoy swimming ashore from a sinking ship and then trying to live through the winter out there." Eric gestured towards the bleak peninsula of Melrakkasletta. "Nothing to eat, a wind that howls straight from the North all winter, spending your time stumbling through the darkness hoping to find enough driftwood dry enough to burn so you will stay alive one more night. And that's if no Icelandic peasant kills you for that fine cloak on your back. No boy, a little patience now or a short miserable life on a barren beach."

Orm looked at the barren landscape and shivered. "Who lives there?"

"Here? No one, except outlaws. Oh, there are a few scattered farms, but I know not on what they live, except for dried fish."

"Is all of Iceland the same?" Orm gestured towards the barren landscape.

"This is the worst, but in truth there is little here except grass and rocks. You should walk with care when we leave the ship. The people who settled Iceland were those Norway could not hold, men who could not bear a king or men fleeing a king's wrath. This is a hard land, full of hard people. You carry your father's sword like a man, but carry it with care here for there is no mercy in this land."

Harald made his way slowly to the bow, stopping to chat with the people crowding the deck. Eric watched him approach, a sour look on his face.

"What's he doing?" Orm asked, puzzled by the expression.

"See a king at work," Eric explained, "He binds this ship and everyone on it to him, as surely as a fisherman casts nets."

Orm watched more closely, saw Harald slap the back of a grizzled veteran, stoop to play with a toddling child, bow with exaggerated courtesy to an ancient farm wife.

"What? I see but a man among his people."

"You see a carpenter, inspecting his tools. You see a farmer, caring for his stock."

"You mean, that is all just a play?"

"No, I did not say that. A farmer can feel for his stock, a

carpenter can treasure his tools. But when this ship finally makes port, every person on it will be willing to die for Lord Harald. And make no mistake about it, boy; Lord Harald is an expert at this because he's had to do it so often." Eric turned to face Orm, so there would be no mistaking his meaning. "He has needed to replace the people willing to die for him, many times."

Harald reached the bow, a slight smile on his stern face.

"So, Eric, what is our course?"

"Straight west, my lord, until we see the seabirds of Grimsey, then outsouth. If the wind holds we arrive at Skagafjordur tomorrow."

"And our port tonight?"

"None, I think. We can drop sail and drift under the bare mast. There is no decent landing beach within reach and I dislike approaching a rocky coast in the darkness."

Harald nodded. "So, one more night with dried fish and sour beer. Orm, go tell Arnora to hold her course due west."

"Yes, my lord." Orm carefully picked his way across the crowded deck. Arnora was at the stern, hands gripping the tiller and her back resting against the rising strake that went up to the dragon's tail. Her red hair was curled and tousled by the salt air. Her cheeks were now more tanned then rosy and Orm could see tiny lines forming in the corners of her eyes.

"My Lady Helmsman," Orm said, and bowed. Arnora said nothing, but her smile showed that all was right with her world.

"Lord Harald says to stay your course, straight west until we see the seabirds from Grimsey."

Arnora nodded. Orm looked over her shoulder and saw only one ship following them.

"Who remains?" he asked. "When did we leave the others?"

"They have been dropping off one by one. Lord Harald says that they have friends or kinsmen at scattered farms up in the fjords. He says this country is too poor to keep us all in one spot for the winter. Strykar is the only one left."

"Eric calls him 'King Harald's Dog.' He says he is never far from Lord Harald's side."

"I've seen him only once," Arnora said. "He frightens me."

"That is his trade," Orm said, remembering the scarred face and hard hands. "Lord Harald has many enemies. Strykar discourages the cowards and kills the brave."

"He didn't kill you."

"A king's whim, Arnora. Still, if he is King Harald's Dog, he remains on a short leash, and of all on this ship, you certainly have nothing to fear from him."

Arnora blushed. "Another king's whim. I know he favors me, but when we leave this ship and he joins the chieftains in Iceland he will soon forget my name."

The October sun began to set. The ship sailed on, the sound of the waves mingling with the murmurs of the crew until the darkness was complete.

Then all was quiet. In the night a black and white whale surfaced, inspected the vessel, and then vanished into the sea.

CHAPTER FIFTEEN

IT WAS A FINE, FRESH morning. The breeze billowed out the great sail and the ship cut through the waves like a swimming snake. Eric was back at his post, one hand on the dragon's neck as he balanced against the roll. Harald approached, Orm trailing in his wake.

"There my lord," he said, "Drangay Island."

Harald looked closer. The island towered out of the sea, six hundred feet of vertical cliff, with seabirds whirling all around. "So that is Grettir's Island. It would appear to suit him."

"Did you ever know him?" Eric asked.

"No, but his brother came to Byzantium seeking revenge on his killer. Do you know the story? Grettir had a good sword, with a distinctive blade. His killer took it and fled first to Norway, then to Kiev, and finally to Byzantium. Thorstein followed him every step, although he didn't know what the man looked like. While in Byzantium they both served under me in the Varangian Guard. One day Ongul was showing off the blade. Thorstein asked to see it, saw it was the same, and cut off the murderer's head. A good joke, that."

"And then?" Orm asked.

Harald glanced sideways at the boy. "Nothing much. We held counsel and decided that because he had traveled so far to seek his revenge; it would be unmanly to punish him for it. He stayed on and later moved to Jerusalem."

Eric laughed, "Tell the boy the story of his woman. I still think you had a hand in that little tale. Neither of them was smart enough to plan so well."

"Thorstein fell in love with a married woman. And let that be a lesson to you, boy. Woman in general are much trouble, but the married ones are many times more trouble."

Harald continued the story, "The woman's husband suspected something, but could prove nothing, until one day he had witnesses who had seen the two together. By the time the husband had broken down the door, Thorstein had escaped through a trapdoor. Still, no evidence, but the man publicly accused his wife of adultery. She swore she was innocent and offered to risk eternal damnation to prove her innocence. She dressed in her finest clothes and escorted by her friends she walked to the cathedral to swear her oath before God that she was wrongly accused. On the way she came to a muddy ditch. There was a beggar lounging in the shade and she paid him to carry her across so her clothes wouldn't become soiled. The man slipped and in order to save his fee, grabbed her by the thigh and threw her to safety. She kicked him in the face for his impudence and continued to the cathedral, where before the Bishop she swore no man other than her husband had ever touched her—well, her husband and that beggar. She suffered no harm and was declared innocent. Then, for his great insult, asked to be divorced from her husband."

Eric began to chuckle, in advance of the end of the story. Harald glanced at him and finished. "It wasn't until months later that it was found out that the beggar was really Thorstein in disguise. So, her oath was true, but she had been guilty none the less."

Orm asked, "What happened then?"

Harald shrugged, "It was too good a joke to ruin by punishment. They were married and traveled to Jerusalem on a pilgrimage; I think to make amends to God for their trickery. I believe they are still there."

Eric chuckled again, and then turned his attention back to the sea. Suddenly, he stiffened and pointed.

"My lord, what do you make of that?"

Harald and Orm turned their gaze to what Eric was pointing at. A moment's silence then Harald said, "It looks like wreckage to me. It can't be from any of our ships, none could have been here ahead of us." Bellowing to gain Arnora's attention, Harald waved towards the floating wood.

"Drop the sail," he commanded the crew. "Oars in the water. Let's take a closer look."

The mat of floating wreckage was soon abreast of the bow. The ship bobbed up and down, at the mercy of the waves.

"What is it?" Orm asked.

"I'm not sure," Harald said. "It's not the remains of a ship, not anymore. We'll drag it on board."

"Why? It's just wood," Orm was puzzled.

Eric snorted, "Just wood? Boy, if this wood were on shore men would die for it. Look around you. Do you see any trees, wood of any kind?"

Harald looked around, too. "What is your counsel, Eric? Do you remember the laws of this land? I confess, I do not."

"I think the driftwood rules do not apply on the open ocean. It becomes property only after it is near a beach. I think it is ours to claim, or if it goes to law we can make a case."

"Good enough. Get it aboard quickly." Harald himself grabbed the top strake and, judging the roll of the ship, leaned far over the side to grab a piece of the floating wood. Further along the boat, others followed his example. In only a few minutes the deck was covered with dripping pieces of driftwood. They were oddly uniform in size, a little taller than a tall man and as thick as a strong man's wrist. Harald ordered the sail raised and they continued their journey.

Once under way, Harald took a closer look at the wood, a puzzled frown creasing his face.

"What do you make of this, Eric?"

"I do not know, my lord. Why would anyone ship a load of kindling?"

Harald picked up a stick and bent it experimentally. Drawing a knife, he scratched at the surface.

"Why, this is yew," he said, "perhaps Iberian yew. Someone lost a whole cargo of longbow material."

"Of what use is a whole cargo of bow blanks?" Orm asked.

Harald smiled, tipping his head back so the red, raw, arrow wound on his throat showed clearly, "I do not know, boy. This has the feel of a king's cargo, someone who needed to outfit an army. A bowman has his uses. Without archers, I might this day be king of England. This requires some thought, but until I decide what to do, treat this wood very carefully. If I'm wrong, we can still buy our welcome with firewood."

"And if you're right?"

"We can make a home in a strange land. All of us."

The ships continued up Skagafjordur. Drangay fell behind them. Harald watched it carefully for a while. He finally turned his back on the bleak, lonely island and faced the future.

"Where should we land?" Harald asked.

"I think we should go to the mouth of the fjord," Eric said, "All the land around here is under the hand of Asbjorn Arnorsson. After we present ourselves to him we will know the way of this land."

"Very well. Up the fjord till you see a suitable landing site. I'll leave the choice in your hands. Much depends on our greeting. I'll go to prepare."

Harald headed for where his own sea chest waited. He caught Orm's eye and jerked his head. The boy hurried to his side.

"Attend me, boy. Open the trunk."

Orm fumbled with the straps that held the wooden trunk closed. While he was doing that, Harald unfastened the belt at his waist and pulled the plain woolen tunic off over his head. He loosed his baggy trousers and slid them off. His pale skin began to goose bump in the fresh sea air.

"The bucket, boy. Fill it with sea water."

Orm filled the bucket and dragged it back on board. It was all he could do to get it over the rail without spilling it. Harald washed his face and hair in the water, then held it over his head and dumped the contents down his body.

He sniffed, "More water, boy, I still smell myself."

This time Orm stood on a sea chest and sluiced the water over the king. It took many buckets before Harald was satisfied. He'd had lost much weight while recovering from his wound. His muscles moved smoothly under taut skin. Seeing him close up, Orm was amazed again that he'd tried to kill this man. He was truly a giant, with a network of scars giving testimony of a life spent in battle. His arms and shoulders were covered with fading bruises from his last fight and the scars from the arrow wound through his throat showed red and angry, front and back.

He rummaged in his sea chest and found a fresh pair of trousers. He pulled them on over his dripping body and fastened them. Next came a tunic of finely woven wool, a deep sky blue in color. Harald fastened his sword-belt around his waist. The scabbard hung empty.

"My sword, boy."

As Orm picked it up he examined it briefly. It wasn't the sword he expected a king to carry. The pommel was quite plain, iron with only a faint outline of a flying raven made of hammered silver. Plain leather straps, woven tightly and stained with sweat, formed the grip. Harald must have seen the disappointment in his eyes. He laughed. "Did you expect gold? Perhaps it should be. I have been given many golden hilted swords in my time, and I've given them most of them away. Most men are happy to receive them from my hand. I prefer good iron. Swords are like men. Most people don't learn to look past the glitter. But the glitter means little—it is the edge and the strength that matter. This sword came from Byzantium with me. It was made for me by a one-eyed Saracen smith, although I had to get one of our own to do the engraving. He had been outlawed from his own land. Look at the blade." Harald held the sword up to the light and Orm saw the faint pattern of the Damascus steel, subtle shimmering patterns and a thin gleaming edge. "It was made from iron that fell from the sky." He laughed at Orm's look of disbelief. "No, boy, I speak the truth. I heard the story from the man who found it, in a hole still smoking from the fire it set as it fell. I've known a few stories of what falls from the sky. Usually it's just rock or the like, but the best of iron is found that way. That's what makes this a king's blade. After the smith finished welding the steel edge to the iron blade, he quenched it in blood. He said there was no better way to temper a blade, for the proper balance between hard and flexible. He wanted to use the blood of a slave. That seemed a waste to me, so we slaughtered a cow instead." He twirled the sword in the air, rolling it across the back of his hand, the steel seeming to leave a trace in the air after it disappeared into the sheath.

"After the smith tested this blade he said the cow's blood had worked as well as human." Harald laughed. "If he'd known that before, he might not have been exiled." Finally, Harald reached into the chest and pulled out a brilliant red cloak of fine silk. Five gold threads were woven into the edge of the fabric, winking in the soft northern light. It hung lightly on his shoulders. An ornate brooch, another raven, this one in gold, fastened it at the top of his right shoulder. Harald checked to make sure his sword arm was free and then drew on his shoes. He straightened and shook his wet hair back from his face.

Orm was transfixed by the transformation. Harald had almost blended in during the long sea trip, wearing the same clothes as everyone else, and wearing them for the whole trip. Now, gleaming in red and gold, he was once again a king. Even his eyes seemed different, guarded and aloof. They fixed on something beyond Orm's sight. "Leave me now, boy," he said. "I need time to think."

Orm nearly bowed as he backed away. The entire ship quieted as Harald moved to the stern, the only sounds were the creak of the rigging and the impertinent cries of the seabirds.

"When passing a door post, watch as you
walk on, inspect as you enter
It is uncertain where enemies lurk
or crouch in a dark corner."

—THE HAVAMAL

CHAPTER SIXTEEN

THE UNINVITING SHORE WAS CLOSE. The ship was silent as
everyone watched the land approach. They had landed on
Iceland a dozen times, to cook food or get drinking water,
but this was different. This was the place where they were
going to spend the winter and it looked just as inhospitable
as the rest of the island. Orm could see the bleak, eroded
slopes of the mountains towering above the narrow strip of
lush grass, ending on the black, rocky, strand. Sheep dotted
the hillsides even though the snow cover reached halfway
down the slopes. From the ship, Orm could see only three
widely scattered clusters of buildings. Made of turf, they
blended so thoroughly into the countryside that the eye slid
past them without noticing, unless a slight plume of smoke
from the chimney gave them away.

"We're done sailing," Harald said. "Drop the sail, unstep
the mast and get the oars out."

The silence broke as people scurried to their places. A
month of practice had made the women and children more

accustomed to their roles. No shouts or cursing disturbed the sound of the waves as the shields came down, the sail was furled and the mast unstepped. All of them knew where their oars were and it took only a couple of beats before a rhythm was found. Arnora's hands no longer bled when she rowed. Between the exertion of rowing during calms and the long hours steering her hands were calloused in places a spinning wheel or loom didn't affect.

She and Orm sat side by side on what was now Orm's sea chest. They rowed easily, the calm waters of the fjord making their task simple. Their muscles were used to the work and they could maintain the same pace for hours without tiring.

Harald was at the tiller, watching Eric carefully. A stream wound its way through a valley of its own making and they were headed for a black beach near where it met the sea. Eric clung to the dragon's neck, watching for rocks under the clear water. A wave of his arm and Harald slowed the pace of the rowing. A shout and all stopped, oars in the air. Orm felt a grating through the soles of his feet as the keel struck land. A dozen men at the bow leaped into the water and split into two groups to haul the ship ashore. The big iron ring riveted into the keel beneath the dragon's neck held the ends of two thick ropes. Each group grabbed a free end of a rope and moved onto dry land at a slight angle from each other. The others at the front of the ship moved back to crowd the stern. The shift in weight brought the prow of the ship up slightly and at a command, the remaining oars beat the water while the men heaved. The ship moved forward, a third of its length on dry land. Suddenly all the grace and motion and life were gone. It lay still, a dead thing of wood and rope. A ship's length away, Strykar's ship grated onto the rocky beach. His crew was more complete than Harald's and the ship ended up even further ashore.

"Stir yourself, boy." Harald's voice shook Orm from his reverie. "We have much to do this day, and not much daylight to do it in." His voice rose so the whole ship could hear. "Get this ship unloaded. Find a place for tents, get some men on guard and meals cooking. I go to see about our welcome."

Without waiting for the gangway to be stretched out, Harald swung ashore, his big feet hitting the pebbled beach with a rasping impact. Strykar leaped down in a like manner. Dressed all in black, he fell in step on Lord Harald's left. The two men walked along the beach until a path up the bluff presented itself. They were soon lost from sight.

Orm bent to gather his gear. He wasn't able to lift the huge sea chest he'd been bequeathed by Harald, so Arnora grabbed the other end and they made their shaky way down the gangway. They carried the chest up beyond the high-water mark and added to the pile of belongings already there. Arnora set her end down and took a wobbly step, the land moving under her after the long weeks at sea. Suddenly turning her back, she bent and vomited. Orm looked at her. "Arnora, you're supposed to be sea sick, not land sick." He turned back for another load but Arnora remained bent over, her view of Iceland confined to the fouled stones in front of her.

Harald and Strykar paused when they reached the top of the bluff. A large river valley lay in front of them. Half a day's walk away the mountains rose up and the men could see the glint of the river disappearing into the highlands. They stood on a faint path that led along the edge of the fjord. From the looks of it, not many travelers passed this point, but fresh sheep dung proved it was still in use.

"I see a crowd has gathered to welcome us," Harald said. "It is well we dressed for the occasion." In truth, no humans were to be seen anywhere about.

"What do you think?" Harald asked.

"We could do worse than stay right here." Strykar pointed inland. "We could build two or three long houses there against the slope above the water. Water to drink, turf for the houses, close enough to the shore to gather driftwood for a fire. I don't know about peat, but the locals should be able to tell us of that. Food, I do not know. This is not a lush country."

"We have the stores we brought, and we have much silver."

"They pay their debts with wool cloth. Hard silver should purchase a great deal in this place."

"That is my thought as well. Eric has said this area is under the hand of Asbjorn Arnorsson. Do you know him?"

"Know of him. He's a man of middle years, started with little, has much, wants more."

"Then, we know him very well. We have met him many times." Harald said dryly. "A man to approach with caution, perhaps?"

"I think so, my lord."

"It may be wiser to just pour our silver out before him and buy his friendship. That much wealth will serve to make him a man of power in this land."

Strykar frowned. "Walk with care, my lord. Have you looked at your crew? Asbjorn has perhaps a thousand men pledged to him. We lack a tenth of those numbers. It would be a mistake to try to buy him and fail. You might humiliate him and incite his greed. Not a good combination. If the gift you give him is greater than he can repay, no good will come of it."

Harald glanced at the veteran. "It seems to me, that a man of your delicate diplomatic ways should not have quite so many notches in his axe blade."

Strykar threw back his head with a laugh. "Very well, my lord. If you wish to supervise your people I will find a man of this land who can direct us to Asbjorn's holdings. It is good to be ashore. We will have a hot meal and a bed of soft grass instead of ship's timbers and in the morning, you will secure our supplies and safety for the winter."

Strykar headed down the dim path. He had loosed his axe from its scabbard and it rested lightly over his shoulder as he walked. He was entering a strange land full of people who lived by violence yet his walk was carefree and his step was light. His black cloak waved behind him and in the dim light he looked all too much like an angel of death.

"Strykar," Harald shouted, "we seek to make friends of these people. Try not to kill anyone just yet."

"As you wish, my lord," Strykar replied. "As always, I will be an example of restraint."

Harald laughed, then moved to the edge of the bluff and waved his people to the top.

* * *

It was full dark when Strykar returned. He was riding a shaggy little horse and mounted on another by his side he had a guide.

The camp was noisy. Between the two ships there were nearly one hundred and fifty people and they were all glad to be safely on land for the winter.

Tents had been erected around a large driftwood fire. A massive iron kettle hung from an iron pole that stretched across the flames. Porridge bubbled in the pot and loaves of bread baked in the ashes at the edge. Boys had shot waterfowl with blunt-tipped arrows; the birds were strung on iron rods that had been stuck into the ground and leaned over the coals. Children darted in and out of the shadows, glad to be released from the confines of the ships. Men sat in those shadows, faces turned away from the fire, armed and watching the darkness. One of them directed Strykar to the center of the camp.

Harald leaned against his sea chest, a fur robe under him and his long legs stretched out in front of him. He held half of a duck spitted on his knife and he alternated bites with drinks from a wooden cup. By accident or intent, he was the center of all.

"Lord Harald," Strykar said formally, "I bring you a visitor. Thorkal Kodran has a farm further up the valley. He claims this land we are on for his winter pasture."

Harald stood and stretched to his full height, settling his cloak around his broad shoulders. Thorkal's eyes widened and he took a slight step backward.

"Greetings," Harald said. "I thank you for the use of your land. We are in your debt. As you can see," and he gestured around the bustling camp, "my people are very glad to be on dry land."

"What brings you to my farm?" Thorkal asked, "It is late in the year for traveling."

"We seek a place to spend the winter. That we came to your farm is happenstance. Our navigator knows Skagafjordur and we've heard of the generosity of Christians around Holar. There is no need to worry. We will leave in the spring and you will be the richer for offering your hospitality. As soon as the ice breaks we leave for Greenland and beyond."

"Beyond, my lord? No one goes there anymore. The pagans were too strong and the distance too great for trade."

"Trade can wait and we have some little experience in dealing with pagans. Perhaps we will do better than Eric's daughter."

Thorkal smiled slightly. "So, you've heard the story?"

"We've heard that all who sailed with her died, and she returned to Greenland with a short crew and more gear than she had rights to."

"She went mad," Thorkal said, "and made her husband and his men kill all who weren't of their ship. It was an evil omen, and it ended the settlements in the new land."

"I would hear more of this, but I fear it will be a long winter, with much time for the telling of stories. There is great deal that needs to be done before we spend our time drinking beer and singing songs." He opened his sea chest and removed a small leather pouch. He turned and threw it to Thorkal. "As I said, we're in your debt. If we are to stay here we will need permission to fish and build houses. It is a great favor we ask of you. Will this help ease your burden?"

Thorkal weighed the pouch in hand. Years at a time passed without feeling so much as one small hack-piece of silver; now he had what felt like at least a mark in his hand. From what he could tell through the leather, these were actual coins, too. He spread his arms wide. "You are guests on my land. I will surely do all that I can to help you through the winter."

Harald bowed, "Thank you for your generosity. That purse is but a host-gift. Of course, we will also pay for any sheep or other goods we get from you."

"It is a small matter. This time of year, we have more sheep than we can feed and with your extra hands we can put up more hay and butcher the excess animals quickly. Do not worry. As my guest, you can rest easy."

Harald laughed, "Then, my host, stay with us tonight and tomorrow you will be our guide in this fine land of yours."

He offered Thorkal his cup and took a different one for himself. Strykar threw another log on the fire and sat close to it, the leaping flames casting dangerous shadows across his saturnine face. Harald leaned back against his sea chest and took another drink, followed by a bite from the roast duck. *A good beginning*, he thought. *If the new land has people as easy to buy as this one we are on a simple quest indeed.* A hand came up and unconsciously rubbed the arrow-scar on his neck. Over the camp sounds, he could hear the faint noise of waves on the beach. Already the sea ice was forming and soon there would be no travel possible. He stretched his legs and felt his knees crack. These were the days he missed Byzantium, with its warm winters and constant sunshine. Soon it would be light for only a few hours each day, and then they would enter the tunnel of winter. He had immediate issues to deal with, right in front of him. Houses to build and heat, food to set aside, alliances to build. It would be a long winter, and there would be plenty of time to wonder about what would meet them in this new land toward which they were heading.

In the beginning was the Word, and the Word
was with God, and the Word was God.
He was in the beginning with God.
All things were made through Him, and
without Him nothing was made that was made.
In Him was life, and the life was the light of men
And the light shines in the darkness, and
the darkness did not comprehend it.

—JOHN, CHAPTER ONE, VERSES 1-5

CHAPTER SEVENTEEN

TIME OF THE FIRST MOOSE HUNT
KTAQMKUK, LAND OF THE MI'KMAQ

SAMOSET AWOKE. He slept like a hunter. No fuzzy pause
between sleep and waking, simply total rest and then complete awareness.

He lay on his back, a fur robe pulled up to his chin. He
didn't move immediately, but kept his eyes closed and let
the universe sweep through him to fill him with its message.

The air of the wigwam was warm and close. Later in the
season there would be a need for a fire all night long, but
right now, early in the fall, the warm breath of the dozen or
so inhabitants were enough to keep it snug and comfortable.

Thank you, Great One, Samoset thought, *for the gift of the*
birch tree. The bark builds our houses, our boats and even our pots.
Truly, a blessing.

All those in the wigwam were blood of his blood and

he knew the sounds of their breathing as well as his own. Listening, he was the only one awake.

No, not quite. Noshi, his father, breathed like a man awake, though he lay still with his eyes closed.

Let the others sleep. Stars could still be seen through the smoke hole.

Samoset let his senses drift farther away, beyond the wall of the wigwam. He could hear the clashing of tree branches. It must be a great wind to disturb them here in this sheltered inland valley. How fortunate that the time for fishing was over. Much better to track game on dry land than navigate a canoe on the open ocean in waves like there would surely be today.

He felt his youngest son squirm against his side. Wate automatically turned the boy to offer him her breast. He nursed and soon fell back asleep. He was doing that less and less lately. Nearly four, he had begun to wean himself and nursed only in the nighttime for comfort's sake.

As soon as the child lay quietly, Samoset disentangled himself from the robes, stepped over his sleeping wife and slid quietly out the skin flap of the wigwam. He stretched, and took a deep, cleansing breath of the cool, salt-tinged air. It would be a good day for hunting. He would take Chogan along today. The noise from the wind would keep the game unaware of small noises made by inexperienced feet. It would be warier as a result, but in the balance, the wind was an ally.

He automatically turned to face the east. The slightest tinge of orange was discernible in the ridgeline in front of him, harbinger of the coming dawn.

His father joined him.

"Good morning, Father," Samoset said. "The Creator sends us another good day."

His father grunted. "Tell me, son, how do you decide whether a day is a good one or not, so near its beginning?"

Samoset was surprised. "A good day is when you can draw a deep breath, when your family has food and shelter, and when you have a chance for a day's hunt."

"Perhaps," his father said. "Perhaps you are right. But perhaps there is more required than you think."

He straightened up painfully and then moved slowly off, seeking privacy for the morning rituals.

Samoset watched him go. It was an odd thing for the old man to say, but lately he had been talking in the same vein more and more. Perhaps he grew weary and sought the Journey. Samoset dismissed the thought. He would grow better or he would grow worse. Either way would make clear the path to follow. Patience was all.

He bowed to the newborn sun and began his morning prayers.

"Ho! Ho! Ho!" he exclaimed, offering the traditional Mi'kmaq greeting. "Father of the Day, greetings. I ask your protection for my family." He held his arms outstretched to the rising sun. "I ask for good hunting, luck against my enemies, and a long line to my posterity."

He bowed again. "With Your blessing, today I take my son on the hunt with me. We seek one of your children, a moose, for our winter food. We do this with respect and out of need." He bowed one more time then stood very straight. The sun had cleared the hills to the east. Its rays gleamed off his black eyes and sent reflections shimmering across his long dark hair. He closed his eyes and felt his awareness expand. The long night's solitude amongst his dreams was over. Once again, he could feel the harmony of the woods around him, could reach out to the sea a day's travel away and taste its salt. His senses branched out in a dizzying spiral, touching the trees around him, the rabbit crouching in the grass and the red-tailed hawk hovering in the morning air currents. Unconsciously, his arms reached out at waist height, his hands turned up in a gentle cupping motion, as if to cradle the whole world. His consciousness soared and he became one with the world, feeling all the life that surrounded him. He soaked in the sensations, reveling in his awareness of all that existed.

His senses came crashing back as he regained his body. His eyes opened and were at peace. Once again, the universe was as it always was, and he knew his place in it.

He turned at a slight noise behind him. Wate had left the wigwam and was standing, sleep still misting her eyes. She walked into his arms. He embraced her and buried his head in her hair. He loved the smell of her hair—wood smoke, baby, and woman—mingling gently into a scent that meant home.

"Today is a good day," he said.

"Was there ever any doubt?" She reached up and pressed her lips against the side of his neck and walked off into the woods to relieve herself.

Noshi rejoined Samoset, his own morning prayers complete. Samoset looked into his eyes and was disturbed by what he saw. The dark eyes did not look good—the whites were nearly yellow with no peace in them.

Samoset pulled a piece of deer meat off the drying rack and threw it to him, then took one for himself. They squatted by the fire and ate without talking. It was still strange to sit by the morning fire after first prayers with only his father. The other men in the camp had been slain earlier in the summer by the evil ones from the south. The loss of Noshi's other sons had been very hard on him, and had begun his decline.

The old man finished first. He sat back and lit the pipe, using an ember from the fire. He took a few puffs and then passed it to Samoset. Samoset inhaled deeply and passed it back. "Today the boy will seek his first moose," he said.

His father nodded, but said nothing.

"It will be good to have another man by the fire," Samoset added. The old man grunted, then got up and walked to a birch bark container hanging from a tree. A dipper hung from a leather thong; he used it to take a deep drink of water.

Wate came back to the fire. Samoset looked up at her.

"Tell the boy that this would be a good day for him to kill a moose, if he wishes to."

Wate nodded, anxiety and excitement warring in her eyes. She re-entered the wigwam through the woman's entrance and a few moments later Chogan erupted out the man's entrance.

Samoset smiled with his eyes. "Slow down. A hunter who needs to run is a bad hunter."

The boy skidded to a halt, then nodded nonchalantly and squatted by the fire next to his father, watching him eat. Chogan would not eat; he had been fasting for two days to purify himself for the hunt.

It was full light now and the calls of birds echoed through the woods. Samoset let the human silence continue for a bit and then he began to talk.

"Today I thought we might set a snare for moose along the ridge trail. We will spend the day watching and if there is no movement by nightfall we will try to call a bull down by the swamp." The boy nodded. "When you have finished your preparations, bring your bow to me. We go to kill one of the Sun's children and we need to take care that all is prepared properly."

The boy nodded solemnly, his eyes alight with excitement.

The dew was still on the ground as the three men moved along the ridgeline. The path was clearly defined; sharp deer hooves had cut through the sod over the years. Chogan was in the lead. Today, he would lead the hunt as much as possible. He had already passed by two good places for setting snares, but neither of the men had said a word, although Samoset could sense how the climb was affecting his father. Finally, Chogan slowed and stopped. He looked back at Samoset. Samoset looked around, as if seeing the site for the first time. Two young white birch trees, their trunks about as thick as a man's wrist, stood on opposite sides of the trail, about the right distance apart. He nodded in agreement and the men stepped off the trail and further into the woods. Pulling their stone knives, they quickly stripped some branches off another white birch tree and wove them into a large noose. Back at the trail, Samoset climbed one of the young trees and Chogan climbed the other. Hanging from the branches, the tree bent with their weight until they met above the trail. Noshi tied them loosely together, then tied the noose firmly to both trees about a man's height above the ground. Samoset and Chogan gingerly climbed back down. The trees straightened slightly, then stopped, held by the noose. Chogan stepped back and carefully surveyed the area and then nodded, satisfied with his plans. The two men and the boy retreated from the trail again. They squatted on the ground and waited in silence.

It was a long day. Two deer had passed by the snare, but because they traveled with their heads held low, they had passed unharmed. The sun had begun to drop behind the ridge when Samoset heard the faint sounds of a moose approaching. A moment later, Chogan heard them also. He stirred to quivering attention, an arrow nocked on his bow. Samoset put a calming hand on his shoulder.

A moving spot of brown was all they saw at first. The moose was nearly to the snare when they could see its head. A large cow, she ambled along the path. The faint smell of man lingered in the air, but the moose had often smelled man scent on the trails and it usually meant no threat. Without pausing she walked directly into the snare.

When the noose settled around her neck she gave an impatient shake of her head. The two trees tore apart and sprang upright, pulling her front feet off the ground. She hung there, momentarily, bellowing, then with a massive effort tore the noose away from first one, then the other tree. She disappeared down the trail, kicking her heels and shaking her head, before any of the hunters could shoot an arrow into her.

Chogan ran to the trail and listened as the irritated

animal plunged downhill and out of hearing. Sick with disappointment, Samoset came and stood beside him. Noshi walked over and looked at the ruined snare. Hearing a soft exclamation from him, Samoset joined him. Noshi extended his arm and pointed. The knots that had held the noose to the young tree had both failed. Old fingers had simply not tied them firmly enough. Seeing that, Noshi turned and walked off without a word.

After a few moments Chogan asked, "Grandfather made the knots poorly?"

"Yes. It was not your fault. The snare was placed correctly."

"I thought so," Chogan said. "I saw what he did and feared that they would not hold, but I did not know how to correct him."

Samoset touched his shoulder. "Come. We will go to the edge of the swamp and finish the day trying to call a bull to us."

Chogan nodded and once again led the way down the trail.

Samoset paused long enough to tear off a square piece of birch bark. As they walked he handed it to Chogan and the boy began to form it into a trumpet-shaped tube.

Samoset let the boy lead. He finally stopped walking and looked back. Samoset smiled. Chogan smiled back in return and indicated a spot where they could sit. Settling down with their backs against an oak tree with a low hanging branch, they waited for dusk. Every now and then Chogan would sound a tentative grunt through the birch bark horn. As the shadows lengthened he began to call more often, varying the calls, going through the entire range of whine, wail, bawl and bellow that a female moose would make.

It was nearly dark when one of the calls was answered by a deep coughing grunt from across the river. Chogan put the horn to his lips again, but Samoset touched him with a warning hand, motioning downward. Patience, make him wait for the call.

After a short wait Chogan made the call, softer and quieter. The bull answered and shortly the two heard splashing and saw the shape of the moose coming towards them. Samoset touched Chogan's arrow quiver. When the boy turned his attention to him, he held up three fingers and pointed upwards. Chogan nodded and gave one last soft wail on the moose call. In slow, deliberate motion, he picked up his bow and nocked an arrow.

Now the bull moose began to emerge from the water, moving slowly and sniffing the air. It was only a few man lengths away and it was enormous, towering over the two hunters. He was deep into rut and Samoset could smell the urine-soaked mud that covered his shoulders and flanks.

Samoset sat, his shoulders tense. This was not the right moose for his son to kill. It was massive, twice the weight of the cow that had so easily torn free earlier in the day and unlike the cow, when challenged it would not run, but would seek to destroy its attacker. Samoset did not know what to do. The thought crossed his mind to stand up, break a twig, do something to disturb the hunt, but it was too late for that. Startled, the moose was just as likely to attack as to flee. His son had summoned the most dangerous animal in their world and now sought to slay it.

The moose took one more step and Chogan's bow twanged. The arrow sank deep into the moose's chest. Chogan's young fingers flew to his quiver and, in a moment's time, one and then another arrow joined the first. The moose caught their scent, bellowed, and charged. Samoset threw Chogan into the oak tree and then ducked behind it. The moose thundered past, slipping on the leaves and forest muck. Its enormous feet threw a shower of vegetation and Samoset felt the slightest touch of its antlers as he rolled frantically away. Above him Chogan put arrow after arrow into the neck and shoulders of the bull. Samoset regained his feet and made a leap for a tree branch. The moose's antlers brushed his feet and he rode their force up into the tree.

"Father!" Chogan yelled, the first sound either of them had made for an hour.

"I live," Samoset said. "Now we wait."

The bull raged around the bottom of the tree, bellowing and rearing up to swipe at them. The darkness was nearly complete and Samoset had to track the animal's movements purely by sound.

The bull moved slower as the bleeding from the stone-tipped arrows took its toll. It sank to its knees directly under Samoset, reluctant to leave its cornered enemy. Finally, its gasping breaths turned to a rattle and with one last groan, silence descended on the shocked forest.

"Give me your bow," Samoset said. "Mine is still below."

Chogan handed his bow around the trunk of the tree. Samoset reached down with a cautious arm and poked the body below. When there was no response he dropped lightly to the forest floor. He stood quietly by the massive body. His son joined him. Chogan landed next to the moose's head and the antlers towered taller than his height.

Samoset reached out his hand and clasped his son's shoulder.

"Truly," he said, "you have become a hunter today."

The boy simply stood, puffing from exertion and excitement.

"I will go back to camp and bring help," Samoset said. "There is far more here than we can carry. Start a fire to guide us back. We will all camp here tonight and feast on your kill."

"I can go to the camp," Chogan said. "There is no need for you to travel through the dark."

"It is your right as the hunter, and your responsibility, to stay and make the proper offering to the Creator for his blessings. I will return soon."

Samoset moved slowly through the darkened woods. It was a long time before the sound of his son's voice, offering up the prayer of thanksgiving and his apologies to the spirit of the moose, trailed away into the night.

CHAPTER EIGHTEEN

THE MEAT NEARLY OVERLOADED the drying racks. The bull had been old and massive so it was not as tender as the cow's would have been, but there was nearly twice as much of it. Even the hide had weighed more than a man could carry. The family camped by the kill site for two days while the meat was ferried back to their winter quarters and the hide was being scraped and prepared for tanning.

Early in the morning of the third day, Samoset and Chogan greeted the sun together. Noshi had not been seen in camp since his failure with the moose trap. Samoset could still feel his presence during morning prayers, although he seemed sorely troubled.

The father and son stood side by side. This deep in the swamp, the first rays of the sun could barely be seen filtering through the trees. Samoset nodded to Chogan to begin the ceremony. Standing next to a hole he'd dug the day before, he held up one of the moose's massive thighbones.

"Greetings, Creator," he said. "I thank you for the gift of

your child the moose. His food will keep us fed through the cold, and his hide will give us moccasins and leggings. We respect your loss and regret its necessity. We pray that the spirit of the moose will be reborn and to help its spirit we will bury the bones, so no dog can desecrate them." Chogan gently placed the bone in the bottom of the hole. Samoset helped him with the antlers and skull, but the boy buried the rest by himself.

Samoset joined him in smoothing the dirt over the grave, then the two finished their morning prayers and started the journey back to the winter camp.

When they arrived, Noshi was sitting by the fire, staring into the flames and chewing on a piece of dried meat.

Chogan nodded respectfully and then went into the wigwam to drop off his weapons.

Samoset folded his legs and lit his pipe. After a few puffs he passed it to his father. Noshi inhaled deeply.

"The boy did well," he said. "I followed your hunt."

Samoset said nothing.

"You both did well. That was as large a bull as I've ever seen. You gave him his kill, but kept him from harm. A delicate task."

Samoset shrugged and smiled. "I had a good teacher."

Noshi said, "I've decided. It is time for me to make the Journey."

Samoset had been expecting this.

"Are you sure?" he asked. "There is no need. We should have plenty of food for the winter."

"Yes, I am sure. I have waited longer than I should. I can not pass my water; my legs do not let me keep up on the trail and my eyes have faded. Truly, this home I live in is worn out," he said. "I want a new one. I wish to travel to Wa'so'q, see all my old friends and feast and dance again. There is no need for me to stay here longer. Even without Chogan you could keep our people fed, and now that he is a man our family is even more secure."

"So," Samoset said, "when do you wish your funeral?"

"I will begin my fast today. In three days, I will be ready."

The three days passed quickly. Noshi stayed near the camp at all times. He was friendly with all, spending more time with the children than had been his custom, but it was clear he had begun his withdrawal from the world. He was up earlier in the morning, his prayers lasted longer, and he had a peace in his eyes that had been missing for a long time.

On the evening of the third day, there was a distinct chill in the air. The fire was built larger and everyone wore their finest clothes. Wate had made a stew of deer meat and roots and everyone ate to bursting. As darkness fell, the family began to dance. Chanting and moving gently to the rhythm of a small drum, they celebrated Noshi's life. When the youngest and oldest were winded, Samoset nodded to Chogan. As the newest adult, it was his role to begin the eulogies.

"My Grandfather taught me how to fish. He taught me the ways of the forest and the sea. He showed me how to make a moose call and he did it well enough that with the Creator's help, I was able to kill the great moose. There is much I have yet to learn, but he has showed me the path toward knowledge."

Then it was Samoset's turn to speak. "My father guided our family for many years. He decided when we would hunt deer and moose, when we would move to the streams for spawning fish and when we should go out onto the deep sea. He kept us safe and showed me how a man should live. He fought off the invaders from the south and the camps he chose were by sweet water and near much game. Our family has prospered and kept its faith and its honor."

Samoset talked a long time, telling the story of his life and how Noshi had guided him through all the years. When he finished, no one else spoke, and after a few moments of silence he took his place in the circle

Noshi smoked another pipe, slowly and thoughtfully. He

passed it to Chogan and then got up and moved into the fire-light. He was carrying his a'ptuan, which for many years had hung by his bed. A simple stick, with bright feathers on one end and a soft covering of weasel fur on the other, it was the symbol of his authority and had been touched by no one but him ever since his own father had given it to him.

"I have had a good life," he said, "but now I am tired. I can no longer do what a man does and life has lost its joy for me. I want my free-soul to follow the Spirit's Road to the afterlife. I want to hunt, feast, sing, and dance with those who have traveled before me. I do not want my free-soul to stay on earth, but as soon as my life-soul stops, I wish my free-soul to begin the Journey. I am content." He stepped away from the fire and walked over to Samoset. He held out his a'ptuan; Samoset reached out and took it. Noshi then disrobed, giving his clothes to members of the family. He stood for a moment in front of them, naked as the day he was born. His shrunken old man's body was treated kindly by the leaping shadows from the fire. Samoset did not see him. His mind was full of the man his father had once been, poised to spear a porpoise, breaking the neck of a wounded deer, leading the attack against the bad ones from the south.

Noshi looked around the fire and at his family. Then, wiping them from his mind, he turned away and walked to the edge of the clearing. He sat with his back to a tree and said no more.

The fire slowly died down and the family drifted off to sleep. Samoset was the last to enter the wigwam and as he did, he looked back over his shoulder. By the embers of the fire he could still see the faint gleam of his father's eyes.

The next morning when Samoset and Chogan came out into the brisk air for their prayers, Noshi hadn't moved. His eyes were still open, but they didn't move to watch the two men. All day long, the life of the camp went on in front of him while he remained apart. Another cold night, and another day, and still he sat. The third day when Samoset emerged from the wigwam, Noshi had fallen over, but Samoset could hear the rattle of his breathing. Late that day Wate called him aside.

"Your father needs help," she said. "This is bringing shame upon our fire. Your father is a strong man and his life-soul won't let his free-soul depart. You need to do something."

Samoset did not reply, but that night he stayed out of the wigwam, tending the fire after the others had gone to sleep. He looked across the clearing at his father's form, now huddled on his side, his breathing loud and tortured through his dry mouth.

He took the water bucket from its place and walked over to where Noshi lay. When he got close enough, he could see his father shivering in the crisp night air, a small cloud forming in the chill air with every labored breath.

"Father," Samoset said, "I do this out of respect, because your life-soul is so strong."

His father looked up at him, his eyes glittering in the firelight, but said nothing, not even when Samoset carefully poured the bucket of water all up and down his father's body. The shaking grew worse as the water ran off his skin and pooled around him.

"Good night, Father," Samoset said, and walked off to sleep.

When he came out into the morning for his prayers, he was relieved to see that sometime during the night his father had made the Journey.

"Chogan," Samoset said when his son joined him, "today we will bury your grandfather. I think we should take him to the top of the hill, where he'll be able to see the ocean."

"I think that is a good choice," Chogan said.

CHAPTER NINETEEN

AFTER MORNING PRAYERS, Samoset and Chogan began the weary task of getting Noshi to his grave.

His withered body weighed very little, but Chogan was still a boy and the weight wore on him almost from the start.

They wound their way through the trees, climbing steadily uphill. They stopped to rest several times before they reached the peak.

Finally, they came to the crest of the hill; in the distance they could see the glimmer of the ocean. Samoset looked around and said, "I think this is a good place. And you?"

Chogan was tired of carrying his grandfather's corpse but he still looked around carefully. "This place is good," he said, "Grandfather can see the ocean, yet he is among the trees and sheltered from the wind."

"I agree," Samoset set his end of the body down, then straightened up and stretched his back. The climb had been a long one, and he'd been careful to try and shoulder most of the load so Chogan would not be shamed by failure.

The wooden shovels they used to dig the grave were small, meant to be used mainly for digging clams in soft sand, so the digging took a long time. Samoset had to stop to use his stone ax to chop through tree roots several times, and they had to discard one grave and move a few feet to one side because they hit a rock that was too big to move.

The sun was nearly overhead by the time they were finished and they were both covered with sweat.

Noshi's body was stiff so it was difficult to force his limbs into the correct position. This was the first burial that Chogan had ever helped with and Samoset watched him closely to see how he was doing. Even though Noshi had technically been dead since his funeral, dealing with his remains was still an emotional experience.

At last, the task was done. Noshi was seated cross-legged in the grave, his weapons on his lap and a water bottle by his side. He was covered with a cloak of fine leather from a large deer he had killed. He faced the ocean that he had loved so much and he was sheltered under a strong oak tree. Samoset laid a gentle hand on his shoulder, then climbed out of the grave and began to fill it in.

"Isn't there something else we should say?" Chogan asked.

"What? We said all we needed to say at his funeral. His life force and his spirit force have both fled his body and are now reunited. This is just a shell, like an empty clam. We bury it as a sign of respect, so the dogs and the wolves don't desecrate it, but your grandfather is gone now to be with the Creator. He left us in a way and at a time of his choosing. From this time on we honor him with our deeds, not our words. We live as men, as he taught us to live, and that is our final prayer for him."

Chogan didn't speak anymore, but moved to the other side of the grave and began to throw in shovels full of dirt. The grave was filled much faster than it was dug and soon there was just a slight mound of dirt at the base of a tree, with a view of the ocean, to remind anyone of the resting place of Noshi of the Mi'kmaq, leader of his family and provider for his people. It was a peaceful place, untroubled by ghosts, and this was a clear indication that Noshi was truly at rest. Samoset covered the grave with rocks gathered from the surrounding area. He used the biggest rocks he could lift, so no dog or other predator would be tempted to dig up the grave. A bear might be able to move them, but if a bear happened this way and caught the scent of the body, there was nothing that anyone could do to prevent it from digging it out; the act was simply the will of the Creator.

Samoset dropped the last rock into place, picked up his stone ax and wooden shovel, and headed back toward the winter camp. Chogan paused for a moment, took one last look at the winter sea, and then quickly followed.

Samoset paused by the first stream they came to. He washed his hands over and over in the cold water. When he finished he sat for a long time on the bank of the stream, staring into the woods on the other side.

CHAPTER TWENTY

A THIN SKIM OF ICE EDGED the calm water at the edge of the stream.

The family had been busy. The moose skin was now tanned leather. It had taken many days and the livers from a number of birds before the huge skin was finished. They had all taken turns rubbing the skin over a pole, working the tanning solution into it and bending and creasing it so it would be supple. The old moose hide that had been the floor of much of the wigwam was removed. The branches underneath it were also taken out and replace by a thick mat of fresh greens. Chogan's moose hide became the floor of the wigwam and the old floor was used to make clothes. The grease from spilled food and constant foot traffic had made it more flexible and durable than the new skin.

Everyone had new moccasins and leggings and a thick pile of new fur robes lay in the wigwam. Camp socks made of muskrat skins with the fur turned inside were ready for the cold winter days.

All of the moose meat was cured and stored in baskets. Chogan had also killed a deer, with a snare he made himself. The winter sun was no longer strong enough to reliably cure the meat, so the family had feasted for three days until all the fresh venison was gone.

Wild carrots had been dug and the children had stolen many beechnuts from the chipmunks. Cranberries, huckleberries and blueberries were gathered and prepared for winter. They were boiled for several hours, pressed into flat cakes, and dried in the sun. Several geese had been killed and their flesh was cut into thin strips and hung by cords over the fire in the wigwam. It was now well smoked and delicious.

No one had made a winter camp at this spot for many years; they had an abundance of firewood. The young ones spent their days dragging the branches that they could move closer to camp. Today the whole family was helping. The weather felt like snow and after the first big snow firewood would be much harder to find.

Samoset and Wate cooperated to drag larger branches. Chogan stayed in camp, using his stone ax to break the wood into smaller pieces. His younger sister, Wyanet, tended the small children while preparing the evening meal. She had filled a large wooden kettle with water, meat, and roots. The kettle was one she'd made herself, her first. In the center of a large fallen tree, she hollowed out a small depression. Then she built a fire in it and tended it carefully, not letting it get too big. Several times she had let the fire go out and then scraped the inside of the log. It had taken her an entire day to get it deep enough.

Periodically, she used two sticks to remove heated stones from the fire and place them in the pot. She fished the cooled ones out and put them, in turn, by the fire. The stew was bubbling now and the stones retained their heat longer. The smell permeated the clearing, accented by the crisp air and hint of snow.

Samoset stopped and stretched his back next to a big branch they had pulled to the pile. He looked around, content for the moment.

Wate came and leaned against his shoulder.

"I think we are ready," she said. "We have as much food preserved as ever, and now there should be plenty of wood."

Samoset grunted, turned around, and rubbed his itching back against the branch.

Wate laughed, "Are you a bear now? Scratching your back one last time before your winter's sleep?"

"Perhaps, I feel like I could sleep the winter away." He leaned backwards and looked up at the cloudy sky, the sun almost hidden behind the trees. "I miss Noshi's presence. I miss my brothers. I fear this will be a long winter."

Wate replied, "The men who matter are left. You and Chogan remain. The others? It was Noshi's time to make the Journey and your brothers died defending us from the evil ones. Would you prefer to have died with them, and leave us all alone?"

Stung, Samoset said, "You are a hard woman."

Wate said, "I am a woman, and so I am not allowed to wish for what I cannot have—I have to be practical. And," she put her arms around Samoset and put her head on his chest, "as a practical woman I am glad that you are here. The winter will be long, but we will not be cold or hungry or in danger. You and our children are with me and all will be well. I grieve for your brothers, but we are providing for their widows and children and we are together."

She pressed hard against his chest as his arms came around her. The silence held for a moment and then Samoset's stomach growled. Their eyes met and they laughed together.

"Come, the day's work is over. Wyanet's stew is calling to me."

Wate laughed and slapped his stomach, "And your stomach is answering!"

Soon the entire family was gathered around the fire.

Birch bark bowls filled with venison stew were being passed from hand to hand.

Everyone knew that it had been a good day and the conversation around the fire was animated. Samoset was the only one who noticed the snowflakes in the darkening sky.

CHAPTER TWENTY-ONE

THE SNOW LAY HEAVY in the woods. Few tracks other than those of the rabbit were visible. The other animals were either sleeping or staying in the deep thickets where there was ample browse and no predator could come upon them unawares. Samoset and Chogan stood side by side at the edge of the clearing, finishing their morning prayers. It was the shortest day of the year and Samoset basked in the sunlight, knowing that in a few hours it would be dark again. It was very cold. Samoset's nostrils crackled when he filled his lungs and his breath was a thick mist in front of his face. He huffed out and was pleased by the thickness of the fog.

With winter upon them, the outside fire was no longer lit. It took too much wood and served no useful purpose. The family spent most of their time in their furs around a small fire in the wigwam. They told stories and sang songs. They played games and slept a great deal, their life moving to a quieter, gentler, winter rhythm.

"Today," Samoset said, "we will take our spears and see

if we can find a bear."

Chogan nodded, his excitement contained. He had been on many bear hunts before, but that was when there had been more men in the camp and he had been kept safely away from the bear until all danger was over.

They returned to the wigwam. Everyone lay wrapped in their blankets. The air was still and warm, humid with breathing and thick with smoke. Wate was the only one awake. She was leaning against a roll of furs, smoking a pipe when Chogan and Samoset came in. The two men sat by the fire, ate some dried moose and shared a cake of dried berries. Wate watched as Samoset and Chogan put on their beaver skin cloaks and gathered their weapons.

To her questioning look Samoset answered, "Chogan and I go in pursuit of a bear. We need the fat for the rest of the winter."

She only nodded, but her eyes followed them when they left the wigwam.

Their snowshoes leaned against the outside of the wigwam, lest they be covered by an unexpected snowfall. This was the first pair of snowshoes Chogan had made entirely by himself. The frame was of birch bent to shape and the thongs that made up the mesh were strips of moose hide, from the moose he had killed. He'd spent nearly a week patiently carving the joints in the frame and getting the correct square-toe shape. The distinctive mark of their snowshoes identified each passing tribe and Chogan had been careful to make his to match those of his people.

He used heavier straps to tie the snowshoes to his feet, picked up two spears with strong flint tips, checked to make sure his knife was hanging around his neck and then looked at his father.

Samoset closely examined the spears. The spearheads were made from flint that had been scored then thrown in a fire until it cracked along the scratch marks. The resulting points were worked with a smaller stone until the edges were even and sharp as a razor. They were as long as Samoset's hand from the wrist to the tip of his finger, and, at the base, were almost as wide. Each shaft was a piece of birch a man's length long, straightened and split at the end. The tips were inserted and then carefully bound with moose hide thongs.

All looked well; the edges were sharp, the tips unbroken and the shafts strong. Samoset nodded, "So, let us see if the Creator wishes us to eat fat this winter."

He led the way into the forest. A week ago, on another particularly cold day, he'd seen a large tree with what looked like an occasional puff of steam coming from its base. It could have been a vagary of the wind and fog, but it could also be the winter breath of a bear sleeping in a hollow of the tree. He'd kept his distance that day, but marked the spot for a future hunt.

Even with the snowshoes it was slow going through the light snow.

Today Chogan followed Samoset. The two did not talk as they made their way through the woods. The sun was directly overhead when Samoset stopped and motioned Chogan to come up next to him. He silently pointed to the base of a large ash tree. Chogan saw nothing; then a faint puff of white fog came up out of the snow. He nodded and the two men moved forward side by side.

It was difficult to tell how deep the snow was at the base of the tree. Any landmarks were obscured so they could not tell if the bear was inside the tree or in a hollow in the ground.

Samoset held his spear in two hands and made a thrusting motion, then pointed at Chogan. The young man nodded and moved forward slightly. Samoset laid his weapons on the snow close to hand and began to burrow down through the snow, pulling it back one handful at a time. Every few seconds a puff of fog would come up through the snow as the slumbering bear took another breath.

Soon the men were standing in a hole that was nearly

shoulder deep. Samoset was still kneeling, still pulling the snow back one handful at a time.

Now he could hear the faint snores of the bear. A final layer of ice-encrusted snow and then a gust of warm, wet, air, thick with the scent of bear.

Samoset moved even more slowly. Now he could see that the base of the ash tree was hollow and the bear lay curled up inside. He slowly enlarged the hole until the mass of black fur began to sort itself out into some sort of anatomy. The bear appeared to be large, but it was difficult to tell how large.

Samoset looked up at Chogan. He raised an eyebrow. *Can you see where to strike?* the look asked.

At Chogan's nod, Samoset rose and took his own spear back into his hands. He laid the spare on the snow next to him.

Next, they moved back and forth together to trample down the snow so they had more room to maneuver.

Finally, Chogan took a deep breath and drove his spear into the sleeping animal. He was aiming for the heart and lungs, but in the dim light he missed his target and the flint tip splintered on the bear's shoulder.

Chogan stumbled back, his fingers tingling from the impact of flint on bone. The sleepy bear began to stir, slowly coming to wakefulness. Chogan grabbed his other spear and drove it downwards with all his strength. He missed the mark again, but this time the spear penetrated deeply into the bear's stomach. The resulting pain brought the bear fully awake and he stumbled out of his hole, wrenching the long spear out of Chogan's hands. He reached for his tormentor and Chogan rolled frantically to one side as the bear bit chunks out of his fur mantle. Samoset was in a bad spot, but he stood on the tips of his toes and with all his strength, plunged his spear down along the bear's spine, trying to reach the heart from the back side. The bear's thick fur and heavy fat slowed the spear, but it wounded him badly.

He was howling now, frantically twirling in the snow hollow, trying to destroy these creatures. Samoset was able to give his spear a twist and a further shove before he was knocked off his feet and sent rolling. He popped up out of the snow just in time to see Chogan raked across the face by a reaching front paw. The boy fell backward, nearly disappearing into the soft snow and the bear went for him, grabbing and biting whatever he could reach, tearing off one of his snowshoes. Samoset grabbed for his other spear, yelled, "Ha!" and came in low and hard; his spear went in under the ribs and destroyed the bear's heart. The mortally wounded beast spun back around. Samoset, clinging grimly to the spear haft, spun around with it and was lifted off his feet. The last thing he saw was a blurred impression of the tree trunk coming towards his unprotected head.

Then a soundless splash of light and he was unconscious.

* * *

Chogan staggered to his feet. He blinked his eyes, trying to clear his vision. He rubbed his face and winced as his hand came back covered with blood. More gently he wiped his eyes with his sleeves, blinking away the blood until he could see. The bear lay still, broken spears jutting from his body. Samoset, too, lay still in the snow at the foot of the tree. Chogan lurched over and turned him face up. He rolled, boneless and relaxed, but his chest rose and fell. Chogan slumped back against the tree, one hand to his wounded face. The winter noises of the forest returned, the soft creak of branches in the wind, the nearly silent rustle of snow sifting across the ground, a raucous blue jay's distant cries. Chogan pressed a handful of snow against his burning wounds. The cold bit deep, but it seemed a cleansing pain and his senses cleared. In front of him Chogan saw one of his snowshoes, its rim shattered by the bear's jaws. He reached out and drew it to him. Still shaking, his hands made repairs, almost of their own will. When the task was finished Chogan looked about him once more. Samoset still lay unmoving. *He will wake, or he will not,* Chogan thought, *as the Creator wills.* He looked at the great bear, dead in the snow. He crawled through the snow to its body and began his prayers of thanksgiving for the successful hunt.

* * *

Samoset slowly opened his eyes. A thick pain shook his world when he tried to turn his head. The roaring in his ears diminished and he could hear a voice. He slowly sat up, propping himself against the tree. His clothes were covered with snow and he was very cold.

A few feet away Chogan knelt, facing the setting sun.

"Thank you, Creator, for the gift of the bear. We killed him because of our need for his fat and flesh to sustain our family. This was done out of need. We will show him the proper respect so his spirit will return to you."

"So, we live," Samoset said. "I saw the bear strike you."

"I did not see him strike you," Chogan said, still kneeling. "I was upside down in the snow."

He turned around and Samoset saw four deep claw marks across his cheek. He'd pressed a handful of snow into the wounds and it appeared the bleeding had slowed. Samoset looked closer. The wounds missed his eye, mouth, and nose. Praises for that, but even so they were deep and still oozing. With great care, Samoset turned his head. The bear lay only a few feet away, its blood staining the snow a deep red. Samoset stood, very slowly, leaning against the tree to keep his balance.

"Are you able to you walk?" he asked Chogan, "Because I fear I cannot."

"Yes. What are your wishes?"

"Fetch Wate and some of the children, with toboggans. I will stay with our friend. If we leave him all night there will be nothing left for us by morning."

Chogan nodded, "I will hurry."

Without another word he turned and headed down the trail.

Samoset eased himself back down. If he moved too quickly he became dizzy. Now that he was still and the moment was passing, he could feel the other aches and pains in his body. He reached out a tentative hand to pat the bear.

"So, my friend," he said, "my family lives through the winter because of you. My thanks."

He rested a while longer, then retrieved his knife and slowly began to butcher the bear. He had loosened the pelt and had much of the fine fat cut off and piled on the skin before Chogan returned. Wate was with him, pulling a toboggan and Wyanet, came behind, pulling another.

It was a huge bear. The pelt and the fat made a full load for one toboggan and the carcass was a big load for the other. It was a long walk back to camp. The two men were staggering from fatigue by the time they reached the wigwam in the late night dark. They stood outside until the women cut the thongs that held their snowshoes. Their clothes were too stiff with ice and frozen blood for them to bend over and their fingers were too numb to untie anything.

Wate undressed them by cutting the thongs that held their frozen clothes together, and they crawled into their sleeping robes. They did not stir until their full bladders forced them awake, many hours later.

It was many days before Samoset's pains went away. Chogan's wounds healed quickly, but they left scars across his face that would be with him always. The family ate the bear meat in three days of feasting, while the fat was melted and stored in a birch bark box. Chogan buried the bones as deeply as he could in the frozen earth and said the farewell prayers for the bear's spirit. Winter cold made the bear hide harder to tan, but Wate and Wyanet worked many hours, scraping and kneading it so it would remain soft.

More snow fell and soon the bloody ground was once again white; only the tracks of a few rabbits spoiled its surface.

A moon passed and the days began to lengthen. The cold still held but the seasons progressed. Chogan and Wyanet killed several beavers by chopping a hole in the ice, and, while Chogan stood guard with a bow and barbed arrow, Wyanet jumped up and down on the beaver house. Because she was so slight, she had to jump for a long time before the beavers were disturbed enough to leave their house. When they finally did, they headed for the hole to take a breath. Their furs joined the bear's and each of them made one day's meal for the camp.

Fish came at the proper time to spawn under the ice, and Samoset began to relax. They still had food in reserve and from now on the sources of food would be more varied and more available.

One morning he left the camp as soon as his morning prayers were finished. After several months of winter, the wigwam was beginning to feel extremely full. Taking his bow in case a deer presented itself, he wandered aimlessly all morning, always trending uphill, and was surprised to find himself at midday standing under the oak where his father was buried.

The view was different than the fall day when he and Chogan had been here last. In front of him was a world of white and brown, with a band of pine trees adding a touch of green. Far in the distance the gray of the winter ocean blended with the gray of the winter sky. Samoset spent a long time looking at the water. In two or three moons it would be time to leave the winter camp and head back to the shore. All manner of fish would be spawning, and shortly after the sea birds would return to lay their eggs. There would be cod and large numbers of shellfish. The other families would be returning from their winter camps. Perhaps some of his brother's widows would leave his camp, or would bring men to his. Either would help, although he would hate for his small nephews and nieces to leave his fire. If the evil ones returned, and they always did, his family needed to be small enough to hide or large enough to defend themselves. Now it was neither.

It would be good to get back on the ocean. The sea had always been good to him; he wondered what it would bring this spring.

CHAPTER TWENTY-TWO

HARALD EXAMINED THE WINTER ocean. Drift ice cluttered the fjord and crashed against basalt towers on the shore. A stiff wind was blowing out of the north. Low clouds scudded downwind, obscuring an already dim and distant sun.

It was the shortest day of the year. At midday, the sun had little strength and it would not be long before it was dark again.

The close confines of the hall had begun to wear on him and he'd been forced to leave for a time lest he go mad.

The ships were far up on shore, safe from storm-driven ice. They lay sadly on their sides; their masts bare and their decking removed. The sails were gone, used to roof their winter quarters and all the cargo was unloaded and under shelter. Off shore, a few sea birds bobbed on the water and in the distance Drangay was barely visible through the sea mist.

Harald's fine red cape was stored away. He was huddled deep into a heavy gray cloak made of sheepskin as he faced into the wind. The cold salt air filled his lungs and he breathed deeply, trying to expunge the taste and smell of the crowded hall.

He didn't bother to turn around when he heard boots crunching on the snow behind him. His customary alertness was beginning to fade a bit. Ambush was difficult in this wide-open land and particularly in the winter when people's energies were focused on staying alive. Besides, he was always under Strykar's gaze and had heard no warning.

"My lord," Orm said, "a rider brought word that you will have a guest tomorrow, weather permitting."

"Who travels this land at this time of year? He must be a fool."

"I do not know his name, only that he is a bishop from Holar. He comes to perform the Christmas Mass for us."

"So, is this an honor for our illustrious selves or does he fear so deeply for our souls?"

"My lord?"

"Never mind. Tell Strykar I will return after dark and that he is to take charge of the preparations for our Bishop. Tell him," he paused for thought, "that I do not wish the state of my soul to disturb the Bishop's Christmas peace."

"My lord?"

"Just tell him."

"Yes, my lord."

Harald continued to stare out to sea as the boy's footsteps diminished and finally disappeared. Drangay still loomed on the horizon, its sheer cliffs massive, forbidding, and distant. Harald watched until it was gone into darkness and then waited a long time more, until the cold had soaked through his shoes and numbed his legs. It was quite a distance back to the winter hall. He heard no sound save the ice and the waves the entire way.

CHAPTER TWENTY-THREE

THE SMELL WAS WHAT FIRST struck him. After that, the noise. Harald entered the hall through a narrow passage. The walls were of turf, a man's height in thickness, with a door on the inside and the outside. They had built two halls, one for Harald's crew and one for Strykar's. They had found enough driftwood for a ridgepole, and used decking from the ships for roof boards. The sails served to make a roof and a final layer of turf on top had made it warm.

A dim fire in the middle smoldered day and night. Most of the smoke escaped through a small hole in the roof, but a constant haze remained, thick enough so it was difficult to see the length of the hall clearly. They'd excavated the center for fire pits and used the dirt to make sleeping platforms along the wall. Harald slept behind a curtain at the end of the building, but everyone else was in one common room. A huge iron pot of barley porridge was their main food, with mutton and dried cod for variety. One of the men had built a hearth of small, flat stones laid between two of the fire pits;

it was used for baking bread.

This land held nothing to hunt and few fish could be found in the fjord during the winter. Harald's silver had purchased the best this farm had to offer, but that was little enough. Several looms had been set up and the women passed their days weaving. During the sparse daylight hours most of the children were ushered outside. There had been no livestock on Harald's or Strykar's boats so the men had little to do during the day. The smiths stayed busy mending armor and weapons but for the others there was mead, games and stories. When the sun shone and particularly after storms, men stayed alert for driftwood. Regular patrols went out and even the smallest stick was brought back to the hall and divided according to where it was found and who had rights to it.

Harald made his way to the high seat at the end of the hall passing by the trestle tables set up for the evening meal. Everyone waited until he began to eat. The plate set before him held cheese, a raw, dried fish smeared with butter, and some hard rye bread. He shared a jug of mead with Strykar, who sat at his right hand. Orm was on the floor in front of them.

The noise level dropped as everyone began to eat and soon the audible sound of jaws munching dried fish and hard bread filled the hall.

"Tell me," Harald said.

Stryker said, "A rider came, half frozen. He said Bishop Isleif wishes to see to our faith by providing our Christmas Mass for us. Evidently, word that we had no priests with us has spread beyond this valley."

"What are your thoughts? Is this a man of God concerned for our souls or has he heard of our trunk of silver coin?"

"Perhaps both. That is not impossible. From our time in Byzantium, it seems as though even men of God yearn for silver—as much as they do for Heaven."

"Speak with care," Harald nodded his head towards

Orm. "Watch your tongue lest you shock our young companion and make him cynical."

Strykar looked at the boy and laughed. "The boy lost his faith in princes when his father gave his death-rattle. He proved it when he tried to take your head off. Tell me boy, are you surprised that a bishop would take interest in a chest full of silver?"

"I know the priests ate well when we starved, and I knew of their plans to build even grander churches when we lived in a rotting hut. They spoke of gifts to the glory of God, but I saw gold trimmed robes and little of Paradise." The last came in a rush, the peasant's deep black hatred of the powerful breaking through his customary reserve.

Harald chortled out loud, a deep braying that made everyone in the hall turn to look.

"Boy, you and Strykar are brothers under the skin. But remember the Havamal—'Much nonsense a man utters who talks without tiring; a ready tongue unrestrained brings bad reward.' Keep that sharp tongue still while the bishop and his men are here. It is long until spring and I would keep their good will if I can."

Arnora bent over their table with a jug of mead. With the ship beached, she had rejoined the woman and their tasks.

"No, child," Harald held his hand over the top of the mug. "I do not drink tonight. Orm, how are you progressing with your bow?"

"It goes slowly, my lord. Never before have I made a bow."

"Fetch it. There is no better time than now to learn."

Orm went to his sleeping space. Harald followed him with his eyes, and then shifted his gaze to Arnora as she moved from table to table. He was still watching her when Orm returned.

"Here it is. As I said, I have small skill with a knife."

The wood no longer looked like a piece of kindling. It had been cut down to roughly Orm's height. The tips were whittled down to no thicker than the width of a thumb and gradually it thickened until at the middle it was as thick as a strong man's wrist. Harald examined it carefully.

"You have not done badly, Orm. This is a weapon, not an ornament. The yew will not allow you do a smooth job of carving, the grain is too rough. But see," he pointed out a spot, "remember, you need both the heart of the tree as well as the youth to make a good bow. The young growth will stretch so it needs to face the enemy; the old wood is strong and thus it needs to be on your side. That way, when you pull the bow it will not break and when you loose the old wood will send the arrow strongly. It is a lesson boy, neither piece of the tree alone makes a good bow and if the young and the old are not in their proper places, the bow will be weak and easy to break."

"What do I do next?"

"Now, form the side toward the enemy flat and curve the edges that face you. After that you need to carve nocks for the string. Either bone or the tip of a horn will do. Look to Gunnar's bow, it is as fine an example as I know."

Arnora was returning to the kitchen area with her jug.

Harald beckoned her. "Girl, come here, I fear your hands are growing soft again. You too should make a bow."

"My lord," Strykar said.

"No, I have thought on this much. We go to a strange land, full of pagans who know how to kill. Every hand should be of use. A bow like Gunnar's is needed to kill a man in armor, but remember, the tales speak of naked savages. Even a child can pull a bow that will kill a naked man." Harald raised his voice. "All of you, women and children too, come to me. I have new duties for you."

When all had gathered, Harald said, "Orm, teach these others what you know." He stood away from his seat and walked the length of the hall, fastening his cloak as he went. Strykar followed him out into the darkness.

The wind was even colder now with the full dark. Only

a few stars were seen and the air smelled like snow and storms.

"I am still your marshal," Strykar said. "Tell me of your plans."

"There are so few warriors left to us and many of them are either crippled or worthless. I do not go to seek battle in this strange land, but we have seen much of the world, you and I, and everywhere we have traveled the stranger dies if he cannot defend himself. So, if we cannot fight as we choose, we need to fight as we must." He motioned with his head to the hall behind him. "These people cannot close with an enemy. They have neither the strength, nor the skill, nor the weapons to survive that. But an arrowstorm from behind stout walls will discourage most foes."

"I do not make this trip to live behind walls," Strykar said.

"Nor do I, but until our strength grows we will need caution,"

"Tell me, my lord, when did you learn caution?"

"I have learned many things in my life. Truly, this is a fool's quest we are on, but now that we have begun the journey I cannot help myself; I wish it to succeed."

"And this bishop who comes upon us? I have never known a bishop to concern himself overly much with the souls of a few travelers, let alone to travel in this land in the winter for naught but pity's sake. What do we do with him?"

"Same as always. Buy him, bury him, bully him or ignore him. Although, there is a chance that he is a man of wisdom and charity. Perhaps we will sit at his feet and gather his wisdom."

Strykar snorted, "Perhaps. I'll sharpen my ax, just in case. And your new army?"

"Advise them a little. Encourage them to work slowly. If nothing else, it should keep them quiet for a while."

Strykar laughed. The two men walked further from the buildings, as the wind out of the north tugged at their cloaks.

They talked of small things, of distant battles and far off lands. They talked of comrades long dead and of women long unloved. The northern lights shone wild and bright, raining subtle colors down on the barren plateau atop Drangay.

When they returned to the hall the fire had been banked. Already snores were emanating from those sleepers who'd had too much mead.

Arnora sat alone by the fire, staring into the coals. She didn't look up when Harald passed.

Perhaps she didn't see.

CHAPTER TWENTY-FOUR

IT WAS MIDDAY WHEN the Bishop's party approached. They came down the valley, from the direction of Holar. They followed the course of the river, but stayed on the high ground above. The sturdy little horses plodded through the snow, grabbing a bite of grass whenever a tuft presented itself. The storm had blown itself out overnight and the sky was clear and blue.

"They must have made a rough camp last night," Eric said, "or perhaps they chose to travel in the dark. They could not have come far since dawn."

"How many?" Strykar asked.

"Twelve," said Eric, his seaman's eyes picking out the details in the distance.

"Is it Christ with the disciples or is Judas leading the way?"

Eric was shocked. "Do you think it wise to mock the Lord on his day of birth?"

"It is a poor God who would take offense at a harmless

jest. I fear there are other sins that will send me to Hell before this one. My question stands—what are your thoughts on this visit?"

Eric said, "I don't know. Lord Harald is a great man and has been good to these people. It would be peculiar if the people in authority did not pay their respects. On the other hand, this is a strange land, of independent people. Harald is the first king to come to these shores and he has no army to enforce their respect. Truly, I could wish no visitors at all this winter."

"I think your worry is without merit," Strykar said. "I see only a dozen men and half of them priests. I would barely fear a dozen men if I stood here alone. No, calm yourself. Today promises much amusement. Lord Harald is still fey, and while these people may be powers in this land, this is a very small land. Come, let us bid them welcome."

Strykar and Eric walked forward, away from the hall, to properly welcome the guests. Two men, one in black and one in blue, one slender and tall, the other grizzled and thick, but both with long handled war axes across their shoulders.

The ponies picked up the pace as they saw the bulk of the camp. They flowed across the rugged land, with a smooth gait that seemed too fine for their uncouth appearance.

The lead rider was a big man; his legs dangled nearly to the ground. He pulled his horse to a stop and looked down on Strykar and Eric.

"I am Asbjorn Arnorsson and all here are under my hand."

"I am Strykar Knattarson, Lord Harald's marshal. Welcome."

Asbjorn looked around the barren landscape. "Where is Lord Harald? Did he not come to welcome us himself?"

Strykar smiled, "Lord Harald sits on the high seat, where he has sat for many years. Truly, he has never needed to seek men out. In time, they all come to him."

Asbjorn frowned, "You speak boldly, for one who lives

under my protection."

Strykar lifted the ax off his shoulder. "This is the only protection I live under. As for the rest, you are welcome to Lord Harald's table. A feast awaits you in a warm hall. How long do you wish to remain in the cold?"

A fat man in a fine robe spoke. "I am Bishop Isleif. The word came that you had no priest to perform Mass for you. King Harald has always been a friend of the church. He sent us grain during the bad years when famine threatened us all and he provided the timbers for the church at Thingvol. I come to bring him our thanks and to consult with him about his plans."

Strykar bowed. "Our welcome, Bishop. Lord Harald awaits you in his hall. Come, it will soon be dark."

The small cavalcade made its way down the rocky trail to the rude turf buildings.

Harald greeted them from his high seat. He was dressed once again in his finery, sword swinging free by his side. Strykar came and stood behind him at his right and Eric took an even position on his left. Even though Harald did not stand when the visitors came to him he towered above all in the hall.

"Greetings," he said, "I welcome you to my hall. Thank you for making the hard journey for no better reason than to see after our well-being." There was no discernible trace of irony in his voice.

"Please, be seated," he went on. "The night is long and there will be much time to talk. First let us eat."

Women and girls moved to bring food to the men.

When his first hunger was satisfied, Asbjorn Arnorsson said, "The word is that you are here only until you can sail on in the spring. Is this true?"

Harald nodded, "I have no interest in your domain. I seek only provisions and guidance to lead my people to the land Bjarni discovered and Leif the Lucky sought to settle."

"It is true then. I could scarcely believe my ears," Asbjorn said. "The land is there, and rich beyond belief, but it is too far from our shores, and we too far from Norway, for any worthwhile trade."

"I do not seek trade—I seek to make a home for the people who travel with me. We go, and we do not return."

"Aye, that is like enough," said Asbjorn, "but just because you do not return does not mean you will thrive. How do you plan to succeed when others have failed so badly?"

"Perhaps we will not. Perhaps, we will disappear under a horde of pagans and no one will even survive to sing our song. Or perhaps, the reason no one has succeeded is because the right man has yet to try."

Asbjorn laughed, "Lord Harald, you are as the songs say. I fear you have overmatched yourself. Still, what we can do we will do."

Harald nodded at Strykar. He turned around and picked up a heavy sack.

"I appreciate your generosity," Harald said, "but I cannot expect you to give of goods your people need. Please, allow me a gift in return."

Strykar dropped the heavy linen bag on the table and, as if on cue, it split and spilled its contents.

Silver coins from a dozen countries rolled upon the table and onto the floor. Asbjorn's mouth dropped open. There was more silver on the table than he'd ever seen before. In a land where the unit of currency was more often than not homespun cloth, it was a fortune.

Harald waved a casual hand. "This is a gift to you, in exchange for your favor. My people are scattered throughout your domain and they need much to survive the winter and the coming year. It is a great favor you do us, far more than I can repay."

"Do you seek to buy me?" Asbjorn said, a dangerous edge to his voice.

"By no means. You are no slave, but a man of power. I seek only to give you a host gift and a Christmas gift, in partial payment for your hospitality. Your people have been open-handed with us; I seek merely to do the same."

"But this—this is enough to buy a kingdom."

"I had a kingdom," Harald said, "I gave it away. I do not seek another kingdom, I wish only your friendship." His voice was quiet and reasonable but the restrained power in it filled the room.

The hall was very still. Even the smallest of the children were silent. The night hung on an edge of pride, greed, and persuasion.

Harald stood and held out his hand. It was the first time that night he had risen from his seat and he dominated the room with his size and his presence. Asbjorn stared at the outstretched hand. A legend was before him, a man about whom songs had been written for thirty years was offering his treasure and his friendship. As if drawn by a magnet, Asbjorn stood and took his hand.

The tension in the hall relaxed. Men took drinks from forgotten mugs and children began to run and play. The hall soon became noisy with the sound of conversations. Orm gathered up the scattered silver and placed it in a pile in front of Asbjorn. Strykar and Eric remained standing behind Harald, a slight smile on Strykar's face and a mild look of disgust on Eric's.

Bishop Isleif could not take his eyes off the pile of silver.

"The Lord could do much good with that amount of silver," he said.

Harald cocked his head. "The Lord does not require silver to do good. That seems to be reserved for his servants."

The Bishop flushed. "You edge towards blasphemy, my son."

"How is that, Bishop? I have read the scriptures, in both Latin and Greek, and I find no mention that our Lord required treasure and fine clothes. And yet, everywhere I go, I find the men of God seeking more and more treasure and more and more power. Please, Bishop, these things trouble me. We have a long winter's night ahead of us. Let us discuss the scriptures. You can correct my errors. I have a copy of the Gospels in my baggage—a gift from the Patriarch of Byzantium. I am sure he would be gladdened to know we were studying it together. Of course," he added gently, "it is in Greek. A difficult language, Greek. It required years before I felt fully fluent in it. But such a gracious language for reading the word of God, do you not agree?"

Bishop Isleif paused before answering. He hated to be made a fool of, but he didn't know a word of Greek and he felt in his bones that this arrogant outsider would put him to the test if he tried to bluff.

He snapped. "His Holiness reads the scriptures in Latin, which is good enough for me. We do not care in what language the emperor of Byzantium conducts his business. His church is run by heretics, and its patriarch has been excommunicated. I would not place much faith in anything you learned in that place."

"Very well," Harald said, "Let us discuss in Latin. What of 'cumque prope esset ut ingrederetur Aegyptum dixit Sarai uxori suae novi quod pulchra sis mulier' Of course, you know the rest. Why do we base our church on such a coward?"

Harald turned to Orm. "The verses are from Genesis. When Abraham went into Egypt he was worried that his wife Sarah was too beautiful and that the Pharaoh would kill him and take her for himself. So, he told his wife to pretend to be his sister and Pharaoh took her as his concubine."

"What?" said Orm.

"It is the truth, boy."

"Stop confusing the child," Isleif said. "It is not your place to interpret the Scriptures. That is a task that rightly falls to the church."

"Did I quote the Word wrongly? It seems straightforward, cowardice that the least man of my men would not dare commit. How is a man to be a man if the Word of God tells him to be a coward? Please, guide me." Harald was vastly enjoying himself. Isleif was so obviously torn between his indignation and his greed, tormenting him was more enjoyable than anything he'd done in quite some time.

"It is a lesson." Isleif said. "It is proof that even the greatest of men can fail, can fall short in the sight of God."

Harald's laughter turned bitter in his stomach. He stood.

"Perhaps. Perhaps you are right. Still, the silver is Asbjorn's now, not mine. He can determine what belongs to you and God." He gave a small, formal bow. "Now, excuse me." He left the table and went into his sleeping chamber. Once behind the curtain he slowly disrobed, carefully, methodically folding his fine clothes. He held his red silk cloak for a long time. On the other side of the curtain he heard the hubbub of the Christmas feast getting louder and louder. With luck, no one would die this night, although with the combination of mead and the constant winter darkness it sometimes took much luck to avoid bloodshed.

"My lord." A voice said from beyond the curtain.

"Come in, boy."

Orm squeezed through the edge of the curtain.

"My Lord Harald, how, how do you dare to argue with the Bishop?"

"Because my knowledge is as much as his, because I have traveled far and listened much. I dislike the priests for they seek to keep the word of God to themselves, and tell us only what they want us to know. Remember, Orm, know as much as you can, trust only as much as you need to."

"How did you learn to read?" Orm asked.

Harald cocked his head. "The same way you will learn to read. I was taught. But not tonight. Tonight, I am tired. Leave me."

In the hall, Strykar and Eric had left their posts behind the high seat and had begun to circulate. The ten men who had traveled with Asbjorn and the Bishop were clustered together at the end of the hall. In this hall of cripples and women they stood out as young and whole. Strykar paused by them. They had been drinking since their arrival and now their faces were flushed and raw.

Strykar nodded gravely to them and the youngest said, "This does not seem to be the hall of a king."

"Well," said Strykar, "King or no, Lord Harald wishes you to enjoy his hospitality."

The young man raised an eyebrow. "What, we dine on our sheep and our mead in our land and it becomes Lord Harald's hospitality?"

Strykar examined the youth closely. "Perhaps," he said. "You have a point. But you should know, that whether this is Lord Harald's hospitality or no, you draw another breath only because of his mercy. This morning before you arrived he made a special request of me that I try not to kill any of our guests."

"So, the name is right. You are King Harald's dog."

"You fool," Strykar said. "How have you lived so long?"

A flicker of the old man's eyes and the young warrior rolled backwards off the bench, doing a somersault and coming onto his feet, his sword at the ready.

Strykar laughed. He had not moved or even shifted the weight of the ax across his shoulders.

"If I am a dog, you seem to fear my teeth."

The other men were on their feet too, weapons at the ready. Strykar turned a casual eye toward them and then looked back.

"Sit down, boy. You tempt me beyond all measure. Finish your drink and fall asleep. I tell you the truth," he continued. "It might be your only chance to wake on Christmas morning." He waited, relaxed and ready, for whatever decision the boy might make. "You might, pretend to sheathe your sword and then cut for my legs. That might work, if I hadn't seen the trick tried a dozen times. You could lunge for my chest to kill with the point, like a Roman, if your blade wasn't so dull. There are many things you might try, but know this boy, I've seen them all and none of them would work."

The tableau held for a moment, then the young warrior dropped his sword point and walked back to his bench. Strykar looked away and the boy swung his blade two handed, the steel making a vicious sweep toward Strykar's neck. Strykar dropped to one knee and his long ax came around in its own vicious arc.

The boy shouted in pain as the heel of the ax crashed into his kidney. He dropped to both knees and bent over, gasping. His head touched the floor.

Strykar regained his feet, looked down at him for a moment, and then pulled him up by his hair.

"Congratulations." he said. "It appears that you might live to see Christmas." He released him and turned to face the boy's companions, bouncing lightly on the balls of his feet. "Using the heel of my ax instead of the blade was my Christmas offering. I see no need to make another. What are your wishes?"

He smiled merrily, but his eyes showered tiny sparks from the firelight. "I have no particular desire to kill you all," he said, "But then, I have no particular desire not to."

Two of Asbjorn's men helped their young comrade. The others sheathed their weapons. Women moved among them, refilling their drinking horns. Strykar completed his circuit of the hall and then took his post in front of Harald's sleeping closet.

CHAPTER TWENTY-FIVE

"*Confiteor Deo Omnipotenti, beatae Mariae simper Virgini, beato Michaeli Archangelo, Beato Ioanni Baptistae. . . .*"

Bishop Inigmund droned on, the Mass finally coming to an end. Harald, irritated, shifted his feet as he stood. The Bishop's Latin wasn't fluent, in truth nearly unintelligible. The hall was small and crowded, full of unwashed bodies and the smoke of an ill-burning fire. His thoughts drifted back to other Christmases. He could barely remember his childhood, but the celebrations would not have been much different. Crowded halls and ill-trained priests.

Christmas in Byzantium was another matter—dressed in the finest clothes and armor money could buy, standing in the Hagia Sophie while the Patriarch conducted the Mass in perfect Greek, the flawless, awesome dome soaring overhead. After the services fine food and finer women. The wealth of an enormous empire was his to draw from and the recognition that he was its strong right arm. Constantinople, a city of gold, where the powerful were sometimes subtle and always dangerous.

Then there had been a Christmas in Jerusalem, the day shared only by his men, a few ragged pilgrims who'd been under his protection, and a horde of curious Saracens. The smell from the bodies of the robbers he'd hanged from olive trees had wafted over the scene. The Saracens had allowed pilgrims to the Holy Land, but they'd done nothing to protect them, so over the years almost all the helpless pilgrims in their tattered white robes had been robbed of all they had. Harald had put a stop to that, festooning so many trees with captured robbers that they were called "Lord Harald's Fruit." After the Mass he had bathed in the Jordan River and then returned to his duties.

So many Christmases in muddy fields, wearing full armor while taking Communion, the Christmas feast rotten scraps stolen from starving peasants.

He came back to himself. It was time for the offering. He strode to the makeshift altar and laid a small bag of gold in front of the cross. Asbjorn followed behind him and left another small bag of the silver that had come from Harald. One by one they all, down to the last and the least, made their way to the front until the altar was covered with gifts of gold and silver, bread and grain, cloth and carvings.

Bishop Isleif said, "*Et Verbum Caro Factum Est, Et Habitavait In Nobis. Et vidimus gloriam ejus, gloriam quasi Unigentit a Patre, Plenum gratiae et veritatis. Deo gratias.*"

After a moment's silence people broke from their ranks and began to set up the tables so they could break their fast. Strykar and Eric disassembled the rude alter, turning it back into Lord Harald's table. Asbjorn, Harald, and the Bishop took their places and were served porridge and black bread.

Asbjorn ate rapidly, giving occasional glances toward Harald. Finally, he chuckled. "This is passing strange. I never thought to break Christmas fast with a king, at least not on my own lands."

"Perhaps you sought to one day be a king in your own

land," Harald said, "Stranger things than that have happened in this world."

"This is not a land of kings," Asbjorn said. "We have laws, and the Althing, and a lawspeaker. With these we rule ourselves quite nicely."

"Tell me of this," Harald said, "I have never seen a land ruled without nobles. How do you settle disputes?"

"The land is divided into four Quarters and in each quarter, there are thirty-nine godar, or godly ones. These are men of power and reputation who provide houses of worship. They settle disputes at assemblies in the spring and in the autumn. The laws are written by the Logretta which meets at the Althing. It contains one hundred forty-four of the righteous and powerful and it is in their hands alone that the law is given."

"I still do not understand. Let us say, I have a dispute with my neighbor. He is breaking one of the laws, harming me and mine in the process. What can be done?"

"Much. You bring suit at your local assembly and three of the godar will hear your case. If you do not get satisfaction you can bring it to the Althing where the final word will be given. If your neighbor has harmed you, he will be ordered to give you restitution and if his crimes are serious enough, he can be outlawed."

"To continue the example," Harald said, "Perhaps my neighbor has killed one of my horses, and all agree he should repay me its value. How do I collect what is owed?"

"You collect your family and all who owe allegiance to you and you go to your neighbor's farm. If he does not pay, you can take what is owed you, as well as his life. All you need to do is report what you have done to the closest farm, lest you be considered a murderer for killing in secret."

"And what if I have not the strength to take what is owed?"

Asbjorn shrugged again, "Then your claim would likely not have been allowed, for why would the godar rule against one of their own, a person of power and influence?"

Harald persisted, "But what if my claim were right and honorable?"

"If you do not have the power to compel payment, you will not get paid. Such is the way of the world everywhere. At least in Iceland we have the laws, so all are protected, but those who have a certain station will not be dragged down by some foolish lawsuit by an eager peasant. That is as it should be."

Harald laughed, "So, even here, in this land without kings, this land of free men and laws, the rich live under the protection of the law and if that fails, under the protection of their liegemen and you are only right if you are strong enough to force your will upon others."

Asbjorn, stung, said, "Show me a land where it is not so."

"I cannot," said Harald, still laughing. "All the world over the powerful make the laws suit their whim, if there are laws other than their whim. I just find it amusing that you speak with such pride of your freedom, when you really have only as much freedom as you have family and allies."

"Why would you want it any other way? Why would a man strive for wealth and influence, if it was to do you and yours no good?"

"Why indeed," said Harald. "Enough. It is Christmas. Let us get drunk, sing songs and tell tales. Soon spring will come and there is much to do before we sail." He raised his mug and Arnora hurried over with a pitcher of mead. She did not meet Harald's eyes as she poured, and she scurried away as soon as the table was served.

Harald watched her go. His eyes were thoughtful as he took a long, deep drink.

CHAPTER TWENTY-SIX

ASBJORN, THE BISHOP, AND their men left in the morning, their horses saddled before daybreak. The morning sun was barely clearing the mountains to the south when they made their farewells. The horses stamped in the cold, worked the iron bits in their mouths and hunched their backs against the saddles.

"I will send word throughout my domain, that wherever your people are quartered they shall be well treated and given all they require," Asbjorn said.

Harald inclined his head. "My thanks, Asbjorn Arnorsson."

Asbjorn bowed his head in return and then they were gone, taking an extra horse for the silver.

Harald watched them leave and then turned toward the fjord. Drangay stood tall above the water, its sides lit by the morning sun.

"How long was Grettir an outlaw?"

"Nearly twenty years," Eric said. "When he was killed he

had but a short time left in his term."

"Twenty years is a long time to have every man's hand against you, in a land like this."

Eric said, "He was very much a man, stronger than two ordinary men, so the songs say. Cunning and vengeful."

"I think of him much," Harald said. "Is it enough, to live a life of struggle and blood, to end with nothing but a song?"

Eric shrugged, "Many men have ended their lives with less. Grettir chose his course."

"Did he? Or was it as the old ones said, that his fate was ordained?"

"He was a prideful man, unwilling to turn aside for anyone, so perhaps his fate was sealed."

"A hard road though, to end your life on a barren rock in the middle of a cold sea."

Eric was puzzled. "And how do you think our lives will end?" he asked. "Truly, Grettir's end might seem one of great wonder for us, since we are likely to drown or starve, lost at sea, or die from a barbarian's arrow in a dark forest far from home."

Harald smiled, a grin of purer amusement. "Perhaps, you are right. I feel much better now. I've been mourning the waste of Grettir's life, when in fact I should have been mourning ours."

The two men laughed heartily together, while far down the fjord Grettir's island warmed under the winter sun.

Back in the hall, Harald checked the progress of Orm's bow. He was pleased to note that the boy was a careful worker. The arrow nocks for the bowstring were made of horn, which had been carefully whittled to size. Orm was rubbing the bow with a mixture of tallow and wax; the yew was almost glowing, the wood a gentle gold in color. Orm had wound several wide strips of lamb skin around the middle of the bow for a firm hand grip.

Harald hefted the bow, bending the limbs experimentally. "So, have you tried to string it?"

"No, my lord," Orm said, "I did not know if I should."

"It is meant to be used, boy," Harald said. "Not to be looked at. Have you a bow string?"

"Yes, my lord."

The boy produced a bow string made of silk and slipped both ends over the limbs of the bow. He put the string in the nock on the bottom and then put the nock against his instep. Pulling mightily, he was barely able to get the upper end of the string slid up the limb and seated in the top nock. Harald watched in silence. When the bow was strung he said, "Arrow?"

"Here, but where will I shoot?"

"Move aside." Harald bellowed, and everyone near the fire scattered back up onto the sleeping benches. "There, boy," he pointed, "aim for the post in the center of the hall, about chest high."

Orm looked at the crowd of people watching expectantly. He took a deep breath and then nocked the arrow, letting the shaft rest on his fist.

"No, boy, don't point your feet at the target. They should be to one side. And tilt the bow a little to be certain it clears the ground. Then the arrow will rest more easily on your fist." Orm nodded and adjusted his stance.

"Now," Harald continued, "pick a spot on your target. Make it small, the size of a man's eye. Look only at that spot."

Orm's young face was intent as he brought the bow up and drew it back. It bent easily for a hand's breadth, and then Harald saw the boy's shoulder muscles begin to tremble.

"Be a man," Harald whispered, for Orm's ears only. The bow came back the rest of the way and Orm released as soon as his thumb touched his ear. The arrow hissed the length of the hall and disappeared up to its fletching in the turf wall, an arm's length to the side of the post he'd meant to hit.

"Not bad, boy. If you'd brought your father's bow instead of his sword when you came to kill me, I might well be dead now."

"I think not," said Strykar, "Look where the arrow hit. If he'd come to kill you, I would be the one dead."

The hall erupted in laughter. A boy ran to pull the arrow from the wall. Orm flushed as Harald pounded him on the shoulders.

"Remember this, boy," Harald whispered, "You will never make a more difficult shot. A never-used bow, a hall of spectators and a skill you barely know. Truly, you have a gift."

"I did not hit the mark."

"That will come. Soon, the arrow will go where you look. With a bow, it is important to do everything the same way, every time. You need not have the same form as others, but your form has to remain consistent."

"I was not able to hold it steady," Orm said.

Harald nodded, "It is too powerful for you. Were you a man grown, I would suggest you shave more wood from the limbs to make it a little weaker. Since you are a boy, I think your best course is to simply grow stronger."

"I will grow stronger."

"Every day, boy, every day." Harald's voice rose above the crowd, "All of you, witness what Orm has done. We go to a strange land, where every hand may be raised against us. Anyone who fails to learn to use a bow will not sail with us in the spring."

"My lord?" a woman questioned.

"Yes," Harald said, "I mean what I say. All of you, down to the last and the least, will make a bow for his strength and learn to use it. Before we leave this place, that post will fear us all."

The hall fell silent once more as everyone bent to their work.

Harald watched the activity for a bit and then turned to Strykar and Eric.

"Attend me," he said and left the hall.

The two men followed him and together they walked

across the barren landscape.

"When will we sail?" Harald asked.

"It is difficult to tell. We need to retrace our route, picking up our fleet as we go, and transit around the south. The sea ice will be too thick to take the direct route to Greenland. It will do us no good to leave too early, for the waters around Greenland will be dangerous and the Greenlanders will be too short of food for us to tarry there. Late April, perhaps even early May to be safe."

"If we are to plant a crop in a new land, I think we need to leave earlier than that."

Eric threw his hands up. "I cannot melt the ice, Lord Harald."

"We will do the best we can. If needs be, we will live on fish for another winter. What of our other supplies?"

Strykar said, "For grain and livestock, I think all will be well. Tools the same. We will need arrows and armor."

"Arrows will be easy, but armor may be difficult. I doubt if much is for sale and question if we can find many smiths capable of competent work."

"Most of the men have some armor. The women and children, even if you wish them to be warriors, are not strong enough to wear chain mail."

"We will not worry overmuch about armor," Harald said. "but, my byrnie was reduced to shreds at Stamford Bridge."

Strykar looked up at him. "We certainly will not find a mail shirt to fit you. I think our wisest course is to let the men see to their own armor. We have too few warriors for any kind of a shield wall. If it comes to that, we will have need of a fortress or a grave. You, though, my lord, should commission a new byrnie, for if there is to be talk with these pagans, you will be exposed."

Harald nodded, "Perhaps a mail shirt, but with a high collar."

"About this high?" Eric asked, holding his hand a bit above the arrow scar on Harald's neck.

"At least that high," Harald laughed, "or else I need stand behind you."

"You are too wide and too tall to shelter behind me," said Eric. "Perhaps if Strykar and I stood side by side and you bent your knee."

"I've bent my knee once in this lifetime. It did me no good, and I did not enjoy the sensation. Find me a smith who can make chain mail."

"Yes, my lord," said Strykar.

"Leave me now," Harald said, "but send Arnora Asbrandsdottor out. I wish to speak with her."

The two men left and Harald continued his slow pacing, ending up near the horse pen. He had purchased several of the small, tough horses to be used for winter patrols. They, too, were living on winter rations and when he approached the fence they came to him, looking for food. They looked not at all like the sleek, fast war horses of the Saracens, but they were strong, tough, and intelligent. He planned to take as many as possible to the new land. If needs be, they could be eaten and, if not, they added an immense mobility to patrols and would help plow the fields.

He was rubbing their forelocks and talking to them gently when he heard Arnora's footsteps behind him.

"Yes, my lord?"

He turned and looked down on her. "Tell me," he said.

"Tell you what?" she asked.

"Tell me who the father of your child is," he said.

"My lord," she said, "I am not with child."

"Yes, you are," he said. "Either you lie to me or to yourself. I see it in your eyes, the way you walk, in every line of your body. You are with child and you need to tell me who the father is."

Arnora's lip trembled and without warning she collapsed to the ground. She sat staring up at Harald, panic in her eyes. Her face twisted and she suddenly rolled over, gagging. She remained on her hands and knees, retching and sobbing.

For several long moments, Harald stood quietly where he was, watching her with his careful eyes. At last he walked over and offered his hand to her. She ignored him at first but when he touched her shoulder she grasped his hand and climbed slowly to her feet, wiping her mouth with the back of her hand.

"What am I to do?" she whispered. "If you know, everyone knows. I thought, perhaps, it would just. . .go away, that I was wrong. I mean, I knew, but still, I hoped. . ."

"There is no great shame in this," Harald said, waving his hand in an all-encompassing motion, "do you think that all the women who travel with an army, particularly a losing army, know for certain the father of their child? Still, you know the law. Your child does need a father. I need to know, and if he does not, he also needs to know. Is it Orm?"

"NO! We have never. . . . I mean, I have never. . ." Her voice trailed off and she stared bleakly into the distance.

"Arnora," Harald said, "I will give you as much time as I can, but before your child is born, you must tell me who the father is. It is the law, and it is a good law."

"I cannot," Arnora said.

"I told you once before," Harald said, "there is no 'cannot.' You do not wish to tell, but in time you will need to. Now, come with me. You spend too much time in the hall. The air is foul. It does you no good. Let us walk and I will tell you of our plans for the coming spring. When we reach the new land, you will have a child and he will sit in a basket at your feet as you are at the helm of the finest ship in the world. It is not a future that should frighten you."

He led the way into the darkness. Arnora hesitated a moment, but she took quick steps until she caught up. The two walked and talked for a long time, under the cold winter stars. The wind blew and occasionally their path was obscured by drifting snow, but overhead the northern lights danced and glowed.

When they returned to the hall, Orm was still practicing

with his bow. There were several holes in the post where an arrow had struck, and a pile of dirt on the floor marked the times he'd missed.

CHAPTER TWENTY-SEVEN

THE SEASONS CHANGED. The post at the end of the hall was soon scarred so badly that Harald feared for the hall's collapse. He found another, thicker one and practice continued. The store of bow blanks was virtually exhausted and there was an abundance of kindling before everyone had a useable bow.

As the days grew longer, people spent more and more time outside. Tempers flared less often and everyone spent more time staring out to sea. A pod of killer whales came into the fjord; Eric took a crew in a small boat out and harpooned one of them. The fresh meat and fat were a welcome addition to their bland diet.

Arnora grew larger. She moved slower, weighed down by more than the baby in her belly. She spent much of her time alone, moving through the crowded hall in a soft circle of despair. After their long walk through the winter's night, Harald spoke little to her. The exception was when Eric and Strykar talked of navigation or ship handling. He then consistently called her over to listen and asked her questions afterwards.

Orm, too, moved alone. Soon the bow was no longer too much for him to handle and as his shoulders broadened he had to dig into Gunnar's trunk to find clothes. Arnora cut them down to fit, but their easy friendship was gone. He was puzzled by the changes beyond her growing stomach and her new silence. She was living a world he could not visit and he did not understand why. When he was not practicing with the bow, he remained Harald's shadow.

Harald seemed to have little to do. After so many years of leading vast armies, as well as countries, the ordering of a few hundred people was a small challenge. He, too, spent much of his time alone. There were the usual disputes caused by people crowded together under a winter sky, but no serious fights and no one had been killed. Many tedious hours passed while he was measured for a mail shirt. The smith then spent many more hours coiling wire into rings, and forging them together until his new armor took shape.

People grew used to seeing his immense frame dwarfed by the landscape, moving slowly, lost in thought. He spent many hours staring out to the north, watching Grettir's island through the winter fog.

Orm joined him one day.

"My lord," he said. "For what are you watching?"

"I am just thinking," Harald said. "I think much of Grettir."

"Why? He was just an outlaw and many of his stories are merely that, lies and songs for drunken men."

"He was far more than that, boy," Harald said. "He was a hero, in many ways a perfect man. He was strong, brave, cunning; he stood aside to no man and he always did only what he thought he should do. To many men, he was everything a man should be. And he died, killed by treachery, and left nothing behind save a song. He left for the worse almost every thing he touched. It is a lesson, yet I am not sure what the lesson is."

Orm was silent for a time and then he said, "Lord Harald, why did my father die?"

"You were there, boy. He died a straw death, taken by wound fever."

"Yes, but, why. . ." his voice trailed off.

"You want to know why he was wounded, what we were doing in the north of England in the first place? Really, you want to know why I got your father killed."

"Yes." Orm met the flat blue eyes squarely.

"I have seen the world, Orm, or at least a large share of it. Everywhere, the small and the weak are held in thrall by the large and the powerful. In Byzantium I saw an empire, and it had the power to do much but it did little, because it was run by weak and foolish people. Even so, I could see that the north could never be what it should be, until all the countries were one. Norway against Denmark, Sweden against Norway, Denmark against England, Scotland against England, all the wars, uprisings, insurrections, treacheries and betrayals. All of it was pointless. Perhaps we of the North are like bears, strong but always too independent to ever come together under one flag. But unless we do, blood will always flow, and always for stupid reasons, and we will be left helpless before our enemies." Harald paced back and forth. Below him the surf waves boomed against the basalt rocks. "So, Orm, your father died because I sought to make one country of the North, to make one empire where all would have their place and could stand together. And, truthfully, where I would rule. And, I was right, boy! I know I was right. But I could not succeed." He turned and grabbed the boy's shoulders, gripping so hard that days later there were still bruises, "So tell me, Orm, am I a man of vision who was betrayed by the weakness of those who share my blood or am I a man like Grettir, doing great deeds while spoiling all I touch? The evidence is clear—all I have built is gone. My daughter is dead, dead at the moment that I sought to rule

England. My wife chose not to share my fate, my kingdom has lost most of its young men and answers to another's word, and I stand in this barren land, my only people a group of crippled warriors, desperate widows and children. And in a few months, do I lead another group of believers to their deaths because of my ambitions?"

Orm could say nothing. Harald laughed a short, bitter laugh when he saw the boy's expression.

"You learned more than you wanted to, didn't you, boy?" The two were still alone, far from camp. "Are the stories still told of the old times, when we had many gods?"

"Yes, but they are stories for children," Orm said.

"Do they tell of Odin, master of the Gods? How he was called Odin the All-Knowing? Do they tell how in order to get that name he hung himself on gallows for nine days and then plucked out one of his eyes? That is the cost of knowledge. The more you know, the more pain it brings. And yet," he went on, loosing his grip on the boy's shoulders and spinning around to stare at Drangay again, "it is always better to know than to not know, no matter how much it hurts. That is the real story, that knowledge is pain."

Again, Orm could think of nothing to say. The two stood in a hard silence.

"Come, boy," Harald said. "The day grows dark."

As they neared the hall they were met by a woman.

"Lord Harald," she said, "the girl is giving birth."

"And the father?" he asked.

"She remains silent."

"Very well," Harald said, "I will speak to her."

The first rain of spring pattered around them on the grass and snow. They left the sea behind them. Drangay was lost in the mist.

CHAPTER TWENTY-EIGHT

THE HALL WAS FULL WHEN Harald entered. The cold rain had brought everyone inside. Preparations for the evening meal were in process. Arnora lay in her sleeping robes, against the wall near the middle of the hall where two midwifes attended her.

Harald lifted an eyebrow as he approached. One of the midwives shook her head.

He knelt by the girl. "Child," he said, smoothing her hair with one massive hand.

Arnora looked up at him with confused eyes. She opened her mouth to speak, but another pain hit and her words were lost in a soft shriek.

Harald looked around the crowded hall and then gathered the girl up in his arms and took her to his sleeping room. Orm ran ahead and swept the curtains back.

He set her down gently then stepped back to let the women take over.

"Keep me informed." He stepped out of the room, pulling the curtain closed behind him.

Neither Harald nor Orm ate that night. The hall stayed quiet throughout the evening. No one, not grizzled veteran or boisterous child, was willing to face Harald's eye.

The fire was no longer needed for heat and after the evening meal was prepared it was allowed to die down. Soon the darkness was marred only by sporadic flickers from the fire and occasional soft gasps from the girl behind the curtain.

"How long. . .?" Orm asked.

"There is no telling, boy," Harald said. "Perhaps soon, perhaps days." A flicker of bleak humor crossed his face. "It is best that women not become warriors," he said, "for their courage would put most men to shame."

Everyone was asleep when the midwife came to get Harald.

"The girl still has not spoken. The babe does not have a father."

Harald nodded and left his place in the high seat.

He went behind the curtain and knelt beside the girl.

"Arnora," he said, "your child needs a father. It is the law. I do not understand your silence, but I have respected it, until now. Now, you must speak." The force behind his voice had cowed armies and emperors. Arnora could resist no longer.

"My child needs a father," Arnora said.

"Yes."

"Have I your vow, that you will not harm the father of my child?"

Harald was puzzled, "Yes, child, I have gone to much bother to ensure your child has a father. It would make little sense for me to do him harm."

"You must swear!"

"I, Harald Sigurdsson, swear by God, before these witnesses, that I will not kill the father of your child. Will that do?"

Arnora whispered, "The father, is my father."

Harald sat very still, became stillness. "Asbrand brought you to this state?"

"It is not his fault," Arnora said. "He was drunk, it was after my mother got sick. I. . . I didn't even know what he was doing. I doubt if he knew."

Harald stood. Arnora clutched his hand frantically. "Please," she pleaded, "you swore, you would not leave my child without a father."

"I will not kill the father of your child," Harald said. "Clear your mind. You have much more work to do this night." He bent over, smoothed her hair back and smiled into her eyes. "All will be well." He left the bedchamber and the curtain swung shut behind him.

"Here, boy," Harald handed Orm a torch. "Light this and follow me." When Orm took the torch, he was surprised to see that the big hand was trembling.

Harald and Orm walked slowly the length of the dark hall. Harald peered into each sleeping closet. He found Asbrand close to the far end. He was sleeping on his back, an occasional snore rattling the quiet.

Harald stood over him for several long moments, then took a firm grasp of Asbrand's hair with both hands. His eyes flew open and Harald pulled him from his bed, flinging him as a dog flings a snake. He hit the wall, half a man's length high, and bounced off to the dirt below. He landed on his hands and knees. Harald shook the loose hair from his hands, and took a long step forward and kicked Asbrand in the stomach. The kick lifted him off the floor and sent him into the wall again. He rolled over and tried to rise. Harald kicked him again; this time he did not move, but lay still, choking and gasping.

Silently, Harald looked down at him, then grabbed him by the tunic and lifted him to his feet. His eyes were unfocused and he had vomited down his front. Blood trickled down his face from his torn scalp. Harald held him until his breathing eased and he became aware of his surroundings.

"Asbrand," Harald said, "your daughter told me of your actions. Truly, you are a man of most extraordinary fortune, for before she told she made me swear not to kill the father of her child. Know this, your life hangs by a thread and that thread is in your daughter's hands."

Asbrand opened his mouth and Harald said, "Shhh," his voice soft as it would be to soothe a babe, "your daughter is in childbirth. You would not wish to disturb her, because the vow was only to leave you alive." His voice dropped to a whisper, "I can find a great deal of room between dead and not quite dead. *I am an expert at that.* Do you understand?"

Harald released him and he sank to the ground. Harald kicked him again, more out of disgust than fury.

"On your knees, and stay there till I release you. Spend your time in prayer for your daughter. Recite the most sincere prayers of your life. Do you need me to tell you that if she dies, you die?" Harald took his knife from its sheath and inserted the tip into Asbrand's nostril.

"If you are lucky, lucky beyond all measure, I will merely make you pay through the nose for this, this, abomination."

Harald twitched his knife blade up and Asbrand rose high on his knees. Harald looked at him wearily. "If God answers *your* prayers, it will be truly a miracle." He looked at Orm. "Boy, string your bow. If this one leaves his knees, kill him. No," he amended himself, "if he moves, shoot him through the stomach. We will make wagers as to how long before wound rot kills him."

"Yes, my lord."

The night faded slowly toward day. A woman woke, stirred the fire, swung the big iron kettle over the flames and began making porridge. Harald sat in the high seat, staring into the flames. As the hall awoke, people would look from Harald to Asbrand, and then hear the occasional slight outcries from Harald's sleeping chamber. Explanations were quietly passed from mouth to mouth and everyone who could leave the hall soon did. No one talked to Asbrand. He had never had many comrades and he had fewer this morning, for no one had the courage to brave Harald's stare.

Arnora's labor continued. No one re-entered the hall and those who had stayed maintained a self-disciplined silence. An unfocused violence hung in the air. It was midafternoon before Asbrand moved and that was only to topple sideways, his hands cradling his bruised stomach. Orm had not left his post the entire day and when Asbrand moved he nocked an arrow.

"No, boy," Harald said, "leave him."

Orm nodded, his face without expression. He unstrung his bow and left the hall.

As darkness fell, people filtered back in. The hum and clatter of the evening meal was noticeably subdued. Asbrand lay on his side, saying nothing and moving not at all.

Harald slept in the high seat. Orm returned to the hall and slept at his feet. It was near morning when the noises awoke him. The harsh panting from behind the curtain sounded like a deer run down by dogs. Asbrand was gone from his place on the floor. Harald walked the length of the hall and saw that his gear was also gone.

Harald returned to the high seat and sat, idly toying with his belt knife. At his feet Orm stirred, then sat up, alarmed. Harald put a cautioning hand on his shoulder and the boy relaxed.

In time, the noises reached a crescendo, then stopped. Harald sat very still, but no other sound came.

A midwife came through the curtain. She had been with Arnora for two days and she was bloody and exhausted.

"What news?" Harald asked.

"The child was stillborn."

"And the girl?"

"She sleeps or is senseless, one or the other."

Harald nodded, his face showing nothing.

The midwife hesitated, then went on, "The birth did her great damage, my lord. She is too young for a child."

"Will she live?"

"Yes, unless the birth fever takes her, but she will be a long time healing."

Harald nodded again. "When she awakes, give her my best. Tell her that I have been called away, but I will return as soon as possible. Bury the child." He went on, the barest shadow of a threat in his voice. "Take care of her, woman."

He turned to where Orm sat sunken in misery. "Orm, come with me."

"Where do we go?" Orm asked.

"We go to find Asbrand."

"What will we do when we find him?"

"Kill him."

CHAPTER TWENTY-NINE

IT WAS FULL DAY BY THE time Harald and Orm left the hall. Drangay loomed on the horizon, but no figure moved in the landscape around them.

"How will we find him?" Orm asked.

"Men are no different than deer. If you know how they think, you can hunt them." Harald gestured around. "Four directions. He cannot go to sea, and snow still plugs the mountain passes. He bears his crime like a scar upon his brow, so I do not think he will go up the valley toward the larger settlements. I think he will go up the fjord."

"What is there for him?"

"Nothing, but Asbrand is a stupid man, not accustomed to thinking beyond the reach of his sword or his drinking horn. He knows what he has done, he knows he has been found out, and he knows my will. He will think of nothing but escape." Harald settled his sheepskin cloak on his shoulders. "This could take some time. Are you ready?"

"Yes, my lord."

The two headed north, keeping to the narrow strip of flat land between the sea and the mountains. By the time the sun was directly overhead, the crusted snow in front of them was unmarked, except for one set of tracks.

Harald set the pace, Orm followed behind him. They walked in silence for several hours.

"My lord," Orm said, finally.

"Yes?"

"You talked of Byzantium, and of the worth of an empire. Why did you leave there?"

"Because my home was in the north and I sought to make myself king, not the servant of an emperor. In addition, Constantinople was no place to be a man. Empress Zoe was a fool, an evil, stupid, woman whose thoughts never rose above her waist, yet her word and her whims were law throughout the empire. It was as though half the energy of the empire went into satisfying her whims and the other half went into cleaning up the stench from them. A sane country would not have given her the power to rule over a dung heap, yet because she was clever at manipulation and ruthless in her demands, she kept power while those more able fell to her. I have seen it many times—a king can be a stern and good ruler, but if he founds an empire, it is with a sword, so is not built on rock, but sand. And if his sons rule after him, they are usually lesser men. In time they forget all but their power. These Icelanders are mad, but they have found something here which could work."

"Why do you call them mad?"

"Because all is law to them; you cannot turn around without someone bringing suit against you, but it means nothing. The powerful remain careful to retain power so should they break the law; no harm comes to them. They call themselves free men, but notice that none of them get an arm's reach away from their weapons. A man is not free if he cannot rest his head without fear that all he has may be taken from him. No, they do not have a country here and, as a result, they will always be vulnerable."

"What makes a country?"

"Something that holds people together, from the last and the least to the greatest. A small country is often bound by blood ties and common interests, but to create an empire more is needed. The Saracens seem to have it in their belief in their God and Mohammad, yet they, too, squabble over power. The Jews have a powerful faith in their God, but have never had an empire. The Romans united half the world under their flag, but in time they forgot themselves and became degenerate. Most great empires are forged with blood, but to last they must either be ruthless or make the lives of their subjects better for their rule. Attila did not have it, nor did the Vandals. The Greeks under Alexander lost their way when he died."

The sun had set and still they walked, guided by a rising moon.

"When will we catch him?" Orm asked.

"Soon, I think. He took no supplies and has no allies."

"What of your vow to Arnora? She does not wish her father killed and you gave your word."

"I swore not to kill the father of her child. She has no child. And Orm, you need to understand, I was humoring her so she would have her strength when she needed it. Her wishes are not paramount here. Asbrand is a blight upon the earth. I have known him for many years; he is both foul and a fool. Arnora is safe from him now, but what of the next child that falls under his hand? He dies to save that child, not to save Arnora." Harald paused, and then clarified himself, "I kill him to protect the other children. I'll enjoy it because of Arnora."

They walked until a bank of clouds came in off the sea and all was dark.

Harald stopped, "I have lost his trail," he said. "We will rest here until dawn." They tramped back and forth until the snow was firm beneath their feet. Harald laid a tightly woven wool blanket on the ground and they lay on it, wrapped in their cloaks. Harald placed his sword next to him and dug some bread and dried meat out of his pack. He pulled the hood of his cloak up and rested his head on the empty pack. The man and boy lay side by side, eating their meager meal while gazing at the dark, empty sky.

"My lord?"

"No, boy, not now," Harald said, spitting out a fish bone and settling his cloak over his face. "Now I want to sleep."

Far away, waves crashed upon the beach and beneath them the snow creaked with every move they made. Orm did not know when he went to sleep, but eventually he had. He awoke, shivering. There was a faint blush of dawn on the horizon. Harald had already risen.

"Come, boy," he said. "You can eat while you walk. I have found the trail."

By early afternoon they occasionally saw a faint figure in the distance. By dark they knew that they, too, had been spotted.

They stopped at an earlier time that night.

"We stand too great a chance of losing him or walking into an ambush." Harald said. "He is slowing now. Tomorrow he is ours."

A slight mist filled the air. "A cold, dark, camp. I have killed men for that alone."

It was not much of a joke, but Orm found himself laughing. Their groundcover had not dried from the previous night and its clamminess permeated his entire body. The bread was soggy and the dried mutton stringy.

"Tell me," he said through chattering teeth, "Why do we go to this new land."

"Why not, Orm? None of us leave anything behind. Our people have always had their eyes on what lies beyond. Truthfully, when we first set out I had no grand plan—I simply thought to leave pain and failure behind. Now that we have come this far, I believe perhaps we did the right thing."

"What will we do?"

"We will move into an empty land and make it our own."

"And the pagans?"

"I think on it much. We cannot conquer; we are not an army. We will need to find another way. If they are truly savages, there is much we can offer in trade. It will not be easy—we will be like a man walking a narrow rail. If we are too strong they will despise us, if we are too weak they will kill us and take all. That is yet another reason to kill Asbrand. We cannot afford many fools, for one man's actions could ruin all. I have seen it happen, more often than not."

"My lord, you have been all over the world, spent your life walking with the great and powerful, yet you talk as if they were nothing but sheep herders, squabbling over summer pasture."

"They are, Orm, they are. Men are the same everywhere and at all ranks. They want their bellies full, they want women, they want more than they have. And to get what they want, they often do that which guarantees they will not succeed."

"Eric says you see people as a tool, like a carpenter looking at his chisels."

"He does, does he?" Harald thought for a moment. "There is some truth in what he says. Keep in mind, boy, since I was younger than you, my life has been spent learning how to bend people to my will. I do it as naturally as I breathe. Part of it is knowing your will. A man who knows what he wants always has an advantage over one who does not. There are usually many paths from which to choose, and some people cannot or will not choose. Thus, they are doomed to always follow in the path of one who can. The problem comes when the man who has the will chooses poorly."

"And how often does that happen?"

"Ask your father."

CHAPTER THIRTY

IT WAS RAINING WHEN they caught him. He was finally trapped by geography, pinned between them and the headland at the mouth of the fjord.

Drangay was very close. Although rain muffled the sound, it was possible to hear the cries of seabirds, returning to nest.

"Perhaps you should swim, Asbrand. Grettir did, to this same spot. Remember? He was afraid of the dark and he swam to fetch fire. I give you leave to try." The waves crashed below, but Harald's voice carried easily above the noise.

"No?" he continued. "Then here you die. I always knew you were a fool, but if I had known what you really are, this day would have come years ago."

Asbrand shouted in defiance. "Come and kill me then, if you can." His defiance melted into self-pity. "Harald the king, Harald the high and mighty, Harald the HardRuler. Making judgments, making the law. You have nothing left, you're a fugitive from your own land and still you seek to rule. And you judge me—I was drunk, my wife was sick, what was I to do? I barely remember it. The girl suffered no harm. How dare you force yourself into what happens between her and I? You know nothing of what it is like to be me. You were born to be a king—always the best weapons, the best armor, the finest food, the best women. I would like to see how bold you would be if you were like me, born with nothing."

Harald looked at him in amazement. He held up his sword. The silver raven gleamed in the stark iron pommel. "This? Do you think this is what makes me a king?"

The sword twirled in the air and stuck deeply in the turf. He dropped his shield beside it, then his cloak. His new mail shirt came off and then, to Orm's shock, he continued to disrobe. In a few moments he stood, naked in the cold rain. His big feet splayed, gripping the earth.

"See me, Asbrand. I stand before you, owning nothing but my soul. I am still your better."

He turned to Orm. "Orm, there is a chance he might kill me. If he does, put three arrows through his heart and kick the carcass over the edge of the cliff."

He turned back, "Your death approaches, Asbrand. Try to face it like a man."

Asbrand rushed to meet him, his cloak billowing behind him and his sword held high. He planted his feet and took a vicious swing, the sword slicing the air toward Harald's neck. Harald took a quick step forward, deflecting the blow, then grabbing his wrist. He stood, towering over the smaller man. Their pose held for a few moments, straining against each other. Then Orm heard the bones in Asbrand's wrist break and saw his sword fall harmlessly to the ground. Harald shifted his grip to throat and waist, and lifted him high in the air. Orm could hear the gasping of their breathing along with the cries of the seabirds.

Then Harald broke Asbrand's back across his knee and

dropped him to the ground.

Orm hurried over and he and Harald looked down on Asbrand. He lay motionless on the ground, a dark stain wetting his legs. His eyes were open but unfocused. They shifted to Harald and he began to talk. "Do you think by killing me you get my daughter? You are no better than me after all." He went on, mouthing obscenities, his voice rising. Harald said nothing, but suddenly his bare foot lashed out and with his heel, he crushed Asbrand's windpipe. The voice stopped and his face blackened with his efforts to breathe. It was several long minutes before he lay still.

Orm looked in shock at Harald, whose gaze had not shifted from Asbrand during entire time it took him to die. He sensed the boy's stare and turned to meet it.

"I think I will dress now," he said. "This rain should melt the last of the snow. Perhaps spring has finally arrived."

He picked up his wet tunic and struggled into it. "We need to find the nearest farm and report this. It must to be done lest I be declared a murderer. True, we are leaving this land, but I would hate to leave as a criminal."

CHAPTER THIRTY-ONE

STRYKAR CAME TO MEET them as the halls came within sight. The two were exhausted, muddy, and hungry.

"Asbrand?" Strykar asked.

"Dead."

Strykar nodded. "He used up his luck long past. Truly, that he remained alive so long was a miracle."

"And the girl?" Harald asked.

"She lives. Beyond that I do not know. She is still in your sleeping closet; I thought that would be your wishes. The women are caring for her. The babe was buried against the mountain with the others. The farmer says he will fetch a priest when traveling is better."

"Good," Harald said. "Well, Orm, this will be hard. Never postpone an evil day." He led the way back into the hall.

Arnora lay on Harald's bed, her hair greasy and uncombed. She was very pale and her eyes were closed.

Harald stood over her. He did not look much better. His clothes were foul after a week outside, his beard untrimmed and his hair matted.

And he smelled.

After a silent moment, Arnora's eyes slowly opened.

"My lord," she said.

Harald nodded gravely. "How do you fare, child?"

Arnora closed her eyes. "I am weary unto death, my lord," she said. "My limbs feel like water, I cannot stand. I hurt, all over, and my child is dead. What sin have I committed that I suffer so?"

"No sin, child, just ill luck. Your wounds will heal, your strength will return."

"And my father? Will he too, return?"

"No. I killed him for what he did to you."

"I knew you would. Even though you promised you would not. It was only my weakness that made me tell you what he had done. If I had kept my will and my silence, he would still live."

"Arnora," Harald said sharply. "You did not cause the death of your father. He lived as long as he did only because of you." He hesitated. "I did not wish to tell you this, it seemed an unnecessary burden, but in truth your father did the only good he ever did in this life when he fathered you. He was a weak, drunken fool, who fled from the brave and tormented the weak."

"And yet, he was my father. I have memories of him coming home and laughing with my mother. I remember the time he brought me a doll, a little one made of rags with a carved wooden head. It is true, when he drank his temper was terrible and sometimes he hurt us, but that was not his fault—he had spent his life a'viking and had many harsh memories that he needed to drown before he could sleep."

"Arnora," Harald said, but she did not stop, did not even appear to hear him.

"This was his chance, this new land we go to. He would not have needed to drink, he could have found a woman to replace my mother, the evils would have left him and we would have had a good life together. And now, because I could not stay quiet, all is gone. My mother is dead, my father is dead, my child is dead. All gone, all my fault."

"No fault lies with you, Arnora."

"No? Would you have hunted my father down and killed him like a dog if I had kept my silence?" Harald said nothing. "I thought not."

Harald tried once more. "Arnora, a man chooses his own path. God gives us free will. Your father chose to leave you and your mother poor, because he preferred to spend his silver on whores and mead. He chose to beat you, neglect you and abuse you, not because you deserved it, but because you were an easy target for him. He sinned: against you and against God, because he chose an evil path."

Arnora met his eyes and it was Harald who looked away first. "And yet, I did not wish him dead. But even so, you killed him. Do you believe you did it for me? Or was it merely for your own pleasure?"

"I acted because a man who would do to you what your father did is a man who has forfeited his right to life."

Arnora was starting to drift off, her voice sagged with weariness. "I think you killed him to avenge your daughter. You have yearned to kill someone ever since you heard of her death; don't you think everyone in this hall could read that in your eyes? My father was unlucky enough to cross your path. Did you think that if you killed my father I would become your daughter?" Her eyes closed and her voice became very soft. "I would have liked that, my lord, being your daughter. I felt like I was living a dream, at the helm of the ship with you standing close by, patient and kind, instructing me, trusting me. I could have sailed that way forever. But you murdered my family; I will always see their faces when I look at you. So, a good day's work for you—you take away my father and my child, but you also take from me the man who has made me feel like I could do anything. I think you should rest now." Arnora turned her head slightly

and lay as if asleep.
    Perhaps she was.

CHAPTER THIRTY-TWO

HARALD LOOKED AT THE remains of the hall. With the roof off, the boards and sails back on the ships, little was left. The turf was already crumbling and, in a year, or two there would be nothing left but a pile with a few fire blackened stones buried where the fire pit had been.

The mountains were still the same as when they'd arrived, but everything else had changed. The snow was long gone, spring grass was intensely green, the air alive with the sounds of seabirds returning to nest, the fjord full of fish.

The sun was warm on his back, but he had kept his sheepskin cloak on. Once out to sea he would be comfortable again.

Everyone else was aboard ship. Strykar had his ship away from shore already, and even as Harald watched the great sail was raised and the morning breeze filled it. The ship heeled over and headed up the fjord, out to sea.

Harald walked slowly down to the beach. The black volcanic sand crunched under his boots. The gangplank was drawn up inside the ship, but the anchor rope still hung over the side. Harald jumped, grabbed the rope and swung himself aboard. Without another glance back he said, "Let us leave this place."

With a clatter of oars, the ship pulled out to sea. By midday they had passed Drangay and the sea opened up before them. Eric was at his accustomed place, one hand on the dragon's neck; Arnora had the rudder.

Harald walked to the bow and stood next to Eric as they passed Drangay. A seal kept pace with them, his brown head and black eyes watching their every move. The gulls hovered overhead, somehow holding their position yet remaining motionless.

"So, Eric."

"It is good to be at sea again, my lord. I weary of this land."

"I will remember that, after we have been at sea for two weeks and the water is stale and the fish foul."

"Then I will be weary of the sea. I do not see your point, my lord." Harald laughed and clapped him on the shoulder, then made his way to the stern.

Orm stood near Arnora. The winter and his incessant practice with the bow had given him depth to his chest and shoulders that matched his height. Harald nodded at him and then turned to the girl.

"Arnora," he said, "I need to make amends to you."

"My lord?"

"The law of the land in Iceland is that the family of a man killed is entitled to compensation, in the form of a mark's worth of silver." Harald held out a coiled silver armband. "I had this made for you. It contains a mark's worth of silver. Take it."

Arnora reached out her hand and he dropped the armband into it. She examined it closely. The silver gleamed in the morning air, drops of condensation already appearing on the surface. It was sized to circle her upper arm twice and the ends of the coil were finished with fine silver heads, birds of some sort.

"Do you know the story of Odin's two ravens that circled the world and brought him back to him knowledge of all that had happened?"

The girl nodded.

"It is your compensation, but it is also a lesson. Knowledge is all. It is always better to know than to not know, even when ignorance would be vastly more pleasant."

Arnora met his eyes as she slid the coil onto her upper arm. The weight was strange and she shifted her shoulder slightly.

"It fits, but it is not comfortable."

"As it would be." Harald nodded at her and turned his back. Orm and Arnora watched him walk away.

"Truly, he earned the name the Hard Ruler," Orm said.

"I believe," Arnora said, "for better or worse, in this life we always earn what we are given."

She rubbed the cool silver with her fingertips, feeling out the details of the ravens' heads. She altered course slightly to the east and soon Drangay was lost in the distance, behind the headland at the mouth of the fjord.

Harald was the only one who saw it disappear.

CHAPTER THIRTY-THREE

IT WAS GOOD TO BE BACK to the sea.

Samoset stood at the edge of the woods.

Their summer camp was at the end of a long, narrow peninsula. It was heavily wooded its entire length. The ground dropped off quickly to the shore, with only a narrow strip of beach which nearly disappeared at high tide. It was low tide now, and the children were running up and down gathering shellfish from the mud flats.

Samoset liked their summer campground, especially since last year's raid by the evil ones. The water on three sides made it difficult for enemies to approach unnoticed and the base of the peninsula was narrow and easily defended.

The bay to the south was very wide and had good fishing. To the north it was narrower, but the adjoining peninsula had suffered a forest fire a few years back which had destroyed all the underbrush and young trees, leaving a ghostly forest of black and white trunks, with grass growing thick and tall between the stumps. In the summer, many deer grazed there. Samoset used it as a reserve, never hunting it unless the grounds further away failed and they had a need for food.

Their peninsula stuck out into the ocean proper, so if whales passed by they were easily spotted and occasionally pursued.

The summer wigwam was back in the trees. It was much larger than their winter lodge and more oblong in shape. No one spent much time in it this time of year. The weather was mild enough to sleep outside and most of the family did, reveling in the space after the close confines of the winter quarters.

"Father," Chogan said.

"Yes?"

"I think the canoe is seaworthy."

"Then it is. Should we try for some fish while there is yet daylight?"

Chogan tried not to show his eagerness. He loved the sea, and had loved it since he was very small. This was the first year that the repairs of their canoe had been left in his hands and he'd been busy all day repairing the winter's damage. With birch bark, spruce roots and tree sap, he had fixed the leaks and rotten spots that had developed since the craft was last used.

The two slid down the bank to where the canoe waited. Theirs was the first family to reach the summer campgrounds so theirs was the canoe at the water's edge. It had the distinctive design of their people—modest upturning at the bow and stern and a rising hump in the middle. Samoset took the bow, leaving the stern to Chogan. This, too, was a concession to his manhood, for the canoe was steered from the rear, with the front paddler providing the majority of the driving force.

They headed directly out to sea, the canoe breasting the small waves easily. They paddled without speaking until the children on the beach were nearly lost in the distance.

Samoset pointed ahead at a disturbance in the water and Chogan headed the canoe toward it. As they approached, Samoset laid his paddle down and took up a short line of fine braided sinews with a copper hook on the end. A small, tattered streamer of deer hair was fastened on the hook. Samoset flung it over the side and he had a strike before it sank an arm's length. The cod had recently spawned and their hunger had brought them up from the depths to feed. The first fish Samoset pulled in was as long as his arm. More came, as quickly as he could pull them in.

Chogan did not fish, but kept the canoe facing into the waves. Soon the bottom of the boat was covered with flopping fish and only a few inches of freeboard showed above the water.

"Enough," Samoset said, digging his paddle from beneath the pile of fish. Together they timed the waves, dug hard into the water, and turned the canoe for shore. Paddling with the waves, but with a much heavier load, it took them as long to return as it had taken them to get to where the fish were feeding.

Chogan steered them around the curve of the peninsula and brought the canoe ashore in the sheltered water. Samoset hopped out and pulled the craft up on the beach, taking care not to drop it on a rock that might puncture its fragile bottom. Chogan jumped out on the other side and together they pulled the boat completely out of the water. They paused to catch their breath and looked at the boat full of fish. Many days' food, ready to be cleaned and dried, and all for a short afternoon's work.

"Almost as easy as bear hunting," Samoset said.

Chogan grinned. The wounds from the bear claws had healed well, although they were still red and raised on his face. He had kept the claws that had wounded him and wore them on a leather thong around his neck.

"Indeed," he said, "the Creator has blessed us with great bounty. At least, in the spring. But why do the fish leave in the fall, when we need the food?"

"Winter storms are no time to be fishing. Perhaps the Creator is concerned we will come to harm on a winter sea. Perhaps it is a test, to prove we are worthy hunters. Or perhaps, the fish come and they go and their course has nothing to do with us at all."

Chogan smiled and bobbed his head. They were merely a part of the web of life and possibly not even the most important part. The rebuke was gentle, but earned and well-aimed.

The rest of the family had watched as they returned and could tell how heavily laden the boat was by the way it moved through the water. They came now to help carry the fish up to the camp site. Soon the camp was alive with flying entrails as everyone cleaned fish. A soup made from the beach shellfish simmered next to the fire.

Two of the drying racks were quickly filled with fish and everyone leaned back to smoke an evening pipe, their bellies full and their hearts content. The waves crashed on the beach and overhead the night breeze whispered through the trees. A few random sparks floated up to the sky.

Samoset was well pleased. The smelt had come up the streams as they should and now the cod had arrived. The sea birds were nesting and for a few weeks their eggs would be available. It was the best part of the year. It was too early for raiding parties from the evil ones—they had their crops to plant and tend. Their visits tended towards late summer, after the crops had matured but before the harvest. In the heat of summer, they would have to watch for them, but now in the late spring they were as safe and well fed as they could be. There would soon be more families and some of the responsibilities could be shared with the other family leaders. He settled back more comfortably into his seat, the tanned deerskin soft beneath him, and drifted off to sleep.

CHAPTER THIRTY-FOUR

THE LONGSHIPS BOBBED up and down in the slight swell. Strykar had bound his ship to Harald's and they were conferring. Behind them, the icy mountains of Greenland loomed. Ahead of them, at the mouth of the fjord, the rest of the fleet had already set sail. They were proceeding with caution, wending their way through the scattered sea ice that still cluttered the protected water.

"What is our route?" Strykar asked.

"It depends on how long this wind lasts," Eric said. "If it holds, we could have an easy crossing. I do not know these waters, though."

"Out to sea," said Harald. "We will keep together as best we can. At night we will sail with torches. It will never get truly dark; there should be little danger."

The day was bright and clear.

"Is that wise?" asked Eric.

"We know our destination," Harald said. "The Greenlanders told us where the new land lies."

"Knowing where it is and getting there are two different things. We will need five days sail to make landfall, and that's with much luck."

"We have had weather luck so far," Strykar said. "Iceland to the west of Greenland and only two ships lost."

"It is called luck because you never know when it will leave," Eric said glumly.

"Enough," Harald said. "At Herjolfsnes they told us the route to follow. We wish to go to this new land and a strong wind blows directly toward it. The water kegs are full, the ships are nearly foundering from the weight of the food, we take the chance. Take the lead, Strykar; we will again play sheepdog. Heading straight west or southwest. If we stay that course we will make landfall sooner or later."

Strykar nodded and ordered the lines cast off. His crew set sail and were soon overtaking the heavily loaded freighters.

Harald's ship followed suit, but at a more leisurely pace.

"My lord," said Eric, "you take a great risk."

"I choose between risks," Harald said. "The season advances. With five hundred people to feed, we need to find a place where, with luck, we can get a crop yet this year. If we take the time to beat our way further north till this strait narrows and then come all the way back down, we will find ourselves in a cold hut with little to eat."

"A cold hut or the cold sea."

"I thought you grow weary of the sea."

Eric laughed. "Indeed, thus I would not desire to spend eternity floating in its currents."

"That would never happen," Harald said. "The whales and the sharks would eat your bones soon enough, and there would be naught left but your soul, wafting to Heaven."

"Ahh, my lord, you are, as always, a great comfort."

Harald clapped him on the shoulder and headed back to the stern to give Arnora her instructions.

They cleared the mouth of the fjord and entered the open

sea. The swell was half a man's height and the ships rode from wave to wave, skipping along in weather that seemed to have been ordered just for these ships. The big sails bellied full. Their fleet had diminished since leaving Scotland. Many people had found homes among kin in Iceland, and a few were unaccounted for. There was still more than a score of ships, each with a different design on the sail, and they made a proud sight. The spray from the bow waves scattered like diamonds flung in the bright summer air.

They'd been at sea over a month now and Arnora had regained her health. She made a fine figure, her hood down, her red curls windblown and her cheeks tanned.

"Arnora," Harald said, "we sail for the new land." He nodded across the sea, toward the land clouds. "I want us to stay behind the slowest ship. Our job is to keep everyone together and give aid if necessary."

"Yes, my lord. Do we reef the sail?"

"I think not. Practice sailing with the wind. You'll not get a finer day for it."

Arnora nodded and set course across the rear of the fleet. Orm was sitting on Gunnar's trunk, a chunk of dried meat in his hand. Harald raised an eyebrow at him.

"I yearn for land," Orm said. "I tire of nothing but water."

"Back to Iceland then, boy?"

"No, I want land, real land, with trees and soil; land that can be farmed."

"So, you are a farmer after all?"

Orm nodded, "I think I am, Lord Harald. I want the feel of soft dirt, I want the smell of crops growing, I want the sound of a warm barn in the middle of the night when all are comfortable."

"Not I," said Arnora. Her health was back, but there a shadow remained across her spirit. "I would sail forever if I could."

"Well, Arnora," said Harald, "I hope you do not get your wish. Certainly, not until the rest of us find some good land." Harald had not addressed Arnora as "child" since he had killed her father. They had only begun to have anything close to a casual conversation, but the silver coil with the raven's heads never left her arm.

"What will this land be like?" Orm asked.

"You heard the Greenlanders," Harald said. "Depending on where we land, it will be almost anything. Barren ice, grassland, or forests."

"And the people?"

"Greasy pagans, say the Greenlanders, but you will notice that they have not chosen to challenge them. No, we best think of them merely as people and walk with caution until we know their ways. I met many peoples when I killed for the emperor. Some were greasy, some were pagans, but all would take weapons to hand when a stranger threatened. I hurry this crossing because I wish to travel far enough south so we reach a land that has been little bothered by the Greenlanders, for I think there has been much blood between them and the natives."

"And how far south are we now?"

"Arnora," Harald said, "answer Orm's question."

"By the height of the sun at its highest and the depth of the darkness at night, I would say we are already further south than Norway."

"If so, why is it so cold?"

Harald shrugged, "Much depends on the sea. These are strange waters to me, but with all the ice, I think this water is colder than the waters around Norway. There are currents in the sea, just like the flow of a river, and perhaps in this land the water flows down from the North. If so, our trip to this new land may be easy, but we might spend much time in sailing far enough south to find your farm."

The day wore on. Evening came, but never complete darkness. Arnora sought her sleeping robes and Harald took the helm. Orm, too, went to sleep and soon there was only a lookout at the bow and two men midships keeping watch.

In the middle of the night the stars were visible and Harald checked the course against them. In the distance he could see the glimmer of a torch from Strykar's ship. He, too, must have been waiting for the stars, because soon he trended a bit further south. The wind beat strongly against the sail, making the ropes and mast creak. The ship was running with the wind and needed little guidance. A slight sea mist had formed, but visibility was still adequate. Harald rubbed his thumb over the dragon's head carved into the rudder handle. The hard oak was deformed, the carving nearly worn away.

Orm is right, Harald thought, *the land calls for me, too. I have spent too much time at sea, sailing through waters where all are my enemy. I want to sit beneath a tall tree, feel the sun on my face, and listen to children laughing in the distance.*

His hand squeezed hard on the thick oak handle, carved to fit his hand and his alone. *But none of them will be my children.*

Orm slept nearly at his feet, Arnora a little way beyond. His gaze fell on the handle of his sword, leaning against his sea chest. The silver raven seemed to wink at him in the dusk. He looked again at Arnora, pulled out his belt knife and set to work.

He never did wake his relief that night.

CHAPTER THIRTY-FIVE

THE SEA MIST THICKENED toward morning. The wind held steady, pushing them hard to the southwest.

"Wake, boy," Harald said, stirring Orm with his foot. His eyes popped open, but he didn't move.

"Up," Harald said. "I want the watch strengthened. We must track our ships. Wake Eric and tell him my wishes."

Overhead the sky was clear and blue, but at sea level, visibility was little more than a boat's length. The thick, white mist was pervasive.

Orm pulled himself out of his sleep sack and made his way to the bow. Soon the sound of a horn shattered the morning calm. After a few moments other horns could be heard. Harald cocked his ear. Everyone he could hear was still ahead, and on the right course.

Arnora stirred at the sound of the horn and arose. She stretched and went to midships. She and some of the other women took turns holding up a cloak to provide privacy while they managed to relieve themselves over the side.

She returned, balancing easily on the pitching deck. The breeze was stronger, causing the ship to twist and plunge like a living thing as it rode the waves. The constant mist from the spray over the bow dewed her hair. She was chewing on a piece of dried walrus they'd obtained from one of the settlements on Greenland. Harald had used the last of his Byzantium silver there, purchasing whatever they had for sale. There was little, except for the walrus meat and some meadow hay for the animals.

"Why are you at the helm?" she asked. "Did you wake before me?"

"I had something to do and sleep did not appeal to me. Here, it is yours. Hold this course. I'll order the sail reefed so we do not overtake the freighters."

Arnora nodded and reached for the helm. Her eyes widened as she felt a difference in the familiar wood. She looked down to see that worn dragon's head was gone. In its place was a stylized raven's head, much like the one on her arm. She looked at Harald, a question in her eyes.

"The dragon was worn beyond recognition. I had an idle evening and decided it was time for a change."

Arnora said nothing. She took the handle more firmly in her hands, a handle now carved to fit her hands and hers alone.

Harald watched her for a moment.

"I have little skill in wood carving. The raven is ill done, but it should fit your hand better now."

"It is thinner. Will it have enough strength?"

"I'm not worried about the strength. It has strength, and strength to spare."

The ship crashed through the waves and the morning mist. Off the bow, a family of small white whales kept pace with them as they sailed into the west. The mournful sound of the ship horns echoed off the sea.

CHAPTER THIRTY-SIX

SAMOSET AND CHOGAN WERE saying their morning prayers. With them now were a dozen other men with them, facing the sunrise. There was a slight morning mist, but the sun showed promise of rising clear above it. They stayed far enough apart so their prayers to the Creator were theirs alone, but even so they could feel each other's spirits reaching out to the rising sun. All was good. It was warming to feel the presence of so many other men, after the long winter and before that the bitter times with the death of Noshi and his brothers. The churning pressure of complete responsibility for his family was lifting. Three other families had joined them now, with plenty to eat and the summer's work well in hand. Samoset's hands reached out, waist level and palms up. He rocked backward as he felt the power flowing into his body. His eyes flew open and he took a shaky breath. He gave a slight bow to the sun and turned to leave the beach.

Slowly, he walked back to the campground. The women had stirred up the fire. Samoset took a piece of fish off the drying rack and sat down. The other men soon came wandering up as their finished their prayers. They ate and smoked a pipe. Dogs and children meandered in and out of camp.

"Noshi is dead," Ahunu said. He and his family had come to the summer camp late this year. They'd waited for a spring baby to grow large enough to travel safely.

"Yes," Samoset said. "He made the Journey even before the winter came."

"The summer council will be soon. Who will speak for our clan with the other chiefs?"

Samoset answered, "Someone must."

"He was our chief. And your father."

"That may be," Samoset said, "but the choice does not have to run from father to son. It is the village council's decision who represents us at the district."

No one said anything. Chogan continued to whittle on a harpoon point. A dead minke whale had washed ashore and from the jawbone Chogan was making a harpoon for sturgeon. The point was already complete and he was nearly finished with the barbs. All that remained was to use a sharp piece of flint to drill a hole for the line and then attach it to a staff of ash. Wyanet was braiding moose sinew to make the line.

"The evil ones killed your brothers last fall," Ahunu said, "yet you brought your family through a hard winter well-fed and safe. You helped your father to make the Journey and your son is now a man. It is right that you be our chief."

There was a murmur of assent from the other men. Samoset nodded and stared into the fire while he smoked a pipe.

"Very well, then," he said at last, "as you wish. I will speak for the village when the district council meets." He tapped the ashes out of his pipe and set it down, then walked off to see what had been captured in the fish traps overnight.

Chogan completed his harpoon shortly before dark. He and Samoset walked down to their canoe. The sun had already set behind the hills. They were in deep dusk where they stood, but it there was still daylight out on the ocean beyond the reach of the hill's shadow. There was not a breath of breeze and the sea was unusually flat and calm. Across the bay, where the sun still shone, the white trunks of the dead trees cast ghostly reflections.

The two didn't speak, but carefully carried the canoe beyond the reach of bottom rocks and then climbed aboard.

"Will I be chief one day?" Chogan asked.

"Perhaps," Samoset said, "after I make the Journey. Do you seek the position already?"

Chogan turned his head and grinned at his father. Because he was to use the harpoon, he had the front of the canoe while his father steered.

"What does a chief do?"

"Very little," Samoset said, "and that is as it should be. Do you need a chief to tell you when the salmon spawn? Can a chief order a moose to walk into camp when the snow is deep and there are hungry children? There are some decisions that need to be made, and in the usual course of events they can be made by any man with good sense."

"If that is so, why do we need a chief?"

Samoset thought for a moment. "Three times. First, a chief says what needs to be said. If everyone were to decide on their own when to move to winter camp, we would straggle for weeks. The exact day we move matters little, but that the decision is made on time matters greatly. Next, a chief is needed to mediate between clans. We live in a harsh land. If the same clans were to use the same hunting grounds, the game would be used up. Finally, a chief is needed when no one would want to be a chief. When the deer cannot be found in winter, old people need to be convinced to make the Journey so children can be fed. When we need to flee from the evil ones the weak and slow must be left behind, a chief is needed to make the hard choice, choosing between one life and that of the clan."

Chogan sat quietly for a bit, his paddle moving noiselessly through the water.

"I would not want to do that," he said at last.

"Good," Samoset said, "for anyone who truly wants to make choices like that should not be a chief."

Around them the darkness deepened. Samoset took up a birch torch from the bottom of the canoe. A small stone container with live coals in it sat next to the torch. Samoset carefully blew on the embers until they stirred into life, and then lit the torch. He held the torch above the water and Chogan took up his harpoon. They sat in silence. The moon rose and the stars moved. Finally, in the depth of the night there was a stir in the water. A great shape circled the canoe, drawn to the light. In the light from the torch, the sturgeon's stomach shone as it turned. The small, soft scales of the belly were the target they were waiting for.

Chogan rose slightly, gripped the harpoon with both hands and thrust down. The tip penetrated and the barbs held fast. There was a flash of fins and a swirl of water and the line started to run out. Chogan sat down, grabbed the line and braced his feet against the front of the canoe. Samoset threw the torch over the side and picked up his paddle.

"Slow the line, if you can," he said. Chogan nodded, grimacing as the sinew sped through his fingers. The sturgeon was badly hurt and it sought the depths. Chogan grunted and was pulled half out of the canoe when the fish hit the end of the line. The bow of the canoe dipped and was almost pulled down until its buoyancy checked the sturgeon's dive. As it rose towards the surface the canoe bobbed back up and began to speed through the water.

All was darkness, with the exception of the stars overhead. The moon had set and Chogan could only dimly see the bow wave as the canoe rushed toward the sea.

Once the first rush was checked and the line held, Samoset began to trail his paddle in the water, slowing the canoe and tiring the fish.

Chogan felt the line go slack in his hand

"It is gone," he said, but then the line came alive again. "No, it has turned; hold on!"

The line came up short again and the canoe was jerked sideways, nearly spilling the men into the water.

The sturgeon towed them far upstream, far enough that the river began to narrow and the current became swift. Finally, the fish rose to the surface and Chogan was able to pull him next to the canoe. It lay still, dark blood staining the wound where the harpoon had entered. Occasionally, there was a slight twitch from the huge tail.

"He is longer than I am," Chogan said, easing the ache in his clenched fingers. "I thought he would swim forever."

"A good fish," Samoset said. "Hold tight, he may yet fight. I will get us home."

It was well the fish had chosen to swim up the river, because even with the current's aide it was a hard paddle dragging the giant fish next to the canoe.

They went slowly, Samoset finding his way back to camp more by guess than anything else. A slight whiff of wood smoke and a change in the sound of the sea told him he was close. Soon they recognized a tall pine looming near the water's edge. Samoset eased into the water on the far side of the canoe and came up behind the sturgeon. He quickly wrapped a loop of line around the tail and waded ashore, pulling the fish. It made one final protest, but Chogan added his strength and soon they had it safely away from the water.

Samoset was mildly surprised that he could now actually see the fish. They had passed the entire night on the water.

"Come," he said, "it is time for morning prayers. The women can butcher the fish."

The sun rose over a calm blue sea.

CHAPTER THIRTY-SEVEN

THE SUN SET ON A CALM BLUE SEA.

The fleet sat becalmed, sails limp. To their west mild waves washed up on a white sand beach. Close to the beach was a rocky shore where trees grew tall and thick.

"Is this the new land we seek?" Orm asked.

"No," Harald said, "not quite."

"We cannot sail on forever," Eric said. "The animals grow thin and weak and your people grow restless."

Harald nodded towards shore. "Do you see pasture land, land for fields?"

"No," said Eric, "but do you know that land exists anywhere? Perhaps from here to forever is naught but rocks and trees."

"We sail on," said Harald, "but not till morning. We moor here. I want the animals to stay on board; the people can gather seaweed for them. I do not want to risk losing the cattle in the trees."

"What do you tell your people?"

"I tell them that we sail on."

Orm walked the length of the ship to tell Arnora the instructions. Eric unfurled the line and weight and began testing the water's depth. They were very practiced by now. Without further guidance, the oars went into the water and the crew took shallow, careful strokes. Now was no time to stave in the hull on an unseen rock. When the keel grated on the sand, men leaped into the shallow water and tied the bow lines to the biggest trees they could reach. Soon the whole fleet was aground and preparations for the night begun.

It was only a matter of minutes before the ships were empty except for the livestock, protesting because they could smell the land. It had been nearly two weeks since the animals had been let ashore to graze. It took time to gather food for them, but not as much time as loading and unloading.

These waters were rich in fish, so the crews had gotten into the habit of trailing fishing lines while under sail. Soon the fish they'd caught during the day were on grills over campfires. The children scattered along the shore, looking for birds' nests. They'd found many before, further north on small islands, and everyone had feasted on eggs, but this was a different country and the seabirds were warier about where they nested.

As was his custom, Harald wandered away from the main group. As was his, Orm tagged along behind. A quiver hung from his waist and his bow was in his hands. It was seldom far away.

"My Lord," he said, "how much farther south are we going? We are already further south than England."

Harald flashed him an irritated look, "Do you think I deceive these people? I know not how far we are to go; I have never before been to this land."

"But everyone grows tired of the ships."

"It matters not. Look around—we are not an army, stealing food from peasants, and we're not a band of hunters living off the land. We need land, land we can farm and defend, we need a safe harbor, we need good fishing and tall grass. None of that is here and wishing it so will not make bad land suitable. Patience, boy."

Orm made a slight sound under his breath. Harald looked at him and nearly smiled.

"You must learn, boy. There is a time to plunge ahead, there is a time to throw caution away, but that time comes seldom. You must learn patience or you will die. Fortune does not favor the careless and hopeful. Make your plans, heed wise counsel- only then should you cast your lot with the Fates."

"Is this always your path?"

Harald laughed out loud. "No. Not always. Still. . .careless is dead, more often than not."

The shadows lengthened, stretching far out to sea. The smell of broiling fish reached them where they stood. The livestock were quiet, reconciled to another night aboard ship. The camp, too, was quieter as people spread their clothes on tree limbs to dry and began to eat their evening meal.

"Come, boy," Harald said. "We will eat, fall asleep on a bed of soft moss, and tomorrow make an early start to find your farm for you."

They ate, made beds on the soft moss of the forest floor and soon all the camp was asleep. Except the guards.

Except Harald.

CHAPTER THIRTY-EIGHT

"WE WILL MAKE AN EARLY start in the morning," Samoset said. "A pod of the small whales has been seen off shore. Your harpoon worked well on the sturgeon. Shall we see if it works as well on larger game?"

Chogan simply nodded, but couldn't conceal the excitement that rose within him. Any day on the sea was a good one for him and their people hunted whales only occasionally. Much depended on the man who wielded the harpoon. He needed to strike a killing blow on a whale that was too small to drag the canoe under. It took judgment, strength, and luck. The rich flesh and blubber were highly prized, but was most often obtained only from stranded corpses.

"I will check the line," he said, rising from his place by the fire.

Samoset settled down comfortably in his skin seat. He was smoking his evening pipe and eating a strip of smoked sturgeon. The drying racks were full of fish and the hardship of the previous winter seemed far away. The spring spawning runs were over, but the clams were as thick as ever. It looked like the beginning of a good summer season.

He took a long drink of water, then another, lay down in his sleeping robe and was soon asleep.

His full bladder woke him. All around the camp was quiet. He could hear nothing except the breathing of his family. Even the normal night noises seemed quieter.

The coals in the fire pit still glowed. He threw a few sticks on and stirred it to life. A few moments later, Chogan joined him by the fire.

"Are you ready?" Samoset asked.

"Yes," Chogan said.

"Very well."

They walked through the woods to the shore. The tide was low and they had to carry the canoe across mud flats to get it into the water. With luck, they would be bringing a whale back at high tide. Samoset took the steering position again. Chogan knelt in the front of the canoe. He paddled steadily, the harpoon and two spears lying next to him.

The moon still shone and Samoset could see the ghostly white shapes of the dead trees across the bay. Samoset was a dark shape in the front of the canoe and the sea was barely visible. He headed the canoe into the waves. The shore was almost out of sight by the time the sun rose.

"Stop," Samoset said. Chogan put his paddle down and sat up straight. Samoset kept the canoe pointed into the waves. It rode easily, high in the water. The raised gunwales made it a thing of the sea, not just calm inland waters.

They knelt in silence, waiting.

"Nothing," Chogan said.

Samoset turned the canoe and they began to quarter across the waves, heading back toward shore. The land rose out of the morning mist. Samoset could just see the tallest trees becoming clear and distinct when he heard the sound.

Chogan heard it too, a series of deep grunts and thuds seeming to come through the skin of the canoe.

"There," Samoset said, pointing. Against the dark green of the forest, Chogan saw an inconspicuous double stream of mist rising about a man's height above the water. They paddled slowly, the canoe rocking from side to side as it passed over the waves. In a few moments they saw the spout again.

"I think it swims alone," Chogan said.

"Yes, but it may be too big," Samoset said. "It will serve us little to harpoon a whale that can drag us to the sea bottom."

Samoset saw the boys back stiffen. This was more dangerous than the moose or the bear. Even a small whale was the size of the canoe and could, if it desired, crush the fragile birch bark with ease.

The whale came into sight. It was on the surface, swimming slowly along, feeding, and seemingly oblivious to the canoe and its occupants. Up close, it *appeared* huge, fully as long as the canoe. Samoset saw with relief that, for a whale, it was small, perhaps a yearling that had just left its mother. It was dark gray on top, with a white band on each flipper.

"Get ready," Samoset said.

Chogan lay his paddle down and picked up the harpoon. They were very near the whale now. The breeze picked up the wet fishy stench of its breath and blew it over them.

Samoset was able to keep pace with the whale paddling by himself, angling closer and closer. Suddenly, the whale arched its back and Samoset said, "Now!"

Chogan had been poised, the harpoon above his head. Now he rose to his feet and thrust down strongly with both arms.

The harpoon struck true and deep. The whale disappeared in a flurry of spray. Chogan held onto the line and leaned back away from it. Samoset, too, leaned away from the whale, balancing his body far over the gunwales while stroking heavily with his paddle.

They waited, watching the line Wyanet had made streaming over the side.

When the whale hit the end of the line and the harpoon bit deeper, Chogan was nearly pulled over the edge and the floor of the canoe was awash in sea water. The whale gave in to the pain and headed back for the surface. The line stayed tight. The whale blew and dove again, shallowly this time, pulling the craft strongly. Chogan again leaned back, his feet braced against the ribs of the canoe. Should he slip, he would likely put his feet right through the bottom. The bow of the canoe dipped towards the sea. Samoset leaned far over the stern, feeling for the right balance. The natural buoyancy of the big canoe pulled the whale up short and he gave up trying to dive away from his tormentors. Instead, he swam, faster and faster. The ride the sturgeon had given was nothing like this; they were pounding through the waves, the canoe rocking from side to side. Chogan gripped the line with both hands, straining back against the pull. Samoset rose high on his knees, trying to anticipate the rocking, and shifting his weight to keep the canoe upright.

The ride went on, the whale heading out to sea and deep water. Slowly it weakened, the barbed harpoon wearing it down.

Chogan's whole body felt on fire. His legs were cramped and trembling from the effort of keeping his balance. The line had cut deeply into his hands and small drops of blood fell to the canoe where they were diluted in the water washing back and forth.

Finally, the whale slowed and rose to the surface. It blew again then lay motionless in the water. Samoset and Chogan sat in the canoe, connected to the whale by a thin leather line twice the length of the canoe.

"Do not move," Samoset said, "The whale might yet dive if his spirit is strong enough."

Chogan said nothing, but nodded. He changed his grip on the line, rolled his shoulders to relieve what tension he could, and stayed in his crouch.

Samoset bailed out the canoe with a wooden dipper. He

saw with relief that no more water ran in. The seams had held tight. He took up his paddle and stroked the canoe backwards. The line stayed tight. Chogan braced himself tighter against the strain, but then the whale gave in to the pressure.

"Good," Samoset said. "Give me the line."

Chogan unlaced his fingers from the line with difficulty.

Samoset settled his grip firmly, feeling his son's blood on the leather.

Chogan picked up one of the spears.

"Not yet," Samoset said. "Work some strength back into your arms first."

Chogan nodded, a trace of relief on his face.

Gulls hovered overhead, screaming. When Chogan picked up the spear again, Samoset slowly began to take in line. The canoe closed in on the whale. It lay quietly in the water, blood streaming out from around the harpoon. Its stocky body and sharp-pointed snout were easily visible in the clear water.

"Do you know your mark?" Samoset asked.

Chogan nodded, and then struck hard. The lash of the whale's tail sent a wave of water over the canoe. It dove. This time it was Samoset's turn to brace for the impact. He leaned far over the gunwale. The whale hit the end of the line, pulling Samoset nearly upright, then the tortured line snapped and Samoset somersaulted backward into the water. He went deep, the cold water a shock. He saw the blue sky above and the dark shadow of the canoe gliding above him. He struck for the surface and came up next to the canoe. Chogan gave him a hand back in the canoe. They sat, alone, on the sea. Even the gulls had left.

CHAPTER THIRTY-NINE

"What is that?" Eric asked.

"Your eyes are better than mine," Harald said. "What do you think, boy?"

Orm squinted, "It looks like a boat, a small one."

Today, Harald's ship was in the lead. With its shallow draft, it had floated with the tide before the heavier freighters. It was a fine clear morning and they were running before the wind. The great sail boomed overhead and everyone was wet from the spray coming over the bow.

This part of the coast had many sand bars and rocks so Arnora kept the ship well to sea in hopes of avoiding the worst of them. They were still within sight of land.

"In Iceland," Orm muttered, "I thought I would die for want of a tree. Now, I see nothing but trees and I long for anything else."

Eric and Harald exchanged amused glances. "Go tell Arnora we want a closer look at that boat."

"Yes, my lord."

Orm walked the length of the ship. He paused for a moment amidships to let the slaves dump another bucket of bilge water over the side. Apparently, the seams on the ship had opened a little, because the slaves spent more time bailing than they had previously.

Arnora stood at the tiller. Her cloak was green and her red hair, curled by the sea air cascaded down her back. The gleam of the silver raven's head peeked out from beneath her sleeve. She cocked her head, but said nothing as Orm approached.

"Lord Harald wants a course to pass by that boat," Orm said, pointing.

Arnora squinted, "Are you sure it is a boat?"

"Perhaps," Orm said, "if we were closer, we could tell what it is."

"Perhaps," Arnora said with a smile. She altered course slightly, away from the coast. Now they were running nearly straight downwind and the object in the water was soon close enough to identify.

"It is a boat," Eric said. "We have found your pagans, my lord."

The boat was small, about three man lengths, with two occupants. It had an unusual shape, the bow and stern rising a little like a longship but there was also an upward swelling of the gunwales amidships. No oars visible and the boat appeared to be made of some type of wood or bark.

The passengers were brown, with long, shiny black hair that swept straight back from their brows. They were naked, except for some sort of leather garment around their waist. Knives hung from leather straps around their necks.

"Savages," Eric said, "nothing but naked savages."

"Perhaps," Harald said, "but they are a long way from shore in a very small boat. They may be savages, but they do not fear the sea." He looked around and Eric saw him stiffen. "There," he said, "at long last, there is what we need." He pointed toward shore.

They turned their attention away from the pagans to look. A wide, low peninsula appeared. Unlike the many others they had seen, this had no trees and was covered with tall grass.

"This," Harald said, "is worth looking at."

He turned and bellowed, waving his arm. Arnora caught his gesture and altered course. The ship swept by the small boat, but all eyes had turned away.

All except Arnora's. As the helmsman, she automatically watched the small boat as it was the closest obstacle to the ship. They passed near enough to make eye contact. The savage in the front of the boat would have seemed very young, had it not been for some vivid scars that angled across his face. *Anyone with scars like that is no longer a child*, Arnora thought. His eyes were black and steady.

The savages forgotten, the longship turned toward shore. The rest of the fleet saw the course change and followed suit.

CHAPTER FORTY

"What is that?" Chogan said.

"Where?" asked Samoset.

"There, coming along the coast."

The canoe sat rolling in the waves. The whale was nowhere in sight. Chogan's hands were badly cut by the line and he was wrapping them with strips cut off his leggings.

"I do not know," said Samoset. "I've never seen anything like that. Is it a canoe?"

The two fell silent, watching the strange vessel coming toward them.

It was huge, bigger than a dozen canoes. The bow was carved into the shape of a monster and the sides glittered gold in the sun. The gunwales were scalloped like the edge of a clam shell, no, not scalloped, Samoset saw, rather it had round pieces of wood, like slices of a tree trunk, fastened along the top. Above all was a strange, colorful . . . something.

"What flies above the canoe?" Chogan asked. It looked

like a huge cloak, billowing in the wind.

"I do not know," Samoset said. "It serves no purpose that I can see."

"Father, what is it?"

"*I do not know!*" Samoset said.

Chogan was stunned. It was the first time in his life that he had heard his father raise his voice.

The huge craft rushed upon them. It moved of its own volition, no paddles to be seen at all. The huge cloak was hanging from sticks stuck in the bottom of the ship.

"Is it crewed by dogs?" Samoset asked. The ship was close enough now that they could see its occupants. They were clothed, but incredibly hairy, with fur covering even their faces.

"No, they are men," Samoset answered himself, "but like no men I have ever seen."

The ship was very close now. The man in the bow was a giant with long yellow hair. His eyes were on Samoset and he could feel their intensity. The crew was lining the railing, as many people in one place as Samoset had ever seen. Suddenly, the giant turned away and pointed toward shore, bellowing something in a strange tongue, his voice a deep, hoarse shout. The crew turned their attention from Samoset and Chogan, and the ship itself began to turn away.

The canoe rocked in the wave from the vessel's passing. The only member of the crew who saw it was a strange creature standing in the stern, her hand on a wooden handle. She had strange, fair skin and her hair was an outlandish shade of red, like a sweet tree in the fall. She was near enough that Chogan could see her eyes. They were as bizarre as the rest of her, an odd pale color, like winter ice. They stayed on Chogan and his on her until the ship had turned completely away. Dark eyes and light ones, connecting across the sea.

"What did they see?" Chogan asked.

"The children," Samoset said, his voice choked with panic. "They must have seen the children."

He snatched his paddle from the bottom of the canoe and it fairly leapt forward. Chogan was caught off balance, but soon he, too, was digging deep into the water. His hands began bleeding anew and the blood soon stained the gunwale.

"There are more," Samoset grunted between strokes.

Chogan lifted his head and saw what seemed like an endless stream of the ungainly vessels, stretching nearly back to the horizon.

"Perhaps they mean no harm," Chogan said.

"The evil ones cut off the heads and eat the hearts of the ones they kill," Samoset said, "yet, they are men like us. I think I will not trust these strangers' good will."

The ships came closer. He now saw that they differed in some details. They were wider and shorter than the first vessel and many did not have the high prow carved into a monster. They were upwind now and Chogan wrinkled his noise as a strange, foul animal smell came from them, like moose dung only stronger. Strange giant cloaks hung from sticks above each one and all were headed in the same direction.

Straight for his home.

CHAPTER FORTY-ONE

ORM HAD REJOINED HARALD and Eric at the bow.

"Tell Arnora that we will break out the oars when we lose the wind. I want to beach at the inner point of the bay."

"Yes, my lord," said Orm. "Is this our home?"

"Perhaps. It is the best site I have seen on this coast."

Orm nodded and worked his way through the excited crew back to Arnora.

He passed on his message and she nodded.

"Did you look at the pagans?" she asked.

"Only for a moment," Orm said. "then Lord Harald pointed to land. Why?"

"No matter. I have never seen a savage before. I wonder where they come from?"

Orm pointed toward their destination. "From there, Arnora. For better or worse, I think they are our neighbors."

"How can one be neighbor to a savage?" Arnora asked. "We come from a land that is soaked with the blood of Christian killing Christian. These pagans will be worse."

"Arnora," Orm asked, "how much worse can they be?"

She looked at him, a frown on her face, but when she saw the laughter in his eyes, she began to laugh out loud. "Truly, Orm, you are wise. How much worse can they be?"

They passed within the shelter of the arms of the bay and the sail began to flap as they lost the wind.

Eric uncoiled the lead line and Harald made his way through the hubbub to the stern as the sail was lowered and the oars put out. He stood next to Arnora, but did not take the helm from her.

The ship slowly worked its way up the bay, with Eric testing the depth and watching for rocks.

"It goes slowly," Orm grunted between strokes.

"Better slow than to drown this close to the end of the journey," Harald said, "but I think you fight a current. A river must empty into the bay and make its way to the sea."

Eric shouted and pointed. Harald followed his glance and waved back to him.

"There, Arnora," he said. "There is room for the fleet to beach and unload the animals." A long, gentle, grass-covered hill sloped down to a narrow beach at the water's edge. The grass was tall; a ghostly forest of dead trees sprouted in its midst, their black and white trunks gleaming in the sunlight. A small stream, narrow enough that a man might leap over it, wound its way to the sea.

"What happened here?" Orm asked.

"It matters not," Harald said. "Were I to guess, I would say it was a fire, perhaps caused by lightning. You can see," he pointed, "there are young trees sprouting already. This must be good ground, to support such a forest. Haa!" he yelled, "too fast!"

He picked up a small drum and began to beat a slower rhythm for the rowers. In the bow, Eric repeatedly threw and retrieved the weighted line.

"It looks like high tide," Arnora said. There was very little beach showing, the grass starting a man's length away from the water.

"No better time to land," Orm said.

The keel struck a sandbar, grated over it and then stopped, the ship solidly aground.

The crew rested on their oars as Harald slowly made his way to the bow. Once there, he grabbed the bowline and swung to shore. Everyone watched as he walked, alone, up and away from the water.

Harald absentmindedly pulled a few strands of grass and nibbled at them. When he was well away from the shore he pulled his sword, brandished it above his head and thrust it downwards. It penetrated deeply, nearly half its length. He pulled it back out, the bright iron obscured by the brown soil clinging to it. He turned and made his way back to the ship, rubbing the blade clean and rolling the clods around in his fingers. He looked up at the row of heads waiting eagerly for his word and he almost smiled. Everyone had grown tired of the sea and it had only been his will that had kept them traveling for so long, seeking the perfect site. At the water's edge he called out quietly, "Unload the ship. Here we stay. Tell Orm his farm is found."

He turned away and began to walk uphill, wending his way through the dead forest, seeking the high ground. Behind him the crew happily pulled the ship sideways to the beach, stretched the gangplank and began unloading the vessel. Ship after ship entered the bay and each found its own place along the beach.

The livestock smelled the fresh grass and began calling excitedly, the lowing of the cattle mingling with the high whinnies of the horses and the quieter baaing of the sheep. They needed little urging to find their way down the gangplanks, although once they reached land they staggered uneasily, brought off balance by the long weeks at sea. Dogs raced up and down the shore, sniffing at dead fish and strange scents. Several cats sat quietly along the ship's rails, washing themselves and watching the excitement with distant eyes.

Strykar found Harald at the crest of the hill. He was seated with his back to a huge dead tree. In front of him stretched the panorama of the land beneath, the bays on both sides, and the heavily wooded peninsulas that bordered. The wind was still blowing and the waves had gotten bigger. The savages' canoe could no longer be seen.

"So, my lord," Strykar said.

Harald grunted, "I'm looking at the sea, Strykar. Did those waves begin in Norway?"

"Perhaps," Strykar said, turning to look. "It matters not. Wherever they began, they have brought us here. A good place, unless I miss my guess."

Harald stretched his legs and his joints cracked.

"It needs be good, for we have much to do and little time to waste. Do the people need to be told that the animals must be watched lest they bloat on the fresh graze?"

"There is time for that. They will be easier to fence if they are allowed to feed a bit first."

Harald nodded, and said nothing more.

"What of the pagans?" Strykar asked. "It appeared you were very close."

"Naked, but for bits of leather. A good boat for the size. I saw what looked like a stone headed spear. Dark like a Turk, straight black hair. They neither called out nor rowed away. I think we were strange to them."

"As would be," Strykar said. "None of the Greenlanders come this far south when they gather timber. These people know naught of us."

"Then let us be careful. We have no retreat. Make certain that all know; I would prefer allies to enemies."

"Yes, my lord," Strykar said.

"I mean that," Harald said, "Allies over enemies."

Strykar removed his sodden woolen cloak and stretched it over the stump of a massive tree. He sat down carefully on the ground and stretched his own legs out. His axe stayed, as always, close to hand. A gleam of color caught his eye.

"Are these strawberries?" he asked.

Harald glanced down.

"Perhaps," he said. "Or perhaps they are some strange deadly fruit that is spawned by the devil just to tempt sinning travelers in a strange land."

"And do you have an opinion, my lord, which?"

Harald shook his head. "No, I was waiting for you to come to test them for me."

Strykar laughed out loud.

"Truly, my lord, being in your service has always been a blessing to me."

Now Harald laughed. "I think only of you, Strykar. If these are in fact strawberries, you will get the first taste. And if, in fact, it is deadly fruit sent to tempt sinners, what better sinner than you to yield?"

The two hard men leaned back against the dead trees, nibbling on wild strawberries, while below them the beached freighters rolled back and forth as their crews carried load after load of gear down the gangplanks to their new home.

CHAPTER FORTY-TWO

"They turn," Chogan said between gasps of exertion.

Samoset looked up. The first vessel had turned away from their campground. As he watched, the huge cloak came fluttering down onto the deck and strange, long paddles, many of them, sprouted along the sides.

Despite their best efforts, the vessel moved nearly twice as fast as they could force the canoe through the sea. As they approached the tip of their peninsula, the second ship was making its way into their bay.

"We will land on the far side, out of their sight," said Samoset.

Chogan said nothing, but bent to his work. He had a sudden flash of insight.

"Those huge skins, they pull the canoe along with the wind," he said.

"What?" Samoset asked.

Chogan was sure he was right.

"When you stand in the open in a high wind, you can

feel it press against your body. That is how they move; they use the wind."

"It matters not," said Samoset. "We will talk of these things when we know the children are safe."

Chogan was stung by the rebuke, but he said nothing. *I know I am right*, he thought. *They make the wind serve them.*

A few more paddle strokes and they were hidden from the intruders by the tall trees at the tip of the peninsula. This side was not protected from the prevailing wind and it was harder to make a safe landing. Samoset gave no thought for rocks, but merely drove the canoe as hard as he could for shore. There was a crunching noise and Chogan saw a boulder break through the bottom of the canoe, right between his knees. The cold water rushed in, but Samoset gave it no mind, leaping over the side and waiting impatiently for Chogan to help drag the canoe up under the shelter of the trees. By the time Chogan picked his spear up and turned around Samoset was nearly out of sight.

He ran as fast as he could, dodging through the thick underbrush, but he could not catch up.

They burst into the campsite, chests heaving from exertion, and there was no one to be seen.

All was quiet. Samoset's mind skidded back to the ambush site, where his brothers had been killed by the evil ones. That had been silent, too, but his brothers had been all too evident, their headless bodies with gaping wounds where the evil ones had cut out their hearts for the victory feast.

"Samoset," he heard. He spun around and saw Wate beckoning him from the underbrush at the edge of the camp. Her hand was clamped over their youngest child's mouth. Her dark eyes were wide and scared.

"You live," he said.

"Samoset, what are they?" she asked.

"They are men," he said. "Just men, but strange looking. Where are the others?"

236

"The children are safely hidden. The men watch the bay."

She held out his weapons, his bow and a hardwood club.

He grabbed the war club. "Go to the others," he said and ran out of the clearing.

Chogan took his bow and followed. One of the dogs ran with them, excited by the unusual activity; soon it began to bark loudly as it bounded along. Without pausing Samoset swung the club in a vicious arc, silencing it.

Chogan ran past the dog's body, trying to keep his father's pace.

All has changed now, he thought, *the dog did not know. But I do.*

There was a flicker of blue water ahead, dimly seen through the screen of thick trees. Samoset halted his headlong plunge and dropped to the ground, crawling slowly, hidden from any observer.

"Here," Ahanu said. "We are here, Samoset."

Samoset froze in place, Chogan at his heels. He remained motionless for long moments, waiting till his chest stopped pounding and his pulse cooled. Then, slowly and deliberately, he made his way flat on his belly to where Ahanu watched.

A thin screen of bushes obscured their vision slightly, but it made them invisible to anyone more than a few man's lengths away. Ahanu wiggled sideways to make room for Samoset and Chogan. On both sides of them, a line of men lay silently, patiently watching.

Another strange craft beached itself.

"All the canoes are hidden," Ahanu said. "We were watching your struggle with the whale, so we saw them coming. I do not think they know we are here. There would be a few footprints in the sand, but the high tide washes them away."

Samoset grunted. Across the narrow bay there were strange cries and animal calls. Four-legged beasts were coming out of the vessels and staggering onto shore, some large, some small, some with horns and some without. A steady stream of the strangers was carrying all manner of objects ashore. They saw fires kindled and more of the huge cloaks strung between trees to make shelters.

"What are we to do?" Chogan asked.

"I do not know," said Samoset, "but this does not look good. That does not look like one night's camp to me. I think these strangers plan to stay."

"If they stay, we cannot," Ahanu said. "Look at them; they are as thick as ticks on a sick moose. They will eat the forest empty of deer. There are as many as there are people in our whole district. Are they truly men?"

"Yes," said Chogan, his voice firm. "They are men. They are very strange, it is true. Look at them, they must have come from very far away, but none the less, they are just men."

"I agree," said Samoset. "Even though they travel with beasts, they are still men. But indeed, they are very strange."

"So, what do we do?" Ahanu asked.

"We watch," Samoset said.

CHAPTER FORTY-THREE

"What do they do now?" Samoset asked.

"It makes no sense," Chogan said. "They have enormous blades. I do not know of what they are made. They use them to cut the grass and put it in piles. Then they rip up what is left of the grass, pulling the dirt and all, and making long piles. I have watched all morning and truly, they seem mad to me."

"Do they show any signs of leaving?"

"I thought so. Two canoes left with the tide this morning, but I think they merely went to sea to fish."

Samoset grunted. The bay was narrow enough that sounds and smells carried clearly to where they lay in hiding. The strangers had a noisy camp, and a smelly one. The dung odor had diminished, but there was a constant level of unusual sounds and smells coming across the water.

"See," Chogan said, "They are tearing some of the ships apart. They do not make wigwams, but they use pieces of the ships to make something."

"Another thing," said Ahanu, "have you noticed how few men there are?"

Samoset turned, startled.

"I know not from where these people came, but it is not an easy land. There are many women and children and most of the men bear scars."

"So," Samoset said, "at last, we have something in common. Women, children and a scarred man. Perhaps they are of our lodge."

Ahanu laughed. "Perhaps," he said, glancing sideways at Chogan. "Although I do not see many other resemblances."

"For how long do we watch?" Chogan asked. "We are eating our winter fish and the children grow restless."

"Yes, already we have lost the berries from where they landed. We need to be here for the fall fish run, but even so it will do us little good if we dare not tend the weirs."

"What are we to do? There are so many. They scurry like ants whose hill has been crushed."

The camp across the bay was busy, every person rushing about on one task or another. Samoset had heard them stirring during his morning prayers and there was unceasing activity until dark.

Ahanu said, "The giant—I think he is their chief or sagamore. See, he sits and watches all, but throughout the day people always find their way to him. He was the first one ashore. He ate some dirt, then all the others came ashore."

"Perhaps they are farmers, like the evil ones," Chogan said.

"If so, they are fools. We are too near the frost for corn or squash to ripen."

"Look, there!" Chogan said. "They do it again! See the beast, like a fat deer or a small moose? It is tame as a dog. They put a robe on its back and climb on. I think they use its four legs to travel faster. But only those, the other beasts they leave alone"

"I agree," said Ahanu. "Now watch, the one on the beast

disappears up the peninsula. I think they are looking for something. Every day this happens and every day the man and beast are gone for a longer time."

"What manner of men are these?" Samoset asked. "They do not pray, so they are clearly savages, but are they magicians that they bend animals to their will? They are like children in the woods, their camp is as noisy as a flock of seabirds, but their ships are things of wonder."

Chogan's eyes gleamed, "I would like to ride in one of those ships. Such a vessel could take me anywhere. They surely came a long way to reach us."

"What do we do if they cross the water?" Ahanu asked.

"We watch. If it is one or two, we can kill them. If they all come, we must flee. They are too many to fight with just our band."

"I weary of watching these strangers," Ahanu said. "I weary of cold, dry fish. I think I will go inland and kill a deer."

"I will stay." Chogan said. "There is much to learn."

CHAPTER FORTY-FOUR

"Are we being watched?" Harald asked.

"I think so," Strykar said. "We've seen no one, but surely your pagans know we are here, and it would be almost beyond belief that they would not be wary of us."

Eric said, "But where are they? Our patrols reach farther every day and they have seen nothing."

"I would be in the woods, across the bay," said Strykar. "True, they run the risk of being cut off if we attacked, but the cover is good and perhaps they do not think like an army."

"I agree," said Harald.

"What should we do?" Orm asked.

The four men were sitting at the crest of the hill. The sun had set behind them, leaving them in shadow while the sea was still lit, the water glimmering with gentle tones of gold. Below them, the camp was settling into its evening routine. The livestock was safe and contained with sea on three sides and a rope fence on the fourth. The children were playing amongst the trees. There were camp fires scattered across the slope. Hard against the fence were massive piles of hay. The outlines of a dozen longhouses were laid with turf. There was a small area of tilled ground, a larger area where the turf had been removed and a much larger area where the grass had been cut as short as possible.

"About the savages? Nothing," Harald said. "Tomorrow the first wheat seeds will be planted. Soon after, the oats, barley, and flax will be seeded. We cut the grass for winter hay, use the turf beneath to build our houses and till the bare ground for our crops. We have enough to do and more without trying to provoke our neighbors."

"We need a wall," Strykar said. "Granted, this is a good camp site, with clear vision all around, but without a wall we will be at the mercy of arrows in the night."

"Perhaps we should not ignore the savages," Eric said. "We could land a force at the base of the peninsula, cut them off, put our ships in the water with plenty of longbows and clear the woods. There would be little risk. If need be we could fire the woods. This land would then be ours, without fear of who is watching."

"It is true," Strykar said. "It would be a little thing to remove those watchers. If we dispose of them we would certainly have time to build a wall before others came."

"First the crops," Harald said. "We know not how soon the frosts come in this country, we dare not tarry or there will be nothing to harvest. Once the crops are planted we will have all summer for building walls and dealing with pagans."

"It will be good of our enemies," Eric said, "to wait until it is convenient for us to receive them."

"What comes, comes." Harald said. "We need the crops to survive the winter. We are working as hard as we can. The wall must wait. We just need to maintain a proper guard."

Strykar said, "About the guard—there are too few men to keep a proper watch by night and still get a day's work done."

"Then we will use women."

"My lord?" said Eric.

"Why not?" asked Harald. "They need to stay awake, sit quietly in the darkness and sound the alarm if danger comes. We are not asking them to challenge the pagans to single combat."

There was a moment's silence, then Strykar said, "Very well, my lord. Never before has it been done, and perhaps you underestimate the task. For a woman, to sit quietly. . ."

The men burst into laughter. They regained their feet and walked down the hill to the fires. All was dark now, except the glow of the fires and the soft reflection off the waters of the bay.

Quiet shadows left the fires, the evening guard headed out to the perimeter of the camp where they would sit, backs to the fires, to search the darkness. In the middle of the night they would be relieved, this night by women. Mothers for the most part, women who were fully aware of all that could come in the dark to threaten their children. They sat quietly, and they did not sleep.

CHAPTER FORTY-FIVE

EVEN UNDER THE TREES, it was very hot.

Chogan lay quietly, the sweat running off his face, as he watched the savage's camp.

He had grown used to the sight of men beginning their day's labors without morning prayers, but he still could not understand why they would want to.

Samoset slid down next to him.

"Is anything different today?" he asked.

"They continue to work on the wall," Chogan said. "They must fear someone and they are clearly making this their home."

The peninsula had changed greatly in the past two moons. There were vast expanses where all the grass had been removed which were now covered by strange crops, like nothing any of Mi'kmaq had ever seen. Longhouses made of grass and dirt rose in a straight line. Some of the big canoes had been torn apart and the wood used in other places. Across the neck of the peninsula, the strangers were building a wooden wall, more than a man's height. Every day ships went out to fish and rack upon rack of split fish were drying in the summer sun.

The band had also begun to fish again. They kept their distance from the strangers and landed their canoes on the far side of their peninsula, but there was no hiding when they were on the water. So far, no contact had been made between the groups.

The young of the seabirds had begun to flutter, trying their new feathers. In one more moon it would be time to begin pondering the move to their winter camp.

Ahanu and his family were the only other members of the band who had stayed. The rest had been unnerved by the strangers and sought fishing grounds elsewhere. Samoset was not sure why he stayed, although Chogan's great curiosity certainly had a place in it.

"The girl," Samoset said, "is by the great canoe again."

"Yes," Chogan said. "She spends much time there. She was the one who steered the day they arrived; she treats it as if it were her own. It is very strange. At times the others help her, but usually she works alone. It is as if she repairs the winter damage to a canoe."

"Their canoe is so big, it takes her much time. But why would a girl do the work of a man? And why would a girl be given the management of their great canoe?"

"I know not. I think that is the chief's vessel. It is never used for fishing, and in truth has not left land since they arrived, but always it is kept in readiness."

"It is very strange. See, some work only the women do, like the cooking, and some work only the men do, like riding their animals, but otherwise it is difficult to decide what is men's work and what isn't. And stranger yet, they all, even the women and girl children, practice with those huge bows."

"That I have never seen," Samoset said, "What purpose do those bows serve? How would you carry something like that in the forest? They are as long as a man is tall."

"Neither do I understand their arrows. They shoot them into that old tree, and use the same ones over and over again. It is as if the points do not chip or shatter."

"It is soon time for the summer council," Samoset said. "I will speak with the other chiefs about these strangers. I dislike the feeling of being trapped between these furry men and the evil ones."

"What can we do?" Chogan asked.

"I know not," Samoset said, "They are too many to attack. Perhaps before we leave for winter camp, we can burn their food stores and force them to go back where they came from."

"Would you do that?" Chogan asked.

"They are not our people. We will have no sweet berry cake this winter because of them. The deer have moved their feeding grounds and we dare not tend the fish traps. I care not what happens to them. My responsibility is my family and the tribe. Beyond that, I care not."

Chogan said nothing.

Samoset sniffed the calm air, "There will be a change in the weather, perhaps a storm. Be careful in your watching. These furry savages may have strange ways, but I do not think they are fools. They see our canoes on the water; they know they have been discovered. You have chosen the best spot from which to watch them, but they will know that as well. Take no chances, you can escape them in the woods, but it would be difficult to flee with the children and our summer's catch."

Samoset clapped his son on the shoulder and slid back from the bank. He stayed on his belly until he was far behind the screening trees. The woods crackled with his passing, dry leaves crunching beneath his feet.

Wate was waiting when he got back to their camp.

"Is there any news?"

Samoset shook his head, "Chogan still watches. He

knows more about these savages than anyone else. It seems he cannot take his eyes off them."

"How long must we stay here?" Wate asked. "I dislike having the children so close to danger."

"We still need more fish before winter. As for the danger. . . I do not know. The evil ones are my greatest concern and I doubt if a mere raiding party would wish to challenge the strangers. Perhaps we are safer here in their shadow than we would be elsewhere. Besides, the district is full of our people. Where would we go?"

"Nevertheless, I dislike staying."

Samoset paused for thought. "Perhaps we can spear some seals. We will boil their fat, store it and then we could leave early for our winter camp."

Wate said, "Perhaps. It would be good to leave this place. The furry men worry me."

Samoset said, "And me. Very well, prepare some baskets for the seal fat. When the weather changes, Chogan and I will spear some seals."

He sniffed the air again and cast a wary eye at the sky, "I think it will rain soon."

CHAPTER FORTY-SIX

HARALD SNIFFED THE AIR, "I think it will rain soon," he said, "The air is very heavy."

"That would be good," said Strykar. "The crops need the rain."

The sea was calm; disturbed now and then by a long swell. There was very little activity below them. The children stayed in the shade while the adults found light work to be done around the camp.

"These seasons are not so strange," said Harald. "The grain should have time to ripen before fall."

They leaned against the wall. A short distance behind them they heard the twang-thump of Orm practicing his marksmanship.

"When will we clear the pagans out?" Strykar asked. "Our defenses are nearly complete, harvest is soon to come, we need to make our borders secure."

"Are they not secure?"

"We are watched. We know they are still there, because

we see their small boats on the sea. It is not a village, for we would have seen evidence of it by now. It must just be a few scattered hunters. If I spent as much time as they have merely watching a city, I would know all its secrets. We are beyond reinforcements; we need to be cautious about our security."

"I am trying to be cautious," Harald said. "The Greenlanders slew without reason and were chased from these shores."

There was a slight edge to his voice and Strykar subsided. They sat in silence for a bit and then Harald said, "Who is that coming up the hill?"

Strykar squinted, "It's your helmsman, the girl."

Harald nodded. "What grieves you so about her?"

"She is apt to drive me mad with her questions. She will wear out your ship climbing about."

"It was a long voyage," Harald said. "There was much to repair."

"But my lord," Strykar said, "she is a girl, a child."

"She has buried her parents and her child. You can't get much older than that. Besides, she learns fast and works hard. Can you find fault with her efforts?"

"Granted, but she is still a woman. What point is there in giving her this leeway? Her duties are to give birth and cook meals. She has no need to know how to rig a ship or clean a fouled bottom, unless it belongs to a child."

Harald laughed. "Do you fear for your place? You need not—Arnora may be a natural born ship's captain, but she will never be able to make heads fly off bodies the way you can."

Strykar grunted, but said nothing.

Arnora reached the crest of the hill where they sat.

"My lord," she said.

"Arnora, how goes the ship?" Harald asked.

"That is why I came for you. I believe it is finished. The rips in the sail are repaired, the bottom clean, the planks caulked. I have replaced the rudder line, it was badly worn, and Eric told me that we needed a new yard so Orm helped me install that. All the shrouds are now good and I scoured the water barrels with sand and refilled them. One of the midships oars was cracked, but I replaced it with one from the ships we scrapped. I believe we could sail back to Iceland if we wanted."

"And is that your goal?" Harald asked.

She shuddered. "No, my lord, I never wish to see Iceland again. But, I fear I am not a farmer. The sea calls to me."

"Do not answer, at least not for a while. We have too much to do before winter for you to go a'viking. Still," he got to his feet, "Let us examine your work. A blade is best kept sharp, even if it does naught but rest in your scabbard. ORM!" he bellowed, "come, leave off your torture of that target and come with us."

"Yes, my lord," He retrieved his arrows from the dead tree he'd been targeting. Harald noticed in passing that even at a distance of fifty paces, the arrows were grouped in an area little larger than his hand.

They walked down the hill. A sudden gust of wind cooled them as they entered the sunlight and neared the boat.

Harald made a show of inspecting Arnora's work although, in fact, he had been watching the entire process, unwilling to let her damage the finest ship in the world merely to practice ship care. To his surprise, she had not committed a single error, working carefully and asking for help when she didn't understand what to do or have the proper skills.

The ship was in good shape. It sat calmly at anchor, bow and stern lines out. The mast was stepped and all the shrouds were tight. The yard was swung out, and the sail was ready to be raised. The bilge was dry and the ballast was properly arranged. He rubbed his hand against the arrowhead in the mast while he took a drink from a water barrel.

"You did well, Arnora," he said at last. "Truly, I can find

no flaw."

"Thank you, my lord," she said. Another gust of wind, this one stronger, rocked the boat.

"Look at the clouds," Orm said, pointing.

An evil looking line of wind clouds cleared the hill. Behind them the sky was dark and ominous. A heavy rumble of thunder sounded and with it a spattering of rain. The gusts steadied into a hard offshore wind. In the bay, the waves built and began to crash upon the beach.

"This could be bad," Strykar said.

Eric came down from one of the longhouses.

"This feels bad, my lord," he said. He had to raise his voice over the wind and the thunder.

Harald stood still, taking in the situation. All the other ships were safely beached, above the reach of high tide. The animals had shelter and the longhouses were complete. His ship was all that was in danger, no matter how bad the storm. He laid a hand on one of the anchor lines, thinking.

"Orm," he said, "fetch our crew. We should beach the ship before this gets worse."

"Yes, my lord," he said and ran off toward the longhouses.

"What is that smell?" Arnora asked.

CHAPTER FORTY-SEVEN

"WHAT IS THAT SMELL?" Wate asked.

"Only smoke," Ahanu said. "The wind gains strength. We must smell the smoke from the savage's cooking fires."

Another gust of wind pushed the smell away. Everyone was crowded into the summer wigwam. Above them the trees clashed and grated against one another.

Chogan came through the door and fastened the flap behind him.

"The storm comes quickly," he said. "Already the waves are too high for a canoe to survive."

Though it was still midafternoon, the sky was very dark, lit only by the flicker of lightning. There was an occasional spatter of warm rain on the bark walls of the wigwam, with a few drops finding their way through the smoke hole. It was crowded and close inside, dark and noisy. There was no fire in the fire pit, but everyone sat with their backs against the walls, feeling the flex and pull of the poles as the wind swirled above them.

The smoke smell returned.

"Chogan," asked Samoset, "was the cooking fire burning when you came in?"

"No, I checked, because the woods are so dry. Even the ashes were cool."

"Something is wrong," he said. "The wind is from the wrong direction. We should not be able to smell the furry one's fires." He left the tent, followed by Samoset and Ahanu.

Outside the smoke smell was much stronger.

"Where does it come from?" Samoset yelled. It was becoming difficult to hear. The wind reached a higher pitch and horrified, Ahanu pointed. Samoset whirled around and saw a faint glimmer of red through the woods.

"The woods are on fire!" Ahanu yelled. "It must have been the lightning!"

"Get the others!" Samoset said. "Ahanu, get the canoes down to the water! The fire will cut us off!"

They scattered in different directions. Samoset raced through the woods, branches lashing his face. The storm howled like a living thing above him. Soon he could hear the fire, as well as smell the smoke.

He was too late. The blaze had started beyond the narrow neck of the peninsula and already was burning from shore to shore. There was no passing it on land. The high winds would sweep it the full length, leaving nothing but scorched stumps in its wake.

It was getting harder to breathe, the smoke a smothering cloud around him. He turned back toward camp. A rabbit passed him by, and a few moments later a deer, both blind to the human, fleeing a greater danger.

The camp was empty when he reached it. He looked around frantically.

"Father," Chogan yelled, "this way!"

Samoset followed him through the trees. The fire was louder and closer, making its own wind now, leaping from tree top to tree top, consuming all in its way.

They reached the tip of the peninsula. Everyone stood on the rocks, waves crashing against their feet.

"We must hurry!" Samoset called over the wind.

"Look!" Ahanu said, "We cannot. A canoe will not live in these waters."

Samoset looked out and his heart sank. The waves were taller than a man, tops white and torn by the wind.

"We have to try!" he said. "There is no other way!"

"We have," Ahanu said. He was screaming now, his face only inches from Samoset's. "The waves took the canoes and smashed them to nothing! One was ripped from my hand and flew through the sky like a bird! We must find a way around the fire."

Samoset looked at him, his eyes wide and unseeing.

"There is no way. The fire burns all. We cannot face it and live."

The two men stood, face to face, their minds racing. They no longer heard the wind, the waves, or the fire.

It was Wyanet's scream that brought them back. The monster came crashing out of the mist and sought her with angry jaws.

CHAPTER FORTY-EIGHT

"There," Arnora said, "over there. The woods are on fire."

She pointed across the bay. In a moment everyone saw it—a cloud a lighter shade of gray and a tongue of red fire reaching up.

"That is what happened here," Strykar said. "A dry forest and a sudden storm."

Harald's crew was coming down the hill, hurrying through the storm. Orm was the first to reach the harbor.

"What are your wishes, my lord?" he asked. "Do you wish to beach the ship, or will the anchor lines hold?"

Harald faced into the storm, testing the wind and the clouds. The deck pitched beneath his feet.

"Perhaps I sent you on a false errand. I would not wish you to be in this water now. It would be too easy to get crushed beneath the hull."

"We should put out two more anchors," Eric said. "Then the ship should ride out any storm."

They could hear the fire from across the bay now, a

crackling roar that grew progressively louder.

"Look!" Orm shouted. "There were pagans in the woods."

He pointed to the tip of the peninsula. People appeared out of the trees. The waves were crashing around their feet as they were trying to launch their small boats. One made it a short distance off shore before its bottom was ripped out on a rock. The occupants struggled back to dry land. Another boat was torn away by the wind and went skipping across the water, rolling end over end.

"They are trapped," Harald said.

"The storm does our work for us," Strykar said. "Soon the fire will sweep them away."

"They are helpless," Orm said.

"Not true," Strykar said. "They can choose between drowning and burning." Arnora glanced at him, horrified.

Harald's crew gathered around, awaiting their orders. Harald noticed that even the slaves had come down to help secure the ship. A sudden fey mood swept over him. Perhaps it was the sight of the small figures among the large, clinging to the rocks across the bay.

"Arnora," he said, "I would test your work. Perhaps a short voyage is in order."

She looked at him oddly, then awareness dawned.

"Yes, my lord," she said.

"Are you mad?" Eric screamed. "What are you doing? Would you rescue rats from a sinking ship?"

"I agree," Strykar said. "These are pagans, and a threat to us. This is very poor strategy, my lord."

"As may be," Harald said. "Still, it is my wish."

"Look at the sea!" Eric's face bloomed red. "This is no summer squall! I have been feeling this storm build for days, we all have."

"We waste time," Harald said.

"I will have no part in this!" Eric said. "Let your children and women man your boat." He turned and stalked up the hill without looking back.

Strykar came close and spoke for Harald's ear alone.

"If you still wish to die," he said, "there are simpler ways."

Harald cocked his head and smiled.

"Perhaps easier, but this is the death I choose."

Strykar shrugged. "Very well, my lord." He reached for an anchor line.

Harald's big hand stopped him.

"No," he said, "my crew is enough. This is a fool's task, and I need you to take care of my people."

"My lord," Strykar protested.

"We waste time," Harald said.

Strykar tilted his head, then nodded and took his place on shore.

"My people!" Harald shouted, "my wish is that we save those pagans from fire and wave."

"But why?" came a voice from the crowd.

Harald smiled and leaned over the side of the ship.

"Why not?"

And then he laughed.

It was the first laugh, untouched by irony or bitterness, that had crossed his lips in. . .how long? Years, certainly. It came from deep in his belly and his throat ached from the force of it, but it was sweet to hear.

"You know who you are," he shouted, "and you know from where you come." He waved his arm toward the raging sea. "In all the world, there is no one else who would dare this. I have seen the world, from the Holy Land to the frozen North and there is no one with whom I would rather cast my fate!"

He continued, "Stay if you wish, but come with me if you must, for they will sing songs of this voyage!"

His people streamed aboard ship. The slaves climbed over the gunwales and headed for the bilge.

"Stop," Harald said. "I will take no slaves on this trip."

The older of the two looked up at him and said nothing.

"If you come on this trip, you come as free men. And if we return, you earn the freedom of all your fellows."

The slave opened his mouth, but then shut it without a sound. Water stood in his eyes as he took his place in the bottom of the ship.

Arnora was at the helm, Orm by her side.

"Your wishes, my lord?"

"Straight down the bay until we near the open sea," he pointed. "Then we will come about, and beach at the tip of the land. After we get them loaded we will try to beat our way back to this anchorage. Orm," he said, "I will take the bow. I want you at midships to relay my word to Arnora. NOW," he shouted, "oars out; I dislike this spot!"

They were able to free the ship from shore by pulling on the anchor lines. Once out in the bay, the wind caught it and swept her toward sea.

Harald clung to the dragon's neck and peered through the mist. He licked his lips and tasted salt. The rain had not yet begun, the wind was just whipping the sea. He turned around and looked at the backs of his crew. Women, children, a dozen grizzled warriors, a boy who had tried to kill him relaying his messages to his helmsman, who was a girl who wished him dead for killing her father. He laughed again and rode the bucking deck, judging the wind and the waves, pitting his will against the sea.

"NOW," he screamed. "Come about!"

CHAPTER FORTY-NINE

WYANET SCREAMED.

The monster came out of the mist and crashed down, the noise thunderous.

Samoset spun, and realized it was the ship of the savages across the bay. The carved wooden head gaped, high above him. The giant himself was swinging over the side.

The ship was even bigger than he had thought; it towered over the beach. Another wave came in and the vessel crashed down again, this time Samoset heard wood splinter and crack.

The giant screamed something, his voice a harsh roar, and waved towards the boat.

"He wants us to come along," Chogan said.

"We cannot!" Samoset said. "What do they want of us?"

"If we stay," Wate screamed through the smoke, sparks falling past her face, "the children die!" She took the first step toward the wild-eyed giant. She held their youngest in her arms and the giant plucked them both from the rocks and hurled them over his head and into the boat. Wyanet was next. The giant grabbed her under the arms and lifted her high over his head. Wate reached down and pulled her over the side.

That broke the spell.

"They cannot stay!" Ahanu yelled. "Even this ship is but wood, soon it too will be smashed to nothing!"

The people swarmed aboard the ship, climbing over both rails.

Once aboard, they were in an utterly mysterious world. They stood on wood, hewed flat and smooth. The crew was bizarre, an odd mix of sizes, age, and sex. They were seated on square wooden baskets and they held on to the long wooden paddles. Their clothing was of an odd design, made of materials other than leather. Both groups stared at each other. The wind whipped overhead; it was becoming difficult to see and breathe.

The giant swung aboard and screamed in his strange tongue. The crew dug their paddles deep and pulled hard. Samoset saw that a portion of the paddles had two people on them and some only one. One had three children sitting side by side.

The ship did not move. Another wave hit and the ship crashed again. The splintering was louder this time.

"Take a paddle," Samoset said, "We need to help or we will all die."

The Mi'kmaq found places and together all pulled. The ship moved back. The next thud was not as shattering and the following wave the keel did not strike the bottom at all.

Chogan had found a place near the end of the ship. He pulled when the others pulled and watched the girl who stood there. Her arms strained on a wooden handle. Samoset suddenly realized that what she controlled was a huge paddle, hanging straight down. She guided the ship as if she were the rear paddler in a canoe going downstream. He marveled, even as he strained at his oar, to see a woman given so much authority and power. Her hands were small and white, but steady and strong.

The ship was now going straight back. Every time they went into a trough water towered over the top of the ship.

What now? Samoset thought. *We cannot paddle backward across the sea and we cannot go upstream against this wind.*

He heard the giant yell again; saw him storm by. He spoke to the girl and turned to face the paddlers. Shoving people aside, he grabbed the two paddles at the back of the ship and stood, holding both. He shook one, then the other.

"He shows us when to paddle and the direction," Chogan yelled from behind Samoset. "He must mean to turn and run before the wind."

Samoset was transfixed by the giant's eyes. They were blue, blue like a summer lake, and as Samoset watched, they filled with power, shining through the mist and smoke. His yellow hair hung in sodden streamers. A huge scar swelled a vivid red on his neck. He nodded several times, judging the waves Samoset realized, then suddenly bellowed and dug forward with one paddle and back with the other. Even as tall as he was, he had to hold them high over his head for them to strike the water. He screamed with effort. The crew took strength from his. Samoset pulled strongly, and again. The ship rocked sickeningly as it turned sideways to the waves. The giant's shoulders swelled and his shirt ripped across his chest. The girl swung her paddle hard and the ship was around, running before the wind.

The crew pulled their paddles in. By the time Samoset had figured out how to get his inside the ship, the crew had raised the huge cloak. The ship gathered itself like a startled doe and then fairly leapt through the water. In a heartbeat, Samoset was moving faster than he'd ever moved in his life.

He sank to the deck and looked around. His family was here, they were not dead, and it appeared likely they might live a little while longer.

The giant went past, hurrying to the front of the ship.

He was laughing.

"Courage is half of success"

—HEIMSKRINGLA,
THE SAGA OF THE KINGS OF NORWAY

CHAPTER FIFTY

HARALD MASTERED THE SHIP, he mastered the storm and somewhere, perhaps on the trip across the bay, perhaps when he saved the child from the flames, he mastered himself. The long winter of torment and despair was behind him. He felt his will run back into his body, felt the pain and lethargy that afflicted him drain into the sea, emptying out like a lanced boil. The hot blood poured through his veins and he once again felt himself a king.

He looked down the long length of his ship, crowded with people whose fate rested in the palm of his hand. *This is who I am,* he thought. *How could I have forgotten that? And, God help me, this is what I do.*

"We need to come about, and run before the wind," he shouted to Arnora.

"We cannot! We will broach," she screamed. "The waves are too high."

The wind howled through the rigging. Waves crashed over the stern, soaking them.

"NO, we will not! Watch me," Harald said, willing her to believe. "We have one chance."

For a moment Harald indulged himself in his wish for the crew that had left Norway for England. The king's finest, the best sailors in the world, tested by battle and storm; they could have done this maneuver. But that crew was dead. They had stood next to him at Stamford Bridge, and the last of them had fallen protecting what they thought was his dead body.

He looked down the row of benches. The savages had all found places and rowed next to his people. *They do not know this ship, but they know the sea,* he reminded himself. *They will know what we must do.*

"Look at me," he shouted into the wind. "LOOK AT ME!"

He snatched the rear oars from the women closest to him and pulled them inboard. He rowed a few strokes, his people and the pagans focusing on him. He watched the waves, felt them, waiting for the moment. "NOW," he screamed, his voice rising over the wind. He dug deep, one oar forward and one back. The thick wooden handles bent beneath his fingers. His nostrils flared as the thick sea air swelled his chest and filled his lungs.

The ship rolled, sideways to the waves, the mast tipping and reaching for the sea. The yards actually touched the water, and then she answered to the rudder and the oars and came around. One last sickening wallow and the ship turned and ran before the wind.

"Set sail," he ordered, his voice carrying through the storm. The crew scurried to obey and he turned to Arnora. He pointed a massive finger at her and she stared back, transfixed by his gaze.

"Well done," he said. "Finally, now, you know. Never again, never till the day you die, will you need to say the word 'cannot.'"

"I could not have done what you did," Arnora said. Her thick red hair was plastered close to her head and her eyes were wild.

"It matters not how I did it. What matters is that it was done. One day, your time will come. You will be faced with a crisis that cannot be solved, a question that cannot be answered, and you will *remember* this moment and *remember* that you were at the helm and then you will find your own way to do what cannot be done."

He turned and hurried toward the bow, oblivious to the stares of the exhausted rowers. His torn shirt flapped against his arms and he tore it off.

The ship was very crowded. At least a hundred people were on board, nearly half of them pagans.

"The bilge?" he asked the slaves. They stood in the bilge, their heads level with the deck boards. They were standing in water, their faces white with strain.

"The hull is whole," said one, "but there is much water coming aboard."

Harald grabbed a half-dozen people, those closest to him, regardless of sex, age, pagan or Christian.

"Bail," he said. "This ship does not sail under water."

He grabbed Orm by the elbow and together they went to the bow. The ship slid sickeningly down the back of a wave and then squatted as she climbed the face of the next. Spray was breaking over the bow in solid sheets.

"Stay here," Harald said. "There should be naught between us and Norway but open sea. Still, I dislike sailing without a bow lookout. I want your face in the wind and one arm on the dragon's neck. Do not stir from this spot and watch EVERYTHING. We have no margin for mistakes."

Orm nodded, his face pale except for two red spots high on his cheeks.

"Boy," Harald said, "I walked past a hundred people from the stern to the bow, and from them I chose you to keep the watch. My people and my ship are in your hands. Can you take the watch?"

Orm looked at the steady eyes and inclined his head

slightly. "Until I go blind, my lord."

The wind grew stronger yet. Harald ordered the sail taken in and soon he ordered it furled altogether. They sailed under a bare mast. Surrounded by towering waves, the ship rolled from side to side.

Fairly dancing with energy, Harald moved from one person to the next, cajoling, admiring, criticizing. He made his way from the bow to the stern, his will galvanizing all he passed.

Two of the pagans were standing near Arnora, waving their arms and speaking their gibberish.

Harald went to her and asked, "What do they want?"

"I do not know," she said, her face taut with strain, "but it seems important to them."

They turned to him. They were of a height, but one was much older. The younger had long scars across his face and both were excited.

What are you saying, Harald thought, *is it pointless superstition, or do you see something I do not?*

The older one pointed back toward shore and made a sweeping motion with his arm.

Harald shook his head. "No, we can not go back, not in the face of this wind."

Now the man swept both arms over his head. The ship went into a trough of the wave and all in the stern were soaked again.

The ship wallowed, heavy with water, wavering before the wind, threatening to roll.

"I must tend my ship," Harald said. "Be patient. With luck we will return you to your home."

He turned to leave, but his arm was grabbed and held.

Harald slowly turned around and looked into the eyes of the younger pagan. Harald had spent a lifetime reading men's faces and he could see that this boy was terrified of him.

Harald looked down from his great height, "I am unaccustomed to being grabbed, boy."

The older pagan spread both hands out in front of him. Then he grabbed the stern of the ship and shook it. He waved his hands in a remarkable imitation of a bird in flight, and pointed at the waves towering behind the ship. As if for emphasis, another wave broke over the railing. The younger pagan still held Harald's arm and now he shook it.

Arnora looked from one to the other. It was the boy with the scar she'd seen their first day. She couldn't believe he'd grabbed Lord Harald by the arm. No wonder he had that scar, if he had so little caution around dangerous beasts.

Harald could have screamed from frustration. Both men were scared, of Harald and of something else, but they were not panicked. Harald held his own arm out and waved his fingers in a gentle, come along, motion.

The older man nodded, went through his gestures again, more slowly, but this time he finished by smashing one hand down on top of the other. Then he picked up one of the anchor lines, still attached to a ring in the stern.

"Yes," Harald yelled, "yes, you are right! Arnora, cut the anchor off that line. We need something to hold us before the wind. A sea anchor will steady us."

Arnora did, throwing the line over the side to drag through the water. The ship did not slow appreciably. Harald pulled the line back in and tied an old cloak on it then threw it out again the water. The ship slowed and the ride smoothed out. It did not skip from wave to wave as quickly as before and the vast pitching eased.

Harald grinned at his passengers and they smiled back.

"You may be filthy pagans," Harald said, "but by God you are seaman too!"

Harald tapped himself on the chest and said, "Harald Sigurdsson."

The older pagan cocked his head, looked at him, then tapped himself and said, "Samoset."

They ran before the storm for four days. It was two

weeks more before they found their way back to camp. By then, they had all learned a great deal.

"A guest needs giving water,
Fine towels and friendliness
A cheerful word, a chance to speak
Kindness and concern"

—THE HAVAMAL

CHAPTER FIFTY-ONE

"THE CROPS STILL STAND," Orm said.

"The hill," Harald said. "It provided protection from the wind."

The crew rowed the battered longship slowly into the bay. There had been progress since their departure. A dock now sat in the water with two freighters tied to it. The remainder of the fleet was still beached. The houses were intact and the sound of axes came across the water to the ship.

"Arnora," Harald said, and pointed toward the dock. She waved and put the rudder over.

A crowd of people streamed down the hill to greet them. Strykar handled the line that drew them in.

"Greetings, my lord," he said. "How was your trip?"

"Eventful," Harald said. "We have guests."

"Guests or prisoners?"

"We have guests, perhaps allies," Harald said, "Beyond that, I know very little. Come aboard and meet them."

Strykar stepped lightly aboard ship and followed Harald to where the Mi'kmaq stood.

"My second," Harald said, putting his hand on Strykar's shoulder, "Strykar."

Strykar and Samoset were of a height, but there was little resemblance beyond that. The Mi'kmaq had black eyes and long black hair. He wore a leather tunic and a breechcloth with soft leather shoes on his feet. His only possession was his flint knife that hung from a cord around his neck. He was lean and dark from the sun.

Strykar's full beard was grey. His blue eyes gleamed beneath massive eyebrows. He wore blue leggings and a gray wool tunic. A large knife hung in a sheath on his hip and his axe swung gently from one hand. A huge scar seamed his forehead and he was missing two fingers on his right hand.

Strykar spoke to Harald while gazing steadily at Samoset.

"Their language?"

"Like none I have ever heard. They appear to have experience in communicating with strangers; they can almost talk with their hands. The children, theirs and ours, learn quickly."

Strykar smiled, "And a little child shall lead them?"

Harald laughed. "Perhaps. I wish them to stay with us, but I will not compel them."

Strykar said, "They may have no place else to go. Look at their camp."

* * *

"Look at our camp," Wate said. "There is nothing left." Their home was black and desolate. The fire had consumed everything; only a few blackened stumps marked where their former camp had stood. Their hard-earned food was gone, along with all their tools and possessions.

Ahanu spoke, "The Creator jokes with us. He sends savages to save us from the fire, only to let us starve this winter.

Samoset, who is this dog-faced savage who came aboard?"

"I do not know. He could be a lesser chief. He and Harald confer. Perhaps he led in Harald's absence."

Chogan said, "Perhaps he is their sagamore, and Harald is just a chief."

Samoset snorted. "Do you think so? If Harald is the lesser, I know nothing of men. Here, Harald brings him to us."

The Mi'kmaq turned from the ship's rail to face the new-comer.

Harald put a hand on the man's shoulder and said, "Strykar."

Samoset took a step forward and introduced himself. The two locked eyes for a long moment and then Strykar smiled and waved his hand in invitation. He turned and led the way off the ship.

"What is that he carries?" Chogan asked. "It looks to be made of *iron*," he stumbled over the strange word, "like their other weapons, but it is a strange shape."

"I know not what it is called," Samoset said, "but it is made to kill. And it fit his hand."

"Who is he?" Chogan asked.

"He is a killer," Samoset said. "He may be a chief or may not. He may be a good man or bad. He may be our friend or our enemy, but know this my son—he is a man whose first solution to any problem is to kill."

"They want us to follow," Ahanu said.

"We have no choice," Samoset said. "It is almost time to begin to move the winter camps. The other bands will be separating, who will take us in? Besides; do you not wish to see what other wonders these savages have?"

It was a slow walk through the camp. Everywhere, peo-ple stopped what they were doing to gaze at the strange pagans. Three weeks on the storm-tossed ship had broken many of the barriers between the Norse and the Mi'kmaq. The children who had been on Harald's ship led their new friends by the hand, eager to show off their homes.

Wate clung grimly to their youngest, but soon all the other children were out of sight, scattered throughout the settlement.

"Samoset," she warned.

"I see no point in caution, now. When Harald threw you and the babe over his head onto his ship, we cast our lot with these savages. They could have left us to burn, they could have thrown us into the sea, they could have bound us when we landed. If these were men like the evil ones, the children would be dead and I would be running a gauntlet. I do not understand it, but I feel we have little to fear. For now."

The small group of adults wound their way uphill, toward the long buildings made of wood and turf that nestled together near the crest of the hill. All around them the Mi'kmaq saw things that they had witnessed from across the bay, but still did not understand.

"Father," Chogan said, "I do not understand how these people bend animals to their will." All around them were the sheep, cattle, and horses that had come to the new land.

"Truly, it is a wonder," Samoset said, "yet look, they do not respect the spirit of the animals." He pointed at a pair of dogs, quarreling over the carcass of a horse that had died of bloat.

"I want to see how they make their *iron*," Ahanu said, "I do not understand how it is worked. It is neither stone nor wood."

"What do they want of us?" Wate asked. "Why save us from the storm and now give us leave of their camp? Would you have done the same?"

"No," Samoset said. "I would have watched them burn and thanked the Creator for removing the threat to my people."

"I think," Chogan said, "that whatever their reason, it comes from Harald. He is their chief and their law. They all answer to his word."

Samoset looked ahead.

"Where do they take us?" he asked.

* * *

"Where do you take them?" Strykar asked.

"We will give them one of the longhouses," Harald said. "I want them to feel safe. Truly, Strykar, these people can do us much good."

"These pagans?"

Harald laughed. "These pagans pray far more than you do."

"That is not such an accomplishment," Orm said.

Harald threw his head back and laughed again. "Strykar, each day on the boat all the men rose at dawn and prayed to the rising sun. While the storm raged they faced where the sun would be had they been able to see it. Water over the bows, each bailing for his life, the storm howling through the yards, and they prayed. When they finished praying they would smile and begin their efforts to keep from drowning. I speak the truth; I know not to what they pray, but their pains would please the pope."

"What more did you learn?"

"This is their summer camp; they move inland to hunt in the fall. They have enemies to fear; most of their men were killed a year ago by a raiding party. They live off the sea and forest, they know nothing of farming. They are no fools. They learn quickly. Particularly the boy with the scars. After three weeks aboard he could sail my ship to England."

"I marked him," Strykar said. "He is very young, yet it seems they listen to his words. Orm, it might be well for you to learn more of this boy. It would appear the two of you are of an age."

Orm was unaccountably nettled by the praise for this strange pagan. "I know not what makes him unique. From all I see, he is a naked pagan with a stone knife."

"Yes," Strykar said, "look at that knife. And then look at his face. Those scars come from a bear or a lion, or something of the like. I know not what killer animals this land holds, but that boy faced one of them, faced it head on with his eyes open and with no better weapon than a stone knife." He glanced sideways at Orm. "You did much the same when you sought Lord Harald's head. You two may have more in common than you think."

They were nearly at the crest of the hill. Harald stopped near one of the longhouses that had been completed, but not yet occupied. He turned to the Mi'kmaq and waved them inside.

"Yours," he said. "Eat, rest. Sunset, we talk."

He nodded and walked off. He needed his own bed. After three weeks at sea the land continued to roll beneath his feet. He needed to rest and prepare. Tonight, would require a clear head and a clever tongue.

CHAPTER FIFTY-TWO

HARALD LEFT THE LONGHOUSE as the sun disappeared behind the hill. The sea was still lit and he could vaguely make out the forms of a pod of whales, far offshore. The camp sounds were muted, as if the dying light also calmed the world.

He was back in his finest. The red silk cloak from Byzantium hung from his massive shoulders and at his waist the silver raven's head winked on the pommel of his sword. His blond hair was clean and combed, swept back from his forehead. He had trimmed his beard and he was as clean as cold river water could make him.

He stood alone, looking over the camp. At the sound of hoof beats he turned his head to see Eric approaching.

"My lord," he said, "I was patrolling. I heard of your return."

"Eric," Harald said, smiling.

Eric's face was taut, strained.

"I prayed for your return," he said. "I mastered my temper and returned to the bay, but you had already put to sea.

I should have been with you."

"Your temper and your choice were both reasonable. I hold no ill will. The crew did well. You trained them admirably."

Eric nodded. "I see you returned with your pagans. What are your wishes?"

Harald said, "I am not yet certain. These may be the allies I sought, but perhaps not. There is a chance we are choosing sides in the wrong war, with the wrong side. I think we will just let this run and see where it leads. If nothing else, this is their home; they will know things we also should know. We will hold counsel this night to find what their wishes are."

Eric asked, "*Their* wishes, my lord? Dirty, naked, pagans? Will your people understand why you pretend to counsel with such as these?"

"There is no pretense; I desire the good will of these pagans. They are naked, but they are not fools. If *any*," he gave a subtle emphasis to the word, "among my people cannot see the wisdom of this path, send them to me. Or should Strykar explain my policy to the doubters?"

"Strykar can be persuasive," Eric said dryly, "but I do not believe he will be needed. Your wish is still our law."

"For now," Harald said, "but only for now. Spread the word—the counsel is open to all. I will keep no secrets and I wish no confusion."

"Yes, my lord." Eric nodded warily and rode off.

"You heard all?" Harald said, staring off towards the darkening sea.

"Yes," Orm came out of the longhouse and stood beside Harald.

"Then go and make my wishes known. Particularly to Arnora. I want both of you at my back tonight."

"My lord?"

Harald turned and looked at him.

"I need people I can trust. Strykar will be by my side, but he would be there if I were to leap off a cliff. Eric will also be there, but he thinks I am being a fool. You and Arnora know my mind and my will. The rest? They will be led. Most people want to be led. The women want only for their children to be fed and safe. The men want full bellies and peace or glory, depending on their ages. Besides, it will take young eyes to see these pagans as people and it will take young ears to learn their tongue."

"My lord, I am no counselor. Nor do I wish to be."

"I care not what you are, boy. I care only for what you may become. I care even less for what you wish. A man does what is needful. That is what makes him a man."

Harald looked the boy up and down.

"You are a man, you know. You became one the day your father died and you sought my life. If not then, when you left your mother and traveled to Iceland. If not then, when you helped me track down Asbrand. If not then, when you put a hundred people in your hand by accepting the watch during the storm. Look at yourself. It has been less than a year since we left Scotland and already you could pull Gunnar's bow if you wished. You see everything and say little, you do what needs to be done, and Orm, you hold my trust."

He turned to walk away. Orm's voice stopped him.

"My lord, what happened on the ship?"

"What?"

"You are different now. And it happened during the storm."

"I have decided to live." The answer was flat and unequivocal.

"That is well." It was almost, but not quite a question.

"Perhaps. Life is pain, Orm, and death comes to us all. It is much else: joy, duty, the sea in a storm or the quiet of a soft snowfall, the laughter of children and the screams of the dying, but above all, to be alive is to accept and welcome the pain that will surely come." Harald was looking at something very far away, but then his gaze shifted to Orm. "Now go, we have much to do. If we are going to pay the price, we need to make sure we receive full value, and we cannot do that by wasting time."

"Yes, my lord."

"None is so just and generous
As not to gladden at a gift.
None so abstinent or open-handed
To refuse a just reward."

—THE HAVAMAL

CHAPTER FIFTY-THREE

THE FIRE CRACKLED, BANISHING the darkness. As the word spread, all of the camp, down to the last and the least, gathered on the hillside overlooking the flames. Orm led the Mi'kmaq to the counsel site and left them. They took their places, the men dropping to the ground cross-legged, the women in a rank behind. They had reclaimed their children during the afternoon and now held them close.

Around them were more people than they had ever seen in one place, all of them strangers and very strange.

Samoset asked, "What will this evening bring?"

Ahanu surveyed the ranks of watching Norse above them on the hill and laughed. "I know not what comes tonight, but the past days have been passing strange. Perhaps tonight they adopt us as their children or perhaps boil us for their meat in one of those *iron* kettles."

Samoset laughed with him, "If we are to make the Journey, we will have many stories to tell in the Other World."

"Someone comes," said Chogan.

The crowd quieted and parted. Harald came through. He was transformed. He was wearing a long cloak of flowing material, a color like nothing the Mi'kmaq had ever seen, more vivid than a sweet tree in the fall. It hung nearly to the ground and was altogether the most remarkable garment they had ever laid eyes on. By his side swung a knife longer than a man's arm. It was made of *iron*, but had a strange carving of a bird on the handle. It gleamed in the firelight, as did the shirt he was wearing. His shirt was even more peculiar than the cloak. It appeared to be made of tiny circles of the *iron*, looped together. Taller than any human being they had ever seen, the flowing cloak and shimmering metal made Harald seem larger than life itself, like a god.

The storm had broken the heat spell and in the past two weeks the seasons had begun to turn. A slight chill was in the air and the heat from the fire was pleasant.

Behind Harald came Strykar and Eric. Both were dressed in black and both carried fat bladed weapons made of *iron*. Arnora and Orm followed. Arnora was wearing her green cloak and her red hair cascaded down her back in curls. Her cloak left one arm bare and a strange silver ornament circled her upper arm. Orm stood beside her, tall and lean, carrying a bow as tall as he was. He was dressed from head to toe in unadorned grey. A thick bladed knife swung from a sheath on his belt. All five were quiet and somber. Harald entered the circle of the fire alone, then he turned and waved the others forward to join him. They seated themselves, not on the ground, but on rough seats of hewn logs.

Harald beckoned all to come as close as they could.

"Come," he said. "All need to hear tonight's conference."

The crowd murmured and moved closer, silent ranks on the hill above the fire, faces dim in the night.

He turned toward the Mi'kmaq.

"This will go slowly," he said, "for all need to understand."

Across the fire Samoset nodded.

"Yes," he said, struggling to put the Norse words together, "all need to understand."

* * *

The talk continued long into the night—a mixture of Norse, Mi'kmaq, and sign language. There were many pauses for thought and clarification. The fire died down and was replenished, but no one left.

"So," Samoset said, finally, "is it agreed, that we cast our lot with these strangers?"

"One thing still bothers me," Ahanu said. "These people have no faith. They never join in morning prayers. We do not know from where they come and we have no idea where they are bound."

Samoset turned to Harald.

"What," he asked, "do you believe? We worry, you do not greet the sun."

* * *

"What is he saying?" Harald asked.

"I think," Arnora said, "they wonder why you do not join them in their morning prayers."

Strykar laughed, at first just a low chuckle and growing to a full deep belly laugh.

"Do you hear, Eric, these pagans worry we lack faith?"

Eric glared at him.

"They are mocking us."

"No," Harald said slowly, "they are not." He turned to Samoset. "Tomorrow," he said, "I greet the sun with you."

"What!" Eric exclaimed. "Have you lost your mind?"

Harald turned his head.

"What is your concern, Eric?" Harald asked.

"We have given up our country. Now do you ask us to give up our faith!"

"I ask nothing. What would you have me do?"

"Offer these pagans the choice Saint Olaf offered. The Cross or the axe!"

Harold looked up wearily, "Eric, I have killed people for God. I have killed people for an emperor, I have killed people for gold, I have killed for power and Eric, sometimes I have killed for my pleasure." He paused and the silence was heavy around him. "Do you know what I have discovered? The deaths are all the same. The blood pours out, the faces twist, and the souls depart. I weary of the sight. I tire of finding reasons to kill. I would like to try to find reasons to let them live."

He turned toward the Mi'kmaq. "Winter will be long. We will have much time to tell our stories. But tomorrow, I greet the sun."

The fire was dying again. The night air chilled. Harald looked across the fire and saw the young woman, Wyanet, shivering next to her mother's legs. He rose, once again towering over all present. He strode around the flickering fire, removed his Byzantium silk, and wrapped it around the girl, tucking the ends in firmly and patting her gently on the head.

"Wyanet and I are tired," he said, "We will talk again, many times."

He turned and stalked away, up the hill and into the darkness. Astonished silence followed his departure.

"What was that?" Orm asked.

"That, boy, was a king," Strykar said. He, too, rose and wandered away from the fire.

Everyone else departed, walking slowly to their beds, talking of the evening's events.

Eric was the last to leave. He waited for the fire to die completely away, and then went to check the guards.

Overhead, stars glittered. Down the hill the horses and cattle moved slowly about their enclosure, the sounds of their hooves on the ground a muffled echo off the quiet waters of the bay.

Everything on this earth is alive, has a soul.
The animals are our brothers and sisters. They
offer themselves to us that we might live so we
need to treat their bones with respect, lest
they become offended.

—THE STORIES OF THE MI'KMAQ

CHAPTER FIFTY-FOUR

THE SNOW WAS VERY DEEP. In the shelter of the woods it seemed bottomless. Chogan and Orm moved slowly on their snowshoes. Orm had spent much time practicing, but he was still clumsy compared to Chogan. The air was cold, and the snow crunched beneath their feet as Chogan pulled a toboggan behind him.

They were half a day's journey from camp. They had left early in the morning, as soon as they finished their morning prayers and had eaten their breakfast of dried fish as they walked.

The game near camp had long since been killed or had fled. The hunters were forced to travel far afield and few of the Norse were skilled enough to make it worth their bother. Most of the hunting had been delegated to the Mi'kmaq and Chogan was the one who traveled the farthest and fastest. This was Orm's first trip with him and he was getting tiring of the irritated glances from his companion.

Near the crest of a hill, Chogan finally stopped. A few

moments later Orm came up next to him, puffing, his breath a fog in front of him.

Chogan knelt in the snow.

"What are you looking at?" Orm asked.

"The track," Chogan said. "It is fresh, the edges are still sharp. It must be a buck or big doe; see the size of the print? It moved down the hill, in no hurry—you can tell by the length of the stride. I think Sister Deer is headed to find others of her kind." Chogan pointed. "Down there is where they will be. The pine trees are thick and they will feel hidden. They feed off the bottom branches and trample down the snow so they can move freely. This is their pattern in the deep winter; they band together. The wind comes toward us. If you go there—stand with your back against that sweet tree. Remain still, with the wind in your face and the deer will not be wary."

"And you?" Orm asked.

"There," Chogan said, pointing. "With luck, I will drive the deer past you."

Orm nodded and began to move down the hill.

"No," Chogan said, "keep to the trees. This trip will be of little use if the deer sense your presence. The Creator gave them good ears and noses, and they will see you if you move like a man and not like a bush in the wind. Go slowly, pause, listen, then go on."

Orm nodded again and moved more carefully. Chogan watched him leave, and then started back down the back side of the hill to circle around to the other side of the deer yard. He left the toboggan where they had separated.

The shadows were beginning to lengthen when Chogan got close enough to the deer to hear them. It sounded like a large herd, perhaps several hands or more. His steps became even more cautious. He had little faith in Orm's skills and was hoping to get close enough for a shot of his own, lest they return empty-handed to a camp that yearned for fresh meat.

The deer became alarmed. They did not yet smell Chogan,

but they could feel his presence and were restless. Yet, they did not want to leave the safety of the deep woods, where they'd trampled down the snow and could still reach the lower branches of the pine trees.

Soon Chogan could see their dark shadows through the trees as they moved about, sniffing the air, their long ears swiveling.

Chogan nocked his arrow. He had switched from using the stone arrowheads that he'd made himself, his hard-won skills made useless. The iron arrowheads were not as sharp as the flint, but far more durable and able to inflict great damage due to their larger size.

One more cautious step and the snow crunched beneath his feet. The deer squatted and turned to flee, their white tails flashing in alarm. Chogan saw a shot and took it. He saw the white fletching standing bright against the dark hair of the deer and then it was gone through the forest.

He waited, letting his breath slow and his heart rest. The shot was good. He was confident that the huge arrowhead had done fatal damage, but if he pursued too quickly the deer would ignore the pain and flee further and faster. If there was no further alarm it would soon stop its flight and die quietly, close by.

Chogan waited patiently, resting with his back against a tree. When enough time had passed he rose to his feet and looked for the trail.

It wasn't difficult to find. The deer had erupted from their sleeping grounds on a narrow path and the blood trail was thick and vivid in the white snow. Chogan knelt, examined the trail, and nodded in satisfaction. The blood trail was wide and pink, with tiny bubbles evident. He had hit a lung and the deer was no doubt lying dead not far away. Chogan trudged down the path. The blood trail swerved into the deep snow and the deer lay in shadow under a pine tree.

Chogan approached cautiously, another arrow nocked and ready. The deer didn't move so Chogan dropped his bow for his knife. He lifted the deer's head and slit its throat.

"Thank you, my brother," he said. "I have many mouths to feed, and if they are to have fresh meat, it comes from me."

He dragged the deer through the snow back to the path and left it there, while he went to fetch Orm and the toboggan.

The toboggan was gone when he returned to the crest of the hill. He followed the tracks and found Orm loading a deer unto it.

Orm looked up. "You were right. The deer ran where you said they would."

Chogan looked and read the signs. "You made a good shot," he said. "Both lungs and the heart. The spirit of the deer fled quickly."

"I was not so lucky with the other one." Orm said, with a jerk of his head. "He ran much farther before he fell."

Startled, Chogan's head snapped around. Sure enough, another deer lay at the crest of a small rise. "Two deer," he said, "running, and they both die within sight. There was little luck involved."

Chogan took his knife and with a few quick strokes removed the deer's heart. He divided it and the two stood, chewing the warm flesh while around them the woods darkened.

"I too, have a deer." Chogan said. "We must get all three loaded on the toboggan and find a place to camp. It will be dark soon, and we have the smell of fresh blood about us. We will need a fire to keep Brother Wolf from sharing in our bounty."

It was full dark before the meat was loaded on the toboggan. They found a massive fallen birch tree to shelter them. Chogan led the way, showing Orm how to use his snowshoes to scoop snow away from the tree. By the time they had reached the ground, piles of snow surrounded them. Chogan used his knife to cut a great sheet of birchbark off the fallen tree for a roof. Orm started the fire, striking sparks into a tiny nest of shredded dry bark and feeding it with branches ripped from the dead tree. They lay with their backs against the tree and broiled chunks of meat over the small fire. Both had woolen cloaks wrapped around them. The toboggan stopped the night wind and they were comfortable.

Orm laughed out loud.

"What?" Chogan asked.

"I was remembering a night outside in Iceland, the land we came from. Lord Harald and I lay side by side in the rain, shivering, all night. And here we are—warm, dry, comfortable, well fed. Truly, Chogan, your people know much."

"This is my land. What kind of fool would I be, if I could not find food, shelter, and comfort in my own land?"

The howling of wolves disturbed the night, but they had plenty of firewood, their weapons, and their youth. They were not afraid.

"Tell me," Chogan said, "of the. . .book Lord Harald shows you. It means nothing to me."

Orm paused to think. "Today, when you found the deer trail, you told me how big the deer was, where it was heading, when it had gone, almost what it was thinking. Truthfully, to me the track meant nothing. How did you know what you knew?"

Chogan said, "I learned. My father and my grandfather and my uncles showed me the way, corrected my errors, tested my knowledge."

"Lord Harald does the same. The marks in the books are like the tracks of the deer—no more, no less."

The fire popped and flared, sparks heading to the heavens.

Chogan said, "I would learn more of this. Do you think I am able?"

Orm laughed, "Today you led me through a forest, located food for our people, seemingly read the minds of the deer, told me where to stand, caused deer to run directly in front of me, found us warmth and shelter—all without effort. I think you can learn to read."

CHAPTER FIFTY-FIVE

THE FIRE FLICKERED IN THE hearth. Only Samoset and Harald were still awake.

"Speak to me," Samoset said, "of Arnora-Without-A-Father."

"Why do you call her that?" Harald asked.

"What else?" Samoset said. "All of you. . .know your fathers. They are part of you, in your name. When she introduced herself, she called herself naught but 'Arnora.' Is she an orphan?"

"Now she is. Her father was an evil, foolish man. He. . .he. . ." Harald made a universal gesture with his hands, "got her with child."

Samoset drew a deep breath, shocked, "Where is this man?"

"When I learned what he had done, I broke his back across my knee and threw his carcass to the ravens."

Samoset nodded approvingly. "And the child?"

"Stillborn," Harald said, "buried in the land we come from."

Samoset nodded again, "She has a shadow on her spirit," he said. "It shows in all she does. The winter, away from the ship, it weighs on her."

"I feel," Harald said, "that she is not content here. She still flees her father."

"How long will she flee?"

Harald shrugged, "Perhaps she will never stop."

"Perhaps," Samoset said, "it was not good that her father was not buried. His life-force and his spirit-force are not together. While he is uneasy, so shall she be."

A long silence followed while the two men sat staring into the fire.

"And your true children?" Samoset asked. "Where are they?"

"My two sons rule the land I came from," Harald said. "My daughter is dead. She died at the moment I began my attack on the land I wished to rule."

Samoset's eyes widened, but he said nothing.

"I have felt," Harald went on, slowly, "that God took her from me, as a punishment for seeking what I should not have. When I saw my wife's eyes, when she told me of her death, I felt that I had died myself."

"And this?" Samoset asked, touching on his own neck where the scar was on Harald's.

"In my last great battle, I sought victory against all reason. We were outnumbered, no armor, far from our ships. We should have fled but I would not." Harald reached behind him into a quiver, pulled out one of the great war arrows, and handed it to Samoset. "When I saw all was lost, I charged the English chief and one of his archers brought me down. I awoke days later, on one of our ships. My men, seeing me fall, died, almost to the man, to protect my body."

Samoset looked at the arrow. "You should have died," he said. It was a flat statement.

"Yes," Harald said, "I should have."

"On the ship," Samoset said, "when you saved us from

the sea and fire, I saw you change. I saw," he waved his fingers in front of his eyes, "something happen."

"I am not sure," Harald said. "I felt as if I had awakened from a dream. I, too, was fleeing. Now, I have stopped."

Samoset nodded, "It is as I thought. You are a man of great power, a sagamore and more. As a dead man, you brought all these people all this way. Your life-force left you on that battlefield and your spirit-force left when your daughter died. Now you have them back."

Harald rose and added another stick to the fire. A small shower of sparks rose and eddied toward the smoke hole in the roof. A soft whisper of snow came across the roof.

"Now," he said, "I need to know, what do I do with this new life?"

"You have done much already," Samoset said. "My people live because of you. The widows and orphans who came with you, they live also. In the summer we will go to where the chiefs and our sagamore meet and then there will be much to talk about."

"And what will your people say?"

"I know not," Samoset said. "There will be much talk. You are very strange to us. Your ships own the sea. Your tools of iron and your cloth, the way you bend animals to your will—speak in your favor. They will see that you are like children in the woods and they will want what you have. But people will look at you and see war; and they will be cautious."

"There are few men in your lodge," Harald said. "Your people know war."

Samoset lifted an eyebrow.

"Tell me of your brothers," Harald said. "I would know your story, and my people need to know what enemies they face."

"There is little to tell," Samoset said. "It was summer, near the time when the fire came this season. The evil ones are farmers, like you, and they come when their crops are growing. They creep through the woods, strike quickly, and leave."

Samoset leaned forward and rubbed his eyes with his fingers. He propped his head on his hands and stared into the fire.

"I knew they were coming that day," he said. "The animals told us that there were strangers near. We were preparing to leave for winter camp. The canoes were loaded, full of fish and fat. It had been a good summer; there was plenty to eat for the winter. If we had left even one day earlier, all would have been well, and we could have, we had enough and to spare. I was in the first canoe with some of the women. My father followed. I was already far upstream when I heard the sounds. I left the women in the canoe and ran downstream as quickly as I could. My brothers had stayed behind, sending the last of the women and children off." Samoset shrugged. "There was little left. The evil ones take the heads for trophies and the hearts for their victory feast. Noshi and I buried the rest."

"And you did not pursue them?"

"I could not," Samoset said. "There were too many, I was alone, and the women had no protection." He twirled the war arrow in his hand, the broadhead nearly as wide as his hand. "Is that why you command your women practice with these?"

Harald nodded. "One day, your evil ones will return." He stood up and put his hand on Samoset's shoulder. "When they do, we will be ready and we will do the feasting."

"After the Creator made the world and all that was in it, he caused a bolt of lightning to hit the surface of the world. This caused the formation of an image of a human body shaped out of sand. This is how the Mi'kmaq came to the world."

—THE STORIES OF THE MI'KMAQ

CHAPTER FIFTY-SIX

"TELL ME MORE OF YOUR GOD, the One who took your daughter."

Harald paused for thought. "God is the Creator. He made everything and is sagamore over all. He made men to rule the world in his place, but he was distressed by our disobedience and cast us out to make our own way." Harald nibbled on a fragment of fresh venison. Orm and Chogan had returned. The three deer had provided only a bit of meat to everyone so they had left again almost immediately. Samoset and Harald were once again alone, the rest of the camp asleep. "In truth, I know not what to tell you of God. Our priests have much power and constantly tell us of His Will, but often I do not find their words in the word of God. This I know—after many years God sent his son, his only son, to show us his way. Evil ones took his son and killed him."

Samoset hissed, "Truly, do you believe this? What kind of God would allow his son to be killed?"

"What if," Harald said, "on that day when the evil ones

came, it had been Chogan who had been left behind? If the lives of all had rested on his shoulders could you have left him?"

"I know not." Samoset said. "Your God is a hard God, to do such a thing. What does he ask of you, if he will allow his son to die? And how could even a God remain sane, if he were to offer up his child as a sacrifice?"

"That would explain much of my world," Harald said, "if God were indeed mad. Perhaps coming to your shores is no more than a joke by a mad man. Still, to answer your question, he asks as much as we have to give. We are to treat all men as our brothers. We are to feed the hungry, clothe the naked, and tend to the sick. His death was foretold—he allowed himself to be killed that all of us would be saved."

"Like my brothers?"

"Yes," Harald said, "like your brothers. That is very clear—the highest calling is to make of yourself a sacrifice, for those weaker or less fortunate. These are not the words of the priests, but it is obvious to one who reads the words of His Son. The weak, and especially children, hold the favored places in his kingdom. If you serve them, all your errors are forgiven and when you take the Journey, you travel to a wonderful place. If you do not do this, nothing else matters; you are condemned to torment forever."

"And you believe this?"

"I believe that the Creator made the world, that we are his children, and we are responsible for it. I believe that for everything there is a price that must be paid."

"We believe much the same," Samoset said, "but the son, who dies for the others, that is very strange."

"Tell me, of what you believe."

"The story goes, that Gisoolg is the Creator, the one who made everything. Is your God a man?"

"So the priests say."

"That, too, is very strange. The Creator is neither man nor woman. The Creator is beyond us all. To understand the world would be a strange and wondrous thing, but perhaps a very wise man could do it. To create it?" Samoset shook his head, "That is beyond the wisest man."

"You pray to the rising sun," Harald said.

"No," Chogan said, "We pray *toward* the sun. The sun is the giver of life, light, warmth, but it was placed there by the Creator. We do not worship the sun; we salute the power that put the sun in the sky."

"And why are you here?" Harald asked.

"There is no why," Samoset said, "only *is*. All around us has life, all around us has value. The Creator did not send us to rule, as you say yours did, but merely to live. True, we live off the land and the waters, we take the lives of our fellow creatures, but it is done out of need and with respect." Samoset rose from his seat of fur robes and walked around the fire. He put his hands into the small of his back and rolled his shoulders. "Why," he continued, "do you feel that your God took the life of your daughter? This I do not understand at all."

"The priests teach that to be forgiven your crimes, your sins, you must pay a price, you must earn your forgiveness."

"Perhaps there is justice in that, but it is madness to say that your God took your daughter for your crimes. We hear of peoples, beyond the evil ones, near a great river in the center of the world, who sacrifice their children to their God. Is that what you believe?"

Harald shook his head wearily, "I know not what I believe. It used to make sense to me, but now I doubt. I know that my daughter is dead, my woman is as if dead to me, I know that I fled my failure and the contempt in my son's eyes. I sought to care for those left helpless by my ambition. I remember the words of the priests and I read the words of God, and there is much to dispute between them. I do believe in God, my Creator, and in his Son, who died for the helpless. I believe also that priests are men and they may have wants and ambitions that cloud their words."

Samoset shrugged his shoulders. "Then that is enough. You make too much of the world. Think less of why and more of what is. All these people, they look to you for the law. You cannot be cloudy in your mind."

"Are you never cloudy in your mind?"

"Seldom," Samoset said, "for I know my world and my place. Only twice—when I found my dead brothers and wished to run mad through the forest until I found their slayers, and again when the fire trapped us, when you came out of the smoke and the mist, I thought my head would explode."

Harald shook his head, chuckling, "I thought little of how we must have appeared. What made you come so willingly?"

"I would not. If it had been left to me, our scorched bones would be resting on the rocks. Wate made the decision. It is easier to be a woman, I think. There are the children—what is good for them is good, what is not, is bad. Little matters beyond that. It seems an easy way to live."

"And are they wrong?" Harald asked. "And even so, I have known many women who are just as cloudy in their minds as I. One day I will tell you tales of Empress Zoe, and even a woman of my own people, the daughter of Eric the Red. No, you underestimate the cruelty and cunning of women. They can be as foolish as men."

"Then we are doomed," Samoset said, laughing, "We are but insects, crawling across a rock, tormented by your God as a child with a stick torments ants."

"Perhaps," Harald said, "but if that is the case, I think I shall go to my bed now. I want to be rested, for tomorrow I will seek to crawl faster than all the rest and perhaps I can get my jaws into our tormentor."

CHAPTER FIFTY-SEVEN

"There are two uses for the bow in war." Strykar said. "First, you shoot to kill a man, as you would a deer. But also, these bows can fire an arrow at a range far longer than you could be assured of hitting one man. When you fire as a group, at an area, your arrows will fall like rain from the sky. One weapon, two skills. You will learn them both. Begin."

Soon bowstrings began to twang and the sound of arrows hitting targets filled the air.

"No, child," said Strykar, "you are meant to strike the target. You cannot eat a deer you merely frighten and you do not survive an enemy that is unharmed. Close is the same as not at all."

Sweat beaded on Wyanet's face and she loosed another arrow. It missed by an even wider mark.

"Stop," Strykar said. "I see the problem." He turned to Wate, who was next in the line of women and children practicing with the long war bows. "Have you any wax?"

"Wax?" Wate repeated, the word strange on her tongue.

Strykar growled under his breath. He paused for thought. "A little. . . that flies. BZZZZZZZ, sweet food." *God's,* he thought, *I will never get my tongue around this language.*

"Ahh, to eat?" Wate said.

"No," Strykar said. "Its home."

"We can find, one sun, maybe more."

The meadows were thick with spring flowers; it was not long after the children had spread out that one of them saw a bee. He raised a shout and ran after it. When he finally lost sight of it, he stopped and pointed in the direction of its flight. The people gathered and in a short time another bee was spotted and pursued until it, too, was lost. Gradually the arc was narrowed and by late afternoon they found the hive.

It was in the base of an old ash tree, the inside rotting away with age.

"Smoke," Strykar said, and when the bees were stunned he reached into the hive and brought out big hunks of dripping honeycomb. It was piled into a deerskin and hauled back to camp.

"This, we need," Strykar said, holding up a tiny piece of wax. "This, you eat," He let a droplet of honey fall on the tongue of Wate's youngest child. The children giggled and before long the camp was full of young people chewing diligently on honeycomb and returning to spit the wax into a large iron pot. While this was going on Strykar cut the deerskin into pieces as long as his arm and wide enough to wrap around it. He dropped the pieces into a pot of water. When they had soaked he grabbed Wyanet and held her arm out.

"See," he said, showing a bruise on the inside of her forearm. "The bowstring strikes. You, your arm, knows the pain and moves away, so your arrow misses." He wrapped the soaked leather around her forearm, stretching it tightly, and tied it with a string. "Let it dry, and stiffen," he commanded. "Then we use the wax."

The next morning when the leather cuffs were hard, he built a fire under the wax. After it was melted he instructed everyone to drop their new arm guards into the hot liquid. A few moments later he fished one out with a stick and rubbed the wax into the leather, inside and out.

"Do this," he said, "over and over, until the wax has penetrated through the leather. Then, we try the bows again."

When everyone seemed to know what they were doing, Strykar nodded and walked away. He found Eric down by the horse pen, watching the new foals.

He leaned against the fence next to him. For several moments neither of them said a word.

"Do you suppose," Stryker spoke first, "that these evil ones the Mi'kmaq speak of are armed with the same weapons as they?"

"I care not," Eric said. "They are pagans and beyond understanding. Why do you ask?"

"You have seen their bows and the arrow points they use. How long before we have a decent forge and an armory?"

"I know naught of that, either. I know the smith has found some bog iron, but cannot be used for fine work, no matter your skill."

"You agree, then, it will be some time?"

"What is your point, Strykar?"

Strykar said nothing for a long moment, and then continued quietly. "I think that a decent armor could be made, good enough for these stone arrows, out of several layers of waxed leather."

"Why do you care?"

"I care," Strykar said, "because Lord Harald asked me to see to the training of these people. I care, because these people have enemies and we have cast our lot with them. Their enemies will become our enemies as well. And if we are to have enemies, I wish them dead, as fast and as expediently as possible. If our archers can fire volleys without being worried about a stone-tipped arrow piercing their belly, our enemies will die quickly indeed."

"This is almost beyond bearing." Eric said. "Why have we

cast our lot with these savages? Why are we not ruling them?"

"Because," Strykar said slowly, "it is Lord Harald's wish. Because, we have no army to back our demands, no fleet to rescue us and no other option to entertain. There are many reasons, but all that matters are the first."

"Still, and as always, King Harald's dog."

"Perhaps. I can imagine worse fates. Eric," Strykar went on, "you are a fine kendtmann and a good man with an axe. This gives you value, but never imagine that your value is infinite. I may well be King Harald's dog. Do you wish to try my teeth?" Strykar looked up at the clear blue sky, then all around at the early summer vista. "It is as good a day as any for one of us to die. You have your axe, I have mine. A little sport between old companions and there will no longer be a need for this pointless bickering. What are your wishes?"

Eric pushed himself upright and spat on the ground. "Dogs age," he said. "Teeth grow dull. I am not like you, besotted both by your king and this new land. I am still a man, and will make up my own mind and in my own time. Perhaps Harald is right, but perhaps he is merely tired, losing his manhood yearning for peace. Time will tell. But until then, plan your woman's army yourself. I have no need for them." He stalked off down the hill and Strykar saw him push away from the dock in one of the canoes. He paddled until he reached the center of the cove, where he cast a line overboard and began to fish.

Strykar turned to walk back up the hill and saw Wate standing, watching him intently.

"How much. . . you hear?" he asked.

Wate shrugged.

"Eric," Strykar said, "not friend. Of me or Mi'kmaq. *Someday* you may need to," and he ran one blunt thumb across his throat. Wate looked out to the tiny boat. Her eyes narrowed and she nodded slightly. Strykar saw the set of her jaw and chuckled deep down in his throat. "Good," he said, "very good."

CHAPTER FIFTY-EIGHT

"Tell me of this council we attend," Harald said.

"It is our council of clan chiefs," Samoset said. The two rode down a narrow deer trail. Overhead was the first glimmer of fall color. Samoset rode in front, handling the horse with some caution. They traveled slowly, for many of Samoset's clan trailed behind. Most of the Norse were back at their village, although Orm was with Chogan, somewhere in the woods. Strykar brought up the rear, his axe dangling from one hand, the other carelessly controlling his horse. "We talk of hunting grounds and fishing territories. If the evil ones have entered our lands, we talk of that. Our saga-more will, at times, meet in Grand Council with the saga-mores from the other districts. That is very seldom, only if we are faced with war or some other grave trouble."

"And this council?"

Samoset laughed, "There will be much talk. You are strange to us and all will be very curious. Everyone knows of your presence, but no decision has been made."

"Will they want war?"

"I think not. You have much to offer and you did save us from the fire. They will want what you have and I *believe* all will agree that trade is the best way. Still, there will be much talk."

"How will the decision be made?"

"We will talk until all agree. If all cannot agree, there still needs to be a decision that all can live with."

"Your sagamore, how much power does he have?"

"He has as much as we give him. This sagamore is named Keme. He is the eldest son of our most powerful clan, but he has one seat at the council fire, no more, no less."

"When will we reach the meeting place?"

"Not today, but early tomorrow."

"Another question," Harald said, "Tell me, your youngest son—why does he have no name?"

Samoset laughed, "How do you name a child until you know the child? That would be bad fortune. He is nearly old enough for a name, and we think on it often. We are not so many, Lord Harald; we can be patient in choosing a name."

The sun was pleasantly warm wherever it penetrated the forest canopy. The clan moved at a pace suitable for the smallest legs and they made camp well before dark.

The site was on a rocky bluff overlooking a small stream. They found ample water and firewood. Soon the cooking fires were built and Orm and Chogan reappeared with rabbits, ready for spitting and roasting.

It had taken real hunger before the Mi'kmaq would eat bread, but they had begun to acquire the taste.

Harald saw to his horse and then joined Strykar, seated and leaning against a large oak tree.

"Tomorrow should be of great interest," Strykar said. "We will learn how these people treat with strangers who have not saved their lives."

Harald smiled and stretched his long legs.

"What do you learn from Samoset?" Strykar asked.

"I am not sure," Harald said. "This is no king we see tomorrow. They seem more like Icelanders, meeting to talk endlessly. This land is so empty that they need no real government."

"What about the evil ones they speak of?"

Harald shook his head. "It would appear that they come only in raids and not to conquer. They attack, then run, killing a few men and enslaving some women and children. They surely have no army—you have seen how hard it is to get them to go so far as to post a regular guard."

"How much have you told Samoset of the world we come from?"

"I have hidden nothing. There is much that I do not feel he would understand, but he knows that you and I have spent much of our life at war. These people do not go to war, as we know it. They fight for honor and spoils. It is almost a game to them, mattering little except to the dead."

They sat in silence for a bit, watching the children play. Wyanet was easy to spot. She was older than the other children who had joined them, more of a young woman than a child. She was wearing a tunic made from the Byzantium silk, now stained and torn, but still shining a brilliant red.

"Do you remember Sicily?" Strykar asked, his eyes on the girl.

"What part of it?"

"The siege, I cannot name the city—the one we did not conquer."

"Yes, I remember."

"I think often of how after we had surrounded the castle, their king forced all the peasants back out the gates, so his food would last longer."

"I remember. Good tactics. We could not starve him out."

"Then you must also remember that we would not let those peasants through our lines, lest they become a thorn in our sides."

"I remember that, also."

"Lord Harald, I dream of them now," Strykar said. "I dream of those helpless ones, trapped in the open between our army and the castle walls, and how they remained there until they starved. It took a long time, didn't it?"

"Weeks, perhaps a month or more before the last of them died." The memory was clear in Harald's mind. The hot sun, the looming walls of the castle and the horde of bewildered peasants trapped between the stone walls and the iron ring of the Byzantium army.

"I complained only of the smell, then, and the noise. I believe, that when I next saw a priest and confessed my sins, I didn't think to mention that what I had done. What penance do you suppose I would have been given for causing the death of so many who bore me no ill will, especially the children who know not why they should die?"

"None," Harald said. "You were following your liege's orders and making war in the name of the Emperor of Byzantium. You committed no sin."

Strykar laughed, "You believe this? Then, my Lord Harald, you are a fool. For what my dreams tell me is that I will surely burn in hell. Perhaps a priest would forgive me, but do you suppose she would?" He nodded toward Wyanet. "Shall I go tell her the story?" He rose stiffly to his feet.

"Strykar," Harald said, "my dreams are the same."

"I fear, my lord, that we will burn together." Strykar ambled across the clearing, heading for the slope down to the stream. He still carried his axe, but with his free hand he gently touched Wyanet's shoulder as he passed. She gave him a quick smile, and then returned to her game.

Harald watched him disappear down the slope, then looked away. A sudden outcry brought him to his feet. He crossed the clearing in several long strides, but the children were ahead of him.

Strykar lay at the foot of the slope, swearing loudly in Norse.

"What have you done?" Harald asked. "Your noise would

disturb the dead."

"I have broken my leg. Now come and get me out of this damned stream before I drown and complete the embarrassment."

Harald chortled and made his way down the slope. "Is it truly broken?" he asked.

"Yes," Strykar said, "right above the ankle. Help me up; this is not a comfortable bed."

Harald scooped him up, carrying as if he were a child. Wyanet followed, shouldering his axe. Harald laid him down on a fur robe near the fire. He uncovered his leg to assess the damage. It looked bad—lumpy and bruised, with swelling already stretching the skin. Harald laughed again when he saw it.

"I am glad," Strykar said, "that I can serve as your jester. Do you wish any other tricks?"

"No," Harald said, "this was sufficient. The Turks, the Byzantiums, the Danes, the English, and God only knows how many random husbands and fathers, all have sought your life's blood without success. If only they would have known to strew a bit of wet clay underfoot."

Strykar chuckled and then grimaced as Wate began to wrap the limb, "Very amusing, indeed. Now, what will we do tomorrow? Your council calls, and I will detain you."

Samoset spoke up. "The council waits, yet Strykar should not travel. Let him stay, Wyanet can tend his needs, and she can bring him when the swelling is less."

"Did you understand?" Harald asked. "Samoset says you should stay—we will leave Wyanet with you to fetch and carry."

"Wyanet and I are comrades," Strykar said. "We will tell stories of past campaigns until you return."

By now it was full night. The people gathered to eat and soon scattered back out to their sleeping robes. Wyanet took her duties seriously, bringing Strykar food and water. He slept little, the pain in his leg keeping his dreams at bay.

"Bare is a brotherless back"

—THE SAGA OF BURNT NJAL

CHAPTER FIFTY-NINE

THEY DEPARTED AT FIRST LIGHT, as soon as the men finished morning prayers.

Harald paused by Strykar's sleeping robe, towering over all on his horse.

"Do nothing foolish," Strykar said. "I should be there to offer counsel."

"What sort of counsel?" Harald asked. "You cannot speak their tongue and your usual counsel is to kill them all. It is probably best that you stay behind." He waved casually and followed Samoset down the trail.

The morning flowed slowly. Strykar's leg was black and blue, swollen to the knee. Wyanet took the horse out to graze, holding tightly to its lead rope. Strykar shifted uneasily as he watched her and the horse drift aimlessly around the clearing. Several times the horse snorted and sniffed the air. Strykar frowned and watched more carefully. A rabbit started from the underbrush, then swerved and ran away. When a raven flew suddenly from a tree on the other side of the clearing he called the girl back.

"We have trouble," he said, when she was by his side. "Something watches. The horse heard it first, but now even I know that we have guests. Something comes through the woods. Behind you, and over there, something hides."

The girl's dark eyes widened, but she did not look.

"Is there any chance that it could be your people?"

Wyanet shook her head. "They would know our camp. They might approach with care, but they would not remain hidden."

"Help me up," Strykar said. "Stand close to me. We still have a chance. They will not understand me or the horse, so they will be wary."

She tugged and he leaned on his axe, finally standing on one foot with his other hand on the horse's mane. He shifted on his good leg, his eyes darting around the clearing.

The Icelandic horse was small. Even with one leg Strykar thought he'd be able to leap onto its back. He looked down at the girl. Whatever had come through the woods was nearly all around them now, almost cutting off the trail. In the time it would take to haul her up, there would be arrows through them both.

"One can go, or both can die," Strykar said. "I see no other way."

The girl asked, "What do they want?" Her red shirt shone in the morning sun.

Strykar shrugged his shoulders. "They will want my axe. They will want me dead and," he looked at her gravely, "they will want you alive."

"How can you know what they want?" Wyanet asked.

"Be at ease, child," Strykar said. "Pretend we talk of the morning, or the butterflies in the clearing. How do I know what these men want? Because they are men much like me."

"What?"

"You live in a world where darkness presses in all around you, Wyanet. I wish it were not so, but there it is. We choose, all of us, whether we join the darkness or keep it at bay." He rolled his shoulders, loosening stiff muscles.

"Do not be alarmed, child. Do you realize that I have lived my life, waiting for this moment?" Strykar smiled down at her. "Truly," he said, "it is a wonder to have grown so old. Do you know what you must do?" he asked. The girl nodded. "I ask you to perform a service for me. Tell Lord Harald that you are my final gift to him. And be sure and tell him, that my dreams have stopped. His can also."

He held the lead rope loosely, then flipped it over the horse's neck. He turned as if to walk away, then twirled on his good leg and threw the girl across the back of the horse. The horse shied, and he had to push off his bad leg to place Wyanet firmly on its back. The pain shot through his body but he mastered it until the girl was secure and slapped the horse's rump with the flat of his axe as he fell. The horse darted away, Wyanet clinging frantically to the mane, and was gone in an instant.

Wyanet glanced back for one look and saw Strykar, two arrows in his back, on his knees.

Then she saw no more.

* * *

They broke from the trees, racing to the fallen man, each eager to be the one to take the head. The first to reach him grabbed his sagging head and pulled it back, baring his throat.

The blue eyes were not glazed and dying, but burning with a strange, fierce light.

"Too soon," Strykar said, grinning through the blood running out his mouth. The hand that captured the other's knife hand was strong, and his axe hand was steady and quick. "You came too close, too soon."

CHAPTER SIXTY

"THEY HAVE LEFT," Chogan said. He was puffing from his run through the woods.

Harald nodded, "And Strykar?"

"He remains."

Harald spurred the horse.

"There is no need to hurry," Chogan said to his back.

He nodded again, but did not slow.

When the others reached the clearing, Harald was standing over Strykar's body. Orm was standing a small distance away, his bow in his hands.

The clearing looked like a slaughterhouse, with pools of blood drying on the foliage and drag marks through fallen leaves. Samoset dismounted and walked slowly around the clearing, his trained eye taking in the evidence.

"How many?" Harald asked, without looking up.

"About two hands, perhaps a few more. Now, a few less."

"They buried their dead." Orm said. "Back there, in the trees. There are fresh graves."

"We will dig them up," Harald said, "and leave the corpses for the dogs."

Samoset looked down on the body, "They didn't take his head. He must have fought very well indeed."

"But they took his heart," Orm said.

"Of course," Samoset said. "They would want his courage to flow into them. They eat his heart and gain his strength."

"They are fools," Harald said, "but I understand their wish. If eating his body would give us Strykar's will, I would boil his bones myself."

"They took his axe, too." Orm said.

"Good."

The men's heads snapped around. Wate stood at the edge of the clearing. Wyanet huddled close to her side.

"This is not a woman's place," Samoset snapped, shocked and embarrassed that she would speak when men were speaking.

Wate walked slowly forward, her eyes very large.

Harald tilted his head and asked, "Why is it good that they took Strykar's axe?"

"When we find his axe," Wate said, "we will know who to kill. Unless it becomes necessary, I would not wish to kill them all."

"Then," Harald said, "you are a better Christian than I, for I wish to kill them all and burn their lodges to the ground. I wish to make a mountain of their skulls and I wish to wipe their seed from the face of this earth."

Of those in the clearing, only Orm knew that this was no random threat, but something Lord Harald had done before. Something he was willing to do again.

"He was your man," Samoset said. "What are your wishes?"

"We will bury him," Harald said. "On the hill, where he will be able to look down on the bones of those who killed him. Then we will return to our village and tell the others. And then," he said, "we go to war. Your people have taught me much, Samoset, but you have no idea what I am about to teach you."

"Lord Harald," Wyanet said, "Strykar had words for you."

"Truly?" Harald's head snapped around. "As he waited for his death, he prepared a message for me?" His voice dripped with sarcasm and Wyanet recoiled from the sound. "Tell me of this message."

Wyanet shook her head and backed away, confused.

"Tell me, child." Harald's gaze was heavy and the girl wilted before it.

"He said that I was his final gift to you. And he said that the dreams had stopped. And I was to be sure to tell you, that yours could stop, too."

"And was he certain of that?"

Wyanet began to weep. "I do not know, Lord Harald. I did not understand him, I do not understand you."

"Never mind, child." Harald said. He covered his face with one huge hand and sank slowly to one knee, "Leave me now," he said.

"I will dig the grave," Orm said.

"No. I have buried my father. I have buried my child. Boy," he looked up, his eyes red and angry, "I have buried armies. I can bury one old man." They all turned to leave, driven by his voice, but stopped when he spoke again.

"You were right," he said to Wate, "as was Strykar. We will not kill them all and we will not make war as I wish. But this will end."

No one said a word and they left him very much alone.

CHAPTER SIXTY-ONE

"Strykar is dead?" Eric asked.

"Yes," Harald said, "These evil ones of whom the Mi'kmaq speak killed him. It was evidently a small raiding party, sent out to find what it might find."

"It is, hard to believe. Some days I thought there was nothing that could kill him."

"He was on his knees, shot through and through with arrows. They came to slit his throat but he killed three of them, and took the arm off a fourth."

Eric chuckled. "Imagine their surprise, to think they had captured a gray-bearded ancient with a notched axe and a bad leg."

Harald smiled, his first in days. "It could happen only here in this new land. No one who knew him would have walked within range of that axe while there was still breath in his body."

"And what now?" Eric asked.

"You are my second. Stay here and protect our people." Harald said. "I am going to take my crew and the ones Strykar was training and we will go and retrieve his axe. I weary of people who play at war as if it were a game."

"I stay behind?"

"No," Harald said, "you guard our ships, you protect our people and you keep the peace. I need you here. I do not need you to show me how to go to war."

* * *

"He was not able to stand," Wyanet said. "I had to pull with all my strength to get him on his feet."

She sat on the slope above the harbor. Arnora, Chogan, and Orm sat with her.

"His leg was black and purple, swollen like a tick till I thought the skin would burst."

She had been talking for a long time. The others sat quietly, listening. The four were close enough in age and outlook that they had come to spend most of their time together. The sun was setting behind the hill and the cooking fires sent smoke wafting up to the darkening sky.

"Tell me again, what he said at the last." Orm said.

"He said, that darkness presses in all around us, and that we all need to choose, whether to join the dark or protect the light." Wyanet buried her face in her hands. "But then he smiled and said he had been waiting his whole life for this moment. Then everything happened so fast. He threw me onto the horse as if I weighed nothing, and then I saw nothing except the horse's neck. I looked once, and saw the arrows in his back."

"What did Lord Harald say?" Arnora asked.

"He said very little," Chogan said, "but there was death in his eyes. If I held Strykar's axe, I would flee, as far and as fast as I could run. I have never seen. . ." he struggled for words but finally gave up and shrugged helplessly.

"I have," Orm said, "once, and I would have died content

if I'd never seen it again."

"What will happen?" Arnora asked.

"We go to war," Orm said. "I believe Wate's words has saved many lives, but Lord Harald is who he is. He will not leave Strykar unavenged and he will not leave these others thinking we are their prey."

"And to what end?" Arnora asked. "Strykar will still be dead and how many others?"

"I do not think," Orm said, "that Harald kills only for revenge, at least not now—now that his temper has cooled. I think he wishes to live at peace."

"And so, to live in peace you go to war? Please, you do not make sense."

"Yet," Wyanet said, "Strykar saved my life. You know he was right. The others would have raped me and then killed me, and had you been there, they would have done the same to you. What should we do?"

"I do not know," Arnora said, "I DO NOT KNOW! But I feel as though I live in a world of blood and I am weary beyond all endurance." She stalked down the hill. She had rigged one of the canoes with a sail and soon the others saw her heading out into the bay, the wool sails catching the evening breeze.

"What haunts her?" Chogan asked. His worried eyes followed her as her boat sailed to the edge of his vision. "She acts as if she flees a ghost."

"She does," Orm said. "Lord Harald killed her father, for the harm he did her."

"That, explains much." Chogan said. "Is there more we should know?"

"Her father was an evil man. Harald grew very fond of Arnora, I think because of his own dead daughter and the way she learned the sea. She asked him to leave her father unharmed, for her, but Harald killed him. He said that although she was safe from him now, he must still die because of the children he might meet in the future. I think this is what drives him now. Despite Arnora's scorn, I believe he does wish to live in peace, but he will not leave these others thinking there is no price to be paid for their actions."

"So," Chogan said, "Lord Harald leads us to war. What will he teach us?" His eyes still followed Arnora, as they often did, but his thoughts had turned to the new problem.

"You cannot imagine," Orm said, "I have spent two years now, listening to the stories he tells of how he has led his life. He first fought in a battle when he was younger than us, and Strykar carried him off that field wounded nearly unto death. He has been in battles every year, sometimes every moon, since that time. In all that time, he lost only once. These evil ones have no idea what comes."

"Tell me more," Wyanet said.

Orm looked at her. He had learned that while she was young, she was very old in her head and he'd long since stopped thinking of her as a child. "Very well," he said. "Look here." He drew in the dirt with a stick. "I believe, we will march this way, with scouts here, here, and here. He will take everyone who can use a bow. Those who can ride will go here, and here."

Chogan and Wyanet leaned over the map. Their talk continued until full dark.

It was much later when Arnora returned from sea. She was quiet. The peace of the sea seemed to have soaked in, although she had nothing to say.

The fires burned long into the night. There was much to prepare.

CHAPTER SIXTY-TWO

"THE TRAIL GROWS FRESHER, and more obvious," Samoset said. He sat easily on one of the small Icelandic horses. "They feel safe."

"Do you know this country?" Harald asked.

"No. We left our land many days ago. All here is strange to me."

"We will put out more scouts. They will be a screen, like a fish net. They can let the enemy in, but no one who sees our column must leave alive. Orm, you know my will—tell the scouts they will get less rest and will need to be more cautious."

"Yes, my lord," Orm said, and scurried off.

"Wyanet," Harald said, "pass the word. No fires tonight. No noise. From now until we find the enemy's lair, we travel like hunted deer."

"Yes, my lord," she said, and wheeled her horse back down the length of the column.

The line stretched back down the deer trail, most traveling on foot. Each person had a longbow, a quiver of arrows, a knife, and little else. Packhorses carried dried meat and sweet berry cakes.

"The trail has not wavered for days now. Where are they going?" Harald asked.

"They are returning to their home." Samoset said. "Their meeting with Strykar would have been a very bad omen for them. One wounded old man with a broken leg doing such harm, they will think their gods are against them. In addition, they will want to tell their elders of the strangers in the land."

"What do you know of these people?"

"Very little," Samoset said. "You saw the bodies. They do not look like us, they shave off most of their hair. They never come to trade, only to kill. They take prisoners and torment them to death, but once a young man, a Mi'kmaq but not of our clan, was captured by them and taken all the way back to their home village. They adopted him into their tribe and treated him as one of their own. He waited his chance and escaped. He followed the rivers to the sea and finally made it to his home. He tells that they are farmers, like you. They live in longhouses made of bark. Their villages have walls made of trees."

"Why do they come to kill and steal?"

"They prove their manhood. They fight constantly, even among themselves. A man who is not a warrior is not a man."

"Tell me of their leaders."

Samoset rolled his eyes. "I know very little, only tales around the fire. Men rule, but their chiefs are the eldest son of the lead woman of their clan. They say that the women own all in the village, because it is the duty of the men to be elsewhere much of the time. Many of their men are killed, so they replenish their numbers by adopting male children stolen from other tribes."

"Tell me, do they. . ."

"There is nothing left to tell," Samoset said, "and I am

not certain that what I told you is the truth. We are far from our home and all is strange."

Chogan appeared as the trail wound its way around a huge tree.

He fell into step with the horses. "We have found Strykar's last victim." he said. "He was buried by the side of the trail. The wound must have soured. He died at their last camp."

Samoset asked, "How far are they from their village?"

"Close, I believe," Chogan said. "When they eat, they throw away anything burned or rotten. They are not worried about having enough food. And their fires at night are larger; I think they do not fear discovery. We are not far behind; they traveled slowly because of the wounded one and we have not stopped to hunt."

They traveled in silence for a while, the horse's hooves muted on the forest floor, Chogan's moccasins making no sound at all.

"Chogan, I want you and Orm to leave us." Harald said, "Catch up to the enemy and find out where there are going and how far. If they have not reached their village in two days, come back to us and report. Travel off the trail, but close, and stay to the high ground."

Chogan nodded.

"Travel with care," Harald added. "Every hand will be against you and we need what you learn."

Chogan nodded again, and dropped back to the first packhorse to pick up food for he and Orm. A few moments later he trotted by them and disappeared into the forest.

"How much longer can we travel?" Harald asked.

"Not long," Samoset said. "The forest is thick and it will grow dark quickly. We dare not lose the trail."

Nothing was said for a time and then Harald blurted, "I do not do this merely out of a desire for blood revenge."

Samoset looked at him but made no reply.

"It does not seem possible," Harald continued, "to live in

a land where other peoples see you as nothing more than a rock upon which to sharpen their spears. Your people deserve better, and my people are too few to exist without peace."

"I do not disagree," Samoset said, "yet the Creator does not give us all that we wish. At times, we must simply accept the world as it is."

Harald laughed. "That, I have always had trouble doing."

"My worry is that we are far from home. If the enemy falls on us, many will die. It is one thing, to lose my brothers to a raid or to have a child kidnapped occasionally. It would be another to watch as my clan is slaughtered."

"You worry too much. If we are to be ambushed," Harald said, "it would be good tactics if you and I were the first ones killed. Therefore, your worries are pointless; you would see nothing."

It was some time before Samoset laughed, but in the end he did.

Not quite two days later Chogan returned.

CHAPTER SIXTY-THREE

"The village is one day's travel from here." Chogan said. "Orm stayed to watch through the day, then he, too, will return." His face was drawn and his clothes showed evidence of much hard travel.

"How does it look?" Harald asked.

"There are fields all around, like the ones you have planted, though the crop is much taller. They have a wall of upright logs, perhaps twice a man's height."

"Are there gates?"

"Gates?"

"How do they get through the wall?"

"Ah. The ends do not line up. They walk to the wall, turn to the side and walk through the gap. The gap is wide enough for only one man to pass through at a time."

"Are there guards?"

"There are always people watching, but we saw no guards at night. Orm stayed mainly to learn if any come out of the forest at daybreak."

"Good," Harald said. "We will continue our march all this day, and then wait for Orm."

It was completely dark before one of the scouts showed Orm where Harald waited.

"Tell me," Harald said.

"There are a hundred, perhaps one hundred and fifty, in the village. I counted thirty warriors. The houses are long and are made of bark. There is much land cleared. They seem to have cut down the trees to make their barricade, then farmed where the trees had been. There is no gate, merely a gap one person can fit through. I saw no guards, certainly none in the woods and none at night. They do have dogs, and I do not think you could get very close before they detected you."

"Can you get me close enough to see for myself?" Harald asked.

Orm thought for a moment. "No, my lord." he said. "There are always hunting parties coming and going. I am afraid your body is not built for stealth."

"How much closer can we get before we have to worry about being seen?"

"We are too close now," Orm said. "Either we will be found or else they will miss the hunting party we will have to kill."

"What time would we need to leave if we wanted to be in position before first light?"

Chogan spoke up, "A little after the middle of the night would be soon enough."

"Good," Harald said, "Go to sleep, both of you. We will wake you when it is time."

Harald smelled wood smoke first. A moment later Samoset motioned him to get off his horse and stop, then he disappeared into the woods. Harald waited patiently until he returned.

"It is not far now," Samoset said, "and no one seems to be awake."

"Good," Harald whispered, "have each scout take two people with him and spread out through the woods. No one enters or leaves without our permission. Tell Chogan to take the far side and go into the open when all are in position. And tell Orm I want him by my side."

Samoset nodded and left. Harald turned back and waved the others forward.

"We are very close," he whispered. "Pass the word. All of you know your duties."

He handed the reins of his horse to a child and, hand on sword, moved quietly forward. On both sides there were soft rustles as his people moved abreast of him. Ahead was a lightening of the darkness as the trees thinned. Harald fell to his knees and crawled the last short distance, then gently moved the branches of a bush aside.

The light from the morning sun was just catching the top of the village wall. Smoke from several cooking fires curling up through the morning mist. *Perfect*, thought Harald, *the walls are just within reach of our bows.* A small stream wound around the edge of the clearing. A woman was walking back from the stream, a bark bucket full of water clasped in both arms. She didn't see Chogan emerge from the woods and cross the stream. When he saw Chogan, Harald stood up and moved into the clearing, too. All around him, the rest of his small army appeared. Orm and Samoset came and stood next to him.

"What now, my lord?" Orm asked.

"We will walk halfway across the clearing and wait until we are noticed." Harald said. "Our people will stay back here. Samoset, will you be able to speak their tongue?"

"Perhaps," Samoset said. "We should have some language in common."

Harald raised his voice slightly, "Wate, can you hear me?"

"Yes," she said from her place at the forest's edge.

"Very good," Harald said. "Now we wait."

They didn't wait long. In a short time, another woman

came through the wall with an empty bucket. She looked down at her feet, avoiding a small mud puddle, and then raised her head and saw Harald and the others. She said not a word, but turned and raced back to the shelter of the walls. Harald could hear the swell as word of their presence spread throughout the village. Heads appeared on top of the wall and a few moments later a crowd of men came boiling out, clutching wooden clubs and bows. They were shouting and gesturing.

Harald chuckled. "It looks like a hornet's nest, doesn't it? What do they say? I don't understand a word."

"They are calling us dogs, and speaking of how they will feast on our hearts tonight." Samoset said. "They say more than that, but much is repeated."

"Tell them," Harald said, "that we have come for Strykar's axe."

Samoset started to speak, but was shouted down. The tallest warrior stepped forward. His head was shaven clean except for a stiff strip down the middle. He wore only a loincloth and he shook a polished wooden club with a ball on the end of it.

"Try again," Harald said. Samoset began to talk and once again the tall warrior shouted above him.

"Orm," Harald said, "kill the loud one."

"Yes, my lord," Orm said and drew his bow. The arrow flew across the clearing with an evil hiss and buried itself to the fletching in the tall warrior's chest. He dropped straight down, his heart shredded by the broadhead.

There was a stunned silence. Then the enemy released a shower of arrows. Most of them fell to the ground short of the Mi'kmaqs, although one did bounce off Harald's mail shirt.

"Try again," Harald said.

Samoset yelled again, even louder. This time they heard him out and shouted their own reply.

"They say," Samoset said, "that we are dogs. They say

they will keep the strange weapon that they won fairly in battle, and they say they will eat our hearts and put our heads on poles."

"Tell them," Harald said, "that the man they killed was one of our elders. Tell them he was sick, old, and a poor warrior, but we still want his possessions back. Ask them how many of them were lost in defeating the least of our warriors."

Samoset's mouth twitched, but he relayed the message. He was rewarded by another shower of arrows and more screams of anger.

"Wate," Harald said, "do you see that group of warriors that are a little to the side of the others? Kill them all."

"Yes, my lord," she said. There were nearly fifty archers standing in the forest's shadow. They fired three arrows each, the third launched before the first one struck. They arched through the air, the goose feather fletching catching the sun.

"The grey geese fly again," Harald murmured, "I am glad to be on this side of them."

Seven of the enemy fell, their bodies bristling with arrows. Those living broke for the protection of their walls.

"And now?" Orm asked.

"Back into the forest," Harald said, "and wait. Get some sleep and kill anyone who tries to leave."

The day wore on. Harald leaned against a huge oak tree and watched the compound intently. Late in the afternoon, he called Wyanet to him.

"Child," he said, "I have a mission for you." He explained what he wanted done, and then he explained why.

"Yes, my lord," she said, and left, gathering the other young people to her.

As the sun set he moved further back into the forest. "We want them to not know if we are here or not. An enemy you cannot see is more terrifying than one you can."

Just before full dark, a warrior burst out of the village at a dead run. He was nearly to the forest's edge before he fell, a dozen arrows in him.

"Good," Harald said. "I knew they would try to send for help, but I was afraid they would wait until dark. Now, double the guards, but light no fires. Let your eyes become accustomed to the dark. A fire in the night only serves to show others where you are."

The night stretched on. When the sun rose again they saw another feathered body near the forest's edge.

With the sun nearly at its peak, Harald called Wyanet to him.

"Now is the time to try our venture," he said. "We will move out in the open, and let them watch what we are doing."

Wyanet and the other young people brought up many little woven boxes, filled with several different kinds of birds.

"Have all of these birds came from the village?" Harald asked.

"Yes," Wyanet said. "Some from the village and some from nests in the wall."

"Let me show you something that I did long before you were born, in a land called Sicily." He held up a little piece of thread, about an arm's length long. At the bottom was a tiny bundle of tinder held together with pine tree sap. He tied the free end of the thread to a bird's leg and then lit the tinder on fire. He threw the bird into the air and it flew rapidly back to its nest in the village.

"Now," he said, "Work quickly. We want many fires, all starting at once."

The sun had barely moved before smoke from a dozen fires filled the sky. Screams of frustration came from inside the wall, which within a short time was also on fire.

Samoset went to where Harald sat, his face to the setting sun. He settled down next to him, cross-legged in the grass.

"Is this the way you won all your battles, by using the birds of the air?" He pulled three strands of grass and began aimlessly braiding.

"It worked once before. I thought it might work again. They should have built their village around the stream instead of away from it. If water had been available, we would have had to try something else."

The crackle and roar of the flames was getting louder. The houses and wall were all ablaze. Part of the wall collapsed and Harald could see people milling around, uncertain what to do next.

"Tell me," Harald said, "of your brothers. Have these people paid a price for them?"

"I do not understand." Samoset said.

"I know not the customs of your people. Mine require a payment for blood. Either blood or silver. These people, or people of their tribe, killed your brothers. These people here are now under our hand, we can do with them as we will. So," he continued, "if there needs to be payment made for what was done to your brothers, here you can collect that price."

Samoset stared into the flames, listening to the screams, watching the frantic forms trying to save their homes.

"Tell me, my brother from a strange world, when is the price paid sufficient?"

"Never," Harald said. "Truthfully, it seems as if the price you collect never cancels the debt."

"Then let us do as Wate suggests. Punish those who brought blood to our people."

"Very well," Harald said. "We will kill only those who ask to be killed."

When the flames died down, Harald stood up and brushed himself off. "I think," he said, "that it is time to talk to them again. If they will not listen now, I fear they are too stupid to live."

Samoset, Orm, and Harald once again set out across the fields. Nothing was left of the village except the smoke-blackened people standing next to the ruins of their homes.

"Our oldest and weakest warrior killed four of yours,"

Harald said, "and now we destroy all you own, using nothing but the birds captured by our children. Do you wish us to raise our hand against you?"

This time they listened as Samoset translated.

An old man limped out from the crowd. "What do you wish from us?" he asked.

"We want Strykar's axe, and we want the people who killed him."

The old man looked at them and turned wearily away.

"We will wait," Harald said, "while they talk."

There was much talk. Harald stood patiently at ease. Orm stood by his side, an arrow nocked and ready. Samoset stood on his other side, his face without expression. The shadows were growing long when the crowd opened and six men came forward, one of them carrying Strykar's axe.

"They are boys," Harald said.

Samoset asked a question and then said, "It was their first raid. All the men who led it are dead. These are all who are left to take your vengeance upon."

Harald walked forward, drawing his sword as he went. The evening breeze billowed his black cloak out behind him. The silver raven's head winked and glimmered on the pommel of his sword while the Damascus steel blade gleamed. The boys stood their ground as he approached, but when he was close enough that they could see his true size, their eyes widened.

"Tell them," Harald said, "that the man they killed was my brother. Tell them that all that I am I owe to him. Tell them that I valued his life more than my own and tell them that my soul cries out for blood and vengeance."

One of the boys spoke.

"He says," Samoset said, "that you should take them and leave their people. He says that they left the old man's head because he was so brave. He says he is ready to be just as brave, so do as you will."

Harald smiled. He walked closer and held out his sword,

lifting the boy's head with the tip of the blade under his chin. He glared back at Harald, his black eyes holding firm. "Tell them that their blood is not enough. Tell them that they are now members of our tribe and that they must spend their lives trying to earn Strykar's place. Tell them that they are not likely to ever be worthy." He lifted the boy's head higher on his blade. A tiny drop of blood fell. The boy did not waver. "Tell this bold one he can keep Strykar's axe. He will be surprised at its weight.

"Chogan!" Harald yelled, "take two hands of our people and these boys. Take them back to our village and show them all we have done. Have Arnora take them to sea in the longship. We will bind these people to us."

After Chogan led the boys away, Harald turned to the crowd. The warriors that remained blocked his view of the women and children. "Tell them," he told Samoset, "that the world has changed. Their boys will not be harmed. We will only show them our ways and in time they will return to tell all." A muttering came from the crowd and Harald walked even closer, his blue eyes dominating them. "Tell them that my people seek allies and friends." A tall warrior stepped forward and shook his war club. His ridge of hair stood up straight and he was covered with dust and ashes from the burning village. He shouted, his voice trembling with emotion.

"He says," Samoset said, "that we are not allies, but dogs. He says that we have burned his village and stolen their boys and we will all die for it, die strapped to a stake while they cut away our manhood."

Harald smiled and turned to Samoset to give his reply. The tall warrior saw his chance and leaped forward, his war club singing as it swept toward Harald's head. Samoset shouted, but his warning was not needed. Harald caught the motion out of the corner of his eye and pivoted away, his sword lashing out from the blur of his cloak. Still moving, he cut the club out of the warrior's hand. He set his feet and with a vicious two-handed blow severed the warrior's head. There was a shower of blood and the head and body hit the ground simultaneously.

Harald held out his dripping sword, extended toward the shocked villagers. Blood roared through his veins and his chest nearly burst from his desire to kill, to slay and slay until the sight of Strykar's dead body was washed away by blood. "Tell them," he told Samoset, "to send runners to the other villages of their people. Tell them that we will have council here or I will summon our entire army and march from village to village until they are all in ruins. It is their choice. Tell them that my people will have no enemies. They will have allies or they will dig graves."

He turned his back on the ruined village and walked toward the forest. His pulse pounded in his head; it was difficult to speak above the noise. He stopped, his back to the crowd. "Be sure they understand," he told Samoset, "that this day they have received as much mercy as there is in my body." His sword was still in his hand and as he spoke, one sole drop of blood trembled and fell off the tip. "Make certain they understand."

He entered the forest and no one followed.

CHAPTER SIXTY-FOUR

"I MAY GO MAD," Orm said. "This endless talking is beyond endurance."

"We can talk to these people," Harald said, "or we can kill them all. Most days, it seems a simple choice, although I admit there are times I waver."

Outside the wigwam the autumn winds blew.

"Soon," Samoset said, "the time to talk will be over. We are far from home and I would not like to make that journey through the snow."

"You have made a good start." Arnora said. She had recently returned with Chogan, bringing the boys, who were agog with all that they had seen. "I have lost track of the number of tribes who have sent envoys."

"All goes well for the moment," Harald said. "They want our steel and they fear our

bows. What they do not yet realize is that we beat them with tactics, not strength. If it were not for your people," he nodded toward Samoset, "protecting us and being our eyes in the forest, we would have been cut to pieces. They cannot defeat us if we meet in an open field with our full strength and they could not lose if they were allowed to harass us as we marched."

"What is to be done?" Ahanu asked. He, too, had come, leading a group of Mi'kmaq eager to see the homes of their ancient enemies. All carried the longbows with the terrible, killing broadheads. They had built wigwams, expanding the small camp built around the ruins of the village of Strykar's killers. At Harald's insistence, the council fire was built in the center of the ruined community.

"Samoset is right," Harald said. "The time for talking is over. We should return to our homes. This," he waved his arms, "is a beginning. Yet, we need to talk to more of your people."

"What do you want?" Ahanu asked.

"Nothing," Harald said, "and everything." He leaned forward to add another stick to the small fire. "This is not my land, but believe me when I say I have seen its like. You keep the peace among yourselves, but you cannot keep these others from raiding your land."

"Have you a plan?"

"Subjects, allies, or countrymen. Anything but enemies."

"That is not our way," Samoset said. "Always, the clan is what matters for us. We come together only for summer council and then only to divide hunting territories."

"The world changes, for good or ill. Without us, you would have died on the rocks. Without you, we would have died in the winter or been slaughtered like sheep as we tried to learn the ways of your forest. Together, we make something this land has not seen. God has given us this gift; I believe it."

"What do we do with this. . . this gift?" Ahanu asked. He inhaled deeply from his pipe.

Samoset said, "We will return to our village. We should smoke many pipes and talk much of this. Winter comes and there will be time. How would we hold council among so many others, from so far away?"

"I think much on it," Harald said. "I think of the way you set up your council, where each family chooses a chief, and then the family chiefs choose the sagamore of their clan. When there is need, the sagamores of all the clans meet. Could each tribe choose a sagamore out of their head council, and these could settle the issues that affect us all?"

"Perhaps," Samoset said, "but there would be flaws. Not the least, these all around us are not of our blood and are not to be trusted, not yet."

"Agreed," Harald said. "These people want what we have. They will trade for it unless they believe they can take it. We cannot ever let them think they have the strength to take or this land will run with blood."

The evening wore on and one by one the others left until only Samoset and Harald remained.

Samoset lit another pipe and asked, "Tell me. What do your people do when a man and a woman wish to mate?"

"It depends," Harald said, "if they are peasants, they do as they wish, with a priest to bless their union. If they are royalty, their mates are usually chosen for them, to bind two lands together or unite two noble families."

Samoset nodded and stared into the fire. "Among our people, the man lives with the people of his woman for two years, showing his skills in the hunt and on the sea. He has to prove his worth. After that, if all agree, they are mates."

"That seems reasonable," Harald said. "It seems more reasonable than the way our people do it. Why do you ask?"

"I think, that it will not be long and we will need to have an answer we can agree upon. Something else for us to talk about this winter."

Samoset emptied his pipe and rose to his feet. He, too, left the wigwam. Harald watched him leave. He did not have the courage to ask for an explanation.

CHAPTER SIXTY-FIVE

THE SNOW WAS DEEP and the sea a bitter grey. A brisk breeze was blowing and low clouds scudded downwind. The boats were all onshore, lying on their sides, safely above high tide and damage from wind-blown ice.

Arnora leaned on the fence, watching the horses and cattle nose through their hay. Harald came down the hill, following the path trodden in the snow.

"The wind is cold," he said.

"Yes," Arnora said, not looking around, "but it is fresh and clean."

Harald smiled. "Does the winter grow long for you, stranded with so many of your people so close?"

"Perhaps," she said. "Perhaps I have spent too much time at sea, where no matter how crowded the ship is, I can put my face into the wind and feel alone."

He leaned against the fence next to her. They listened to the soft snorting of the horses as they sorted through the hay looking for the greenest stems.

"They say," she said, "that at the village, you cut a man in half with your sword."

"Not exactly," Harald said, "But I killed a man."

"Would you have had to?"

"I am not sure," Harald said, "I thought we had won, that they were broken to our will, but he attacked me. I gave it no thought; my blade moved by itself."

"But he was armed with, what, a wooden club?"

Harald inclined his head, "Yes. Yes, I take your point. I could have disarmed him; I could have defended myself without killing. Would it have been the right thing to do? I do not know. Perhaps he would have been grateful for the sparing of his life and so our alliance would have prospered. Perhaps he would have been so humiliated that his anger would have been a bitter weed, spoiling all chances of peace. No matter, the deed is done."

"They talk of you, the Mi'kmaq and the others, as if you are some kind of god. They say that coming back from the death of your daughter and the wound that almost killed you has made you into a different person, that you have powers beyond the ordinary."

"I have not encouraged that," Harald said.

"But you have used it."

"Yes." The word hung in the air, stark and unadorned.

"You use everything."

"Yes."

"That's all—yes?"

"What would you have me say? I'll use whatever I can. These people are under my hand, their lives are my responsibility. They dream of a new life and there is nothing I will not do, no one I will not use, to make that dream come true."

A long silence followed. No other people were about. The animals had been fed and everyone was inside, weaving, telling stories around the fires.

"This land is immense, beyond all measure." Arnora said.

"I think so."

342

"We share our winter camp with people from many tribes. They tell of more and more peoples, far to the west and south."

"I know," Harald said. "There is a great land and we know nothing of it."

"Your ship—is she truly mine?"

"A gift," Harald said. "She is truly yours and has been since we left Iceland."

"A gift, or a blood-payment?"

"Does it matter?"

"No," Arnora said, "in the end, perhaps it does not." She took a deep breath. "When spring comes, I wish to leave this place. I talk with the others, the other young people, and between us we have languages to sail far and still make ourselves understood."

"Do you look for a land without blood, without killing? I fear you would have to travel far indeed."

"No," Arnora said, slowly, the words bitter on her tongue, "I believe, my lord, that what I need is a land without you."

The silence was heavy between them.

Harald nodded, his face twisting into what some might have called a smile. "The wind is cold, off the sea," he said. "I feel it more every year." His hand reached out towards her and then fell and dangled by his side.

He turned and made his way back up the hill.

One of the horses wandered over to nuzzle Arnora's hands. She scratched it between the eyes and rubbed behind its ears. Its thick, bristly, mane tickled her hot face and its sweet, warm breath disturbed her hair. It stayed still as her tears streamed off her face and dampened its neck.

It was nearly dark before she, too, followed the path back to the longhouse.

CHAPTER SIXTY-SIX

A LONG LINE OF MEN faced the sunrise.

Thank you, God, for the sunrise, Harald prayed. *Thank you for the spring and thank you for the peace for which we search. Thank you for the strength in my body and the wisdom in my heart. I know not what this day will bring, but it will surely be a blessing. Help me to deserve it.* His arms dropped to his sides and he turned to walk away. Samoset joined him and they walked in silence, both taking a moment to return from their time with the Creator.

"Chogan is leaving with Arnora-Without-A-Father." Samoset said.

"Really?" Harald asked. "I would not have guessed that. Your lodge will miss him."

"Lord Harald," Samoset said, "they seek to be mates."

The silence was broken only by the breeze in the leaves and the chattering of a squirrel overhead.

"And does everyone know of this, except me?" Harald asked. They were away from the village, walking on a path through the many small fields that now led up to the forest's edge.

"Perhaps." Samoset continued, "They have spent much time together and see the world in much the same way. Both of them look to the sea and seek to find what lies along the coast."

"And what are your wishes?" Harald asked.

"I do not wish him to leave. Wate also would have him stay. He is a man now, and we looked forward to watching his children join our lodge. Still, he is a man, and much has changed in the past few seasons. When you sighted our bay and set your course, the world changed and it will not change back."

"And would you change it back?"

Samoset frowned, "You talk like a fool. What is, is. Had you not come, the fire would have still burned. Had you not come all of mine would be naught but bones, buried in the sand at high tide. I know not where this path will take us, yet we have no choice but to follow it to its end. And you, Lord Harald, what is your wish? We know what the girl is to you. Do you wish to see her mated with a *pagan savage?*"

Harald grinned. Samoset pronounced the Norse almost perfectly.

"I think that we have moved beyond that. Our peoples have gone through much together. Your son is a fine man. A hunter of great skill and a warrior who kills when there is need and shows mercy when it is possible. He is serious about his religion and his responsibilities. If Arnora were my daughter, I could find no better mate for her."

"So," Samoset said, "they will leave soon." He turned to look back at the sea. Arnora's ship was anchored at the dock. Two birch bark canoes lay upside down on the deck and piles and boxes of gear were everywhere.

"Yes," Harald said, "the time is right for them."

"And for us?"

"Small matter. The world moves on, their choices are

their own." He sat down and leaned against a small tree. He pulled up a stem of grass and chewed on it.

Samoset said, "I return to my lodge now. There is much to do." He walked off through the fields, a dark man of moderate stature, his long black hair held back by a single leather thong. He wore a linen tunic and a loincloth. His deerskin moccasins were silent on the path. He looked back. "Wate and I have decided. Our youngest, he will be called Strykar. It is a name of great strength and honor, for he showed us the law."

Harald watched him leave, and then turned his attention back to the harbor. Strykar's longship was still beached but several freighters were making their way out to sea. With the spring the cod had returned and the drying racks were already laden with cleaned and split fish. The bigger Norse ships made a much safer platform for all types of fishing, including whaling, and the Mi'kmaq had adapted quickly.

Another figure climbed the hill to where Harald sat. Harald squinted his eyes. *It must be Eric*, he thought. *He was not one of those who were at morning prayers.*

"Good morning, Lord Harald," Eric said.

Nodding toward the harbor, Harald said, "There should be no hungry mouths this winter."

"No," Eric agreed, "Even should the crops fail, we have begun to make this land bend to our will."

Harald was vaguely irritated by the comment, but he let it go by.

"Did you wish something?" he asked.

"Are you, in fact, persisting in giving your ship to that girl and her savages?"

"Not all savages," Harald said. "The crew will be about sixty and fifteen will be Norse."

"You know what I mean," Eric said. He had not sat down but stood, blocking the morning sun.

"Yes, Eric, I am giving my ship to that girl and her savages. It is my right and my wish. Beyond that, it is a good idea to learn more of this coast and its peoples."

"What are we to use if we need a warship?"

"Strykar had no kinsmen. His ship is mine and I give it to you as my second. It is a very good ship and it is yours to do with as you wish."

"But it is not YOUR ship, the ship where I was kendt-mann."

Harald looked at him. "I do not need to explain myself. What is mine, is mine and I do with it as I wish. I let it rot on the sand, I set it ablaze or I give it to Arnora. In no case do I need to ask your council." The two locked eyes for a long moment and then Harald went on, in a quieter tone. "What grieves you so, Eric? A few short years ago you were kendtmann of a ship belonging to a dead king and you were facing an English axe. Now you are here, in this fair land, and this whole village is under your hand. You will be a jarl in a fine country. You have a good woman and a new child. What more do you want?"

"I do not know," Eric said, "It is true, I have prospered beyond all measure. Yet, somehow I feel that all is slipping away."

"It is," Harald said, "Eric, it is. We sail with the tide of fate. It is ever so. Do you think I saw all this," he waved one thick hand, "when we set sail from Scotland?"

"Then what is to be done?" Eric asked.

"As always," Harald said, "we do the best we can, Eric. We do the best we can."

CHAPTER SIXTY-SEVEN

THE MORNING BREEZE CHILLED the skin but warmed the soul. The waters of the bay were well-sheltered, but on the open sea a wind out of the north had foam skipping from the tops of the waves. The bright sunshine brought out the diamonds in every wave top.

Harald was standing on the deck of his ship. The crew in front of him was almost as unusual as those who had crossed the ocean. Chogan and Arnora were the oldest, but not by much. Most of them were nearly the same age. They were almost evenly divided among men and women. They ranged from big to slight, from blonde to dark. Some wore their hair long and some had it shaved except for a scalp ridge.

"This is the finest ship in the world," Harald said, speaking over the sound of the wind so all could hear him. "You are not the finest crew. Not yet. Your captain and helmsman know far more than you can imagine. Your fate is in their hands, so their whim needs to be your law. It has ever been thus on the sea and for good reason. Fare you well. I ask one favor of you," Harald continued. "The arrowhead in the mast; leave it there. An assassin sought my life and missed. When I looked for the arrow I found the oak from which this mast is made, a mast which has weathered storms and brought this ship and all aboard safely here. Let it be a lesson. From evil, good can come." Harald looked at Arnora. "When I sought your father's life, I did not know the price I would pay. Even so, I would do the same again. You are an entirely wonderful woman and you would not be so had Asbrand held his hand over you any longer. None could know how many other young lives he would have blighted given the chance. The act was mine—he was a walking dead man and neither you nor anyone else could have stopped or swayed me. I am an old man. Please, let your pain die when I die." Arnora made no reply. Perhaps she could not speak. One hand crept up to the silver raven arm band, still in its place.

Harald turned to Chogan. The weight of his gaze was heavy almost beyond bearing but all he said was, "You hold my world in your hand. Take care." He turned and walked down the gangplank and up the hill. Orm found him later in the day, walking among the trees.

"My lord," Orm said.

"I weary of the sea, of the sound and the smell of it. I think of becoming a farmer, far inland. Do you suppose there are enough of our people who would care to join me?"

"I would, my lord," Orm said, "but I would need to speak to Samoset first."

"Why?"

"I wish to make Wyanet mine, so their lodge must become mine until I have proven myself."

"Well," Harald said, "I will leave within the week. Let me know your decision."

*"But from the beginning of the creation God
made them male and female
For this reason, a man shall leave his father
and mother and be joined to his wife.
And the two shall become one flesh. Then they
are no longer two, but one flesh"*

—MARK, CHAPTER 10, VERSES 6-8

CHAPTER SIXTY-EIGHT

THE LONG, NARROW LAKE stretched out before them.

"How old are you?" Harald asked.

"I am not certain," Orm said, "Perhaps twenty-five. Where were you when you were twenty-five?"

"I was trying to find my way through Byzantium, living in my armor and sleeping in the mud. I had no wife and no lands. See how far you have come? You have lands, a wife, a child, and all is well in your world."

"Perhaps it is best I did not kill you when first we met."

"Perhaps."

"And you, my lord. What do you have now?"

Harald laughed, "No wife, no child, no lands. Sore ears from years of listening and a sore back from sleeping in armor far too long."

"This year's Great Council went well?"

"Very well, I think. Every year more attend, and this year there were fewer threats than usual."

Samoset and Wate brought their horses up next to them.

"Your land looks good," Samoset said. "You have made much progress."

"I do not care about your land." Wate said, "Why do we wait here when your child and our daughter are below."

Their spurred their sturdy horses down the trail to the village. Dogs ran out, barking, to greet them.

The village was not particularly impressive. One longhouse, racks for drying meat, surrounded by fields of growing crops. A few small sheds for the animals. Two canoes were drawn up on the shore of the lake.

Wyanet came out of the longhouse, a child peering out from behind her hip and one hand shading her eyes.

"See what I found on the trail," Orm said. "Lost travelers, seeking shelter."

Wyanet grinned broadly, "Good manners require that we let them stay the night," she said.

"I will tend the horses," Orm said.

The evening lasted long into the night. There was no high seat, as in a Norse longhouse and it was built in a combination of styles, with turf walls but a bark roof. Orm had a small household, only a dozen people in all. Those not of his blood were mainly young people, working to pay their way as they traveled. Since a stranger alone was no longer killed out of hand, young people traveled more than in previous years before they settled down with a family.

It was family alone who sat around the fire after their evening meal. Wyanet sat next to Harald, with her little girl snuggling next to her.

"And my brother, Strykar?" Wyanet asked, handing a pipe to Wate.

"He's man tall now. He stayed behind at the Council Site. He is coming with the main party in a day or two."

"Tell me of the Great Council."

"Many tribes, from every direction. They want our steel and our horses at first. It is only later that they seek to learn of our crops and our ships. But before anything else, they must all learn the law."

"They learn the law, but do they live the law?"

Harald smiled. "It comes, but slowly. The law is simple to explain. We teach when we can, threaten when we must. Our strength grows; I think none except the cities on the great river could stand against us. But that means little; if we need to go to war, then we have already lost."

Orm laughed. "My lord, your patience grows with age."

"Truly," Harald said, "I am a man of mild temperament and moderation."

He stood and stretched. The little girl's eyes widened at how he towered towards the ceiling. One massive hand dropped down and gently touched her hair. "I hope that your household can host us until my ears recover from the noise of the Great Council. I look forward to getting to know this small one. But now, I must seek my bed."

"Tomorrow, I go hunting," Orm said. "Fresh meat for the pot. Do you wish to join me?"

"Yes," Harald said. "That sounds very good."

"I think not," said Samoset. "Tomorrow I sit around the fire and smoke and listen to the laughter of children instead of the mumblings of elders."

CHAPTER SIXTY-NINE

THANK YOU, GOD, FOR THE SUNRISE, Harald prayed. *Thank you for the pleasures of this visit. Thank you for the bright eyes of that little girl and the warmth of my friend's fire. Thank you for the chance to rest, before beginning Your work again.*

In order to catch the first rays of the sun, the family was standing nearly at the edge of the lake. The air was crisp, the lake adding a chill to the air.

Harald noted without surprise that Wyanet joined the men at morning prayers but Wate did not.

The little girl still slept while the adults ate.

"Today we hunt and fish," Orm said, "and then we harvest the squash and the maize."

"I am afraid," Harald said, "that my duties will keep me from digging in the dirt."

Orm laughed. "We first came to this place because you said you wished to become a farmer."

"I did not tell the truth," Harald said.

The horses scrambled up the rocky slopes. Orm was in

the lead, Harald close behind. Once they reached the crest, they paused to let the horses rest.

"And what of Chogan and Arnora-Without-A-Father?" Orm asked.

"Word comes from them. Usually it comes with strangers who bear a truce flag and wish to talk trade. They cannot stop themselves from seeing what is up the next river or across the next bay. The last we heard they wintered far to the south, where the sun was hot even in the depths of winter and the days varied little in length. They, too, have a child, a boy. He bears no name as yet, but has red hair like Arnora's. Chogan has taught all on his ship to read Greek, although he says they speak often of how little use it is to them in their daily lives. He tells that one on board talks of making his own way of writing."

"Is that possible?"

"I know not. There are many tongues in this world. I can write Greek, Latin, and runes. Someone of greater wit than I could no doubt find a way to create a tongue for this land." Orm's horse pawed the ground and they turned back to the hunt.

Later in the morning, Orm killed an elk. He spied it standing in the shadows at the edge of a clearing. It was a cow that took only two steps after the arrow struck. They built a fire and grilled the tongue and then skinned and butchered the animal. It was large and fat. The meat was a full load for one horse, so they split it in two and both walked.

The autumn woods were pleasantly cool as they hiked along. "I have always wondered," Harald said, "why not you and Arnora? You went through much together."

"Perhaps that is why," Orm said. "Truly, we are very different. I had no desire to leave my home. When my father died I was thrust onto your ship and when we finally landed here I knew I was home again. Arnora has never left anything behind that she regrets and she may never find her home. And, I think I stood too closely to you too many times. Perhaps I am wrong; perhaps it is all fate that put us where we are."

Harald shrugged and they walked for a while in silence, the only sound that of the horse's hooves on the fallen leaves.

"I smell smoke," Harald said. "It is well you made this kill. Wyanet must have been expecting fresh meat."

CHAPTER SEVENTY

SAMOSET WAS THE FIRST TO DIE.

He was at the edge of the clearing, idly inspecting the ripe crops, when the arrow burst through his back and tore his heart. He dropped where he stood.

Four of the workers had not gone fishing. They, too, died quickly, although one did get out a shout of warning.

Wate and Wyanet stood side by side in the door of the longhouse. The attackers left a trail of dead across the clearing, gray-feathered arrows sprouting from their chests, but there were too many of them. The end came quickly, with the roof of the longhouse collapsing in flames.

The fishing canoes returned at the same time as Harald and Orm and the marauders fled. It was Orm's young ears that heard the child's cry, but it was Harald's great strength that lifted the still burning roof so she could be rescued.

She had been playing against one of the walls and had survived in a cool pocket caused by a leaking water skin, her face pressed against a hole in the wall where a draft of fresh air came in. She had been dressed by her mother for the evening feast. She was wearing a tunic of Byzantium silk, the red still vivid.

"Never walk away from home
ahead of your axe and sword
You can't feel a battle in your bones
Or foresee a fight"

—THE HAVAMAL

CHAPTER SEVENTY-ONE

"HOW MANY?" Orm asked, his arms cradling his weeping child.

"About twenty," said one of the fishermen, Sucki. "Perhaps ten are left. We found their trail. They lay in the woods all night, watching, I suppose. They waited until most of us had left."

"Let this be a lesson," Orm said. "We forgot the Law."

"What do we do?"

"Prepare for a funeral," Orm said.

The sun had disappeared behind the hills on the other side of the lake before the bodies were prepared. Sucki came to Orm.

"Lord Harald is gone. Do we wait for his return?"

"No," Orm said. "I do not imagine Lord Harald will be here for the funeral."

"Where is he?"

"I do not know. He did not ask my counsel. Lord Harald mourns in his own fashion. I would guess he follows those who have done this."

"By himself? What will happen if he catches them?"

On another day Orm's expression might have been a smile. "They will all die."

"What?"

"I said, they will all die. If Lord Harald is merciful beyond all measure, they will die quickly." Orm's eyes were red-rimmed and Sucki quailed before them. "Take my horse," Orm commanded. "My brother Stryker should be a day's ride to the north. Find him and tell him what has happened. Tell him to spread the word and come quickly. Tell him that after our dead are buried we go to teach the Law."

Sucki turned to leave, but Orm's voice stopped him.

"Tell him," Orm said, "that this day he will earn his name."

* * *

They were all young men—young men who had listened to old men talk of the glories of war. It had seemed wonderful—women and loot, triumph and celebrating around a fire while their captives proved their manhood against pain. They had sought horses and weapons and they had lain through the night in the woods near the small village, waiting their chance.

It was not what they had hoped. Half their number had fallen to the terrible arrows from the women and when they saw the canoes full of men paddling hard for shore they had fled with no trophies and only one horse. The horse had slowed them, spooked and rearing, and in the end had broken away and ran bucking through the woods.

They sat around a small fire, exhausted from their day's work.

Harald was upon them before they could move.

"AHHHHGGG!" he screamed and a head rolled into the fire. They scattered like quail and another died without ever reaching his feet. Harald was huge, bigger than any man they had ever seen, he moved like a forest cat and his sword gleamed silver in the firelight. A stone-tipped arrow splintered against his mail vest; the archer lost his hands and then his head a moment later.

One, braver than most, leaped onto Harald's back seeking his throat with his knife. Harald tucked his head, buried his sword in the chest of another raider and let go of it. He reached behind him, plucked the boy from his back and threw him across the clearing, where he crashed head-first into a tree.

When he regained his senses, all was quiet. He blinked his eyes and the giant's face swam into focus.

"What are you called?" Harald asked.

"Machk," he said.

"Machk," Harald said, "We go to your village. We start now. You will carry that bag."

Machk staggered to his feet. Harald's hand on his throat steadied him until he could stand unaided. He reached down for the leather sack. It was almost too heavy to lift. With a shift in the weight, he realized what was in the bag, and why the clearing was silent.

"I cannot," he said. "I cannot carry this to my village."

Harald held out his sword. The blood on it was still wet and the eyes behind it were insane.

"You will carry the bag," Harald said, "or your head will go in the bag." His voice was quiet and reasonable, but Machk had seen his eyes and did not trust the voice.

"We will start now," Harald said. "Since you are a warrior, you will be able to find your way in the dark."

Machk started down the trail. It was slow going. His head throbbed, the bag weighed almost as much as he did, and he shrank from its touch. Harald said not a word, but whenever Machk faltered, he felt a prick from his sword. By the time the morning light filled the woods, Machk had blood oozing from a dozen slight wounds in his thighs.

"I cannot go further," he said, collapsing to the ground.

"Yes, you can," Harald said. He plucked him from the ground and held him at eye level, his feet dangling above the earth. "You can trust me on this, boy. You never know how far you can go until the time comes. Your time has come now. You will walk until I say we can rest. I do not think you know how great a favor I do you. Your life is mine, to dispose of as I see fit. Do you think I need you to find your village?" Harald shook his head. His beard was stiff with blood and a shallow wound scored his throat. "You will walk, or you will die. And if you do survive, you will never complain of weariness again."

The day stretched on. They did not stop for food and Machk drank only when they crossed streams and he could dip his mouth to the water. The sun was growing dim when they finally stopped.

"Sleep now," Harald said. He lay down next to the young warrior. His right hand clasped his sword and his left lay across the boy's throat. Machk could feel blisters and cuts on the hand and shrank from its touch. "It would be best if you did not stir in the night. If I think you are trying to flee, I might snap your neck by mistake."

The nightmare journey continued for days. They traveled slower and slower. Harald would not stop to hunt and they resorted to grabbing handfuls of plants to chew. Soon, Harald carried the bag and almost had to carry Machk, but he would not stop. Rarely was he silent. He talked of Samoset and Wate, and he talked about Wyanet. He told their stories in greater and greater detail until Machk thought he would go mad with listening.

The trail widened and began to show signs of much use.

"How far to your village?" Harald asked.

"Not far," Machk said. "We are almost there."

"Good," Harald said, and then prodded him with his sword. Machk lifted the bag and staggered forward.

It was almost dawn when they reached the village. Harald did not pause, and the insistent sword pushed Machk ahead, through the fence and to the fire pit in the center of the village.

"Far enough," Harald said. "Your journey has ended."

Machk collapsed to the ground, retching from exhaustion. The villagers were awakened by barking dogs and a crowd gathered around the two. Harald ignored them. He looked like a figure from an evil dream—tall, broad shouldered, his hair and beard a tangled mess, his hands still bloody and oozing from burns. He was covered in ancient gore and he stunk like the dead. He leaned on his sword, breathing heavily.

Finally, he deigned to look around. He picked up the rotting leather sack and emptied it on the ground. Heads rolled everywhere and people jumped aside to avoid their touch.

"Your war party has returned." Harald said.

Into the silence he spoke again. "Who is the chief of this village?"

A man stepped forward. "I am chief."

Harald looked at him for a weary moment and then his arm jumped forward and the people heard the chief's neck bones crack. He fell to the ground, dead.

"This ends," Harald said. "This useless slaughter of innocents ends, today."

He continued, "My people did you no harm. They did not seek your lands, they did not bar your trade, they did nothing to hinder you in any way. Yet you came, and you made war upon children, and it will never happen again."

"IT WILL NOT HAPPEN AGAIN!" he screamed, staggering in a circle. "I SWEAR, BEFORE GOD, THAT THIS IS FINISHED!"

"I tell you the Law," he said, "and you dispute with me at your own peril."

The moment hung, balanced on a knife's edge. The next sound heard was that of horse's hooves.

Many horses.

CHAPTER SEVENTY-TWO

ORM WAS FIRST INTO THE VILLAGE. His horse was lathered and exhausted, but it held a trot until he pulled it to a halt. A dark-haired youth with a long sword in his hand was next. More and more horses followed him, more people than the villagers had ever seen in one place. Different races, different tribes, but all armed, all with closed, grim, faces.

Orm sat his tired horse, taking in the scene before him.

"Lord Harald was guesting at my farm," Orm said, mildly. "He agreed to come ahead to tell you people of the Law, because I was busy with the funerals of my family." He looked around at the silent villagers. "You need to know that your raiding party killed my father, my mother, and my wife, along with four others whose safety I had guaranteed. I know not what Lord Harald has told you, but your lives rest on his mercy, for you will have none from me."

"We have paid," came a voice from the crowd. "Twenty of our young men have died."

"You have not paid," Harald said, staring out from under

heavy brows. "Your young men sought death in trade for what they could steal from the helpless. The Book I was raised with called for an eye for an eye, a tooth for a tooth. Send out your helpless, that I might do with them as I will."

"We will not," a warrior said, and he clutched his war club.

"My daughter lies crying, with strange arms to comfort her, because I am here with you," Orm said. "Your position is not strong." He turned to Harald, "What are your wishes, my lord?"

"I do not know," Harald leaned on his sword, his bleary eyes scanning the scene, "Their war party is dead. The chief, who permitted it, is dead. This one," and he pointed at Machk, "has paid."

Orm nodded, his face drawn with exhaustion and grief. "Your warriors must leave and go to the neighboring villages to tell of what happened. When they return, with chiefs to hold council, your debt will be paid."

"We will not!" a warrior said.

"You will," Orm said, "or you will die. You will or you will die in an instant, and then we will do as we wish with your helpless. Now go." His voice was stern and implacable, but what broke them were his eyes.

Harald fell to the ground and rolled over, his sword still clutched in his wounded hand.

Orm leaped from his horse and knelt by his side. "I am so sorry," Harald said. "I am so sorry for what you have lost." Orm searched for sanity in Harald's eyes.

Harald shifted his gaze. "Young Strykar," he said.

"Yes, my lord?"

"Leave this place. You are the One, who sits with his back to the fire, searching the darkness. You know the Law."

"Yes, my lord," Strykar said. He rose and rode out of the village, into the trees.

"Rest now, my lord," Orm said. "Rest."

*"Let the little children come unto Me, and do not forbid them;
for of such is the kingdom of heaven"*

—MATTHEW 19, VERSE 14

CHAPTER SEVENTY-THREE

ORM GAZED AT HIS DAUGHTER. "You," he said, "are now exactly the same age as your mother was when we wed." Wyanet smiled. "And what was my mother like?"

"She was strong, brave, intelligent, and beautiful. And you are like her in every way. You have more than her name."

Wyanet hugged him. "How many times have you told me that? Those are the first words I remember hearing."

"The truth seldom changes," Orm said, "but tell me, this boy, this Da-Yo-Te, you think he's the one?"

Wyanet didn't speak, but Orm felt her head nodding against his chest.

"He'll lead the hunt today," Orm said. "With Eric and his people visiting, we need much fresh meat. We will seek a moose or elk. He'll have his chance to show his prowess."

"You will take care of him? This is not his land; it is all very new to him."

"No," Orm said, "I will not. We live in a good land, but not an easy one. Before he marries my daughter, I need to know if he can provide for her." He stepped back from Wyanet's hug and looked at her gravely. "And, so does he. I will help him as I'd help any man I hunted with, but I will do no more. To do so would be to cheat him, and you."

They both turned at the sound of approaching footsteps. A dozen men came toward them, with one much younger in their midst. His head was shaved except for a ridge down the middle. His clothes were leather and his only ornament was a bone-handled knife in a sheath at his side. In his right hand he carried a bow and a quiver of arrows. He'd come into their village two seasons ago, seeking the strangers and wanting to learn their ways. When they first saw him he was small, tired, dirty, and on the ragged edge of exhaustion. Although he'd come in hopes of getting a steel knife, he'd stayed for Wyanet.

"Da-Yo-Te," Orm said, "you will lead the hunt. We need meat for the feast."

The boy's black eyes showed nothing. Without looking at Wyanet he nodded and led the way into the forest.

"Wyanet," Orm said, "we should return before dark. Eric and his people camp by the river. He said they want for nothing, but make preparations for a feast tonight. If you need anything, Lord Harald said he was going to spend the day fishing. Work the boys hard so they get over their disappointment at missing the hunt." He brushed an autumn leaf off her shoulder, turned, and followed the others.

Wyanet watched them disappear down the trail, then turned back to the village.

Ulf was waiting for her when she returned.

"Aranck has gone to the river to soak his foot. It's swelling where he cut it. I'm taking this poultice to him." He held up a bedraggled handful of leaves.

Wyanet squinted at it, seeing few plants of value. "Give that to me. Go gather firewood," she said. "Da-Yo-Te has gone to kill a moose for a feast. We will need much wood. I'll tend to Aranck."

"You hope we will need much wood; we might not need any." Ulf said. Wyanet aimed a swat at him as he grinned and ran off. When he was out of sight, she dropped the handful of plants to the ground. She would pick some mullein leaves for a poultice.

She had nearly reached the river when she saw Aranck, but only because he was waving frantically to her from the shelter of a large tree. She hurried toward him, but slowed her pace when he grimaced and put his finger to his mouth. Stepping carefully around the fallen leaves, she made it to his side without making a sound. He cupped a hand to his ear and pointed to the river. Wyanet heard the rumble of male voices; after a moment they sorted themselves into words.

". . .till mid-morning. That should give them plenty of time to get out of sight and sound. With that whelp leading the hunt, they won't be back till late." It was a familiar voice—Eric, Lord Harald's man from the coast. She leaned closer, every nerve awake.

"So, take your time," Eric continued. "Gather the men, get them armed and in their armor. We will make short work of the women and then set our ambush on the main trail. When they return, tired and sore, they will all be dead in a heartbeat."

"Pity about the women and children," an unfamiliar voice said.

Wyanet could almost hear Eric's shrug. "They are all pagans and mixed blood, of little value to us as slaves, but much danger to us if one should wiggle free to warn Orm and his men. Now, off! Today is a great day, the first of many."

Wyanet heard the heavy male footsteps move off toward the encampment by the river.

"Come," she whispered to Aranck. "We must hurry."

* * *

The autumn sun was pleasant. Harald sat on the river-bank, a fishing line held loosely in his gnarled hands. He sat in the sunlight, his rock perch warm beneath him. The afternoon shadows had nearly reached his shoulders, carrying the chill of the coming winter. The small stream made slight noises as it tumbled over stones. Fallen leaves speckled its surface and gathered in small eddies.

"Lord?" a voice said.

Harald looked up with a squint. When boy took a step closer his face swam into focus.

"Ulf, what are you doing here? I thought you and Aranck were going on the hunt today."

"Aranck stepped on a thorn. Orm said he would delay us and must stay behind."

"And you?" Harald asked.

The boy shrugged diffidently. "There will be another hunt and we can go together."

Harald smiled, "Bare is a brotherless back, boy. You were right to stay behind. Have a seat. You can keep an old man company."

The boy did not sit. His voice betrayed a touch of strain as he said, "Sir, Wyanet sent me to find you. She fears trouble and seeks your counsel."

"Trouble? What troubles Wyanet?"

"Sir, some of the old ones, the Norsemen, talk loudly and she fears them. Please sir, could you come?"

"Help me up, boy. We will look into this matter." Harald struggled to his feet. He had been fishing upstream from the village, enjoying his solitude.

"Please sir, can we hurry?" Ulf said. "It took me a long time to find you."

Harald walked faster. The years had taken their greatest toll on his legs. Some mornings he looked at them in amazement, traitors that kept him in bed long hours before he could summon the will to face the pain and rise.

Ulf was almost skipping ahead in his urgency; Harald

walked even faster. As they approached the village, he looked around, struck by the lack of activity. Fires and gardens were unattended. Ulf led him to the longhouse. Harald paused for a moment in the doorway and then entered.

Inside, he waited for his eyes to adjust to the semi-darkness. He heard Wyanet's soft voice before he saw her.

"Lord Harald, your people grow restless." Wyanet was very small; next to Harald she seemed tiny. Her blue eyes gleamed from under raven black hair.

Harald looked around the longhouse. It was full, and to his eye, held all the women and children of the village. Over a hundred silent forms, all with eyes on him.

"My people are in this house. They do not appear overly restless to me. Of what people do you speak?" he asked mildly.

"Eric, your second. Aranck was soaking his foot in the stream and heard him talking. They plan to take what has not been given. They seek to make this land theirs."

"I have seen nothing of this."

"Sir, you have seen what you wish to see. If you doubt me, we can. . ."

Harald held up an admonishing hand. He smiled down at the young woman. "Peace, Wyanet. I never doubted your grandmother, I never doubted your mother and I cannot imagine the day I would doubt the daughter of Orm. Do not worry. I will deal with this. First, I must speak to the guard."

Wyanet's voice held the tiniest tremor. "There is no guard. All of the men left in the village are with Eric. Truly, I fear this. It cannot be an accident."

Harold regarded her for a long moment. Behind him he could dimly hear voices approaching. "Ulf," he said, "I need my sword, and my shield. Quickly." He turned back to Wyanet. "All will be well. No one will harm you while I am alive."

"And how long will that be?"

"As long as need be, child."

* * *

Orm followed Da-Yo-Te through the forest. The lad moved well, picking his way quietly through the autumn woods leading the hunting party out of the country near camp. They moved parallel to the great lake, crossing streams and ravines, always trending downhill. When Da-Yo-Te called a halt, the sun was already high in the sky.

He knelt in the middle of the trail, the rest of the hunting party clustered around him. With stick he drew a little map in the dirt. "I have scouted this area. Ahead of us," he said, "the river slows and enters a marsh. The deer know winter is coming and are beginning to head for sheltered ground. There may also be moose in the river or near it."

The men gathered around him had provided for their families by hunting since before he was born but they simply listened to his instructions and offered no suggestions. It was his hunt and much depended on his success. A kill wasn't necessary, the Creator did not send food on demand, but it was important that Da-Yo-Te order the hunt in a reasonable manner. If he were to be considered a man, fit to wed Orm's daughter, this would be a good test.

Soon everyone except Orm was assigned a task. "And you and I?" he asked.

Da-Yo-Te pointed at the map. "Here," he said. "There is much moose sign here. You and I will wait near the shallows."

Orm was impressed by his courage. Da-Yo-Te was giving Orm every chance to find fault with him. With a nod he motioned for the youth to lead the way.

Luck was with them. They were barely in position, their backs against an oak tree with a screen of bushes in front of them, when they heard splashing. They strung their bows and waited. It wasn't long before a big cow moose ambled around the bend in the river. Da-Yo-Te waited until she put her head in the water to grab a mouthful of water plants before he moved. He slid sideways out into the open and nocked an arrow. He froze as the moose lifted her head. She gazed about, water lilies dripping from her mouth, and then dipped her head again. The bowstring twanged and the arrow leapt across the water. The big cow bellowed and reared, spinning to run. Orm saw the arrow buried to the feathers behind the front leg. As it turned, Da-Yo-Te, moving with the speed of youth, put another arrow in the same spot on the other side. The moose splashed out of the river and disappeared into the forest, but she was already wobbling. The trail of blood was red and thick.

"Well done," Orm said, "very well done."

The boy just nodded, but his eyes were bright with excitement. They waited quietly, sitting side by side in the sun, until the forest recovered from the shock and the air filled with birdcalls. Da-Yo-Te led Orm to track the wounded animal, but it was no great feat. The moose lay in a pool of blood not far inside the cover of the forest. Orm pulled his knife and with a few strokes removed the animal's heart. They each took a bite of the warm flesh and chewed as they silently said their prayers for the cow's spirit.

"When I was very near your age," Orm said, "I stood in a winter forest and shared meat with Wyanet's uncle. It was not long after I first came to this land. He taught me how to hunt and you are as skilled as he." He paused and looked far into the past. "I never had a brother before and I feared I would never have a son."

* * *

Harald stood in the door of the longhouse and waited. The sun was still over the trees. There was no reasonable hope that the hunting party would return before dark. Whatever the problem, it was his to manage. He looked down at his sword and shield. It had been years since he'd held them. They seemed heavier.

Harald's stomach turned as Eric and his men came into view. His quick count put their numbers at nearly twenty, all armed and armored.

"Eric," Harald said when they stopped in front of him, "what is this?"

"I did not wish to make you part of this, Harald," Eric's voice was quiet. "When all was done we would have given you the freedom to live out your life as you wish."

"I wish, to live in a land at peace. I wish, to see an end to blood. I thought you wished the same."

"I grow weary of peace and grow weary of begging for scraps from pagans when this whole land is ready for the taking."

"You are still my liegeman; please tell me your plan."

Eric smiled, but the smile did not reach his eyes. "First, we take this village. When the hunting party returns we will kill them, quickly, from ambush. Here lies the center of the power in this land. From here we will reach out as our strength grows. Not all our people have become old women. When the news spreads, men will flock to my banner and this land will become ours. We have held our hand back for so long these pagans know nothing of what we can do. They cannot stand against our will."

"I believed this trip with all your people was merely your desire to see me, to visit an old comrade before he dies.

"And if your will," he continued, "is to kill the hunters, what brings you here? There are no armed men here. Only women and children."

"Harald, there can be no warning. Everyone here dies. There is no help for it."

"Ah, do you follow Ethelred's cunning? An odd choice." Harald glanced at

Wyanet beside him, "Have I told you the tale of King Ethelred, child? He was master of a land called England. He wearied of the Danes living in his land and developed a secret plan to rid himself of them. He spread the word and one night, on Sabbath Eve, his men slaughtered all the Danes he could find. I first told you this story, Eric. Did you learn nothing of it? Do you seek Ethelred's ending?" Eric did not respond and Harald went on. "Ethelred made one mistake. The king of Denmark was Svein Forkbeard and his family was among the murdered, but Svein was not." Harald smiled. He turned his gaze to Eric. "How foolish are you? Do you not know these people? Ethelred went into his grave and the Danes ruled all England. Your end will be the same, if you are lucky. This must stop. I cannot allow it."

"*Allow* it! You have done it! The whole North knows of the things you have done! They sing songs of the things you have done!"

Harald snapped. "You need not tell me what I have done. Can you imagine that I have forgotten? Can you imagine that in a dozen life times I could forget what I have done? I will not see fire and sword brought to this land. Go now and no harm will come to you."

Eric was astonished, "No harm will come to us? Old man, who do you think you are?"

It was the wrong thing to say. Harald felt the years fall away. The blood sang in his veins and the death joy he'd hoped he had banished filled him to the brim. His sword boomed against his shield and he laughed aloud. "Who am I? I am King Harald, the Hardrada, Master of the Varangian Guard and Ruler of the North. When I lifted my sword, ten thousand swords followed mine and where ever I place my feet, there I am king. DO YOU NOT KNOW ME?"

Though they outnumbered him twenty to one, the men were taken aback. The calm, measured tones were gone. Harald had spoken in his ship voice, his storm voice.

His battle voice.

He went on, a wild light filling his blue eyes. "Eric, why do you wait? Can you not hear it? I can. LandWaster is flying again. I hear the cloth snapping in the wind. I see the raven on a field of red. The raven's claws seek blood, Eric. You are right about one thing. It has been long since we fed the ravens. Why wait? I am only one old man alone."

"Not alone." The voice was young, but steady. Aranck and Ulf were standing beside him. They had armed themselves with battleswords, swords nearly as tall as they.

Harald laughed again. "Now—now you must fear, Eric. Now we are three against you.

"Put the swords down, boys," he said kindly. "They do not fit your hands as of now. But," he said, "draw your knives. You can slit the throats of the men I bring down." His eyes fell on the men arrayed against him. "For know this—this will not be forgiven. No man who continues will live. You cannot win if anyone lives to spread the warning and no one will harm these people while I live."

"Harald, why do you do this? How can you stand against us?"

Harald smiled, but it was not a good smile to see.

"Eric, I stand where a warrior needs to stand. Between the helpless and the darkness."

"Then here it ends."

Harald shook his head, "It does not end here, Eric. We will meet again. And the only question left is, will you wait for me in Heaven, Hell, or Valhalla?"

Eric howled and lunged, his axe whirling around his head. Like a storm, Harald moved to meet him.

* * *

"There is much meat here," Orm said, "more than we can eat. Smoking racks must be set up. I think the camp needs to be forewarned. Someone should run ahead so they are ready when we return. Da-Yo-Te, would you be willing?"

The young man smiled. He knew he was being patronized, but didn't care. Without a word he turned and raced up the trail toward camp.

With excitement lightening his feet, the trip went

swiftly. He stopped at the edge of the settlement to recover his breath. As his pulse eased, he became aware of strange sounds. Walking forward he noticed the stillness and emptiness. Ahead he heard the clash of steel. His caution awakened; he slid to the ground and eased his head around the corner of a hut. He literally could not believe what he was seeing. The visitors from the coast were armed for war, wearing the strange steel armor and carrying heavy-bladed weapons. The old man, Lord Harald, confronted them in front of a longhouse. Da-Yo-Te started forward when he caught a glimpse of Wyanet. Her face shone with fear and she clutched a spear twice her height. Even as he watched, a man leapt to the attack. This was no game and there was nothing he could do against such odds. Orm would know what to do. Da-Yo-Te turned and sped back the way he'd come.

* * *

Wyanet had never seen one of the long war axes used. She could not believe the speed with which it blurred toward Harald's head. It seemed impossible to stop, but Harald moved his shield subtly and the axe ricocheted off it, while his longsword licked out viciously toward Eric's legs. Eric leaped backward to avoid the blow and stumbled. He did a frantic somersault to regain his feet. Harald took a quick step toward him, sword held high, but then retreated to the doorway. He laughed aloud. "Eric, were I not holding this doorway against your men, your head would be rolling on the ground right now!"

Eric moved forward again, axe held high. "Be careful," Harald cautioned. "If you try for my head and your axe catches in the door lintel, God will still be laughing when you reach His gates." Eric's eyes flickered to the top of the door and Harald's sword hissed out and sliced a long line down his shield arm. Eric hopped back and his axe came around again. Harald's shield arm pistoned out to meet it.

The axe blade crashed off the metal boss and stuck in the wooden face. Harald stepped in to Eric, the axe trapped in the shield. They froze for a second, face to face, and then Harald's sword took Eric's legs off at the knee. He fell, the axe slipping from his loosened fingers.

Harald stepped back into his protective doorway and shook the axe off his shield.

Eric's men stared in shock at their leader on the ground. Eric and Harald's eyes stayed locked on each other. "Make your peace with God," Harald urged. "You have but a few moments."

Eric opened his mouth, but was silent. He half-turned on the ground, his face pressed against the packed dirt. The blood poured out of his body, making a pool all around him. His last breath stirred a tiny cloud of dust.

Harald looked at the leaderless men confronting him. "Now is your choice. Flee or fight."

They paused and Harald's voice lashed them. "Flee or fight, you fatherless dogs. Eric was a fool, but he died a man. You are no less fools, but are you also less than men? Do you need help running? Here is an extra set of legs." He kicked one of the severed legs into the crowd, splashing them with blood. One man started grimly forward, axe held high.

Harald smiled at him. "An even bigger fool," he taunted. "You can not fight me with an axe. Eric was the best man with an axe in this land, and now his blood is on your face." The man came in a sudden rush, without a word, the axe slicing in a horizontal arc. Harald dropped to one knee and with a swift figure eight motion sent the axe head falling free from its shaft, followed a moment later by a head rolling free from its body.

Harald leaped back up and regained his position. Wyanet could hear him puffing. He was silent now, but stood forbiddingly, his body and shield filling the doorway. The boys remained in their stance behind him, desperately clutching their hunting knives, their dreams of combat swallowed up by the bloody reality.

The tableau held, then Harald slapped his shield with his sword, "Come along now," he said. "Die now, or die at the stake when your treachery is uncovered."

The man closest to Harald shuffled a few steps forward, then paused. His dilemma was obvious. Only one man at a time could come at Harald where he stood, and no one man was likely to defeat him.

"Spears," he said. "Get spears, and we will finish this."

Harald nodded his head approvingly. "That may work," he said.

A half-dozen men raced off for spears. Harald spoke quietly over his shoulder. "Wyanet, when I go down, grab my shield. Keep the spear; your bow will never pierce their armor. You and the boys can hold the doorway yourselves. Your man will be here soon with the others. Do not disappoint him by being dead when he arrives."

From somewhere in the darkness of the longhouse, came a muffled sob. Harald spoke again, even more softly. "Wyanet, tell them they do not need to worry." He did not turn to look at her, but continued to speak gently. "Today is a great gift from God, my chance to enter Paradise, and I will not fail. God weeps with joy at the work I do this day. All the stories I have told you over the years, and I never told you the most important one. God took the life of my daughter for my sins of pride. Ever since, I have wondered how much penance I need to pay. Now I know—and you boys hear this also. It is a simple rule. For all that we have been given, we owe all that we have. Nothing else will do, nothing else is enough. The only reason we have strength is to protect the weak."

The men with the spears arrived.

* * *

Da-Yo-Te gasped out his story. Orm frowned, "Boy, are you certain?"

He couldn't straighten up; his side ached from his run. "Yes. This was no jest or contest. By now there is blood on the ground."

Orm stood up, his eyes seeing something no one else could see. "Not again," he said, "never again."

Then the hunting party saw nothing but his back, disappearing up the trail. The other men followed. Da-Yo-Te staggered upright, stretching against the pain, and then lurched to follow in their wake.

He fell far behind, but kept his feet moving, using trees to steady himself as he covered the ground for the third time. Wyanet's face, big-eyed and strained, consumed his memory. He careened off a tree trunk as he rounded a corner and saw he was catching up to the hunters. A deep, narrow ravine cut the trail. Too wide to leap, it was slow going, one man at a time, to cross. Da-Yo-Te saw a sapling, little thicker than his wrist, growing on the edge of the crevasse. Summoning the last of his strength, he broke into a real run and launched himself through the air. When he landed on the trunk, it bent beneath his weight and bridged the gap. He hung from the tree, and felt it tremble as the men ran across it. Hard soles smashed his fingers but he didn't let go until the last man was over. He dropped to the bottom of the ravine. Sweat filled his eyes, his lungs worked like bellows and his knuckles were bruised and bloody. He lay staring at the sky for a long moment and then pulled himself to his feet. He missed his grip twice, but slowly pulled himself out of the ravine and staggered on.

* * *

They spread out in a cautious semicircle. The spears were heavy, bear killing spears. At a signal, they began to hurl them. Harald caught the first three on his shield, but they sank deeply into the wood and their weight pulled his shield down just enough that the next spear glanced off his mail-covered shoulder. A few drops of red appeared through the tattered links.

Harald's hoarse shout filled the forest clearing. "Fram! Fram! Kristmenn, krossmenn, kongsmenn!" He dropped the useless shield and leaped forward, holding his sword in both hands and swinging it in great, vicious arcs. He didn't even realize that he had screamed the battle cry of St. Olaf's doomed army.

The rebels, though startled by the war cry of an army dead for fifty years, closed around him.

Harald, now out in the open, used his great size and reach to hold them at bay. Each crashing blow of his sword caused dire injury, but he gave scant thought to defense and was soon bleeding through a dozen rents in his mail.

* * *

Orm was the first to the village, but the others were not far behind. He waited for the last. The ring of sword on steel and the harsh shouts of men in conflict filled the air. Above it all rose something else.

"What's that?" one asked, "Is that singing?" The voice was strong, the words in a language none of the Mi'kmaq knew.

"No," Orm said. "It is death speaking. It calls to us." He rose to his feet and nocked an arrow. "Time to answer." His grey eyes caught and held everyone in the group. "Spread out, know your marks, kill them all."

* * *

Wyanet crouched in the doorway, almost hidden behind Harald's shield. She couldn't hold both a spear and the shield, so the boys sat next to her, each gripping a spear. No one dared turn his back on Harald to approach the doorway. The village was silent, except for grunts of exertion and the crash of blades. Then Harald began to sing, his sword moving as if in time to his gasping voice.

"What is it?" she asked. It was no language she knew.

Ulf said, his face white beneath its tan. "He sings the Death Song of Ragnar Lobroks."

"What is that?"

Aranck answered for his friend. "It is from the old times. Lord Harald used to sing it for us. Ragnar Lobroks was captured by the king of England while on a raid. The king ordered him thrown into a pit of poisonous snakes. As he was dying from the poison, he sang the song of his life." Harald's voice reached a crescendo, and another head rolled upon the ground. The backswing caught a rebel in the ribs and crashed through his armor. The man crumpled to the ground. Harald's sword caught on a splintered rib, and in that one unguarded moment he felt a spear enter his own side. Dropping his sword, he spun; jerking the spear from the rebel's grasp, he turned and thrust it through and through the body of its owner. He shouted the chorus triumphantly. "And DOWN we hewed them with our swords!" Empty handed he spun back to his next assailant. A movement in the distance caught his eye. It was Orm, easing into position, his bow drawn. In a moment of adrenalin stretched clarity, he saw the amount of grey that shone in Orm's hair. He had lines around his eyes and the thick shoulders of a man. Nothing of the skinny boy remained in the man. Nothing except the eyes. They were the same, the steady, direct gaze of a boy willing to kill a king for the sake of his father. Harald smiled at the memory and when a bloody arrowhead sprouted from the chest of the man in front of him, he laughed aloud.

Harald slowly crumpled. It was getting more difficult to catch his breath. He coughed deep in his throat and through dimming eyes saw blood splash on the ground in front of him. He coughed again. The pain was coming now. His head sank and then he laughed at his predicament. "On my knees again," he muttered. "Twice in one lifetime. What kind of man am I?"

He was still laughing as he died.

* * *

Orm walked among the dead, fury rising in his chest like bitter gall.

The fight had not lasted long. Most of the rebels had died, backs sprouting arrows like porcupines, before they knew their peril.

Wyanet stood at the door of the longhouse, waiting for him. Aranck and Ulf stood next to her. Both boys were covered in blood, but seemed unharmed.

Orm stopped to look down at Harald. He lay face first on the ground, his sword close by. His massive body streamed blood from a dozen wounds.

Wyanet moved to stand beside him "He lived long enough to know he had won. He laughed as he died." Her voice was soft and unbelieving. "Father, I did not know this man. All those years, living among us. You would not have believed what I saw. There were twenty of them and he was old, and alone, yet, they feared him, Father."

Orm looked at the carnage. "With good reason, it would appear." To his practiced eye, the ferocity of the fight was apparent. "How did he take his death wound?"

"He held the doorway. They could not pass or cause him much hurt, but he grew weary. I saw the blade trembling in his hand. He finally dropped his shield and rushed among them, swinging his sword with two hands. They swarmed around him like wolves around a moose. He killed a man with each blow." Wyanet's eyes were haunted. "Father, as a child I sat on his lap and braided flowers into his beard. He made me dolls and wrote poems for me; *yet he sang as he killed.*"

Orm turned from her. "Find the people of these men and bring them here," he said.

It didn't take long. A small crowd of women and children stared in shock at the bodies of their men. Orm noticed in passing that there were none of mixed blood among them. *Of course not*, he thought. *Men who would plan this day's work would not sully their world with the offspring of pagans.*

"King Harald is dead," Orm said, "and the fault lies on you and yours. Today, you all die and this weed is finally uprooted, branch and stem. A cleansing and a lesson, both."

He turned to give the order. "Put them in a longhouse. Block the door; burn it down."

"No, father, you will not."

Wyanet moved to stand between her father and the objects of his anger. She had picked up Harald's sword. The blade was notched and dull, but the raven still gleamed in the pommel.

"That sword does not fit your hand," Orm said. "Drop it and step aside."

"I will not," Wyanet said. She pulled a strip of cloth from around her waist and used it to bind her hands to the hilt, pulling the knot tight with her teeth. "Now the sword will not leave my hand."

Orm noticed that the cloth was silk, red, though faded with age. For some reason, that fed his anger.

"Why do you stand there?" Orm snapped, his fury nearly strangling him. "These people sought to *rule* you. You would have been their servant and your children their slaves, IF they had let you live at all."

"Father, you cannot do this thing. If you harm these weak ones, it is King Harald's dream you kill. Father, please, listen to me. Every day of my life, for the rest of my life, is a gift from him. I cannot betray him. I stand where he taught me to stand, *where you taught me to stand*."

Orm stared at his daughter, seeing something very new indeed. Slowly, he turned from her and walked back to Harald. He knelt and with an effort rolled the body on its back.

Harald's features were obscured by blood and dust. Orm sensed Wyanet standing next to him.

"Give me the cloth," he said quietly. "You will have no need for your sword today."

Wyanet handed him the faded silk.

"Did you know," he said, as he tenderly wiped the grime and blood away, "Da-Yo-Te saved you. He is the reason we arrived in time. You have chosen well."

Harald's eyes were closed. His grizzled face was relaxed and it startled Orm to see how very old he looked. He sat back on his heels. "Oh, my friend," he murmured, "what are we to do?"

He looked up at his daughter. "He taught me so much. I imagine, he taught me everything I know. Why did he not teach me how to bury a king?"

"Because it is not important," Wyanet said, tears streaming down her face. "We live in a dream, made real by his will and his life. His body is not what matters."

Orm regained his feet. He put his arm around his daughter and pressed his lips against her hair. He stood without moving for a long moment then raised his head.

"Come," he said, "There is much to do."

"Cattle die
Kinsmen die
All men are mortal
Words of praise
Will never perish
Nor a noble name"

—THE HAVAMAL